Bewildered

Mark Landon Jarvis

Published by Mark Jarvis, 2023.

This is a work of fiction. Similarities to real people, places, or events are entirely coincidental.

BEWILDERED

First edition. February 26, 2023.

ISBN: 979-8986701219

Written by Mark Landon Jarvis.

Table of Contents

To those first believers who always told me I could do this.

Beguiled.
Betrayed.
Bewildered.

00 Prologue

Ashley Elizabeth Winston frittered in her office. Her father, L.F. Winston, had left her that archaic word, *fritter*, along with similarly ridiculous words that popped out of her mouth at press conferences and board meetings and other inopportune times. He also left behind Winston Water Works, the largest individually owned corporation on the planet. She called it 3dub—*he might have called it humongous*—but no matter what one called it, after her mother's untimely passing, it was all hers. The whole kit and kaboodle.

This was the result of frittering: thinking like her father, even in his words.

Ashley scrawled "Greetings from Texas" on monogrammed Water Works stationery, then wadded it up and tossed it at the portal humming nearby. The paper ball disappeared in a flash of blue. It had been ported away.

Poppy would be rolling in his grave.

The thing resumed its patient humming, as if demolecularizing and teleporting something half-way around the world was as simple as filtering air. As appliances went, it was on the large size, bigger than a refrigerator, more blocky than a wardrobe closet. It was a titanium monolith standing in an otherwise elegant office.

Its girth and finish made it a poor fit, but beyond its form, its function set it apart from any other enterprise of her office. TransCorp, the portal's manufacturer and the Winstons' greatest rival, alienated it entirely.

This model, as bulky and garish and alien as it was, had been delivered just hours before as a birthday gift from TransCorp's CEO, Sarah Dawn Parker. It was a two-edged, two-ton gesture. One simply could not decline delivery of such a massive and expensive present. It would be "too uncouth," as Delores Winston would have said.

It seemed the ghosts of both her parents were to haunt her here.

Ashley had them park the portal between her desk and the east windows. If it were to serve no other purpose, then it could block the morning sun.

Throughout the morning, she had sent crumpled messages through it to wherever the portal presets determined. The delivery team told her it was on demonstration mode, that it could send her to Bali or Paris or Timbuktu by simply walking through. They handed her a note, scrawled by Sarah Dawn herself, that read, "Walk through to my tomorrow."

She would do no such thing. That note was the first paper Ashley had wadded up and tossed through the machine.

No Winston, not even Delores, had teleported, and Ashley was certainly not to be the first. She swore by her father's values and wished only he were here to see her at his desk, furthering his ambitions. She hoped he would be proud of what she had already accomplished and planned for the restoration of the company's good name.

Despite the device idling at her side, Ashley wasn't selling out to her father's rival. TransCorp throttled free enterprise and tightened their grip on travel and trade. Winston Water Works showered the world with water. TransCorp was about control. 3dub helped the world go with the flow.

She was sure the portal was the latest model, something elite and to be treasured, but it was nothing more to her than the other gifts littering her desk. Strewn in the wrapping paper and ribbons, the gifts were an odd collection of the antiquated and advanced. Keys from her friend to a vintage car. A brand new HeadGear model she did not need. Desk toys and greeting cards.

She set the pendulum of a Newton's cradle into motion on her desk.

"Newton's balls!" she scoffed.

The balls clicked and clacked, the portal hummed, and Ashley continued to fritter away the time.

Her staff had blocked the morning off to prepare for her address. Her attorney and best friend from childhood, Kyle, had advised that her birthday was the perfect day to make her first public statement since assuming the corporate chair six months ago. She didn't need the time to prepare. Instead, she marked off the minutes by the gifts and cards arriving regularly by courier.

At just ten minutes before broadcast, an especially anxious and persistent courier pressed into her office. "Miss Winston," he said, waving for her attention through the staffers. "For you!"

Groans went up from the denizens in the crowded office. Someone more outspoken said, "Oh, who let him—"

"It's fine," Ashley said, stepping from behind her desk. "What do you have?"

"Set it on the credenza," Kyle directed.

"Oh no, no sir." The courier's uniform was not quite regulation. He wore scuffed boots. "Orders."

"Orders?" Ashley asked.

"My hand to yours, Miss Winston."

She held out her hand, and he handed her a small square box wrapped in a bow. He gave her a sharp nod. Mission accomplished. His shoulders already relaxed.

"Jewelry?" she asked.

"Not mine to know, ma'am," he said and turned to go.

A small smile turned up at the corner of her lips. Ashley hefted the little box. *Something substantial.* She shook it and the item inside knocked about. She pulled the ribbon and removed the lid. Inside was a small red velvet pouch. Nothing else. Stitched on the small pouch was simply "Seymour." She fingered at the pouch, frowning at the embroidery.

"C'mon, Ashley," Kyle prompted.

Ashley untied a string and dumped the contents from the pouch into her palm. The heavy object was a transparent disc, about an inch thick. It looked like a stack of poker chips, but the edges were especially polished and clear. She knew at once what it was. She knew for certain who it was from, too, beyond a doubt: Rory Reed.

It was a Schmidt-Cassegrain telescope lens. To anyone else, it might be seen as a paperweight, but to Ashley, it was a true treasure, handcrafted by Rick ter Horst a generation ago. She could hear Rory's rumbling voice all over again as she reflected on what he had told her about it when they saw one in a CommCorps satellite museum.

She took it to the window and peered through it across the city. She was astounded at just how far it could reach in its view.

And she thought at once that he had again empowered her to see more.

Her agent sneered as he swept bric-a-brac from the desktop into empty drawers. He made one last plea, recommending a virtual setting, saying they could place her in any setting imaginable. Ashley again insisted on the office.

The light wasn't ideal, the CommCorps broadcast crew argued. She made them reframe twice to get the portal out of the background and instead to feature one of her airships. "Pull in from that Stratocumulus to me at the desk. Then I'll talk."

"Unscripted?" Kyle asked.

"It's so bright out there, the contrast may not— "

"I don't care how hard it is," she mocked the camera man's whine. "Just make it happen."

She had waited all day for the Winston Weekly to cycle around to the right place as her backdrop. It was a powerful airship, radiant in the afternoon sun. Airships were the icon of 3Dub, and she was the corporation's bloodline. They needed to see a true Winston back at the helm. So much had been done behind closed doors since her mother had died. Ashley had insisted on this vid, not a simulation or some virtual something, but a straightforward broadcast from her new office, from behind her father's old desk, just as he had done it. This was her statement to shareholders and her public.

She fingered the red velvet pouch as the lights came up and the cameras came on. It made her smile.

01 End of the Rainbow

"Unbelievable!" Calissa said, wide-eyed.

Rory was studying his daughter's face in the reflection of the limo's side window, superimposed on the topiary and statuary and manicured grounds of the estate. It was the same child-like wonder she had when...well, when she was a child, when they hiked the Grand Canyon or swam in the Caymans. The scene outside was spellbinding, no matter how many times he had seen it.

"I am actually on the Estate," she said. "I'm going to Ashley Winston's Birthday Bash!"

They rounded a graceful curve. "The house is up ahead," Rory said. The approach was designed, he was certain, to yield just the effect it had on him: that the mansion was rising from the ground when in fact the roadway was dipping down. However it worked, Rory always imagined a stunning crescendo announcing the sight.

This evening, though, there *was* an actual, unmistakable crescendo of orchestral strings being broadcast from a stone band shell. A large orchestra was working away at a powerful song. The band shell was impressive, having been fashioned at the same time and by the same masons as those who crafted the Naumburg Bandshell of Central Park, New York over a hundred years before. Tonight, it was radiant, with a wash of golden lights.

It was the end of the rainbow.

"Now that *is* something," Rory mused. A giant rainbow extended from far above and away, descending just-so on the grounds, ending at the band shell. Ashley Winston would not have settled for a purely mechanical or electrical light show pretending to be a rainbow. She had one of her company's massive mechanical clouds parked at the right spot, coercing just the right amount of moisture to create the optimum conditions for refracting a sunset rainbow.

Rory spotted powerful banks of lights stationed among the trees to keep the effect just as she would want it to appear. He saw several technicians, heads up, watching the display and chattering in their HeadGear to ensure the rainbow was sustained.

He knew this was more for the two of them than for any of the dignitaries or debutantes who would be along yet this evening. He knew Ashley had it fashioned especially for Calissa's enjoyment, and that made his heart swell.

"Did...did you tell her?" Calissa asked. A tear streamed down her cheek and curved around her smile.

"I might have mentioned it," he said. Calissa had been enamored with rainbows her entire childhood. Her favorite part of every vacation was when Rory would find a waterfall with a rainbow in its spray. And he had made it a point, on every trip, to find her a rainbow.

Now she was starting college, focusing on Ultraviolet Spectroscopy, or, as she told her father, "I study invisible rainbows in space!" Not the most practical degree, Rory had argued once, only to hear enough technobabble to quell his reservations. Besides, it made her happy, and it made her "anonymous benefactor" happy to bankroll it all. Who was he to judge?

"It's perfect!" Calissa said, shaking her head in amazement.

As the car rounded the circle drive, the orchestra switched to "Somewhere Over the Rainbow." The driver had known it was part of the plan, for he had cracked the windows for her to hear.

A footman opened her door with a flourish, and another man more near her age extended his arm to escort her up a short flight of stairs. Rory followed, looking ahead at the sight he had been waiting for.

All the lights and garland, all the garish grounds and swelling music—all of it was nothing to him compared to the beautiful woman at the top of the stairs. She was beaming her most elvish grin at them as they ascended. Ashley Elizabeth Winston was radiant, and the colorful lights played off her in the most amazing ways. She wore a diamond tiara, crowning her shimmering white hair that flowed down to her cleavage. Her dress was an elegant white shift, reflecting the colors of the rainbow.

"Welcome!" she said as Calissa crushed her with a hug.

"Happy birthday!" Calissa said. "And thank you!"

Rory leaned down and gave Ash a peck on the cheek. "You've outdone yourself," he said with a smile.

"*Living a life without limits*," Ashley mused, sharing a Taoist philosophy, "*is the highest state of existence*."

He was again impressed. He took her hand and said, "Ah, the student becomes the master."

"You like it?" she pulled in close to his side.

He did, though he did not think she was interpreting it in its original tenor. Regardless, she was playing his head game. It was Rory's custom to commit quotes to memory, and he had hundreds of them cycling through his mind.

"Wow, wow, wow!" Calissa was saying to her escort. "Daddy, look at this!" Her arms were splayed wide, showing off an atrium of white roses that covered the walls, floor to ceiling. The roses were backlit with golden light. The floor and ceiling marble were inlaid with gold that shined like the sun.

"You ain't seen nothin' yet," Ashley said, and led them across the anteroom to two tall doors. "Open it up, Jeeves! Let's get this party started!"

"Ma'am," Jeeves nodded, and threw open the double doors. The man's actual name was Jeeves. Ashley had had him legally change it just for sport. Rory had asked her, when he learned that some time ago, what she would rename him. She did not hesitate. "I dub thee, 'Killer,'" she had said with a wink.

This room was Rory's favorite. It was a ballroom, and it was fashioned of richly stained wood. The floor was his favorite, an intricate parquet pattern that reminded him of an Escher painting. The flooring created an optical illusion of depth.

Tonight, the room was festooned with yards and yards of white fabric and ribbon draping across the ceiling. Vast sweeps of white bunting whirled around the room. Delicate snowflake pennants hung low like the streamers at a Mexican wedding. The wood and white made for a stark contrast that was only enhanced by candles glowing throughout the room.

Rory shook his head. He knew Ashley had invested her own time in helping decorate the place. He knew she had just rolled up her sleeves and went at it like a parent decorating for prom. It wouldn't have surprised him at all if she had been up all night cutting out the doilies and snowflakes herself.

He pinched his eyes closed and let the overload pass. *Six footmen. Eleven cars, following. Nine technicians. Five security personnel. Thirty-six banners.* Sometimes his propensity for detail wore on him. *Sixty-six candles, thirty of them more recently lit. The first lit was close to the stage, having burned down a little more than others.*

Tonight was about Ashley, not the details. He held her square in his view and relaxed as best he could. She had noticed, however, for she did not miss a beat.

"Need a drink?" she offered. "Maybe a Charm?"

"I'm fine," Rory said, refusing to take his eyes off her.

"It's too much, isn't it?" she pouted. She turned him to a less busy corner of the room. "I told Rafe it was a little over the top."

She was stroking his wrist as she led him around, almost dancing with him as they circled to the stage. He knew the gesture. She was Affecting him, gently, discreetly. She had that gift. When she was applying it as she was now, they agreed to call it a Charm. When she had to use it for self-defense, they called it by other names.

Rory pulled away. "I'm fine, honest." He was counting the stripes in the wood parquet, seeking solace in the pattern.

"You can't be moody on my birthday, mister," she laughed. "Get drunk or get Charmed, but we're going to have fun."

The room was filling up fast. They would all have their time with her, and he would recess into the woodwork and lace. He would be what others already perceived him to be: her bodyguard.

He was alright with that.

"You've met Rafe, right?" Calissa asked by way of introduction.

Rafe and Rory nodded at one another.

"This man is your father?" Rafe replied in his familiar, judgmental tone.

"Rafe says you're ruining the shot. Wanna come with me?"

"Yes, please," Rafe intoned. "Camera six has yet to capture Ms. Winston's best side."

Rory looked from Rafe across the room to Ashley. She was dancing with an elderly man in a tuxedo. "Her every side is her best side," he said, more to himself than Rafe.

Rory looked past Rafe, then to the cameraman, who was waving him away. The best footage was that in which the camera was unnoticed. *Do not look at the camera*, he told himself, but he could not keep from looking back at its beady black lens. He realized, as Calissa led him to the champagne fountain, that he had likely been right in the line of sight. He likely had been blocking the camera from capturing what he was now admiring so very much: Ashley gracefully moving with the equally graceful old man.

Not all that long ago, she had performed a much different dance, one in which she had killed nearly a hundred men. He had not seen it firsthand, but to hear tell of it, she had done cartwheels and pirouettes and other moves that defied either name or description. Witnesses called it the Dance of Death, and they had nothing but respect for her lethal gyrations. Her actions had saved countless lives from the grinding onslaught of mercenaries sent to kill her and the locals.

That man now dancing with her was some kind of distant relative, one who had taken part that night in the Dance of Death. Even if the old man had not kept up her pace, he and a dozen of her Family had fought at her side, a bizarre and elegant battle that had not been seen in hundreds of years.

"Dad?" Calissa asked, handing him a crystal cup of punch.

"Just beautiful, isn't she?"

"You're not fooling me, you know," she said. "Wanna find a place we can talk?"

"Nah." Rory said. "You go have fun. We'll talk in the car later."

"Why don't you ask her to dance? You're a great dancer."

Rory was asking himself the same thing. He practiced for a few weeks in Franklin. He knew he was pretty good. He looked at his reflection in his punch.

"Nah," he said. "This is her night." He looked at Calissa, seeking understanding. "This is her job, kid. She's gotta circulate."

They stood watching her for a while—one dance, then another. Finally, Calissa took away his cup and led him to the perimeter of the dance floor. It was a slow number, and she led. He had taught her well, he realized, as they eased about the edge of the dance floor. People were watching them, he noted. Admiring their poise and style.

The music changed to a swing, and Rory stepped away just as the young man who had first escorted her approached. "Keep up," he said, passing Calissa off to him.

After a while, the band picked up the pace and then doubled it. Dancers were pulling back from the dance floor to leave a large circle in the middle under the largest chandelier. Rory craned his neck to see around people. There, in the center of the dance floor, Ashley had stolen the spotlight. She was dancing now without a partner in a bizarre and yet beautiful range of motion. She executed moves he had never seen before. The crowd was cheering her on now. The band was continuing to speed up the beat. A trumpet and saxophone were vying for the high notes.

People on the dance floor began their own crude and fumbling imitations of Ashley's frenetic and fanciful dance. From the epicenter on out, the crazed dancing caught on. Rory saw Calissa and her dance partner catching the frenzy. Soon even the waitstaff, camera crew, and even security forces were joining in.

Rory was astonished to realize that he, too, was dancing like a madman. At least he knew it was one of her Affectations coursing through the others, stirring also in his head. At least he could revel in it, knowing her emotional state was in him, in all of them, intimately.

It made him cheer with the crowd.

02 100 Proof

"I can have my cake and eat it too," Ashley smiled. "And I can let them eat cake while I'm at it. All the cake."

"You know what I mean," Kyle DuPree said. "And you're mixing together a millennium of metaphors you don't want to mess with. Not at your status."

It was what she would have expected of him, even at her birthday gala. They were leaning on a balcony railing, standing side by side, close enough to hear one another over the band and mayhem in the ballroom below. It was well past midnight, and the crowd had grown rather than thinned. More revelers were wearing HeadGear now and dancing to their own rhythms, and more and more of them were variously intoxicated. The party had come to bore her, so she withdrew to the loft. Kyle had found her looking out over a couple hundred of her closest friends. They had been talking for an hour, and she realized just how much she had missed their conversations.

"Why, whatever do you mean, sir?" she asked like a coy southern belle. "At my status, I can mix my metaphors as strongly as I can drink them."

"It's a delicate status, and you know it. Princess-party-animal-corporate-magnate."

"I prefer mogul," she said. "Magnate literally means 'great man,' and...." she struck a pose for him, "and I'm not."

"No," he appraised, "you certainly are not."

"And besides, I'm getting buy-in. You've seen my ratings."

"I've seen them, yes. I've also heard talk—"

"It's a party, Kyle. I haven't thrown a party since...since I don't know when. And it's my house now, so what's wrong with a little house party?"

They both looked over the rail at the insanity brewing, then smiled at each other. "*Little house party*," Kyle repeated. "How's the bulldog feel about this?"

"He has so much security down there it's hard to tell them from my friends," she rolled her eyes. "Except they seem a little crusty."

"Like that one?" Kyle pointed to a taciturn woman leaning a shoulder against a wall, her eyes scanning the room.

"And that one," Ashley pointed to a man who was studying the room over the lip of his drink. It was comical the way he kept his cup, empty, to his mouth for so long. Clearly, he wasn't drinking anything. He turned his shoulders left, then right.

"He's talking to someone, isn't he?" Kyle observed. "Maybe Rory?"

"Nope. Rory left. Took Calissa and split."

She didn't want to talk about it. Her hulky beau, gone without a goodbye.

They watched over the crowd and made small talk that ranged from her public announcement, her state of the corporation, to the weather, to her gown, to just a little more shop talk. She would allow it. Kyle was, and would always be, her private counsel. If he wanted to forewarn her to keep her image all buttoned down, that was fine. His opinion. As he said, his *informed* opinion. If he had to talk about consumer confidence and trending whatever, even on her birthday, she would smile and nod.

Ashley didn't need anyone to tell her that the big chair was a poor fit, but she was determined to make it work, to assume leadership at Winston Water Works. It was going to be on her terms, with her being herself, cake and parties notwithstanding.

She pursed her lips and looked admiringly at Kyle. He had diverted her attention, if only for a few minutes, from what was a sore spot he'd detected. She hadn't thought of Rory Reed for five minutes.

A shower of sparks burst from below, and a red fireball the size of her head shot toward the ceiling. A reveler below was holding a stick upwards. He had fired off a Roman candle! Those in the crowd who noticed were patting one another down, extinguishing the sparks. Before the next fireball could be released, security revealed itself by descending on the man en masse. They snuffed out his fireworks and lugged him away.

"Looks like Reed was right to increase security," Kyle said.

"Pfft, hardly a threat," she said.

"So casual, yet so cautious."

"What?"

"You're here with me, up here, not ripping up your skirts and sweating in the mosh pit. You're being cautious."

"You're questioning my inner party animal?"

"Hanging with you has led me to question so many things," Kyle began something Ashley found strangely unpredictable. This wasn't his usual corrective tone of voice but something more wistful.

"You're always full of questions," she replied. "*Full of something.*"

"Like, for instance, how long have you been doing your telepathy thing?"

"It's not telepathy. It's more like thinking out loud, only...not."

"Whatever you call it, you admit that you can put ideas in people's heads, correct?" Kyle asked. He was an attorney, and hours of drinking and dancing did not dilute that.

"Yes, and no. I think what I do sort of frees up things in people, brings things to the surface. I wouldn't say I put ideas in anyone's head."

"Not even into my head?" he asked.

"There's plenty of room available in there," she elbowed him. She could jab and jibe him. They had grown up as neighbors and friends. They'd dated off and on. Kyle had bailed her out of so many messes. He had always been there, through the terrible teens, after her father left, through college, and throughout her 'oat sewing days', as he called them. "Besides, I'm better at poking at autonomous bodily functions than reading anyone's actual thoughts."

"Autonomous bodily...?" but before he could reason it through, she Affected him with hiccups. "Right. *Hic.* I remember. *Hic.* Sneezing fits. Coughing. *Hic.* Knock it off!"

"That's not telepathy."

"But really, Ash. How can anyone really know how they feel about you, when you can doctor up their feelings?"

"What brought this on?" she turned to face him, but he continued to look out over the dance floor.

After a while, he asked again, "How long have you been at it? Clear back when we were kids?"

Ashley thought about it. "I suppose I used it a time or two to get my way."

"That's a scary thought. Kids manipulating parents."

Down below, members of the band were crowd surfing. Someone was climbing the bunting draped over a sculpture. Ashley shook her head.

"How long have you been manipulating me?" Kyle asked, looking at her.

"That's a pretty strong word there, counselor," she smiled innocently.

"Because I wonder if this on again/off again thing was ever *really* on, or if you sometimes turned me off." Kyle slid the back of his hand down her arm. His hand turned to cup her waist. She did not move away. They had been hugging and holding each other for over a decade. He was Comfortable Kyle.

"Kyle, I..." she stammered, remembering dozens of times she had manipulated him.

He smiled sadly and shrugged. "I know, right?"

"I was just a girl."

"Yeah."

They stood together, his arm now draped over her shoulder, her arm wrapped around his back. A good, close side hug. The chaos of the ballroom did not reach them. She was feeling guilty and repentant.

She could feel him sigh.

"I kind of wish you wouldn't have, you know. I wish I could have fallen in love with you of my own accord."

"Kyle, I—"

"Or that I could have soured on you on my own if ever I *had* actually loved you. You know, love-loved you."

"You *have* loved me on your own," she said, giving him a little squeeze.

"Not like a sister."

"No, like for real." She inhaled and then recounted several instances in which he had proclaimed his love. She ended with "...and that time in Kansas City, at the fountain."

"You didn't make me love you any of those times?"

She shook her head.

"But you maybe did, say, some other times?"

She smiled sheepishly. "Maybe?"

"And you *did* make me go away, right? Every. Single. Time."

"Nope," Ashley said. "Maybe sometimes, but really, I think you just spent enough time with me you wised up. Moved on."

He chortled.

"What?" she asked.

"I've never moved on, you goof."

They stood together through song after song. Ashley wished she were truly a telepath. She wanted to know what he was not saying, but she didn't want to ask. She wondered just how much he had had to drink.

She noticed his lips were moving, and he seemed preoccupied.

"Are you jacked in? Dammit Kyle, are you?" He wore an antiquated appliance mounted in the rims of his glasses. Sometimes he would read in the retina display.

"I'm rehearsing," he countered. He pulled away to stand toe to toe with her. He said something that was drowned out by an electric guitar riff.

"What?" she said, leaning in closer.

Their eyes locked. He smiled wanly.

"I said, I just hope you're not toying with Rory." He chuckled, adding, "That's hard to say, you know, 'toying with Rory.'"

"I am not—"

"Because, out of all the guys over all these years, Ash, he's the real deal. I don't even *want* to like him—and I don't think you're *making* me like him, don't get me wrong—but I think he's good for you, you know?"

"Yeah?" She took his hands in her own. "Really?"

"Really." Kyle nodded. He regrouped. "I was watching him tonight. Awkward as hell. This is not his scene...but he was here, and he was just as smitten with you as I've ever been...or so it seemed. That's why I'm asking you. That's why I came up here, I think. Is this guy for real, I mean 100-proof in love with you, or are you pulling his strings?"

"You really think he's 100-proof?"

"Not a doubt."

"Then why did he go home?" She felt her lip pouting and pointedly stopped it.

"Guy stayed until midnight. What do you want? Probably had to get up in the morning or catch a train yet tonight." Kyle cleared his throat. "You didn't answer me, Ashley. Are you messing with his head?"

"I am not," she said. "I have learned not to meddle."

"That'll be the day!"

"In *emotions*, okay?"

It seemed to satisfy him.

They danced together and laughed. They were ballroom dancing at two in the morning to heavy metal down below, but it didn't matter. It felt like the old days when they had danced to Bollywood and Broadway shows broadcast through the mansion's vast hallways. When they tired and returned to the railing, the crowd was noticeably smaller.

"I have a hearing in the morning," Kyle said then. "I have to go."

They hugged, then he continued, "Don't hurt this guy, Ashley. I mean it. He's sensitive, not made of the same stuff as you and I. Not gentrified."

"Sensitive," she repeated. "Delicate?"

"Yeah," he said, swinging his jacket over one shoulder. "That's about right."

"You're astute, you are. Nothing slips by you, does it?"

"Love you too," he said, descending the stairs.

Just months ago, that sensitive, delicate man had killed over a dozen men with his bare hands in gruesome hand-to-hand combat. She had learned he was formerly a leader in a rebel force known as the Turncoats. She had some more research done on him and had confirmed that Rory Ray Reed (aka Rory Orman) was an Extractor, a grizzly assassin that removed nodes from the skulls of his targets. She even came to know that his last assignment had been to neutralize her.

It gave a girl pause, knowing that an assassin had been that close to her and not followed through. Assassins from his Corp were renowned for follow-through. Rory was legendary for it, having never broken Contract, so they said. Her sources speculated that whomever had drawn up his Contract must have died in the Franklin skirmish, and that it was now null and void.

Regardless, they had spent days together, hiding out like fugitives. He had played hero, supposedly saving her from her stepfather and his mercenaries and from a mad man Rory had worked for, Stan Combs. That whole time, had he been carrying around a Contract for her life in his pocket?

It made her a little angry he had never quite owned up to that.

Someone was waving a hand in front of her face. It was Calissa Reed.

"What are you still doing here?" Ashley asked, shocked to see the teenager.

"We went to get you a present," Calissa smiled. "Wanna come see?"

Like presidents and ambassadors, she had so very many token gifts given to her they would fill a warehouse. Ashley had her surplus gifts auctioned for charity every year. It was difficult to buy a gift for someone who could buy anything.

"Sure," Ashley said and let the girl lead her through the crowd and out the doors. Her curiosity outweighed her concerns. He could explain away being a threat to her life another time. Right then, she was dying to know what they had found for her in the middle of the night.

"Over there," Calissa said, fanning her to the limousine. The girl stayed on the steps, squirming with excitement.

Rory lumbered out of the back door and assumed his full height. He was so large and so tall, even a limo seemed inadequate for him. He shut the door behind him and put his hands on his hips. He looked the best she had seen him all night.

"Well, Princess, I saw all that in there, and for a while, I felt outdone."

"Is that so?" Ashley smiled.

"I'll admit it. I'm competitive."

"You didn't have to, Rory. Whatever you have in there—"

"Actually, made the connection a couple weeks ago. Wanted to wait until the time was just right."

"Rory, what *is* it?"

"I could tell you weren't really yourself in there, all the pomp and pageantry, all the shallow people and mounds of gifts."

"Dad!"

"I really wanted to give you something special—unforgettable—for your birthday. And crazy as it was to pull this off, especially at this hour...well, I couldn't resist."

"So... let's have it. C'mon Rory!"

"*Some gifts are big. Others are small,*" he quipped, "*but the ones that come from the heart are the best gifts of all.*"

"You are impossible. What's in there?!"

"Not what, but who." He said.

"Whom," Calissa chided.

"PLEASE!" Ashley said.

"Miss Ashley Elizabeth Winston, I present to you...." he swung open the door of the car, "...your long-lost father!"

03 The Gift

The moment was six months in the making. Rory had been studying up on Ashley when he had read that her father, the Typhoon Tycoon, LF Winston, had been presumed dead. Rory was not a man who liked presumptions, so he put part of his team on confirming that her father was truly dead.

The wealthiest man on Earth could afford to disappear, but it was unlikely he would abandon his family and passions. To remain missing so very long would require an elaborate coverup and iron will. It would take a skilled support staff, his closest confidantes, ones he could trust with his very life. They would have been his truest friends in the cesspool of wealthy posers.

Compromising that level of trust was a gift Astar Amin used sparingly. For Rory, she would reach out across a worldwide spidery web of textile merchant contacts, plucking at every thread of hearsay. She was diligent in every project he asked of her and her husband, Zana. This one, however, had come to *consume her* when she presumed Rory's motive was love.

After the Franklin battle, Rory and Ashley had spent time together recuperating in one of her hospitals. It had been a dreamy month, though interrupted all-too-often with Astar's messages, one after another, updating him as to her findings. He was sure she had thought of it as her gift of good news to buoy up his recovery.

Weeks later, over tea in an import store in the Light District, Astar broke the news: she had found him. LF Winston was alive and thriving. He was a groundskeeper at an orphanage in Morocco. It was one he had founded and funded and set up in perpetuity to care for children commonly referred to as 'chattel,' the victims of TransCorp's sweeping progress.

"This was the definitive break for me, Rory Reed, putting together his loathing of the Trans Corporation and his desire to disappear."

"Genius," he told her, sipping at her special blend of tea. "But Morocco? Really?"

"Astar has relatives in Marrakesh." Zana said. "They knew of the orphanage."

"And my cousin knew of a *Nsrani*, a Christian...a foreigner...who fit the description and who persisted there many years working the grounds. I knew it was him when they said that he was terrible at the job and yet was never fired."

"She was so starry-eyed. It did not take that much of her persuasion. We closed the shop for two weeks and went shopping." Zana winked. Shopping was their term for spying, something they loved doing, even as they were now in their fifties. "Besides, I was, of course, able to write off the entire venture from my taxes."

"Of course," Rory said.

"Oh, you will like him," Astar smiled. "He is a man of principle, like you."

Rory had already set his mind otherwise. "I don't like the comparison. The guy ditched out on his wife and kid. Left them holding the bag while he went off to lick his wounds. Estranged for years. Who does that?"

"Perhaps it was as much for their protection as his own self-preservation?" Zana offered. "There was a great deal of unrest then."

"Assassinations, as you are aware." The corner of Astar's mouth turned up. "Indelicate bombings and the like. Mr. Winston was no doubt a target of a few."

They had slipped him into the country shortly thereafter, bringing him up from the Mexican border using an elite coyote operation. He had accepted up residence in the Amin's home, a cavernous salt mine under Springfield that had been long forgotten.

Rory had spent little more than the ride to the Estate with him.

LF Winston was tall and very lean, wearing a middle eastern, ankle-length robe that Calissa called a kaftan. His white hair was long, as was his beard, which he picked at absently. His worst characteristic, by Rory's estimation, was that he talked non-stop, even to himself.

From the Light District to the Estate, LF narrated the sights like a tour guide. His father had been a founding father of Springfield, at least of its rejuvenation. He was speculating, just spit balling, but he thought the Estate might have predated any other stone structures in the city. Wood had been more portable and affordable, at one time, perhaps even locally available.

Rory had interrupted him. "Why now, Mr. Winston? Everyone will want to know. Why are you willing to come back now?"

LF paused, panned the faces of the Amins and Calissa, and settled back on Rory's. "Well...." he squinted at Astar questioningly, and continued, "I was told I'm needed."

"Oh, very much so. Isn't that right, Rory?" Astar nodded. "She is now grappling with your legacy, with all of your fortunes and enterprises. She will need you!"

"It is a daunting task," Rory agreed. In these intervening months, he had seen less and less of Ashley as she tried to wrap her head around it all. Rory shifted in his seat and leaned in a little. He knew he was an imposing figure, and he was using his size to gather LF's attention. "She will need you for more than the bookwork. She will need her father."

"Of course, and she will need us to help her learn her Craft."

"Craft?" Rory asked.

"The Family business," he said, questioning with an eyebrow.

Rory was feeling the lateness of the hour. His eyelids were heavy, and he slouched back in the seat. LF Winston was fading from focus.

Then the car lurched, and he was at attention again.

The window separating the front and back lowered some, and the driver apologized. "Sorry, Mr. Winston. A bit sleepy, I say."

Zana yawned and stretched.

"Ohhhh," Rory finally caught on. "*That* Family business!"

"Yes," the old man said. "I've learned she is quite the rising star."

Rory glanced at Calissa and the others.

"That's why you're back, eh?" Rory nodded. "You're one of them."

LF picked at his beard and looked out the window into the night. "It is, and I am. She will have so much to learn. It will not help that she will feel all the worldly pressures of the Water Works." He sighed and turned back to Rory. "I wish I could protect her from all that."

"You haven't seemed too worried about her before now," Calissa leveled at him.

"Ah. Boyfriends and ball gowns were easy enough to navigate. And she had Delores to help her. College. Some shenanigans I've heard of. Silly exploits. None of that was half the threat she now faces, leading an empire."

Rory felt Calissa take his hand, and he liked it.

"You'd be surprised how tough those things can be," she said.

"I'm sure you're correct, young lady." LF said. He turned back to the window.

Rory wondered if the old man had regrets. Rory had his regrets, and he *had* been there for his girl all the way through. He studied the withered figure. Was he just back to take over again? Had he been hiding from Mitchum or some Contract killer all this time? What had kept him away?

Rory swept his hand toward the old man as LF emerged from the limousine. "Ta-da!"

"Hello, Snow," LF said, holding open his arms.

"YOU!" Ashley swung fast and clipped her father with a strong left hook. Rory grabbed her from behind and subdued her before she could make another connection. She was a furious spitball of profanity, wriggling in his arms.

LF staggered back against the car. The driver steadied him.

"Easy now," Rory said softly in her ear. "Don't let yourself go too far."

He hoped she would catch his drift.

"Let me go," she said through gritted teeth. "I won't nuke him."

Rory trusted that she would not. He had been the victim of more than one of her outrages of Affectations. Once she had blinded him and everyone within a city block. He released her and turned her to face him, saying gingerly: "Happy birthday?"

Rory and the others had given father and daughter some time alone, but the security staff was nearby and kept a watchful eye. Rory knew the job. He knew their loyalties were to Ms. Winston, even if the strange old man claimed to be her father. If a hand were to be raised at her...

An hour had passed, and the party ended inside. By Rory's estimation, it was almost 3 am. Studying the partiers that streamed down the mansion stairs, Rory mused, "*Better class of losers*," to himself. Had the homeless and institutionalized felons of Franklin been suited up in such foppery and finery, they would have fit right in. He questioned Rafe's invitation list, worried a little more about the people Ashley consorted with.

Ashley came to sit by him. She was not as incensed as at first sight. "How long do I stay mad at him?" she asked.

"Maybe until morning?" Rory replied.

Emerging from the crowd, a knot of white-haired, wild-eyed young men and women, their faces covered in ScanTats, made their way toward LF Winston. He was sitting on the hood of the limousine, his scrawny legs dangling beyond the bumper. He waved away the security and welcomed them in for a group hug. The rest of the revelers passed them by without a second glance.

To most anyone at the party, this little group was just an oddity, similarly dressed in black, wild white hair, crazy facial tattoos. Rory knew, however, that the six of them were Family, some way related or otherwise empowered with the same supernatural Affectations as Ashley and LF.

"Did you know?" Rory asked Ashley, who was leaning against him. "He's part of that family too?" They sat on a stone ledge that trimmed the courtyard.

"I had no idea." She shook her head, marveling at the scene. "Lived under the same roof with him for fifteen years and never had a clue."

"How do you hide something like that?"

"How do you hide for *ten years—a decade*? Period." Ashley asked, "And... how did *you* find him? No one's been able to find him. He was declared dead. All his assets were willed to my mother...I mean...*how*?"

"It was all luck," he said.

She turned and swatted his arm. "Luck? I don't think so!"

"Astar knew the right people. It's all her."

"I just cannot believe it," she said. Then a bit later she cleared her throat and said, "Never in my life has anyone done something like this for me, Rory. Thank you."

She buried her face in his chest and sobbed like a little girl. He held her, resting his cheek against her hair. He listened to her breathing settle. She snuggled in tighter yet.

It was better than any dance might have been.

04 Chrysalis

She had not picked his clothes, and she would never have picked these clothes, but Rory was looking trendy, if not utilitarian. Like the Family, he tended toward dark tones, but unlike them, his wardrobe was primarily forgettable. Cargo pants and sweaters. He had stepped it up for her birthday, she noted, to heavyweight slacks and a stylish and soft jacket. She brushed at the tears she'd left on it.

He was so good at waiting. In their short time getting to know each other, Rory had probably waited her out a dozen times. When she needed to find the right words, he never interrupted. When she just needed to cry it out, like she had just done, he was so great at just holding her.

Once last summer at Mother of Mercy, she found him out on a patio one afternoon, gazing up at a tree. She watched him, just standing there, for what seemed like forever. On her approach, he hushed her and pointed at a low-hanging branch. Dangling from it, just out of their reach, was a chrysalis with an emerging butterfly. She started to remark on it two or three times, but he shushed her. They watched the butterfly unfold her wings and articulate her legs. They watched the wings dry and flutter in the breeze. He smiled at her just then, a childish smile of wonder and glee, something she had never quite seen on him before or since, a smile she cherished. He waggled his eyebrows, and then, as if on cue, the butterfly took flight.

He had that kind of patience and that level of observation. Rory had a way of helping her see things she had taken for granted.

"Dew's coming," she said, feeling the chill of the early morning air. Her gown felt damp, and her bare feet were cold. "We could watch the sunrise," she ventured, gesturing toward the sky.

"Except the sun's coming up over there," he thumbed behind them with a chuckle.

That's the way it was with him: disorienting. She knew her home faced west and that the sun would come up on them from behind, but in this moment, she was bewildered. Exhausted from the party. A little tipsy. Maybe, she sighed, maybe a little in love.

"Still a good idea," Rory continued. "Watch the sun come up. Down a couple shots, you know, 'hair of the dog' and all...then I can take you to a greasy spoon in town where we can have some biscuits and gravy."

"You're kidding," she said, "but I like your plan."

The circle drive was nearly empty now. Jeeves had made up a room for Calissa, and she had long ago gone to bed. Rory's guest room was again waiting for him, though he never took the offer.

Old Tharp, the driver, was standing at his limousine, ever on duty, prepared to take the Amins and her father back into Springfield, which was the current plan. Astar and Zana were sleeping inside the car.

LF was strolling the grounds with some of the Family and a security detail. She had no idea what they were talking about or what he was up to. Jeeves had prodded her to offer her father a room in his mansion, but LF declined, saying instead he wanted "to again get to know the place." She smiled at that. Next to the White House Rose Garden, the Estate was one of the best-known properties in the nation.

Rory had nodded and urged her to just let him walk it off. "He's been in a cave for a few days, Ash," he had said. "Let him feel some grass between his toes."

Now they idly watched him and his entourage as they passed through their field of vision. They were dusky shadows with white highlights, while LF was a radiant shepherd, his robes glowing in the fading moonlight. He was escorting them to their cars at last.

"I don't know," she said to Rory. "Will I ever get used to having him around?"

"Hmmm. Dunno..." Rory took an exaggerated look at his watch. "He's only been here a couple of hours. You *still* not comfortable with him being back?"

They both chuckled.

"He's amazing," she thought back to their brief conversation. He had recounted so many rich memories of her childhood, things she had completely forgotten that meant so much to him. "He's just like I remembered him."

"Really?"

"Well, he was clean cut back then. You know. Didn't wear pajamas to parties or—"

A flash of blinding light. Rory enveloped her in his arms and brought her to the ground, sheltering her with his body. A loud explosion slammed them. She felt a wash of heat. A car alarm was blaring. Something dropped to the ground nearby. Debris was falling from the sky.

Rory said something as he climbed off of her. He repeated, "Car bomb!" He was crouched, ready to spring into action. "Stay here," he ordered. Then he glanced at the limo and led her to it. Astar and Zana had weapons in their hands, as did Tharp. "Stay in here, all of you."

Then he ran off toward the flaming cars.

Regaining her wits, Ashley tossed her platinum mane, "Like hell," she said, and rushed after him. Her dad had just been bombed. Her Family attacked—on her Estate.

She had never experienced a car bomb before, but it was worse than she thought. It was worse than anything she had seen in the battle of Franklin. In the light of the flaming cars, she could just make it all out. Debris and bodies all seemed to thrash on the ground in the flicker of the flames. Her eyes were tearing up, and she found herself gasping for breath.

Rory and one other man were dashing about, checking on people. They moved the bodies as they worked. They were shouting back and forth, words she did not grasp.

She was close enough to feel the lashes of heat from the fires. Acrid smoke was billowing from a burning tire laying nearby. More people were streaming toward the crash after a second alarm sounded.

One car's interior was aflame, the doors blown wide open. The other was scarcely recognizable as a car. She stumbled closer, then tripped and fell to the ground. She glanced back to see what had tripped her. A charred hand was clutching her ankle. It was hard to identify the smoldering person, but she could tell it was one of her security personnel. He shook his head, then collapsed, releasing her. "Help. A little help here!" she shouted.

She put her hand on his shoulder, noticing the shirt was burned and fused to his flesh. *He had to be in such pain.* The least she could do was grant him an Affectation of rest and release. No pain. She had learned from another member of the Family, a practicing EMT, to not press this too far into his system, for like any anesthesia, too much could be fatal. It could shut down vital autonomous functions that were on alert to keep him alive.

Someone nearby was screaming, and she rushed to him and applied the same soothing salve of rest and release. The man, this one was one of the Family, slumped immediately into repose. She affected the wounded again and again, quickly learning the system Rory and the other man were using. Face down, beyond help. Face up, do what you could.

A gathering at the edge of the lawn caught her attention. She walked up slowly, expecting the worst. She had yet to find the body of her father. Surely, he was there.

As people noticed her approaching, they made room for her. There were Family members, more staff from the house, a few party-goers. Someone was on the ground, taking a knee beside another body. Drawing closer, she knew it was Zana Amin tending to her father. "Princess, I believe it is a miracle that he fares so well." Zana pulled back and gestured to LF Winston. His cotton robe had holes burned in it, and part of his beard was seared. His eyes crinkled in recognition upon seeing her.

"Poppy?" she said, crouching down beside them. She stroked the rat's nest of white hair back from his face. "Are you okay?"

"I... I am," he said weakly. "You are too?"

She nodded, fighting back tears.

"It is not safe for you out here, Miss Winston," Zana said, below his breath. He glared at her, his dark eyes reflecting the fire. "No one could have known he would be here tonight."

"He's right," Rory said, crouching to help her to her feet. "That bomb was meant for you."

05 Betrayed

"Barbarians!" Astar shouted. Her face was tear streaked. She rushed into the clutch of people, livid. "Who else would do such a thing?"

Zana and Rory turned to her immediately and tasked her with Ashley's safety.

"To the house," Rory said.

"And perhaps downstairs?" Zana added. He helped shepherd the two women inside. A remnant of the security team followed.

"Help me to my feet," LF was saying. The elderly Family member, the one Ashley had been dancing with at the party, was doing his best to help. Rory plucked them both up and righted them.

"You," LF commanded Rory, "walk with me."

Rory surveyed the scene. A butler and a woman in pajamas were dousing the cars with fire extinguishers. Emergency medical vehicles were coming up the long drive. He could hear the sirens.

"For the best," Rory said, surprised he had said it aloud.

The two of them set off away from the bomb site. LF guided them on a thin trail between landscaping and the mansion's walls. As they rounded the building, Rory turned back and appraised the smoldering ruins, now strobing red and blue. He tried to convince himself it was all under control.

He brought his breathing under control.

"Your count?" LF asked.

"Pardon me?"

"You were counting back there," he said. "So... how many?"

Rory scowled. "Seven dead, eleven injured."

"I feel...safe with you," LF began, opening a door that had looked painted over, "...and yes, yes, I know your line of work." LF patted Rory's shoulder. "I want to tell you something I believe deeply. *This* is why I am here now," he tossed his head back toward the bombing. "Your timing in finding me could not be coincidental. I am *meant* to be here now. *You* are meant to be here. We all are."

"You and I, we have suffered incredible loss," LF said, gesturing Rory to a seat in the wine cellar.

Rory sat and said nothing.

"That we can walk away from that carnage...what would you call a man who can do that?" LF was picking through the bottles that lined the room.

"Lucky?" Rory said.

LF chuckled. "Yes, perhaps. But to leave the scene as if it were nothing more than a fender bender...would you say that makes us...callous?"

Rory inhaled the cellar air. Damp, but smelling faintly of cedar. He was counting the floor joists overhead.

"Cynical, perhaps?" LF returned, setting two wine glasses and a dusty bottle on an upturned wine cask. He sat opposite Rory and continued. "I have heard you are a man who mulls things over. That you like quotations?"

Rory nodded. Who had told him this? Ashley? A-Z? "I like to train," he said. "I try to ruminate over wisdom, incorporate it."

"Ruminate over this then: '*We can destroy ourselves by cynicism and disillusion, just as effectively as by bombs.*'" He opened the bottle and poured two glasses. "Timely, don't you think...bombs?"

There were well over 200 bottles of wine in this cellar, by Rory's estimation, and knowing what he did of the Winston family, none of it had a screw-on cap. None of it would be available at the local liquor store.

LF continued, "I fear, like Kenneth Clark, the author of that gem, that civilization is struggling, much more perhaps than when he wrote that a century ago."

"We've been through worse," Rory said.

"Yes, yes." LF Winston sat back in his chair, folded his legs under him. "Mankind has been through worse, perhaps. You and I, however, have been *nearly destroyed*, haven't we?"

"I don't think you know me, Mr. Winston," Rory replied. "And I can't presume to know you at all. We just met in the Amin's—"

"Bah!" LF said, and no more for a good while.

Finally, he continued, "You are a Turncoat. I know more than a little of—"

"No disrespect, sir, but—"

"Not on the field of battle, no, but I do know what you were fighting for."

Rory had trouble imagining the husk of the man across from him had once been at the forefront, once been the literal poster boy for the One World movement. To see him now, sitting cross-legged in a natty robe, more like a swami than a billionaire—it was not synching up for him. Levi Finn Winston had created the mighty airships that had changed agriculture and weather itself. He had fought global superpowers to bring rain to arid wastelands. His invention—his iron will in wielding it for the greater good—had made him an icon. The Rainmaker.

Rory struggled with it. How did that man, that legend, end up as this tiny man pouring wine back and forth from glass to glass, sniffing them in turn?

"I know you don't believe me, Mr. Reed." He sighed and sat a glass closer to Rory. "I *need* you, though, and I would very much like to share our disillusionment for a moment. Would you drink with me?"

"Sure," Rory said. He held up his glass, admiring the blood red of the wine. It was not Brandy, and he felt no need to swirl it like LF was doing now. He would not know what an old wine should smell quite like, so he did not pretend to act like it. It was not a glass of champagne, and he did not think a toast was in order. Rory was more of a whiskey man. He waited on LF.

They drank together.

"Yes," LF said, swallowing. "Just enough phase transition. A good earthy flavor to it."

Rory had nothing to contribute, so he simply nodded and took another drink.

"Maybe it could use a little more air. See, when you first uncork it, a wine like this has to off gas, to degas sulfites. It gets a little less bitter with some air." LF chuckled, "I'd not really thought of it until right now, but we're a little like this too. Men like us need some time to breathe."

By Rory's estimation, it had been a good amount of time, easily half an hour since the detonation. He was concerned about Ashley. Still, out of respect, he sat and listened.

And counted.

They were finishing their second glasses when LF picked up on Rory's impatience. "As I said, we are something of kindred spirits. I know, for instance, you're anxious. You're so young, you have different ideas of how long, say, we need to aerate. You would like to go upstairs and get back into the fray. I understand that."

"It was smart to get you out of sight, anyway, before the police and the—"

"I know, I know. The media. The feds. All of it would spin, spin, spin." LF waved it away. "I am better off staying dead. For Snow, however, I think it is almost time for my resurrection. I believe I may be an indispensable deflection for her."

"'Indispensable deflection?'"

"Yes, yes. We will stage my return. I will be her ex officio...whatever she needs." LF smiled, and Rory saw just a little of that maverick, the Typhoon Tycoon through his beard and wrinkles. "But first Rory—if I may—I need you to better understand me. I need you to defend me, to protect me."

"That's...that's not my typical line of work, sir."

"Oh, I know. There are no Contracts on *preserving* people." LF chuckled and finished his drink in a swig. "I need you to join me."

"I... uh... I don't quite know—"

The warmth of the wine welled in his chest, his neck. His face flushed. Rory tried to continue, to finish what he was saying, but his lips would no longer move. He closed his eyes. His limbs felt heavy and then limp.

Rory was cold, colder than he had ever been. His uniform was not rated for these conditions. He was sad. Betrayed. His men were lying dead all around him, splashes of red on the snow. Infinite snow and cold. He could make out a few of his unit here and there, struggling out of their clothes, then they disappeared.

"You walked out of that station, that cold, isolated station in a Wyoming winter storm, and for what? Ideals? You were ousted. Abandoned. Left to die in a whiteout blizzard, and when you did not die, what happened?"

"They shot us," Rory said. *Our own brothers and sisters of the Black and Blue.*

"They betrayed you. You came to be known as the Turncoats, but it was they who turned." *All that time, fighting. All the blood and treasure. Fighting. Struggle and skirmish. Blood and sweat. Betrayed by your brethren.*

Betrayed, Rory felt a tear but could not brush it away.

What did you stand for?

One World.

What did you die for?

One World.

What did you live for?

One World.

Except...?

Betrayed. There was no one. No One World. Only more greed. Bad guys. Disguised. A guise.

"With me it was worse," Rory heard LF say aloud.

Rory sucked in a breath, for he had not been breathing. He held it. He did not want to know the rest, but it swept over him like a tidal wave. All the knowing. All the knowledge. Omniscient awe and agony.

A lifetime of work. His life's work. And it worked! Joy to the world. For the good of the world. This was his gift. His finest hour. His glad tiding. No more suffering. No starving. No dust bowls or downpours or drought or death. LF Winston would bring world peace. The Rainmaker would bring water to the whole world. Water-bearer. Waterborne. What a boon! Rory's heart was flowing with warmth and love and all the optimism he had swelled with when he signed on to TransCorp in the first place. The Incus taking to the sky! He remembered the day, the first day when they shaved his head and issued him the uniform. The pride and joy. Joy to the world. One World.

Everything was working. One hundred ships were rerouting weather worldwide. No more death and damage from hurricanes. By year three, even tropical storms were tamed. Thousands of lives saved. By the fifth year, crops were growing where they never had prospered. Prosperity.

Then the winds changed and LF Winston, the marvelous man of the hour, was mistaken. First, it was bankruptcy abounding. All those who fed on pain, who banked on imbalance. Belly up banks and insurance and building trades. Premium prices over the barrel were worth less, then worthless. Disrupting the weather, cashiering on crops, was upsetting the fruit basket, spilling the basket. Spilling the beans.

His ships were sabotaged. Some were intentionally infected with waterborne pestilence. Some were grounded. *Faith was waning. Good faith was going dry. Sabotage. Trade secrets. Inside trading. Inside jobs. Insidious. The snare of disaster and the bane of betrayal.*

"Say it with me, Rory Reed," LF's voice demanded.

> *"No one has done good who has not suffered disillusionment,"* they spoke in unison.
>
> Rory's wine glass fell from his hand and shattered on the floor, jolting him awake.

06 Sound Wisdom

Police took statements.

Investigators measured wreckage and took images.

CommCorp was swarming for a story.

All of them were filling the Estate with JackChat, that incessant talking into appliances and HeadGear that sounded like so many disjointed conversations at once. Ashley waited them out in the guest rooms she had set aside for Rory, down the left wing and up two flights of stairs. From here, she could watch the action below and remain afar. She thought Rory would drop in sooner or later, but it was midafternoon, and he was still gone, preoccupied with arrangements for her safety, no doubt.

She rolled her eyes.

Guards were posted outside her door. They were also stationed on the stairs, on the landings, at each elevator... an excessive show of force, and for what?

They didn't know whether the bombs were planted offsite. These were rented limousines, she thought, so maybe the bombs were not even intended for her. Several of the guests were prominent figures in business and entertainment. All but the Family members were known to be terrifically wealthy. She could dream up a variety of vendettas, a hundred scenarios to explain the car bombing. She had been doing so all morning.

It had grown too warm in the window seat. Flopping on her bed, Ashley tuned in her HairPin, her custom-made HeadGear that looked like a delicate tiara but had the operating speed and capacity of a fighter plane. With a thought and intention, she zipped through well-wishers and work memos, then she surfed over headlines. As usual, the Winstons had a good working relationship with CommCorp, and no channel had anything to say about the car bombing. It had not made the news, and thus, it had not happened.

But it *had* happened.

Ashley tossed and turned. She was so exhausted, but she was struggling with the losses. There had been so many in the yard, so many of them were people she knew. Lucid dreams reminded her of the dead and dying in the firelight. She willed them to unzip their body bags and get up again to greet the day. Like LF, *everyone* stood, brushed it off, and returned to the dance. However, she knew it was not like that. A dozen were dead, and all because someone wanted her dead.

She had tried for hours to keep it at bay, but the pain and sorrow poured in. Ashley saw every victim she had Affected now. The dead. The dying. Some burned horribly and others thrown far from the wreckage and otherwise unscathed. Friends. Family. She whispered their names as each came to mind. She held vigil for each in turn. It was about dark when she had basked in her misery so long she had no more tears.

She leaned back against the headboard and sighed. A privilege of her status, protection and privacy kept her aloof. It was also a curse, leaving her alone at a time like this. Any friends lingering after the party had been interviewed and dismissed for their own safety. For her safety.

Rafe was being detained. That was ridiculous. He had worked for her for years. Loyal as they came, but those fascists on the force considered him a threat, and his green card was expired. Kyle Dupree could fix it for them, but not even he was allowed on the grounds, her own attorney and family friend. Astar and Zana were also under scrutiny. She missed them so, for at times like these, they had provided her such comfort.

Her father and Rory had not come around all day. She tried to summon them up on her HeadGear, but neither man was Jacked In. Carl, her closest friend from work, was off on a "research assignment" he had called it, and had not even the chance to return for her birthday.

Someone knocked at her door.

She adjusted her HairPin so that it sat properly on her head. She rubbed her palms into her eyes and composed herself. "Yes?" she said, tempering her interest.

The door opened to her grandmother, who entered the room saying, "Oh dear, are you alright?"

Ashley jumped from the bed and clasped the woman tightly. "I'm so sorry," Ashley cried. "I'm so very sorry."

"Now, now," Grandmother said, hugging back. "It's not your fault. No one blames you, Ashley."

"It is. It is!" Ashley moaned. "It always is. Just like Franklin."

"Oh now," Grandmother held her at arm's length and studied her. "Do you really think so?" She shook her head, answering for Ashley. "People *love* you. They want to be with you. We all want to be with you, despite the risk."

The risk was, it seemed, ever-growing. Assassins and mercenaries, terrible people paid to put her away, had destroyed the entire town of Franklin, far out in the Skirts, just to get to her. Rory's daughter had been held hostage in the manhunt. Now the threat had hit home, the Estate itself, and more lives had been lost.

Yet she was still standing.

Ashley felt she could never apologize enough.

She could feel the comforting Affectation from her grandmother coursing into her, relaxing her forehead and jaw. Her shoulders rolled loose, and she let out a sigh. "Thanks," she said, "but I've been letting myself feel it all."

"That's as silly as refusing medication," her grandmother said, persisting. "Don't punish yourself."

Dinner for two was delivered. As they ate, Ashley brought up the Family and asked after her grandmother's obligations. How could she spare time to be at the Estate like this? She was surprised to hear that the Family was all but gone, having left the country for somewhere more remote and secure. Ashley quickly learned that anything more on that topic was off limits.

"And what of Poppy?" Ashley asked abruptly. "He's...Family?"

Grandmother chuckled. "Why yes, love. He is our flesh and blood Family. He is my son."

"Oh." Taking a drink. Ashley asked, "So you really are my grandmother? Not just The Grandmother, like some matriarchal queen of the gypsies or something?"

"I can be both," she smiled. "I can be all that and more, if I wish."

"So..." Ashley did not want to appear accusatory, but she had to ask, "...you knew he was still alive...all this time?"

"I did not know, but I was led to believe it." She put down her fork and pulled a napkin from her lap. It was not, however, a napkin at all, Ashley realized. It was an ancient cloth, covered in intricate patterns. Grandmother gently unfolded it for Ashley to see. "You must believe what these tell you. Haven't you found yours to deliver sound wisdom?"

"Yes," she said, "and thank you for that. It was so—"

"Unbelievable? Magical?"

"Yeah," Ashley mused, her Grandmother was spot on.

Among Rory's friends, they called it the 'magic hanky.' Gifted to her by her Grandmother when Ashley was on the run and needing direction the most, the cloth was truly Ashley's first encounter with mysticism and magic. Her talents at Affectation could be explained, she thought, and she had studied the science of her craft for nearly ten years now. This was different: a cloth that composed messages, answered questions no one had asked, provided direction that could only have the prescience of the supernatural.

"What's it telling you now?" Grandmother asked.

Ashley had not bothered to look at it for weeks. She carried it with her, always, for she had felt horrible when she thought she had lost it once from neglect. She had all the pressures of the businesses she had inherited. She had been so immersed in all that, and the hanky had been without words for so long, she had quit looking toward it for anything. She felt terribly guilty.

"Go on," Grandmother urged. "I am as curious as you."

Ashley kept hers strapped to her thigh when she wore dresses. She stood, then smiled apologetically as she reached up her party dress to extract it from its garter. They both hovered over as Ashley unfolded it, shook it out, and spread it on the coffee table. At first, the complicated script was a jumble of symbols in a random pattern, but as they watched, the inks threaded and coiled into new symbols and elaborate designs. It reminded Ashley of a kaleidoscope.

"Focus, child." Grandmother whispered.

Characters snapped into one unmistakable word: "Duck."

"Duck?" they asked simultaneously.

Grandmother glanced through the room, low under tables and off in corners, as if she actually expected to find a web-footed duck waddling and quacking around.

The window seat and window glass blasted into the suite. Ashley tackled her grandmother just as a dark shadow shot overhead. The object crashed through a wall across the room and exploded. Wood, plaster, and glass slashed at her from every angle, but she did her best to protect her grandmother.

As the wall caught fire, sprinklers spurted into action, and they were doused with water.

Grandmother turned her head to speak to Ashley. "Sound wisdom," she shouted with a nod.

07 Help Arrives

He stood proudly, surveying his troop. The Franklin militia, led by Captain Kelli Chase, had been brought into shape by her lieutenant, Rory Reed. In the last six months, they had been through a rigorous bootcamp and continued to drill daily under his leadership.

The improvised drill pad, a tennis court on the grounds of the Estate, was crowded with 50 men and women standing solemnly at attention. To anyone else, the motley crew would have appeared to be inmates in a prison yard. In fact, a good number of them *had* served time, and some of them were even escapees. Rory did not care what others thought or saw. He saw their true mettle. They were battle tested and hardened.

The flood lights of the tennis court cast harsh shadows on the troop. Even those with ScanTats looked fierce and angry. They did not have uniforms, but they had scavenged all the useful gear from those who had laid waste to Franklin, so they were, in an understatement, equipped.

For once, Rory appreciated what money could buy. In this case, it was quick access to his soldiers. When the missile hit the mansion, choppers were immediately dispatched for Franklin, and Rory was instantly the new Chief of Security, as per orders from LF Winston himself.

Captain Chase stood at his side now, just out of earshot of the militia. She, too, was glaring at her soldiers, but out of the corner of her mouth she said, "They are so damn happy to be here, Reed."

"We didn't practice for this. We're street fighters, ready for door-to-door tussles." Rory admitted, a tone of concern seeping through.

"They're ready. They're all piss and vinegar, and I'd take that over security guards any day."

He knew she was right. What they lacked in discipline and patience, they made up for in spirit. These men and women were die-hard loyalists, and when called up to defend Ashley Winston, their Princess, they were zealots.

A sniggering erupted from mid-court, and several militia members could not contain guffaws and groans. Rory approached stiffly and stood at full attention just inches from a boy in the front row. People were struggling to get back into position, but they kept losing composure three rows back.

"What's so damn funny?" Rory bellowed.

The boy in front of him stared straight ahead, rigid and afraid. Someone cleared his throat to that boy's side, then said, "Kevin ripped a big one."

"Musta shit hisself," another added.

Several burst into laughter again.

Kevin Jackson was easy to spot. His face was beet red. People around him were punching him in the arm, tousling his hair. Several nearby looked nauseous. Others were grousing about them, falling out of rank.

"Kevin!" Rory shouted, and the young man double timed it to the front, then stood at attention. An awful smell settled in around him. "Damn, Kevin," Rory chuckled, covering his nose with the back of his wrist. "What did you eat?"

"Dawgs and Kraut, sir," Kevin snapped back.

"Never again, you understand me?"

"Yessir."

"Unless we go to chemical warfare," Rory continued. "Then we'll need all you got."

The entire militia collapsed into laughter. They were slapping each other on the back, wiping away tears, giggling like schoolchildren.

"Franklin!" Captain Chase snapped from over his shoulder, and every one of them stiffened, including Rory. "At-ten-shun!"

Rory did not move, though he wanted to twist and see what was going on behind him. His eyes strained far to his left, and he could make out Chase coming into his peripheral view. At her side was someone a foot shorter with radiant white hair. Without seeing more, he knew from the looks on the faces before him. It was Ashley.

She was moving fluidly, not in the wildest imagination moving like a soldier. She came to his side and stopped. "Look at me."

He twisted his head, then almost lost his military demeanor. She was still wearing the party dress, complete with bloodstains and burns. Her hair was a mess, and somehow, a diamond-studded HeadGear was tangled in it and dangling to the side. She had several cuts on her face and arms, and she was barefoot, as he had left her early that same morning. She was frowning at him sharply.

"Where the hell were you?" she said. "I could have been killed! Again!"

He had been kicking himself for hours about it. He turned to face his men and resumed his steely gaze. "I was with Mr. Winston, ma'am."

"Oh, just stand down or ease up or whatever!" she yelled at him and the troop. "And you, Reed, c'mere."

Chase led the two of them a good distance from the tennis court. Rory looked over his shoulder at the troop, shaking his head to see several flopping to the ground, others lighting cigarettes. A couple were still chiding Kevin Jackson.

"Don't dress him down like that in front of the men," Chase stated flatly.

Ashley reared back and almost lit into Chase. Then Rory noted she came to her senses.

"What in the holy hell do you think you're doing, you guys?" she said instead, to both of them. She was waving her arm back at the tennis court. "What'd you do, fly them in?"

"Yeah, we flew 'em in," Chase retorted. "Somebody's gotta take care of things around here."

"I already *have* taken care of things!" Ashley shouted back. "I had it under control."

"This isn't good," Rory said, glaring beyond them.

Rounding a grove of trees, a mass of men in garish suits approached. Rory knew them at a glance. They were casino bouncers, bartenders, knee breakers. The smallest of them was twice the size of any man on the drill pad. He glanced behind him, and his men had seen it too. They had their weapons drawn, and they stood taut at attention. One word from him, and all hell would break loose.

"That's what I'm telling you." Ashley waved her arms emphatically. "I got this. These are my men."

The mobsters squared off in a hulking line that faced the militia. Rory, Kelli, and Ashley were standing in the gap. It seemed like the worst place to be right then, Rory thought.

The mob, too, had weapons drawn, every manner of weapon, from tire chains and pry bars to shotguns and knives. Some of them popped their knuckles. One man was punching his fist into his hand menacingly. Though they were outnumbered two or three to one, it seemed it would be a fair fight—if it came to it.

"You're *overstepping*. Don't you see how this looks? What's LF gonna think?" Rory leaned down and spoke in his lowest tone. "Ashley, do you trust these guys?"

She matched his delivery. "I *own* these guys."

"Inherited from Mitchum's business interests?" Chase asked, her eyes clicking on each of them.

"Yeah, so?" Ashley jutted out her chin. "I needed some muscle. I needed some help here, and it sure wasn't coming from you!" She pointed a finger sharply at Rory.

"I was working on it," Rory said, gritting his teeth.

A commotion from the ranks of the thugs caught everyone's attention. The gang parted, and LF Winston strolled through the gap, wearing a fresh white robe, looking like some old wizard from a fantasy book. He walked right up to the three and smiled benevolently. "Problem?"

"And where were you all day?" Ashley huffed.

"I was getting to know your friend here," LF mused, looking at Rory. "We could not have known there would be—"

"Your own *mother* was with me when that thing tore into the house. We could have both been killed!"

Both factions of men seemed to catch Ashley's fury. They were shouting taunts and profanities at each other.

"Yes, yes," LF said, "I am aware."

"Are you now? Well, are you aware that she may lose an eye? Glass and splinters were everywhere!"

"Are *you* aware," Rory said, "that this was an inside job? Only insiders knew what room you were in—my room rather than yours."

She opened her mouth to speak, then closed it.

"And," LF added, "I tracked the trajectory. That weapon was fired from *our own* silo."

"You have missile silos?" Chase asked, looking from face to face in amazement.

The mob was losing control. They were getting frantic. One of them threw a knife at the militia. Rory turned and noted the cause: a member of his ragtag militia was mooning them.

"Give me the reins," he commanded Ashley.

"What?"

"Tell them I'm boss. Do it. Before it's too late." Rory added, "And I don't care how you do it. Zap them. Hell, give us all a jolt."

"I dunno about that," Chase warned.

The air was already supercharged, with anger arching across from either side. Ashley might let it roll out in a nasty Affectation.

"Pfft," LF said. "That won't be necessary. She's done quite enough to exacerbate the situation, don't you think? Yes, Mr. Reed, do your own work. Don't depend on her so."

Chase put a hand on his arm and stopped him from turning on Winston. "He's right. They'll respect you more for it."

"Fine!" Rory said, pushing past Ashley toward her mobsters.

He was easily as big as any of them, and he had much more professional experience than the lot of them. He did not even draw a weapon as he approached. Rory approached the most intimidating man he could find, a man who had a hollow hatred in his features. He got up in the man's face and said in a deep baritone, "We could use you, or I could kill you."

The man did a double take. The tire chain went slack in his hands. A smile broke across his features, and he said, close into Rory's face, "I know you! You're Combs' boy."

"Was," Rory said, his tone deadpan. "He crossed the line."

"Nick?" prompted another man, a nervous tech tweaker.

"He's alright," the mammoth man, Nick, said. "Belongs over here, you ask me."

"I got a better gig," Rory said.

"Pay better?" one of them asked.

"I'm off Contract and living large."

Nick raised an eyebrow. "You squeezing the Winston girl?"

Rory ignored the question. "So, you in? We all work together and get out of this alive?"

"Fat and happy?" Nick asked.

"Fat and happy," Rory nodded, a smile cracking across his face. This guy was a 'Coat. He was using Turncoat code. It once had meant they would be treated well, fresh grip and better quarters, and walk away with healthy commissions. That led Rory to stick out his hand for a solid handshake.

They were shaking when Rory heard the others coming up behind him.

"So," LF said, closing the distance between them, "have we made a truce or what have you?"

Rory nodded. He saw Ashley walking up with her father.

He hoped she would just keep her mouth shut, but she did not.

"Reed's your boss now," Ashley declared. "I'm his."

08 Tea, Interrupted

In 1662, Catherine de Braganza of Portugal was married to King Charles II of England. She brought tea with her, and it caught on to the extent that tea and England seem inseparable to this day. It is said that in the early 1800s Anna Maria Russell, duchess of Bedford, popularized the afternoon serving known as tea time, for it broke up the long afternoon stretch to the evening meal. Later that century, tea prices dropped to the point commoners could afford it, emulating royals. Morning tea, the elevenses, came along as a tradition in the 1900s.

Grandmother shared this bit of history over their morning tea in the flower garden. Ashley was enjoying her scone and hot tea, but she was loving the conversation with Grandmother, Kelli, and Calissa. Just a day ago, she had felt so alone in the world, and now she was surrounded by friends. The four of them sat at a wrought-iron table in the gardens just behind the house. Ashley loved this little spot, surrounded by beautiful flowering bushes that attracted butterflies. She held out a small silver spoon of sweet water and hummingbirds immediately took interest.

"What a place to grow up," Calissa marveled.

"Fit for a Princess." Kelli said sourly.

They all chuckled.

"I lived here before these gardens were grown," Grandmother said. "It was not so luxurious then. More practical."

"I thought you grew up Amish?" Ashley asked. In saying it out loud, she cringed at her own insensitivity and started to correct herself.

"Oh, I did," Grandmother smiled. "I married into all this when I married Walter. You might have heard him called the Ambassador?"

"Wait a minute," Calissa smiled broadly. "You were, like, Amish, like religious and poor and farming and...and you married into the Winstons?" To her, it was a fairytale. To Ashley, it was family lore she'd never really known.

Grandmother smiled and sipped her tea. "Yes, quite a contrast." She was looking off over the garden, recalling it all. "A leap I nearly did not take. So very different. But it was Walter's love, you know, that won me over."

They pried stories from her. She and Walter met when he would visit the farm, early in his career, bartering for the water rights to their properties. She had been struck by his cavalier attitude. She went for a ride in his Rolls and was fascinated by the television inside. When she went on her Rumspringa a few years later, she broke tradition and spent most of her time away from the Amish, travelling instead with Walter. He was so patient with her, taking her on flights in his plane, eventually taking her abroad for a month in Europe.

He was so kind to her that she shared her secret craft, the Affectations, revealing this gift she had never even told her Amish community. They might have thought she practiced black arts, she said, and she would have rather died outright than be accused of that. The Ambassador, it turned out, knew of a band of Eastern Europeans who were versed in this same magic. He flew her there; she found herself, and she found herself forever in love with Walter Winston. "Walter was so good to me," she sighed, winding down, "teaching, traveling, exposing me to so much culture, to the Family... and...and to tea!"

Ashley's mind was reeling with questions. The four of them seemed spellbound by Grandmother's stories.

"I'm going to be so wired after this," Calissa said finally. She had had several cups of coffee earlier with her father. She said he had just kept pouring more and more to keep her at breakfast. "It's like he never wanted it to end or something!"

Ashley knew Rory had earlier led the troop in PT, yelling at his recruits as they ran circles around the mansion. She could hear him, even now, shouting orders from the courts beyond the garden. He was dedicated to whipping those men into shape, into one unit or team, or whatever he called them.

"Does he always yell like that?" Ashley asked, when all four of them blanched at an especially loud and colorful turn of words echoing across the grounds.

"No," Kelli said.

"They respond well to that?" Ashley asked.

"He's really pissed, if you ask me," Calissa said.

"At his own men?" Grandmother asked. She turned her head far to the left to see Kelli with her unbandaged eye.

"No, he's not mad at his men," Kelli raised an eyebrow at Ashley. "I'd bet he's not mad at any *men*."

"You can't mean me," Ashley said, setting down her teacup.

Kelli and Calissa glanced at each other.

"What?" Ashley asked.

"Did you step on his neck last night?" Calissa asked finally.

"Did I—what?" Ashley shook her head, trying to toss off the confusion.

Calissa gulped at her tea.

"Step on his neck, dear," Grandmother repeated. She seemed to know the term.

"What does that even *mean*?" Ashley looked from face to face for answers.

"You might as well have depantsed him," Kelli said, crossing her arms and sitting back. "I told you not to."

"You mean when I yelled at him? He can't take a little yelling?"

Then, loud curses were exchanged, so far away at the tennis courts, yet so loudly they seemed just on the other side of the hedge.

"He can take it, *and* he can dish it out," Kelli said, "just not from you, not in front of the men."

"Especially not the new men," Calissa added. Everyone looked at her for more. "I dunno," she said. "He went on about something at breakfast."

"Really?" Ashley asked. "What else did he say?"

Calissa seemed a little edgy, almost frightened, then looked past Ashley and smiled up at someone approaching. "Why don't you ask him?"

Ashley turned around and shaded her eyes. Sure enough, Rory Reed was coming up on them, all business. He was soaked with sweat. His hair was sopping. He had on dark sunglasses and a white shirt translucent with sweat, the Winston Waterworks logo stretched across his pecs. He was clenching and unclenching his fists. "Captain Chase," he said in the harsh, curt tone of a drill sergeant, "they're all yours."

He did a kind of soldierly move Ashley did not recognize. It reminded her of a butler announcing a guest. Then Rory turned on his heels and stomped away.

"Oh, that can't be good," Kelli said, rising from the table. She sped off toward the site of the drills.

He had not even looked in her direction, Ashley thought. *What the hell?*

Calissa had headed inside, but Grandmother and Ashley trailed after Kelli. As they neared, Ashley heard curses and exchanges, more vile than those of the night before. "Things seem to be getting worse," Grandmother commented.

"If anyone can handle—"

A shot was fired.

They rushed to catch up to the action.

As they came over a crest in the landscape, Ashley saw Kelli Chase standing on the sidewalk, pistol smoking in the air, yelling curses like a pirate.

The scene beyond stopped them in their tracks.

The men were in two groups, Mitchum's men and the militia of Franklin, with a tennis court between them. At that moment, however, the two collided in a fury of fighting. Fists were swinging hard. Several were trained in the martial arts. It was clear, even from this distance. For them, the fight bordered on graceful violence. Others were blunter and more forceful in their delivery, tossing people down like rag dolls and fighting dirty.

On Ashley's approach, Kelli whirled, her face red and angry. "You!" she ground it into two syllables. "This!" She thrust her gun toward the melee. "This is what happens when you interfere."

Ashley could scarcely take her eyes from the fight.

"It does not seem productive," Grandmother said, averting her eyes.

A young man raised his bloodied face from the ground, moaning, "Cap Chase," and crawling toward her. Someone kicked him back down and moved on. The fight grew in intensity. Ashley was grateful they did not have last night's weapons with them. They were, however, resourceful. One man was using a tennis net to trip and tangle others. Some of them were wielding yard implements they had found somewhere. They had broken into the clubhouse, and several were now swinging rackets and golf clubs.

"Ah, you're right, Gramma," Kelli said, her shoulders slumping. The men were pounding one another without mercy or purpose, and they did not let up.

"Ashley," Kelli commanded at last. "Drop 'em."

"I will not!" she said. "You know I have issues with that...you know...I could hurt them!" The irony did not escape her: the thought of hurting them when they were all punishing one another in earnest. "I could *kill them*, accidentally."

Kelli holstered her gun, put her hands on her hips. She looked from Ashley to the horde, as if she were trying to decide her next move. Ashley half-expected Kelli would dive into the mix.

"You're a damned inconvenience," Kelli groaned. "You're the most powerful weapon we have, but *you don't wanna hurt anyone*."

"Allow me, girls," Grandmother said, stepping past Kelli to address the fighters. "Desist," she said in a normal tone of voice. Everyone fell in unison, enemies from both camps all crumpled together in a pile, unconscious.

"I take that back," Kelli said, a little awestruck. "*Gramma's* the shit!"

Grandmother looked at her, offended. "I beg your—"

Kelli did a little jig as she continued, "Dropped them all and didn't even raise your voice. No fancy gymnastics or hoo-doo. Just BAM."

"It was hardly like—"

"Gramma, you're where it's at!" Kelli held up her hand to high five, but Grandmother just looked at it. "You're Ashley on crack!"

Ashley shook her head and walked away.

09 CommCorp

Rory swept the straight razor over his temples again, leaving a smooth swath of flesh back over his ear. Executives of CommCorp were coming to the Estate, and he wanted to make a statement they could not misunderstand: he was not implanted and he never would be.

Even before joining TransCorp, Rory refused cerebral links. He had been a literal card-carrying member of the international organization, Don't Mess With My Head. Like PETA and other activist groups, DMWMH had committed acts of terror and treason, so they said on their promotional material. The rhetoric and ideals of DMWMH had been inspirational. An assembly of people shared Rory's disdain for implants and their inevitable monopoly on news and entertainment. He did not want to be force fed information, and he did not want information about him being archived like it was for everyone else who had a bolt in their brainpans.

Over the years, however, Rory learned the organization was little more than a fad, and flashing a DMWMH card was worth little more than discounts on fast food or picking up girls.

DMWMH never met, and they never accomplished anything—except for this simple hair styling. What started as a fashion statement had become a clear, defining mark of the anti-CommCorp camp. Every self-respecting Luddite shaved their temples.

He knew it would be an irritant to the CommCorp visitors, but he also expected they would not regard him as Leakage. He would be allowed into the inner sanctum of any meeting, for they would see him as no threat to their information being disseminated without their consent. What could he possibly do, talk to someone, just tell them what he'd heard? That wouldn't even stand up in court anymore.

Patrolling the corridors of the mansion, Rory was pleased that many of his Franklin militia had also cut back their hair. He smiled as he walked through to the gymnasium where all his security force was camped. So many rebels just subtly sticking it to the CommCorp.

Inside the makeshift barracks, he was shocked to see several of Mitchum's men were lined up to get their temples shaved too. Nick, the man Rory had squared off with on their first night, summed it up for him in an old rallying cry: "Eat the Rich."

"Jean-Jacques Rousseau," Rory said on impulse, then continued: *"When the people shall have nothing more to eat, they will eat the rich."*

"Amen, brother," Nick said, giving Rory a fist bump. "And I'm getting hungry."

"Give me your best man," Rory said. "One who's clean, no chips. I want a second set of eyes on this."

Nick looked across the cots. "Spexarth! You're up."

A wiry young man in a sleeveless shirt popped up from a card game and joined them. He did not look like a tech tweaker or a thug. Like Rory, he, too, sported the shaved temples. Different clothes and a different setting, and he could have passed as a respectable businessman.

"What's your name?" Rory asked as they walked outside.

"Steven Spexarth, sir."

"And what do you do—I mean, outside of this?"

"I'm a blackjack dealer," he said with some pride, "and an aficionado of prestidigitation."

"'Aficionado of...'" Rory mused. "Dealers I know are always looking to move on. What's your plan?"

Spexarth looked at him shyly, "Well, er...I would like to earn a college degree and practice medicine someday."

"Medicine?"

"Surgeon, at least that's my goal."

"Ah." Rory nodded. "Hence the prestidigitation."

"Yessir." he said, standing a little taller. "And it's best if the house wins a few at my table, you know."

"Best if the house wins..." Rory muttered, repeating the phrase. The house had always won. Pandering to them now would not solve anything.

Lost in thought, he led Spexarth to the laundry room, a depository for uniforms and dry cleaning. Down one wall was a rack of nice clothes sealed in plastic bags. Another wall had work clothes hanging on hooks. The room was otherwise littered with piles of laundry. "Let's suit you up, Steve."

After rummaging through the racks and piles, they created an ensemble that Rory thought might serve. The pants were a little short, and the cummerbund Spexarth insisted on did not match anything else. Admiring their efforts, Rory chuckled and said, "You clean up pretty good, kid."

Rory was signaled on his wrist watch appliance that the CommCorp advanced team was setting up in the library. "You know," Jeeves' voice drolled, "the big room with all the books?"

Rory pried off the appliance and tossed it in a laundry basket.

"Ditch all your tech," Rory said. "CommCorp's pretty paranoid."

"I'm clean," Spexarth replied. "Not a fan."

"That makes two of us," Rory said.

Around every corner, they passed the Franklin militia guards, and every one of them gave Spexarth a second look.

"What's with the stink eye?" Spexarth finally asked.

"They think I should take one of them inside," Rory said, offhand. "But I need you, Dr. Steven Spexarth. I need your eyes and ears in there to corroborate what I report later."

"Corrobor—"

"Are you up for it?" Rory stopped and sized the young man up.

"Yes, absolutely." Spexarth said.

"Are you credible?"

"Sir?"

"Will your people believe what you say?" Rory elaborated. "Because whatever may come from this, we all gotta be on the same page."

"I believe so, sir."

It was crucial that this worked. His Franklin militia would believe him if he said pink elephants were adrift in the library. Mitchum's men, however, might take more convincing.

"Remember, we're just eyes and ears. Got it? Eyes and ears."

"Just a couple security stiffs, right?"

"That's right." He straightened Spexarth's shirt collar, then said, "Blend in."

The four men at the library door did not surprise Rory at all. Even as they frisked him, Rory could hear the Jackchat scuttling in their earpieces. The man patting down his chest was not all there. His eyes were constantly darting left and right, a side effect of too much time in cheap HeadGear.

Their woman in the library anteroom did not surprise Rory much either. She was meticulous in rubbing their temples, feeling their wrists.

Rory wondered just what was being discussed in this meeting that might justify such measures. He tossed it off to paranoia.

"Clear," the woman said, and the double doors to the library were opened by two *more* CommCorp security men inside.

"Aw hell," Rory rumbled upon seeing a metal framework just ahead. He glanced around the room quickly. He spotted LF and Ashley, gave them a nod, then returned to the double doors. He bore his eyes into Spexarth and said, "You're on your own kid. I'll be right outside."

"But...but..." Rory heard the young man sputter, but he was already through the anteroom and back out to the hall. He nodded at the four guards. "I'm just his bodyguard," he shrugged, then settled into a nearby occasional chair.

There was no way Rory would go through that last checkpoint. It would detect the most minute traces of implants and surveillance gear. It would detect his Clench.

Whatever was happening inside the library seemed to take forever. Rory estimated it had been two hours. The Franklin militia had changed shifts twice, and the sunbeams had gotten long and low across the hall expanse.

He took the time to review his situation. Here he was, signed on under LF Winston, who was back from the dead and sharper than ever. He was tasked most immediately with Estate security, most particularly with the tightest security for one Ms. Ashley Elizabeth Winston, who at the moment he would like to take over his knee for a good ass whipping.

He laughed aloud at that, so loudly one of the door guards must have heard it over his JackChat, for he was glaring at Rory with distrust.

She had stirred up the men by bringing in a gang of thugs. Royally messed things up, Princess. He had told her as much. They had mixed it up more than once with his militia, the last time forcing Grandmother to knock their lights out. Grandmother! Rory marveled at the revelation. He was wondering just how many gypsy telepaths there were haunting around the mansion.

The doors swung open and a pack of men and women in expensive suits cut through the guard unit and continued down the hall right past Rory. In the middle of the pack were very young-looking teenagers, four by his count. They were dressed to the nines, and they had a smug air about them. Their handlers were returning a variety of communication devices to them as they walked. They paid him no mind at all.

Rory turned his attention back to the doors just as LF and Ashley approached. Rory absently slapped at his thigh, caught himself, and smiled.

"Where were you, Mr. Head of Security?" Ashley asked, her knuckles on her hips. She cocked her leg. It was a big question mark with a high heel on the end.

"*Chief* of Security," he corrected. Rory noticed Spexarth leaving the library, standing in the doorway, looking around. Rory stood and waved.

"So?" she asked.

"Detained," Rory replied.

"I'm sure he had a very good reason, Snow, didn't you, Mr. Reed?"

"Ulcerative colitis," Rory said. "I can't endure long meetings."

Ashley rolled her eyes.

"So, was it a good meeting?" Rory asked LF. "Get what you wanted?"

"Hardly," Ashley said.

Spexarth stood awkwardly nearby, shifting from one foot to the other. He seemed anxious. Rory was distracted by his shuffle and began counting the alternating footfalls.

"Diplomacy takes time," LF said. "And time is a potent elixir."

"The two most powerful warriors are time and patience," Rory said.

"Ha!" LF cackled. "War and Peace."

Rory nodded.

Ashley sighed.

Spexarth cleared his throat.

"Let's have some wine this evening, and I'll fill you in, eh?" LF said. "Say, eight o'clock?"

"Yessir," Rory replied. Then he turned to Ashley and asked, "Will you be joining us?"

She adjusted her posture and took her father's arm. "We'll see," she said, and they walked away.

"You left me alone in there," Spexarth said when they turned a corner. "Is it something about the Winston lady? Something you want to tell me?"

Rory fought back a diatribe, saying only, "Nothing to tell."

"Well, I got a lot to tell you!" Spexarth said. "And you're not going to believe it!"

10 Hokum

She walked arm in arm with her father along the terraces of the vineyard that wrapped the west side of the Estate. The sun was going down and the late afternoon was cooling. They were making up for 10 years of small talk, and she enjoyed every syllable. Then, after a while, he turned the conversation to CommCorp.

"You seemed...out of sorts in that meeting, Snow."

"I felt like...like there were too many people trying to lead," she said, "So I withdrew."

"Don't withdraw. These decisions—all of them—are *yours* now, not mine. I have no legal right to anything, not even the clothes on my back. I am dead, honey."

"Please don't talk like that."

"Ask Kyle. I am legally dead."

"You were never dead to me. I always thought you were out there somewhere. I can't tell you how many times I'd hoped you would come back."

"And here I am!"

Ashley stopped and looked him over from head to toe. He was still barefoot, but he was wearing an expensive tailored suit, and his hair was tied back. His wild beard was neatly trimmed. She was glad he was here.

He tended to the grapes a bit. She watched him move and work, strong hands, straight back. He seemed so much younger.

"We've the least to fear from CommCorp, you know," he said, turning back to her. "That's why I started with them."

"The one company that can broadcast anything it wants directly into the heads of millions and millions of Tweakers and scum?"

"Yes, that's the one. That same company could project positivity to people who have never heard a kind word. Wrap a message of peace in the guise of an action movie. Teach kids to read with jingles and rhymes presented for free for the entire world to learn."

"That would be great, dad, but all they see, *all they know*, is what CommCorp censors tune them into."

"They have had global translation for a decade. They have had ubiquitous satellite connectivity even longer. Snow, there is no other power on the planet so potent as one hand clapping."

"Oh, please!" Ashley groaned. "What are you talking about now?"

"One message, one unifying message of love."

"CommCorp is going to broadcast that?"

"Yes," LF smiled. "At least, their technology will."

"What are you saying?"

He chuckled and strode ahead. "Catch up," he said.

Ashley kicked off her heels and carried them by the slings. She caught up with him quickly and asked again, "What are you saying?"

"How far can you...reach people?" he asked, his gesture encompassing the horizon.

"You mean..." she felt an ache in her forehead from her eyebrows straining so.

"Yes, what is your range?"

"I..." Ashley made the realization she felt he was leading her to: "I don't know."

"It is roughly limited to your line of sight...or the distance you can clearly see, though, albeit, even around corners and such."

She nodded her head slowly, wondering where he was going with the topic.

"Mine is intimate. Mother's is to the horizon, you know."

Ashley did not know. Prior to that incident on the tennis court, Ashley did not know Grandmother could Affect anyone without touching them.

"I don't see what this has to do with CommCorp."

"Amplification." He said it as if it were obvious. "It's easy, really," he continued. "We buy them, and then we broadcast our message using their technology."

"Wait, wait, wait," Ashley said, "We *buy* them?"

"Yes." LF said, matter of fact.

"You just got through berating them for everything they do. You nearly made the youngest girl cry."

"It's just business," he said. "Drive down the value, then buy up the product for pennies on the dollar."

"You will not drive down the value by just insulting them and CommCorp."

"Their technology will fail them, and then we will buy them. Today was just part of the courtship. They think you're weak and that water is for dishwashing," LF scoffed. "You don't need HeadGear and all that tech webbery to communicate. You don't need to have implants to have fun."

"And how do you know their tech is failing them?"

"It will, right?" He shrugged. "Food depends on us. Our air ships bring rain and sun in the right proportions. Shelter depends on us—fighting blizzards and hurricanes. Water and weather and wealth will stand independently of communication, dear. We will always find ways to communicate, with or without being jacked in."

"So...you're plotting a corporate takeover?"

He smiled his broadest smile. "Sweet Snowflake, goodness no."

"Then..."

"We will bide our time. When they fail, for technology always fails, then we will buy."

"I'm confused," she said, rubbing her face. "So, what was today about again?"

"Every peak and valley in the stock market is an indication of confidence. Buyers' confidence. No company is artificially managed, at least not yet. Every decision is stood up on emotion."

She sighed and shook her head. "I'm not cut out for this."

"Sure, you are. Listen, I might have been a little brutal in there, but the point was to shake their faith. Everything I said in the library was recorded—I know, I know, they claim to have taken out everything, but who among them do you think does not have a high-end implant? They were Jacked, and everything I said in there went right into their heads...but furthermore into their databanks...and *furthermore* into documentation somewhere in the bowels of CommCorp. When I said they would fail, and I said it with conviction, it was like a prophecy. Did you see that on their faces?"

Ashley did not know what to say. She nodded slightly.

"So now, even a glitch in their technology will plummet their prices and more, their confidence. I had to be firm in there, see? I've rehearsed that for years and years."

The sun was going down over the horizon, and the sunset was beautiful. Ashley took a deep breath and admired the majesty. Maybe she had been around Rory too much, but she was thinking the grapes and the sunset were marvels. The tilting of empires was losing its luster.

Then she remembered and asked, "Our message? What message are you wanting to amplify again?"

"You know the one, Snow. It's been the same message I was trying to share so long ago, when they ran me off."

"One World." she said, flatly.

"Yes, yes," LF smiled, though his smile seemed less benevolent with his beard cropped. "One signal, all languages, One World."

A little girl can get attention and get her way. A beautiful little girl has an ever-easier time of it. If that girl were also bubbling over with Affectations...it would seem the world would be hers to rule. Who could resist a beautiful young lady with platinum hair and a thousand-watt smile? What could stand a chance between her and the object of her affection? Not a man nor woman, not an angel nor principality—only an idea.

Ashley had spent her entire life in the shadow of an idea. She had always been bested by this dream of his for one unified world. That singular thought had possessed him to work at all hours, with no regard for anyone or anything else, even himself.

It had brought nations to ruin. How many millions had died on either side of that concept? Even Rory had been victim to the wiles of One World, courtesy of TransCorp, only to learn it was nothing but hokum.

Sure, Poppy was back, but he brought with him his one true love, his One World.

She wanted to smack him with her shoe.

Ashley pushed another exaggerated exhale into the handkerchief. It drifted up, then settled back on her face. She had puffed it up a dozen times now, and it always settled back over her exactly as it had launched. It shielded her face from the rays of the sunset that poured in through her window.

The dinner hour was approaching, and she needed to get her head in the game. She scoffed, and the hanky fluttered in agreement. It was nothing if not a game, whether it was a dinner party or a corporate coup. She was learning again that she was nothing but her father's pawn, and that did not set well with her.

Ashley was wearing her evening dinner gown but had yet to make up her face. Her father had insisted that she cover the ScanTats, for the guests were a conservative bunch, environmentalists he needed to keep pacified.

Why did they matter now? They had not been at the table in years. She wondered if LF was conspiring with them. Maybe he was going to rile them up? Maybe they were instrumental in undermining public faith in TransCorp?

She pulled the handkerchief from her face again and examined it for some insight. There were no answers, just a squiggle of foreign designs.

The tiara on her nightstand, blinking blue, caught her attention. She sighed, flumped up her pillows and settled into them, mounting the HeadGear and drifting out into the connection.

"Hello, lambchop!" Kyle Dupree's visage pulled into focus, superimposed over her room.

"Skipper," she smiled. "Coming to dinner?"

"Working dinner for me," he pouted, "but yes, I'll be there."

"Seems like it's all work and even more work with him back."

"What's on tonight's menu?"

"You know better than I do. Why's he serving up the Greens?"

"Something to do with Peru," Kyle said. "I dunno. I don't do international relations."

Trees raced by behind him and shadows flashed across his face. He was distracted by something in his field of vision.

"Kyle. Kyle! Are you driving?"

"Yeah," he admitted. "It's fun."

"Don't ping me when you're driving," Ashley said. "Put it on pilot."

He complied, then looked directly into the camera lens. His attention was piercing. "Hey now," he asked, "what is it?"

Ashley looked past him. She thought about bringing something else up. Finally, she asked, "Are you on a Stetson?"

She caught the slightest eye roll. "I'm in the McLaren. Retrofitted with a Halo. Top of the line... why?"

"It'll wait until after dinner."

"Doesn't look like it should," he said, studying her features. "We've got more privacy now than we will after dinner, if that's an issue."

Ashley crossed her room and bolted the door, then returned to her favorite patchwork chair. She pulled a deep breath, then just blurted it all out at once. "He's making a mess of things. I was just getting the hang of it, I think, and all that time, like for the last six months at any rate, I kept thinking what I was doing would have made him, you know, proud of me. Of course, I thought he was dead, right? It was just a fantasy or whatever, that Poppy was like, looking down from heaven or whatever—" she sniffed and chuckled back tears. "But now he is here, and I can't think he's going to like the way I want to run 3dub."

"Legally, he doesn't have a say in—"

She scoffed. "You know that doesn't matter. Hell, the *ghost* of LF Winston would be stronger than anyone in the boardroom. He's legendary...and he's off the chain. You heard him with the fab four. He's callous. He's cruel. And he's got an agenda. Did you know about that?"

"I've not spent much time with—"

"I can't get into it, not on the Beam. Later tonight though, if you have time?"

"Think your security guard will let you out of earshot?"

"My security guard," she recalled, "has an 8 o'clock in the wine cellar. How about then?"

Their HeadGear tapped them both with a suggested meeting after dinner. They nodded acceptance of the suggestion and logged off.

Ashley pulled her knees up and rested her chin on them. Reflecting on their JackChat, she realized he hadn't said why he had reached out to her. It was one of his wellness checks, maybe, or maybe something more. The HairPin's virtual clock reported it to be nearly six.

Just a couple of hours, then they could go for a drive or slip away to the old tree house. Then she'd really sound him out on LF's scheme, and she'd find out just what Kyle wanted too.

11 Dinner Guest

"Ol' Cool Hand Levi lost his wits, you say?" Big Nick asked with a smile.

"Mr. Winston? Yes." Spexarth reported. "Pounding the table, red in the face."

"I still find that hard to believe," Rory said.

The three of them were in a large conservatory, standing near a fountain twelve feet high. This was the central feature of the room. All paths led to it. The ceiling vaulted up at its apex directly above the fountain. It was an elaborate work of Rococo art, swarming with naked cherubs. Splashing with water.

Rory liked it for just that reason—the splashing would help mask their conversation.

"So, if Mr. Winston's crazy, what are we doing here?"

"You work for Miss Winston," Rory corrected.

"We work for you," Nick said, "and I'm asking you. If the old man's gone gaga, what are we doing here?"

Rory stood at his full height and shrugged. "Job hasn't changed: Protect the Princess."

"Her and the old lady are wicked," Nick said. "From what I know—"

"Wicked is relative," Rory said.

"They don't need protecting," Spexarth said, "that's what Nick's getting at."

Rory knew better. He circled the fountain, taking it all in. Somewhere in this mansion, someone was likely watching them on the tiny cameras mounted everywhere. Might as well make it convincing.

"He really called the whole CommCorp infrastructure a wad of bad wires?" Rory asked, returning to the others. "He called the four cousins a bunch of brats?"

"Snot-nosed brats," Spexarth said. "And he told them to grow up."

"And he's still alive to talk about it?" Nick asked, now astonished. "I know people got killed for saying less about CommCorp—for just writing it up in graffiti!"

"These people," Rory shook his head. "I heard of a little kid once got beaten half to death for spitting out gum on the sidewalk where a CommCorp exec was walking. They can take it from each other, just not from us."

"Then why do you work for them?" Spexarth asked.

"Pay's good."

"Ah, you got an angle, don't you, Reed?" Nick asked.

Rory did not answer. He studied the flow of water. From the highest spout, a lily held in the outstretched arm of a cherub. It fell in a cascade to splash on the head of another cherub, who seemed to find it amusing by the look carved in his face. The drops and splashes continued on down, parting the waters all around the fountain. Thirty-two splashes to the basin.

"I think LF's working an angle, but I don't know," he said at last.

"You'll tell us after your wine and cheese," Nick sneered, "right?"

Three days before, his doorman or footman or personal butler—Rory did not know the man's station—had said that he was invited to dinner expressly by Miss Winston. "Formal, if you might bother," the man said.

"You're Jeeves, right?" Rory asked.

"Holbrook, sir. Jeeves works the other wing."

"Right." Rory said. "What if I don't have any formal wear, Holbrook? Didn't pack my tux, you know?"

That had been his first exposure to what he called the laundry room. Holbrook had outfitted him nicely that night, and Rory did his best not to spill anything on it. He was surprised that every morning Holbrook would return his coat, freshly brushed and pressed, complete with a clean shirt and new tie. Somewhere in the mansion, or down through the ages, someone once living here had also had an 18-inch neck. Or, knowing these people, they had custom tailored it all for him.

By tonight's dinner party, Rory was wondering why they called it a party. The novelty of it had worn off and the tedium of eating one course at a time had worn on him. The quiet of the room emphasized the clinking of silverware and sounds of chewing. One guest smacked her food. Another had false teeth that knocked annoyingly when he ate.

A server lifted off a silver cloche with practiced flair. The main course. Rory did not really like pheasant, or duck, or whatever fish was revealed before him on the double plates this time. He longed for a beer and a burger. If the food was terrible, the company was even worse. Rafe, the party planner, was sitting across from him, retelling his horror story of being held overnight downtown. Rory did not know the mousy woman who ate the tiniest bites and said the very least among them. The way she was mesmerized by Rafe's story, however, suggested she was with this upset criminal element. Kyle DuPree, Rafe's liberator, also sat at Rory's table, but he was checked out on his HeadGear. The lawyer was as glittery as the table service... cufflinks, rings, bracelets...clearly showing off his wealth and power.

All the gold and drama had not earned any of them a seat at the big table. Instead, the four of them huddled around this table for the help. It reminded Rory of a card table the kids would sit at for Thanksgiving.

Rory leaned forward to look at Ashley. She pretended not to see him, positioned as she was far down the big table by her father. Rory chewed at the rubbery fish, continuing to stare at her. Finally, obviously uncomfortable, she glanced at him, then asked the person to her left for pepper or something.

For dessert, they brought around thimbles of shaved ice. Rory tossed his back like a shot and was munching on it when a commotion stopped his chewing. Waitstaff was trying to keep an intruder out, but he pushed through them. Once inside, the big man, a Samoan from Mitchum's men, turned his torso left, right, then left again. He made eye contact. He kept shaking off the steward and bus boy and anyone else pestering him. Rory nodded, got to his feet, and approached him.

"What is the meaning of this?" one of the head table diners said.

"Security!" another squealed.

"I am security, ma'am," Rory said, then turned to the big man, saying: "You're Pineapple, right?"

"Yeah. There's trouble in the yard."

Rory gave LF and Ashley a dismissive wave, then followed Pineapple. For his size, the man was agile. He weaved through chairs in a lobby, darted down a flight of stairs, and dodged some people in white who were carrying a large cake. Rory could tell it was something important simply by the man's pace.

He checked in with Calissa on his Clench.

He continued to clamp his teeth and his fists. "Every damn time," he grumbled. Let down his guard even for a dinner party and all hell broke loose.

He chastised himself around every turn. They exited the mansion into a vast back yard, easily the size of two football fields side by side. In the center was a helipad. They made their way down the long left side. "Pineapple, what's the problem?"

"One of your yahoos," he panted, "shot an intruder."

Pineapple led them down a wooded trail. It ended in a clearing. Several of the security force had gathered there, all shining flashlights toward the perimeter wall. As Rory approached, Chavez from Franklin stopped him. He leaned in close and said, "You don't want to see this."

Rory was already getting queasy. He hoped it was just the food. His curiosity was getting the better of him, however, and he approached.

It was a strange and grizzly sight. A person wearing a black skin suit and black fatigues had been hewn in two. Only his upper body was there, a clean cut that had since spilled entrails on the manicured lawn. Rory spasmed and wretched off in the dark, purging his dinner.

"Damnedest thing," one of his militia boys said, "just chopped in two."

"Where's the rest of 'im?" another voice asked.

"We looked on the other side of the wall. Up in the trees..." the militia man said. "Nothing."

Rory wiped his mouth on his sleeve and joined them. He did not look at the dead man but kept his eyes trained on the others. "You said they shot an intruder," Rory said to Pineapple, "not this."

"I shot him." A Franklin kid in ScanTats stepped up. "I told him to freeze, he didn't, and I shot."

"Was he threatening you?"

"He was disobeying me, and if you look, he had pulled his weapon, so yeah, I'd call that a threat."

Rory shook his head. "No ID, right?"

Pineapple started, "Nothing on him—"

"At least nothing from the waist up," someone said, trying to crack a joke.

"Good grip though," said another Franklin man, holding up weaponry he had already harvested off the body. "Least what of it that wasn't cut in two on his belt."

"I ain't ever seen this. It's like he was sliced by a samurai or something," another said.

"Or a laser, maybe," Chavez offered. "It's a clean cut, right through his sidearm and bone and everything."

"What's your name?" Rory asked the shooter.

"Eric Clyborne, sir," the young man replied, stepping closer.

"Clyborne, tell me about it again, from the top."

"I'm on patrol, see, come from the pool, heading to rattle the gate, same as always, when I saw a flashlight, I think, then there's this guy like crawling through the wall at me."

"Crawlin' through the wall? That wall?" someone asked from Mitchum's men. They all looked it over.

"I yelled, 'Freeze,' but he kept coming—"

Rory held up a hand. "You say he kept coming, like he was coming slow?" There was no sign of entry. No ropes dangling from the trees. No tunnel under the fence. The wall was intact. The man was not.

"I dunno. It happened real fast. When he didn't respond, I fired."

"Good job, Cly," a militia comrade said.

"Then what happened, after you fired? How'd he get in this shape?" Rory asked.

"I shot, he fell, and it was like when he fell, just his front half hit the ground, the rest got snipped off, like it was still in the wall or something."

Rory stepped around the body on the dry side and examined the wall for something. Anything. It was the same white stone wall that surrounded the Estate. Old. Solid. There were no marks on the wall to suggest the intruder had been scaling it. No hack marks from a sword or laser in the stone.

Another man was shining his flashlight at the wall, directly behind the fall of the body. "What's this?"

Rory inched closer, the nausea welling up as he smelled the fresh blood.

"Piano wire?" someone ventured.

Two little sticks were poked into the grout. They looked like pencil lead. Dangling from them was a hoop of charred black wire, thin as a hair. Rory snatched it up and tucked it in the pocket inside his suit coat. He plucked out the sticks and put them in another pocket.

"Clean the rest of this up, fast and quiet," he ordered, and started away.

"What do we do with the body?" Chavez asked.

"What body?" another man said.

"Exactly," Rory said.

"Where're you going?" Pineapple asked.

"Gotta call in some research," he said. "This just took a whole new turn."

12 Leavings

In the wake of the security breach, Kyle had been swept away in a rush along with LF and his entourage of guards. "We'll swing from the branches later," was Kyle's only communication with her directly. She replayed it over and over, trying to decide if he meant later yet tonight or simply another time. It was frustrating.

Even more frustrating: Rory had left the dinner party early and without so much as a 'by your leave.' All it seemed he had done was double her guard detail and move her to an interior room of the mansion.

If he was going to be her security, he had best learn to communicate.

She was going to buy him a HeadGear, anything he would wear, and require him to keep it on his person at all times.

She chuckled at the thought of him wearing something lavish and ornate, some HeadBand contraption that glittered with rhinestones like one she had seen on a sheik. Even better, she imagined him in an old school Bobblehead. She sobered up immediately again, angry that she knew he would not agree to it. Sometimes he did not seem to agree to *anything* she suggested. He was a bullheaded man.

She realized she was mad at him for not doing something she had not even asked of him yet. "Maybe I ought to back off a little," she said aloud.

"What's that, dear?" her Grandmother asked. This evening, besides the standard security, Rory had arranged for around the clock support specifically from the Family. First shift, which might have been the one he felt least secure about, was held by Grandmother. Either that, or her grandmother had elected to take this shift, for she was an early to bed, early to rise sort.

"I said, maybe I ought to back off."

"Back off what?" Grandmother was sitting across from Ashley, crocheting.

"Mr. Reed," she said. "Rory."

"Hmm," Grandmother said.

"So, you agree?"

"Levi tells me you have been rather short with him," she said, looking up at her.

"He's a fine one to talk. Did you hear about what he did today with the CommCorp execs?"

"No, I don't believe so."

"He embarrassed me, embarrassed all of us."

"Ah. You saw his temper flare then?"

"So..." Ashley began. "That's nothing new?"

Grandmother chuckled and put down her project. "Your father was famous for his tantrums. I am surprised you don't remember them."

"I was like 5 when he left. All I remember is...well, the good times."

"Nostalgia. Rose-colored glasses."

"All I've ever heard about is philanthropy and kindness. That's what he's famous for."

"Ah, the victors write their own history, don't they?"

"What's that?" Ashley turned down the music in the room with a wave of her hand. That had been a security measure, too, noise-cancelling ambient music to make her harder to find in the building.

"I suspect Levi has crafted quite the flattering public image for himself. And what else would you know of him, right? If not memories, all you have left is what he tells you and what he bought the bandwidth to tell the world."

"Grandmother!" Ashley said, "You don't seem too sold on your son."

"Oh, I love him dearly. He reminds me so of Walter in the early days," she smiled a thin-lipped smile. "Dashing and debonair. So enterprising! And yet temperamental. And... fickle."

"About that...I still can't get it." Ashley said. "It still sets me off sometimes to think of it. Why'd he leave like that, Grandmother?"

"Ashley," she heard him say her name from behind. "Don't you know why I left?"

"I... well...no." Ashley felt her face flush, and she squirmed to make more room for him as he came around to sit beside her on the settee. *When had he come in?*

Grandmother seemed again preoccupied with her crochet work, humming as she made knots with distinctive twists of her fingers. Ashley watched in fascination.

"This might interest you too, mother," LF said.

She did not look up.

"There were threats. Haven't you heard of the threats at least?"

Ashley shook her head, no.

"When Winston Water Works was at the height of its success, when we literally bought the seas themselves, some 'investors' did not appreciate it." He cleared his throat. "Personally, I think they finally came to realize the value of water, you see, yes. Realized water was an invaluable resource.

"They did not appreciate that I was giving it away. They did not like the way it was affecting the imbalances they all thrived on. 'What's that? No more starvation? No more dependency on western technology for agriculture?' Why, they could not sit idle and watch their sand castles fall."

Grandmother smacked her lips and yet said nothing. Ashley could tell that she had plenty to say, for the knotting grew more erratic and powerful. The humming was more fast paced, a little louder.

"But threats?" Ashley asked.

"Yes, yes. Attempts on my life, and by that, terrible danger for Delores, for you, for the entire community."

Grandmother scoffed in the tune she was humming.

"It's true, mother. Do you know we intercepted a full-scale ICBM en route to this property? Not some little scud missile like the one—"

"The one that nearly killed us!"

"Much more deadly. Nuclear warhead, albeit a dirty bomb, only 5 megatons. Plenty to destroy everything here, *everyone* here."

"So, your solution was to run away and hide?" Grandmother said, biting the words off.

"My solution," he said, composing himself, "was to distract them, to lure them away from the Estate. I hitched a ride on a Weekly and fled the country. It took them years to even locate me."

Ashley thought about her own adventures, the many times she had evaded pursuit. She smiled just a little at the thought of them running away together.

"When they did get close," LF continued, "I would route a storm overhead and fly away again."

"You might at least have told us you were alive," Grandmother said without looking up.

"I was better off dead, and you all benefited from that as well."

“Fiddle.” Grandmother said, tossing aside her work, getting up as if to leave. “You were a coward.”

“I could level similar claims against you, you know.” LF said, also getting to his feet. “You left when I was young too. What makes you so quick to judge?”

“I was *truly* a danger,” she said. “I did not know how to control it.” She looked from LF to Ashley, almost pleading. “You were a late bloomer, Levi, not even aware you *had* the Craft until you were married. And you, child, I shudder at the thought of what you might do if provoked.

“So yes, I also left, but it pained me so. I think I broke poor Walter’s heart. I... I did my best to stay in touch, given the times, cards and letters and email...and video chats with you...”

“When I was in college, you said you were returning to the Amish, then after a while, I never heard from you.”

“You never wanted to hear from me by then. Off spinning your own webs. Creating things your father would have been amazed by. Son, you took Water to a whole new level—literally—with the airships. I was so proud of you. I am still proud of you, but you cannot be so disingenuous with your daughter. *It is simply not right.*”

She slammed the door on her way out.

Ashley studied her nails.

LF sat down with her again. “The truth?”

She shrugged.

“I was a danger to you. I was a target. Every corps at the time was teaming up to tear me down, Snow. Vicious rumors had spread, and people turned against me. Have you ever had someone reject a gift you were giving them? That was what it was like. Everyone turned against me. I was so...dejected...that I *had* to go away. It hurt too much.” He took her hand and continued, “You understand, don’t you?”

She was feeling sympathetic, first for young Levi, then for herself, and at last for the old man before her. A growing sorrow was crushing her chest, his pain became her own. She empathized with him. Rejection. Betrayal. Nothing he had was good enough for the world, not even salvation.

Ashley snapped her head and stood abruptly. "That was uncalled for."

"I was just hoping you'd see things my way, dear."

"Talking...*talking* is okay, but don't invade my thoughts like that. If I'm ever to forgive you, it will be on my own terms."

"Your friend, Rory Reed, has seen things my way."

"What?"

"He gets me."

"Pfft. Where's he at, anyway? It's after 8."

"Oh, right." He stood with her and offered to help find him.

"I guess," she said and let him lead her out into the hall. Two guards were in front, two behind. The six of them marched off both wings, all three floors, and did not find a trace of him. Ashley raised Jeeves on her HairPin, finally.

"I wouldn't know," Jeeves said, his expression long faced and passive. "Holbrook says his master has left the premises."

"Left the premises!" Ashley repeated.

"Yes, mum. He said to tell you..." Jeeves consulted another device. "Ah, here it is. He said to tell you he was rug shopping and not to wait up."

"He's gone to the Light District," she said. "He's gone to see A-Z without me!"

"I could not hazard a guess, but he did say one more thing, and this I heard myself."

"What is it?" she snapped.

"He said," Jeeves cleared his throat, "that defending the Estate had become untenable, no, impossible."

She pulled off the HairPin and looked at her father. "Rory's out on the town."

"Surely," LF chuckled. "Surely not."

"Left an hour ago."

"But what of our defenses, our security? He's the Chief of Security."

"Yes, this I know," Ashley huffed. "He'd better have a damn good reason for skipping out like this."

"Indeed," LF muttered.

13 Radio Silence

The Wexler building was an old art deco seven story that sat mid-block in the heart of the Light District, Springfield's reconstituted and flourishing arts and antiques quarter. The ground floor was home to a regionally acclaimed eccentricities shop owned by Astar and Zana Amin. The floors above were rented to ghost tenants and dummy corporations that dutifully paid their bills. Building inspectors, utility workers, repair men—even stray cats—were all bribed amply to look away.

Astar's routine—switching lights, playing music, opening windows, raising blinds—sustained the illusion these floors were occupied. All of this was long ago set up on automation, but Astar enjoyed the routine, saving the automation for when they traveled. Altogether, it kept up their cover, and it kept Astar in shape, for there was no functioning elevator in the Wexler.

Rory was scaling to the top floor when he met Astar on the stairs. She had a small pistol aimed at him as he rounded a landing.

"Ah, Rory Reed. You should have told me you were coming," she laughed lightly. "I would not want to mop up your blood and brain matter from an unfortunate misunderstanding!"

"I told Zana," Rory said, catching his breath. "Sorry."

"He's at the radio," she said. "Again, with the radio. Always with the radio."

"Maybe he's having an affair," Rory said.

"I should be so lucky," Astar laughed, and waved him on up. "Coming down for dinner later?"

"I'd love a burger, maybe," he said.

"Ugh. Well, we can call one in. Come down soon."

She padded on down the stairs, gracefully and lively. She was twice his age but spry.

The corner room on the top floor was furnished as it had been in the 1900s. It reminded Rory of a detective's office in any of a hundred film noir scenes he knew. Woodwork, blinds, frosted glass. An old incandescent lamp cast a yellowed pool of light over a large, messy desk. Zana was sitting there, warming up the old tube-operated ham radio.

"It is a good night for skip," he announced. "If Alex is on, he will be within our range."

"Skip?"

"From the ionosphere," Zana said, as if everyone would know. "I have bounced off the moon, you know."

Zana did not look up from his dials and charts. Rory was grateful for his friend's antiquated hobby. The ham radio had allowed them to communicate undetected for years now. Nothing in InnerSpace nor any bandwidth of CommCorp was secure, but out on the neglected frequencies of amateur radio, they found privacy in the open.

Rory had tried reaching Alex on his Clench for months. A precursor to neural implants, the Clench was yet another passé technology that they had used in the war. Rory and his friends, even his daughter, had Clench implants, but they used them sparingly, always aware they might be tapped.

Zana's ham radio, however, was twice-removed from the attention of CommCorp or any other authority. Steeped in a history of maverick communications, ham radio suited them well. In 1901, Guglielmo Marconi communicated across the Atlantic with a radio device using greater power and giant antennas. Transatlantic transmitting and receiving tests began in 1921 and by July 1960, the first two-way contact via the Moon took place on 1296 MHz's.

Zana had cashiered that same system of relays, over 100 years established, to keep in touch with Alex and Rory, no matter their mission, all over the globe.

"I have even contacted the International Space Station," Zana was saying, "but I cannot reach our friend Alex."

To say their broadcasts were some elaborate, unbreakable coded messages would have made them all laugh. Instead, they relied on a method as old as the game of Telephone. They would issue messages casually, asking them to be relayed, knowing they would be riddled with miscommunication along the way...but they embedded a few key ideas that Alex, should he be listening at all, would catch.

This message, in essence, was RETURN IMMEDIATELY, SOLAR FLARE.

"It is a breach of etiquette to be so cryptic, Rory," Zana said between his attempted contacts. "I feel a fool."

"You have a better idea, Z?"

"This?" He tapped it out on the Clench in his jaw.

"Emergency use only," Rory frowned.

"The Stetson, perhaps?"

Rory had stolen a very expensive HeadGear unit and awarded it to Alex for helping save Calissa. That unit, a Stetson, was the most secure, high-fidelity signaling device of the day, better than the military's or CommCorp issued—simply the best.

"We're not at that level on our end. Sure, he could receive, but he couldn't send, at least not in any secure channels we'd tune in."

"Ah, you are correct," Zana sighed. "I believe we are due such a unit then." He grinned. "It would fit here, no?"

"No," Rory chuckled. "But I'll buy you a drink if you can raise Alex on this old thing."

"You must do better." Zana shook his head. "You know I do not drink."

Rory had brought them together initially. They made the most unlikely team. Rory was a big brick of a lineman, a physical force to be reckoned with. Growing up, had let himself come to believe that was his fate: football player, security guard, possibly a pro wrestler. He had known Alex since high school, when he thought he was defending a harmless techie from bullies. Now Rory found the whole story amusing, how Alex had been a cyber prankster, if not an outright criminal. He was only getting what was due him. Regardless, Rory defended the nerd, and since that day, Alex had bailed him out of countless tight spots.

Alex was flighty, sometimes disappearing for weeks on end, but when he was on, he was on! He was a tech genius if ever there was one.

Astar and Zana had actually found the two of them and saved them from a more severe retribution. Alex *might* have been in Marrakesh to close on a yacht he had swindled from some fat cat. Rory *might* have been along as the muscle. The caper had failed, and they were cast into a horrible prison when Astar discovered them and adopted them on the spot. She had been amused that the massive white guy was acting so cheery, though condemned to death. She liked his style and urged Zana to leverage his clout and assets to free them.

It was Zana who first coordinated them as a team, but it was Rory who took the jobs, ran interference, and did most of the heavy work when it came to it. They were highly successful and enjoying a life of liberating properties. It was a lifestyle they could justify with the occasional altruistic act, a la Robin Hood.

The four of them had been comrades in arms for two decades. They had been through hell together. When discovered to be thieves, A-Z had only two options: expatriation or death. They chose to disappear. Astar's family had been in curation, and an abandoned salt mine under Springfield, Texas, became their new home. Alex arranged for their cover as merchants of antiquities, and Rory maintained their elaborate security down below. Everything had held together. Functional. Then Ashley Winston upended their world.

Just the thought of her—impish and independent—made Rory smile.

Finally, just after midnight, Zana gave up. "He is maybe philandering."

"Philandering?" Rory chuckled. "You mean *gallivanting*?"

"Tom-catting, most likely," Astar said.

"Regardless, he is not responding." Zana powered down his radio. They stood silently, watching the glowing dials slowly go dark. "Another day, perhaps."

"If it's not too presumptuous to ask, why do you need Alex so all of the sudden?"

Rory patted himself down, finding the wire in his jacket pocket. "This was found at the Estate."

Both Astar and Zana blurted out something in their respective native tongues and pulled away from the wire coiled on the desk.

"So..." Rory said, "it *is* something, then?"

He had been with them in a helicopter, as it careened toward the earth and they had faced certain death. He had stood between them vomiting his insides out as they held him on the edge of a mass burial, a horrific scene with mangled corpses decomposing. He had been resuscitated by Astar's love alone when he fell off of a building.

Never, however, had he seen the two of them look so upset.

"You should never have the misfortune of seeing one of these," Astar whispered.

"It would be for the best to leave this situation at the Estate to others and for us all to find another line of work!" Zana rasped.

"It's a wire," Rory said, holding it out between them, shaking it so it formed one large loop. A-Z acted as if it were a coiled snake.

"It is a HotWire, Rory Reed," Astar said.

"A hot—"

"Thank the living gods it is expended," she added. "Otherwise, we would be condemned to leave all we love and go into hiding!"

"Aren't you guys being a little dramatic here?"

Zana seemed to have collected himself. "Rory, this is contraband like none you have ever touched. The highest authority of the most loathsome corporation, your most hated enemies, seek these out without reserve."

"Without mercy," Astar added.

"TransCorp?"

They shook their heads. Had they been Christians, they might have crossed themselves. Astar was biting her lips together. Zana was wide-eyed, his brow furrowed in worry.

"TransCorp put this at the Estate?"

"That is unlikely," Astar said, then looked to her husband for confirmation. "Yes?"

"They will visit the Estate now. Of this, you can be certain," Zana said. "They will have caught the wind of this and seek it out, burned out or no. They will be after whomever mounted it there."

"Where, exactly, did you find this abomination?"

"It was mounted—pinned." He fished in his pockets and pulled out the black pins to show them. He rolled them around in his palm as he spoke. "These pinned it to the wall surrounding the grounds. They're weird, huh, like they've no weight to them at all. Not really all that sharp, but they were sure stuck in that wall, a *stone* wall. How do you figure?"

When he looked up, he realized he'd lost them. They had not heard a word he said. He could see it in their bulging eyes.

"So, these are something too?" he asked.

Zana sat on his desk. Astar leaned against him, her lip quivering a little. "What you hold there, Rory Reed, is more priceless than anything we have ever...liberated."

"These?" he tossed them in his palm. "Why?"

"They, too, are so highly illegal, so coveted by the TransCorp. To have them in your possession is punishable by death. Of this," Zana said, "I am certain."

"Guys, c'mon. Is it just because it's late or something?" Rory scoffed. "Past your bedtime?"

"Those...those pins are the only substance that can hold that wire when it is live."

Astar shook her head, "The only thing worse would be to have the Tic-Tacs."

"Tic-Tacs?" Rory was lost.

"There," Zana pointed at the bottom of the wire loop. "At least these are expensed."

They both breathed an audible sigh.

"These little charred things?" Rory flicked at a bit of black crust on the wire. "What are they? Why do you call them Tic Tacs?"

Astar snapped to attention with a thought, "We must take the pins, take all this, home with us, immediately."

"Yes, that is prudent," Zana agreed. "Somewhere safe...if it is not too late."

Rory followed them, asking questions they did not answer. They were skipping stairs on their way down to the main level, then cutting through the shop without regard for things they toppled over along the way. Rory hustled along with them. "Guys, hey, guys!"

"We will talk below," Zana said curtly, escorting him into an elevator hidden behind a faux bookshelf.

The descent was awkward. A-Z pressed their backs to the elevator wall, as far as they could get from the things Rory was holding. They did not talk.

At last the doors opened, and the trail of yellow lights flicked on, bulb by bulb, from their elevator off into the black void of the salt mine. Once the doors closed, Zana took Rory's elbow. "These together create renegade devices that have been the bane of the TransCorp for years."

"I am certain they are aware by now that these turned up at the Winston Estate."

"They will waste no time in pursuing them," Zana said. "They will be hunting for them at the mansion."

"I would suspect they will then be hunting for you, child." Astar said sadly.

All the bile and bitterness welled in Rory. "I hope they find me," he said.

"Not this time, you do not," Astar said.

"If it were me," Zana said, "I would evacuate the property, even if for a few days. Let TransCorp have the run of the grounds."

"Have Ashley send them all on a vacation," Astar recommended. "You can convince her of that, yes?"

"No," Rory scowled. "I don't think I can convince her of anything right now."

"Her father then, or Grandmother," Astar pleaded. "You can work with them."

Rory folded his arms. "Why run? Breaking into the Estate is a crime."

"What you are holding is stolen property," Zana said.

"What the hell are these, Zana?"

"A HotWire is a random portal. To use one is forbidden."

"A random—"

"And to hold those pegs in your hand," Astar said, "is to hold a little bit of something that is not even of this earth."

14 Indecorous

She could hear the clocks throughout the mansion chiming the hour, ten o'clock. When moving back into the Estate after her mother passed away, Ashley had had so many decisions to make. One decision she was coming to terms with was *not* firing any staff prematurely. It had been four months now in the big house, and she was coming to appreciate intricate hierarchies, divisions of labor, the minutia of responsibilities all doled out to dedicated people. Going in, Ashley had hoped to let go of most of the staff, thinking there could not be a reason to employ someone full time as, say, a doorman.

Listening to the clocks now sounding the last toll, all together in perfect synchrony, Ashley had to acknowledge that the staff member who coordinated nothing but calendars and clocks, Hersham, was very good at his job and certainly worth keeping around.

Ashley had settled in the prep kitchen, the room that seemed it would be Rory's point of re-entry on his return. It adjoined the garages and parking in the rear of the house, the hub of activity for the Estate's staff. Groceries were delivered here. The help ate here. She was sure a great deal of gossip was shared at this table. She imagined it all, her chin in the palms of her hands.

She stared at her drink, four fingers of expensive bourbon. It was not her drink of choice, but she was trying out something new. It had nothing to do with Rory favoring whiskey, she told herself. She had been drinking more whiskeys since her time in Franklin, and she was still seeking one she really liked. Tonight's choice, delivered to her by the on-grounds bartender, Bartholomew Sterling, was a 25-year-old bottle of Wellers' Kentucky Bourbon like she had seen Rory and Kelli drinking from back at her bar, *The Distraught*.

Ashley took a slug of her drink and grimaced. What kind of name was that for a bar, she scoffed. Maybe a good name for a pirate ship, maybe a good adjective to describe the town, but for a bar? She wondered if anyone in Franklin knew what the word meant. They said it like "dis-trot" as in 'this trot' or 'that trot.'

Sterling passed quietly through the kitchen. "Anything else tonight, Miss Winston?"

"Yeah, pull up a chair, Bart."

He stood by the table. Light reflected from the rich mahogany, casting a warm cinnamon over him. "Would you like me to pour you another?"

"I know this is my third, already. I can still count," she said with no trace of a drawl. "Pour one for Rory...and one for yourself."

He retrieved only one glass from the sidebar and filled it to exactly the same level as hers. She wondered idly how bartenders could do that. "Does Mr. Reed like his on ice?"

"Nah," she said. "He says it waters it down. Besides," she sighed, "I have no idea when he's getting back."

"Chilled then?" Sterling asked. "I could use the liquid nitrogen—"

"The guy drinks right out of the bottle, Bart. I don't think he cares."

"Yes ma'am," Sterling said. He looked around a little.

"Where's yours?" Ashley asked him and slid Rory's drink back at Sterling.

"I couldn't," he said with an apologetic cock of his head.

"Why not?"

"If Jeeves were to see me—"

"Jeeves works for me. What I say, goes."

"Yes, Miss Winston, but it's.... indecorous."

"Listen, Bart, I have a PhD, so don't try talking over my head. I don't give a rip if it's improper to knock one back with the boss."

"Yes... well, you are aware, this is a twenty-thousand-dollar bottle of bourbon?" Sterling asked. He was almost drooling for it now. His interest in the drink was no longer so well cloaked by propriety.

"I'll give you another bottle for Christmas if you have a drink with me now," Ashley smiled.

Sterling held the glass to the light for a moment, studying its color. He held it under his nose and breathed it in, his eyes closed. He took a delicate sip of it, then a more generous drink, and beamed. He licked his lips.

"Pretty good stuff?" she asked.

He was clearly savoring the first drink, but when he answered, it was in reverent tones, "Oh yes, Miss Winston. Very good...stuff."

"Vanilla. Why do I taste vanilla?

Bartholomew Sterling tugged at his cuffs and went into an explanation of whiskey barrels being burned on the inside to allow the flavors of the wood to be absorbed. "Those burned longer generate more lignin." He nodded. She nodded with him. "You have an advanced palette, if I might say so, Miss Winston."

"Call me Ashley, Bart, and that's the nicest thing anyone's said to me in weeks."

He blushed and took a bigger swig of his drink.

"What's your story, Bart?"

"Pardon?"

"I mean, you're what, thirty-something?"

"Twenty-nine," he said.

"So, how is it you came to be here? When I left there was some old guy pouring drinks, and he didn't care about propriety at all, let me say. I think he was a lush. Came with the house, I think."

"Rolly, you mean?"

"Yeah, that's the guy."

"He's my father," Bart said.

Ashley practically spit out her drink. "Oh! Gosh. Geez. I'm...I'm so—"

"I am kidding," he laughed.

Ashley gave him a look. She thought about giving him a cramp or worse, but she had learned to keep her Affectations in check when she drank.

"But seriously, Rolly knew my father. They hooked me up. I was wasting my life as a barback after graduating from Columbia's bartending program."

"Ivy league," she said with surprise.

He shrugged.

"You like it here?" Ashley asked.

He took a drink. He was buying time, she thought.

"I like the parties, Miss—Ashley." He cleared his throat. "Otherwise, if you don't mind my saying, err...well...it can be a little tedious."

"Tedious?" She feigned being insulted. "Bart, stay with us a while, eh? You're going to see this place liven up a lot."

"Oh, I already have," he smiled.

"Yeah?"

"The security people are..." he sized her up, "...ass clowns, but they do make my life a lot more interesting."

He left her after "just one glass," had extended to two, but no more, which left her pouting. It was too late to call on her father or grandmother, and the house staff would be boorish at this hour. She tried Kyle on her HairPin, but he did not respond.

"Why am I doing this?" Ashley asked herself. For all she knew, Rory might have entered another way and gone to bed long ago.

She was doing this because she was not used to Rory being miffed at her. She was waiting up for him to explain what he called overstepping. The hired help was here to help him. She was trying her best to help him help her.

She also wanted to find out just what he was up to—and she knew he was up to something. Skipping the CommCorp meeting. Skipping out on dinner. Staying out on the town. She was going to get an explanation.

She might, if so moved, share apologies with him.

If that went well, she might even talk through her strategic plan with him. Yes, it would fly in the face of tradition. Yes, it would be risky, but when wasn't risk worthwhile? LF would lose his temper over her plan, but that was apparently nothing new. Imagining the flare of Rory's temper, however, even the hint of it, made her edgy. When he found out, the foundations of the earth would quake. Maybe she would not tell him too much, too soon.

A while later, the clocks struck one. It seemed funny to her, after counting all the chiming all these hours, so anticlimactic to have a single chime. "Dong!" she repeated, and spun up from her stool, bottle in hand. She was going to his room to see if he had given her the slip. She was going to really give him a piece of her mind for that. "Ding, dong, the witch is dead," she sang, skipping up the grand staircase. "Fa la la la, la la la, la la la," she sang in her best Munchkin impression.

She realized then that the song could apply to her own mother, the grand madame of the Estate, the late Delores Winston. "The witch is dead," Ashley whispered, and laughed.

Rory was not in his room, and she decided she would just surprise him whenever he did come back. She stripped naked and buried herself in the bedding, giggling. He would be so surprised!

15 Cartagena

For a man of his size, Rory could be very stealthy when the situation called for it, as did this one. He was silently navigating the aisles of cots, slipping around the occasional arm akimbo. The Franklin militia were sleeping soundly in the gymnastics center. This crew, formerly Lance Mitchum's men, slept in the basketball gym. The two factions of security had been getting along better, Rory had to admit, but were he detected creeping through their quarters, they would have slit his throat on impulse.

There was no sentry for the security quarters, but several men marched the grounds at all hours, and doubled details were stationed inside the building. Rory knew their schedules and their checkpoints, and he had little trouble eluding them. It had taken thirty extra minutes to get to this gym, as he had counted it out in his head, but staying out of sight was vital.

He found his target after a good deal of searching. It was surprising that twenty-five men could look so similar when sleeping in the dark. This man, the one he was after, was asleep on the floor. It was an old Turncoat preference. They chose the hard floors, giving up gym mats, cots, or mattresses. In the field, they'd have to sleep on the ground. Best be used to it. Rory did the same himself when on assignment.

Nick Grimes was sound asleep, using his thick bicep as a pillow. Rory knelt beside him slowly, carefully. He had his Ruger in hand, one in the chamber, his finger on the trigger. It had to look convincing, he knew, if he was to have a chance in hell. He glanced all around to confirm no one was stirring. Then he leaned down so far that his mouth was just inches away from the giant's ear. He made one last adjustment of his stance, ensuring he had his balance and weight under him despite this awkward position.

"Nick, you're had," he whispered. The man did not respond. Rory took a deep breath, counted to ten, then aimed the pistol between Nick's eyes. He pressed the muzzle gradually harder and harder into the bridge of Nick's nose until the pressure registered a flinch from the pain and Nick Grimes opened his eyes. Shock. Terror. Resignation. Rory nodded. "*A man's been had when his hopes are hardened,*" he whispered.

"Wha?" Nick grumbled.

Rory gestured to him to get up. He held a finger to his lips, encouraging his quarry to stay quiet. Nick frowned but complied. He was menacing, even in his skivvies. Meat and muscle. One shout from him, and Rory would not escape. He knew he could cold cock Nick before a word escaped him, but things would get messy. The odds of twenty-five to one were not in Rory's favor, but he could prevail. He was alert and already in motion while the rest of them would be called to alarm, groggy, weapons not chambered. If it came to it, Rory was confident he could escape, but it would require violence, and it would set back all the training and goodwill he had established. If it came to it, there would be bloodshed. This was not that kind of visit.

They threaded through the cots to a locker room. Once inside, Rory lowered his weapon.

"That's a damn rude awakening!" Nick said, letting out the breath he'd been holding.

"No time to spare, Grimes." Rory said. "Somebody here's dirty."

Nick Grimes swelled with indignation but kept his voice down. "My men? You're blaming one of my—"

"Could be someone from Franklin. Could be someone from the house. Hell, it could be someone slipping in and out right under our noses." Rory sat on a bench and gestured to Nick to do the same.

"What do you mean, Reed? You think there's inside help?" he asked, sitting on a bench across from Rory, crossing his arms as best he could. His muscles were broad and rocky.

"I'm sure of it," Rory said.

"Because?"

"Car bombs. Scuds targeting the room she was in, especially since it wasn't her normal room. Someone is leaking information at the very least...or worse, holding the door open for others to come right in."

"What the hell are you talking about now?"

"That wire." Rory did not know where to begin after all A-Z had told him. "From what I know, it was placed out there by someone, maybe a gardener, maybe a guard—anyway, someone hung it on the wall. Then someone *else*, our unfortunate intruder, was stepping right through it when he was shot. Fell over the threshold of that little wire and got sliced in two."

"Where'd he come from? What are you saying? That he went through a two-foot-thick stone wall?"

"I dunno how it works, Grimes, just that it's like a doorway."

"Huh," he said.

"Huh? That's all you got?"

"I heard stories, just didn't believe them." Nick scratched his scalp. "Portals."

"I've seen Portals," Rory said. They were impressive structures built and owned by TransCorp. "Big doorway things, lights, and titanium. Couldn't move one with a forklift, I'd bet."

"They gotta have some hellacious power to transport the things I've heard."

"I saw somebody roll a dolly of ammunition through one."

"I heard they made them big enough to drive through," Nick said.

"Point is, this *isn't* one of those. This is contraband." He fished the charred wire from his pocket and handed it to Nick.

Nick laughed. "You're saying this little wire is a Portal?"

"I think it's the guts of one, maybe."

"Huh," Nick said with a shrug.

"TransCorp's keeping these on the down low. They wipe out every trace, every story, and that means *every witness* to the use of them."

"So, it wasn't TransCorp slipping in here, eh?" Nick surmised.

"I'm not sure on that, but if it's true that they mop up, I'm surprised they're not here already."

"You think they know about this little bugger?"

"I guess. Maybe they're on some radar or something. If my people are right, though...you see the problem?"

"Uh...we're all dead?"

"That's one way it could go. If they come in here guns blazing, I'm going to need your boys so blindly loyal they'd shoot themselves in the head if we said to. I'm going to need to train all the firepower our little army can muster if we're even going to get out of here alive."

Nick nodded his head. He handed the wire back. "Or?"

"They might wait it out, then come in for a Round Up," Rory said.

"Like Cartagena?"

"Just like that," Rory said, grinding the words.

Twelve years ago, TransCorp had become overpowered, glutted with manpower. Most of the resistance, the Turncoats, had fallen into compliance and joined the ranks. Money kept pouring in, and with it, advanced weaponry. More money, more power.

With such a force, they came to prefer 'peaceful acquisitions,' what had once been known as laying siege to a stronghold. An entire battalion, 400 strong, would encircle the town or mountain or military base—or estate—and just wait. They would throw lavish parties. They airdropped care packages with leaflets promising a better life for those who would lay down their arms. Even as their stocks dwindled, the Coats were afraid to eat the care packages, suspecting they were poisoned. The men would walk by, gawking at such elaborate fresh foods just spoiling.

It did not stop at that. TransCorp used every strategy to encourage surrender, but the most effective was the Smoker. As the weeks would pass and provisions were certainly gone inside, TransCorp's battalions would host "Smokers," which were simply giant barbeque parties. The smell of the food alone would lead holdouts to surrender, join the ranks, and TransCorp would chalk up a win.

Cartagena, however, had held strong for a year. Turncoats were able to negotiate the release of all non-coms and support, leaving just under 100 men and women inside. Eventually some executive at TransCorp decided the Cartagena venture was no longer a good return on investment, and she ordered the Round Up.

When the defenses were torn down and the battalion stormed in, only 40 Turncoats were in any condition to fight. They were emaciated, living skeletons, but they fought with the odds against them, 10-1.

Many men, these many years later, sported faded "10-1" tattoos commemorating the valiant effort.

"I'm not waiting," Nick said. "Not like that, and not for that kind of end."

"Me either. I say we accelerate things if they take that—"

"I'm in," Nick said, standing.

"You don't even know the plan," Rory said.

"Don't matter. You call it, I'm in." He held out his hand to shake.

Rory gestured for him to sit back down. "I want you to hear this, Grimes. It's some high-stakes gambling."

"Sure," he shrugged and sat. "We're probably all gonna die, anyway, right? But fill me in. I'm down for some thrilling heroics."

"It starts with this." Rory pinched a strand of hair from his shirt pocket and extended it to Nick.

"Lice?"

"Yeah. You know the drill, short range, emergency use—

"Unreliable, cheap tech from back when."

"Right, but dedicated bandwidth," Rory said. "They'll let us stay in touch when the time comes."

"When's that?"

"When things are most dire."

"Dire," Grimes repeated, nodding his head and studying the tiny communication tool.

An hour later, he slipped by all the security yet again and trudged into his room. The door was ajar, and the room was a mess. Someone, a woman, had undressed here, strewn her clothes everywhere. Rory had to step back into the hall to confirm that this was his room. He hesitated, deciding not to turn the light on, hoping not to startle her. His mind raced and retraced his latest interactions with Ashley, and it did not register that it could possibly be her.

The bed was frumpy. A bottle of Weller bourbon was leaning on a pillow, and a pair of pink panties were draped around the bottle's neck. He raised his eyebrows and stepped around to the far side of the bed.

In a tangle of satin bedding, in the pane of moonlight, in folds of platinum hair, Ashley slept with her mouth wide open. Rory set the bottle on the nightstand, then climbed onto his bed. He stuffed pillows under his head and just watched her sleep.

He was sorry to have missed the party, whatever it might have led to. He laughed to himself, wondering what it might have been all about. Drunk and naked in his room—it puzzled him, but then, she always did. She was maddening and mercurial, but that's what he liked about her most: he never knew what to expect.

She was always fresh.

Spontaneous.

He couldn't help himself from wondering who she truly was. Debutante. Heiress. Professor. Bad Ass. Angel. He thought about her all the time, but moments like this, when she was asleep, he thought he was seeing the real Ashley: a simple, beautiful girl. He questioned what she thought about him, or if she thought much about him at all.

Rory caught himself about to nod off. He rose from bed and went about picking up her things. He thought about trying to dress her, to help her save face. Then he remembered her calling him a "creeper." Once before, when she was badly injured and unconscious, he had given her a sponge bath, and Ashley had not let him live that down.

He chose to leave the panties draped on the bottle. See her live *that* down!

He settled on placing her clothes in a neat pile beside her when he saw she had something clutched in her hand. He had not seen it in months, and it took him a bit to recognize it in the dark. He gently pried the ornate handkerchief from her hand and spread it on the bed. A word looked to be embroidered on it. He turned it to face him and shook his head in wonder.

The word was simply: *Trust.*

16 Second Breakfast

Morning came even though she had rather it would not. Ashley liked dysphoria. In her many travels, it was a simple pleasure to wake and be so bumfuzzled as to her whereabouts. Except she was not traveling, she was in her own house, and a quick look around the room confirmed what she almost remembered: this was Rory's room. She sat up and looked around. Across the vacant bed, a shaft of light illuminated the bottle adorned with her panties. She had a sinking feeling she had done something stupid. The morning sun compounded that feeling, pounding against her eyes, accentuating her headache.

Ashley dressed and darted out into the hall. Two guards were at her door, and they followed her, absolutely stoic. No judgment, no smirking, no small talk. At the moment, she preferred it that way. How could she begin to justify ending up in Rory's room, naked?

Crossing the Great Room, she slowed her pace considerably and tried to remember. Rory wasn't even home last night. She had waited up for him. Drinking. That bottle. The bartender.

She turned down the wide hall leading to the formal dining area, then cut through to the main kitchen and then stopped in the back kitchen, the one they called the 'make room.' Two glasses sat on the counter, both empty. *Two* glasses.

"Jeeves!" Ashley called out.

"I can hail him," one guard offered. He was a young man from Franklin.

"Sure. Do said, then added, "When were you on duty last night?"

"Just this morning, Miss Winston."

Both of the guards nodded.

"See anything..." she wanted to say 'strange' but thought better of it.

"Oh no, ma'am," the other guard said, conspiring in his tone: "We saw *nothing*."

The younger man reported, half-listening to an earpiece, "Mr. Jeeves is on his way here."

"It's just Jeeves, no mister," Ashley said, on impulse. She walked around the room, trying to recall more details. Both guards stayed at the threshold, looking inert and disinterested.

She heard someone whistling a peppy tune down the corridor. The cloying noise was coming closer, growing louder. She glanced at her guards, then tried to make herself look busy by opening a cabinet. She hoped the whistler was just another guard, or maybe her father, or by even a greater stretch of the imagination, Jeeves, whistling along on a very good morning. The whistling stopped as it entered the make room, and Ashley peeked around the cabinet door, knowing who she would find.

"Why, hello, Princess!" Rory said. "Top of the morning."

"Top of the..."

"I'm looking for some coffee," he looked from her to the guards, who shrugged. "Where can a guy score a cup of Joe?"

He was smiling at her broadly. Clearly, he knew more than she did about last night.

Rory sighed, "I *could* visit the canteen they set up in the gym, drink some of their swill...I guess."

"I can make some coffee," Ashley said, thinking it was just what she needed.

"Allow us, Miss," Jeeves said, entering with kitchen staff. "And would breakfast be in order as well?"

"I believe it would," Rory said. He patted Jeeves on the back. "Thank you."

"I meant for—"

"Yes, breakfast," Ashley said, "for two. And I'll have a Bloody Mary with mine."

She stared down Rory's raised eyebrow. She would not be cowed.

"Where's Calissa?" Ashley said over her coffee.

"We had our brew hours ago," Rory said. "She talked Rafe into going downtown. Shopping for some school thing."

"Hmmm." Ashley said.

"Something about a formal."

"A formal!"

"Semi-formal, I guess." He shrugged.

"Is she in a house?" Ashley asked. "When did she rush? How did I not know?"

"I... uh..."

"Did she pledge Tri Delt? That's my—"

"I think it's just a school dance," he said. "You know she's way the hell out in...." Rory leaned in, so that even the guards might not hear, "Wyoming."

Ashley had forgotten that. It was best that she did, for Rory was vigilant in keeping his daughter's whereabouts unknown. The poor kid, even if she had wanted to, Calissa couldn't have joined a sorority. Too high profile.

They were served fresh fruit and croissants. "It is late, and to not encroach on your luncheon with Master Winston, we thought this best."

"Looks great," Rory said. "Second breakfast!"

Jeeves looked at him, raising an eyebrow. "You know *The Hobbit*, sir?"

"Yeah," Rory said around a mouthful of fruit. "One of Mitchum's men, right?"

Jeeves deflated, "Yes. Yes, sir."

"And here's your drink, Miss Winston." It was the bartender, Bart. He sat the Bloody Mary down on a napkin and turned to go.

"Say," she drew his attention.

He turned back to her, scarcely looking her in the eye. She noticed his glance encompassed Jeeves. "Yes, Miss Winston?"

Ashley looked at all three men, then said to Bart, dismissively, "Thank you."

"Anything else?" Jeeves asked. He was looking at the ceiling.

"It's all good," Rory said, scooping up some blueberries. "Thanks."

Jeeves looked at her. "*Anything*?"

"Thank you, Jeeves," Ashley said, but then as he was leaving, she remembered something he had just said. "Wait... Lunch with father?"

"That's right," he picked at his sleeve. "In the west parlor at noon."

West parlor at noon, she repeated to herself.

"And Miss Winston...I would remind you," Jeeves scowled at her clothes, "it *is* another business meeting."

She tossed her head. "With—-?"

"Sarah Dawn Parker and company," Jeeves said, now reading from his wrist appliance.

"What company, again?" Rory asked.

"Why...TransCorp, of course." Jeeves rolled his eyes but snapped his attention back to his device. "The meeting *you* scheduled."

"Yes," she said, clearing her throat. She braced for his reaction. "TransCorp."

Rory sat straight at his stool.

"What?" she asked. He acted like this, like a hunting dog, when he was worried. In the months he had been with her, she had seen it again and again. Once, when a car backfired, he bolted up like that and had his pistol out. Another time, when a painting fell over in the Great Hall, he jumped between her and the offending sound.

He looked at her, then at the kitchen staff. They picked up, then fled the room. In his deepest, most quiet baritone, he said, "Don't go to that meeting. Don't even invite them in."

"Ridiculous," she said. "What do I have to fear from Sarah Dawn?"

"Just do not go," Rory said.

"Have you been talking to Poppy? Is that what's got you so worked up?"

He looked as if he were about to push off and leave. Before he did, however, he took her hand and said it again, "Do. Not. Go."

"It's my job," her head throbbed as she emphasized each word. "Running Water Works is my job, Rory."

"And my job's protecting you."

She pulled her hand from his, then picked up the large Bloody Mary with both hands. "Like you protected me in the CommCorp meeting? Like you protected me last night? Where were you, anyway?"

"Doing my job," he said, growing uncomfortable.

"How did I end up in your room?"

"I don't know," he said, rising to his feet. "Ask your *bartender*."

"Funny!" she said, also standing.

"I could have you detained," Rory said, tipping his head back toward the guards.

"I could have you fired," Ashley replied. She turned to the others. "All of you."

"Listen," Rory said, "I know things, okay?"

"So, then. Tell me things." She took another sip of her drink.

"Not now. Not yet." Rory was firm. "I don't have enough to go on."

"Then I'm going to the lun—"

Rory was fast. He had her by the elbow and inside the pantry before she could collect herself. Her drink had spilled some. "Good god, Rory!" she said, shaking her wet hand.

The pantry was close quarters, but he pulled her even closer as the door swung shut behind them. He snatched the drink from her hand and sat it down on a shelf. "You gotta trust me, Ashley. All I can tell you is that TransCorp is trouble."

"And you don't think I can handle myself?" she felt the ire welling up inside. She did not appreciate being manhandled.

"No, I do not."

"Forgetful, aren't you?" she snarled and unfurled an Affectation on him. The two of them *both* dropped to the floor, as if their bones had turned to rubber.

"Well," Rory said, flopped over her, "that's new."

17 Comfortably Numb

He did his best not to crush her, but he could only roll off to the side, and in the process, canned goods tumbled from the shelves. In trying to block them from hitting Ashley, he flopped over her again. There they lay, nose to nose, on their sides. Their legs were tangled together.

"Reed," he heard a man slur from the kitchen.

He tried to turn his head when yelling his reply, "In here!"

"Please," she said. "Not in my face."

"We're down, sir," the younger one cried out.

Rory pried his shoulder enough to flop his head away a bit, responding, "It's fine. Just temporary. You boys go get looked at...as soon as you get your bearings."

He managed to slide his foot over to block the door, ignoring anything the men might have to say further. His head settled back to the floor, and his cheek rested in a nest of her hair. He could feel her breathing against him.

Then Rory noticed the tears dripping across the bridge of her nose.

"Are you alright?" he said, wishing he could brush back her hair, wipe her tears away.

He felt her draw a deep breath, as if she were going to answer him, but then she did not. Her eyes turned to his. They had never seemed deeper. In this ridiculous situation, where neither of them could so much as sit up straight, Rory wished he might close the gap to her and kiss her forehead.

They were too close to just lay there, face to face, staring into each other's eyes and not talk. He wanted to relieve the tension and look away, but he could not. She was too beautiful, and in this moment, she seemed to need him.

"I didn't mean to piss you off," he mumbled. "I just want to keep you—"

"I'm broken!" she interrupted. The deep gaze was tempered with fear. Her lips had drawn tense. More tears flowed across her face and pooled in her hair.

"It'll pass." He tried to smile. "You've done it to me before."

"But never to *myself*." He felt a shudder go through her, like she was fighting off a full-on sob. "What's happening to me?"

It had crossed his mind. How many times had he seen her Affect whole crowds without a shrug? Blinded people. Completely incapacitated people. Left people with sneezing fits, mad laughter, screaming in fear—and simply, gracefully walked on through. This time, however, she had Affected Rory, even the two in the kitchen—*possibly more*, he suddenly worried—but also brought *herself* down.

"I don't know what happened," he admitted. Psychic powers were not in his arsenal. He wished they were, for he so wanted to know her thoughts and fears. "I don't even know how you do it."

"Sometimes I don't, either," she sighed. "I'm...I'm sorry for this. Sometimes I just...overreact."

"Everybody does," he said, and this time, he could feel the corner of his eyes crinkle.

Her eyes darted past him in thought. When her gaze found him again, she said: "This really sucks, doesn't it? So powerless."

"Could be worse." He felt a little bit of a shrug in his shoulder. "Not as bad as the loose bowel one you told me about."

She chuckled.

"Could be laying here with, I dunno, Rafe or somebody," Rory added, liking the effect on her.

"Jeeves, maybe." She glowed with her crooked smile now, and although half of her face was pressed into the floor, she looked absolutely stunning.

It had been five minutes, maybe, by his count. In her company, his mental meter was less than accurate sometimes. He figured, by the sensation he was regaining, the Affectation wouldn't last another ten.

"There's nobody I'd rather be numb with," she said.

"*I have become comfortably numb*," Rory sang softly.

Her nose crinkled in that especially impish smile. "Rory Reed! I didn't know you could sing."

"Must be the hoo-doo," he smirked.

"Is that from some album you memorized?"

"Yeah. Pink Floyd."

"Sing some more."

"Nah, I couldn't."

"Please," she was using her coquettish plea, the one that never failed. "Just a little?"

Rory took a deep breath, and with it, he was able to roll on his back. The song coursed through his memory, every guitar chord, the cheers of the crowd. A live recording of the song "Comfortably Numb," recorded in 1979, twenty years before he was even born. Rory relaxed into her Affectation, her irresistible tide.

Never in his life, outside of lullabies, had Rory sung for anyone. Ever. He let out a sigh, shut his eyes, then sang so softly it was scarcely more than a whisper. The mystical lyrics flowed from him freely. When he voiced the last of it, the words scarcely passing his lips, he sighed peacefully.

He could still hear the beautiful, spellbinding guitar solo that closed the song. He was letting it play out in his mind when he felt her clamber onto him. Her hair fell all around them, enclosing them in this dream space. She kissed him, and he kissed her back.

Rory was sure now that he was caught up in the undercurrent of another Affectation, and she, too, was rolling with it. Their kiss became more and more passionate as they tossed about on the floor, and then, just as all hell was about to break loose—

"Miss Winston!" Jeeves said, rapping at the door.

They broke, but as they were only just gaining control of themselves, they flopped back against the pantry shelves. Food stores rained down on them, and the Bloody Mary toppled and spilled all over her.

They sat up, laughing, holding each other.

"Right with you, Jeeves," she said, and kissed Rory again.

After a quick lunch of quiche, it was time to get down to business. The staff had repurposed the main dining hall for this meeting. TransCorp, despite A-Z's forewarnings, was not nearly as uptight as CommCorp had been just the day before. The dining hall was fine with them. No security detail of their own. The entourage featured Ms. Parker and an older man who carried himself like an attorney. They were, of course, flanked by others in suits, all of them wary and calculating.

Their backs were to Rory. He was in the 'cheap seats,' with Spexarth and Zana at his sides. They were sitting among several others looking on, what someone at the dining table had called the 'gallery.' Rory was fine with that. In his mind, this was the best seat in the house.

Framed between the shoulders of the TransCorp people, just across the table, Miss Ashley Elizabeth Winston was holding court. Her father sat on one side of her, while Kyle Dupree and a battery of other attorney-types sat with them on their side of the table.

He knew she would not look at him, *and had she*, he would have looked preoccupied. He did not want to disrupt her composure. This was the richest young woman on the planet, conversing with the head of another corporation not worthy of mention by comparison.

Still, his analytical nature could not stop the comparisons. Ms. Parker was around the same age as Ashley, and like her, had inherited her post. Parker was prim and taut, sitting erect, the balls of her feet on the floor, but her knees were bouncing nervously. Her clothes were correct, buttoned up to her chin. Her elocution was correct. She was poised and all-business. Her makeup was perfect. Her every hair was in place.

Ashley, however, was not her corporation; she was herself. She wore a trim, professional business suit, but the jacket was open to reveal a white satin shirt (Calissa had taught him it was a camisole) and doubtless showing far too much skin by Jeeves' standards. The ScanTats that covered her face and neck trickled out in a pattern like falling bricks down to her cleavage. Her silver white hair was pulled up in a quick ponytail. Her hair and ScanTats together made her look magical, like an exotic genie.

"So, what *are* you proposing, then?" Ashley asked.

"Dear, I hardly think that—" LF was saying.

"No, it's quite alright," Ms. Parker said. Her legs were still. Her accomplice touched her elbow below the table, but she recoiled almost imperceptibly. "It is more of a suggestion than a proposal, really."

"Really?" Ashley asked. Rory heard mirth, almost a challenge, in her tone.

"Yes," the man with Ms. Parker said.

People were squirming to know where this was going. Rory could hear the chairs creak in the gallery. He had heard the briefing, as they had hustled down the hallway after a quick cleanup. Kyle had told her TransCorp would ask for an alliance, and they were in some kind of hurry. He had spoken in hushed, worried tones, but he had turned his shoulder back toward Rory, opening the conversation to him with his body language. It was as if he had wanted Rory to be in-the-know.

"We could become closer." Sarah Parker laid her palms on the table and said in measured words. "Our business ventures could...more closely align."

It was so quiet that Rory could hear LF inhale from across the room.

Ashley tapped a pen on her teeth absently. She was looking only at Ms. Parker now, focused. Rory wondered if she was Affecting her. He cocked his head, wondering how exactly that worked in business dealings, and then again, wondering how it would now work if her hoodoo was backfiring.

"Marry-up. You know, LF." It was the older man at Ms. Parker's side, "like in the old days."

Parker's shoulders dropped. Her back straightened a little more, if that were possible.

"I don't remember the old days being so cordial, Briggs," LF said. Old man Winston looked formidable since he trimmed his hair and went back to suits, but Rory could not ignore his flexing toes gripping and releasing the chair's feet. "In fact, as I remember it, you boys were bucking for it all back then."

"Bah," the assistant, Briggs, was clearly emerging as the true power of the TransCorp team now. "Water under the bridge," he chuckled. "You appreciate that, right? *Water* under the bridge."

"Hmm," LF said.

"Sarah Dawn Parker," Ashley smiled brightly, "are you saying we should hook up?"

Zana cleared his throat softly. He was riveted by the entire exchange, never looking away from the table. Zana had given him that throat clearing warning before. This was his warning, as if to say that Ashley was pushing it.

"I find all this language a little...vague." Ms. Parker said.

"And that is why we have crafted a pre-nup," Kyle DuPree said, opening a folder, browsing over his workmanship, smiling ever so slightly. He was pleased with himself, from what Rory knew of him, probably for pressing the courtship metaphor ever-so-slightly more.

Ms. Parker sighed. She was looking down her nose at his documents across the table.

"Well!" Briggs said. The back of his neck was reddening. "We have our own write up here, too, don't we, Sarah?"

"So, it is a proposal, then?" Ashley asked. She looked up and down the table at her staff. "I'd say if anyone's putting anything in writing, it's more than a suggestion, wouldn't you?"

Everyone on Ashley's side of the table nodded vigorously.

"If we work together, Ashley, we both stand to gain so much." Ms. Parker's veneer was cracking. "Don't you see?"

"*For everything you gain, you lose something else.*" Rory mouthed the words, *just as Ashley spoke them*. It seemed everyone at the table was taken aback. Rory was astonished. She was tossing out quotes now?

"My daughter's up on her Emerson," LF said, quickly recovering. "And she makes a point. What are you asking for in this... *suggestion* of yours?"

He looked from Briggs to Ms. Parker and back.

Ms. Parker stopped Briggs from sliding his file across the table by resting her hand on his.

Rory had been in gentlemen's agreements and battlefield peace treaties. He had sat through tedious negotiations when the Turncoats had been liquidated by TransCorp leadership. None of it seemed as electrifying as this little afternoon tête-à-tête between Ashley Winston and Sarah Parker.

The two women locked eyes across the table.

"Excuse us, won't you?" Ms. Parker said to the room.

"Yeah," Ashley said, smiling. "Time for some girl talk."

18 Accord

Ashley slipped on a pair of sleek sunglasses. The sun reflecting off the dining room table was only adding to her headache. The room was emptying, and she took the opportunity to do some chair yoga. It felt good to stretch the tedium out of her muscle groups, particularly her sides and back. She was working out the lingering numbness.

As she leaned this way and that, taking in deep breaths, she noticed the smells: wood polish and hairspray, but deeper, she picked up notes of beer, tomato juice, and... Rory. She took another breath, remembering the taste of his kiss.

When they had the room, they squared off.

"Ready?" Sarah Dawn asked. "Shall we get down to it?"

"Yes, let's," Ashley said.

"TransCorp has market advantage and flat out leverage on Chomp and Pharma. Surely you know that?"

Ashley took off the sunglasses. "Blah, blah, blah. What do you want from me? From 3dub?"

"3dub?"

"Winston Water Works, of course."

"Oh. Of course." Sarah collected herself, steepled her fingers. "The good thing about us is we don't compete. You guys already own most of the water rights, all the hydro, all the commercial nauticals... and we own all the—"

"You lock down the land."

"Is that something your dad says?"

"I'm just saying," Ashley smiled, "nothing much is moved if not by TransCorp. Isn't that the motto or something?"

"*We Move Masses*." Sarah said.

"But not our airships, and that's why you're here. Right?"

"Ashley!" Sarah said. "How rude!"

"Well, isn't it?"

"I would like to see us collaborate. You know, just work together on a thing or two."

"Because you think my ships can move more than your transports?"

Sarah sighed. She was thinking up a better way to say it, but Ashley had been thinking this through since she had first taken WWW over after her mother's passing. All the corporations were coming to call, and all of them thought they would have a better chance of hitting Ashley up before she got too established. None of them believed she had the business acumen to run a lemonade stand.

"Think of it like this," Sarah began, "the Weeklies are flying at no profit. If you had even a modest surcharge and carried even a fraction of your payload..." she chuckled and shook her head, "I can't even *do* the math on that."

"And yet, you have," Ashley said. "TransCorp would broker transportation, like usual, and our percentage would be what—a sliver of your client's charge?"

"I don't want to quibble over percentages, Ashley," Sarah said. "It is true your ships offer the greatest profit margin, even if they are slow. I'm sure we could find something reasonable and still save what it would cost by ground transportation."

"Don't we have people for this?" Ashley waved it all away with a flutter. Her head was throbbing.

"So... you're okay with it?" Sarah asked, smiling broadly.

"You don't know anything about an airship, that's the problem. You guys just see a big platform that moves across the sky and think you can load it up like a barge."

"I... well..." her smile melted. "Are you saying we can't make this happen?"

"I'm saying you don't get it, Sarah. The payload is not that impressive. Once you allow for the aether, and even if you *could* burden a ship like you'd like to...well...it would be impractical to load and unload."

Sarah got up abruptly and paced her side of the dining room. "I've had this talk with Delores and with Lance...even with LF."

"Let me guess, mom wanted too much. Lance wanted TransCorp, and good ol' LF just said, 'No deal,' am I right?"

Sarah stopped pacing and stood in a full-on, arms-crossed pout.

"Sucks being a captain of industry, doesn't it?" Ashley said.

Sarah looked toward the door Briggs had exited. She took off her FeatherWeight, her high fashion HeadGear that was little more than a barrette. She fidgeted with it in her hands a bit, then asked, "Can we go for some fresh air?"

"Sure," Ashley said, putting on her sunglasses again and pointing to the huge glass doors that opened out to the west.

Sarah's exaggerated move of leaving the FeatherWeight behind was a message: they would be truly alone. Truly able to speak freely.

Together, they walked out on the veranda overlooking the gardens. Ashley looked down at her butterfly garden, waiting.

Sarah stood elbow to elbow with her, feigning interest in the garden as well. "We're working on something big—really big—that will make *this* deal obsolete. When that day comes, we won't need you or your Rainmakers."

"Why are you telling me this?" Ashley asked.

Sarah shrugged, "Us girls gotta stick together, right?"

Ashley scoffed. Their relationship had been strained, at best, their entire lives. CommCorp played off of the two of them, constantly stoking their rivalry, *creating* the rivalry. Daddy's little girls. Competing in gymnastics. Vying for the same boyfriends.... their stories had been hyped since before they could even read.

"Really?" she said at last. "Was my birthday present part of this?"

"No, no," Sarah said. "Well... maybe a little. Making up for a little?"

"LF will explode if he sees that thing in his old office."

They shared a laugh.

"We need to make a splash. Strike a chord," Sarah said. "Nobody's taking either of us seriously. I have a whole board of uncles who walk all over me. You were just taking the reins *from a mob boss*, of all things, and then your dad shows back up!"

"Does feel a little shaky," Ashley admitted. "I'm taking meetings every day. Sharks circling."

"I know, right?"

"So, before your big product roll out or whatever, you want to team up because...?"

"We have to get established. We have to build some credibility."

"Why are you throwing me this? What's in it for you?"

Sarah drummed her nails on the stone bannister. She bit her lips together in thought. "Okay, Ashley, *there's a war coming*, and we'll have the best chance of making it big if we're already teamed up. There. Now you have it."

"You're predicting wars now?"

"We're *making* wars, Ashley. You're not that new to the biz."

"Isn't that profiteering?"

"It's survival. Strange bedfellows and all that, sure, but if we don't...we both lose."

"How's that?"

"TransCorp will still dominate transportation. We'll dropship for all sides—"

"Like any good arms dealer," Ashley interjected.

"—but we'll not make nearly the profit and we'll not be able to ship nearly the payloads without you."

"Profit and payloads," Ashley repeated. "LF would not like this one bit."

"What he's never gotten, and what you're not realizing is just this: your ships aren't invulnerable, Ashley. Join us or someone will shoot you out of sky hopping altogether."

"Is that a threat?" Ashley laughed. "You still don't understand our airships."

"No, no, no! *TransCorp is a mover, not a fighter*," Sarah said. Another slogan. Their wartime slogan. Ashley had heard it a thousand times in history class.

"You *cannot* shoot us down," Ashley said, an idea forming in her mind. "Come see for yourself."

"What? Really? Can we make it look like we're cutting a deal, like a tech inspection or something?"

"Whatever you want... if we're going to end around the old men, you need to see what you're talking about. The scale. The power. The problems."

"Therefore," Ms. Parker said, in summation, "there will be no paperwork drawn up at this time. We have an accord, a verbal agreement, and both parties find that... well... agreeable."

Both attorneys spoke at once. Kyle was stuttering. Briggs was blustering. LF stood, and his chair fell behind him. He slapped his palm on the table between each word: "No. Way. In. Hell." His face was red; his features were contorted.

The room silenced, and he continued. "My airships are *proprietary*."

"*Whose* airships?" Ashley asked, tipping her sunglasses low on her nose to eye her father. "You're dead, remember?"

LF sputtered. "We do not host guests on a Weekly. It is not done."

"Well, seems I remember that you did," Briggs boomed. "Before launch...Gulf of Mexico, Fall of '31."

"That..." LF said, sitting back down, "That was another matter."

Ashley noted the faraway look in his eyes, and she registered the whole thing. He was reliving that time when the world was enchanted by his vision. Every dignitary had toured his first ship, the *Incus*, before it sailed. Every medium the early CommCorp could muster was broadcasting virtual tours. Even Ashley, though only a young girl, had been under his spell. She spent that autumn onboard.

"You've said it before," she said. "It's time to bury the hatchet with TransCorp."

There was a shuffling in the gallery. Zana and Rory were leaning close together.

"Well, that's downright civil of you, Levi," Briggs said. "And long overdue."

LF glowered. "That is out of context."

"I... I believe that was said only in regard to hosting this meeting." Kyle offered.

"Well, then!" Ashley said abruptly, "Good meeting. And good day!"

She rose from the table, and everyone rose with her. She felt like the Queen of England when they did that, but at the moment, she did not care. She snatched up her HairPin and sped for the door.

"ASHLEY ELIZABETH!" her father roared behind her. She waved over her shoulder without giving him so much as a glance.

The guard detail was right on her heels. Those from the hallway did not even have time to ask, "Where to?" and just fell in behind her with the rest. She was on a hard march for the left wing.

"...and NDA's," she heard Kyle over the staccato of heels.

"Fine." It was Rory's bass tone. "But no background checks."

She slowed, and those immediately behind her had to bolt around and ahead. "Mr. Reed. A word?"

He came alongside her. Kyle was right behind them, still talking details, "...impossible before the first of the month, so you'll have that long to—"

"*We board in the morning*," Ashley said.

"Miss Winston," one of her executive board members approached, a little out of breath. "We don't have a ship near here. We won't for days."

"Pfft," she said with a toss of her hand. "We have over a hundred of 'em up there. I'll pick the one I want, and we'll fly there overnight."

Several of those closing around her protested, but she ignored them.

"And I don't want a 'detail.' I want *you* there, Rory."

"I'll be right at your side," he said, "but—"

"And Calissa too."

He nearly tripped but continued, "Ashley, we need to run a sweep, take stations...it's not something you just do, overnight."

"Well," she said, arriving at her rooms, "figure it out."

She cracked open her door just enough to squeeze in, then shut it behind her. There were few rules at the Estate more firmly enforced than this: Leave the Princess alone if she shuts her door.

She rested her back against the door and sighed. Jeeves and his staff had already picked up those clothes she had so quickly shed before the meeting. A cold glass of orange juice sat on the sofa table, beading with condensation. The drapes were pulled, and soft acoustic guitar music wafted through the room.

When Ashley was sure they had dispersed outside, she set the HairPin and her sunglasses aside and kicked off her heels. She pulled off her jacket and tossed it on the sofa, then flopped down in an overstuffed chair. Ah, this chair, her chair, one that had been in her room since she was a girl. It was a gaudy thing that might fit better in a Vårdö-style gypsy caravan, a bohemian patchwork pattern that she just sank into. If she had a throne, this would be it.

She had chosen her inroad, her partnership, and LF would have to accept it. If he didn't like it, he didn't have to join them on the junket. She chose to show TransCorp what and who they were messing with. She would decide on the airship to show, and Rory Reed would step up his game to insure everyone's safety. Bringing Calissa along would guarantee that.

She drifted to sleep, imagining herself in this chair, perched on the front edge of a Winston Weekly, commanding the skies.

19 Emphatically

"Not a word, understand?" Rory said to the six militia men surrounding him.

"Yessir," they said in unison.

"Pain of death kind of deal, get me?"

"Yes, sir!"

"I might suggest they be...harbored next door. Contained," Zana said.

"It would be prudent," Kyle DuPree offered, "all things consid—"

"I trust my men," Rory said over both of them. He frowned at the suits huddled around the attorney. "You look to your own."

They dispersed. Rory's head hung low, wagging back and forth in disbelief. It was an impossible task, trying to protect this woman. She never consulted him first. She just did things. It was infuriating.

"Sir?" one of the Franklin kids questioned.

"Two of you, take this station. Rest of you, look for me in the gym about dark."

The four strode away in a proud little knot, knowing they were chosen for this special mission, whatever it may be. Protect the Princess. Save-the-world-level stuff.

Rory waited with Zana for them to get out of earshot.

DuPree was back again.

"Now what?" Rory snapped.

"This is what you're signing on for," DuPree said, his arms widely displaying the whole estate.

"I just watch Ashley," Rory said.

"She calls me up at the last minute, the final hour! Buys and sells whole corporations over drinks," DuPree said. "Has me draw up things she never intends to sign. She's...chimerical."

"Chimerical," Rory repeated, rolling the word around in his mouth. He liked it.

"It would be in her own safety were our chimera a bit less so," Zana said.

"I'm glad she wants you up there," DuPree said.

He was changing subjects now. Rory was wary of attorneys, acutely aware of their tactics. He waited it out.

"You're a bulldog. I can tell," DuPree continued. "Wouldn't matter if the whole thing fell out of the sky, you'd save her."

"I don't know about that," Rory said. He remembered the Weekly that had stormed Franklin. It eventually crash landed, taking out a swath of land thirty miles wide, a mile across. The debris field was much larger even yet. No one had survived.

"Even Rory Reed has limitations," Zana said.

"I'm just doing my job," Rory said.

"Well, I don't envy you, pal. Hundred ships, all different configurations. All over the planet," DuPree chortled. "We won't even know which one until her majesty gives us the nod."

"Perhaps she will choose to show Ms. Parker a ship nearby?" Zana said.

"Right," DuPree said, doubtful. "And now she's pissed off LF. That can't be good. I mean, I have it hard enough. Between me and the charters, we have to ramp up transport, *global* transport, and all the passports, CorpCharts—the works."

Rory had an idea. His features stretched into a Cheshire smile. "Let's skip all that. I can get her there. Wherever it may be. Off the grid."

"Overnight?"

"Yeah," he said. He turned to Zana then and continued, "Pull up Mac. Have him at the ready."

"Ah!" Zana said, nearly clapping his hands together. "An excellent idea."

"Mac?" DuPree asked. "Is that your service? Part of your old gig?"

"Just trust me," Rory said. "She'll be in good hands."

"Oh, I do trust you," DuPree said, offering a handshake. "Emphatically."

Rory took his hand, and they shook firmly. "Emphatically," he repeated.

Only half of the TransCorp party had left the grounds. A second car and contingent of security remained out front. Rory neared three men his equal in size, likely veterans too, only on the winning side. He swallowed his distaste and approached, saying, "Hello gentlemen. Who are we waiting for?"

"Non-a-ya," one of them said as he took a step closer to Rory. He was chewing his words and a wad of gum. "Why don't you piss off?"

Rory continued, "Ms. Parker or her manager?"

All three men snorted.

"Her puppeteer, then?" Rory asked. They laughed now, more openly.

"He's like her handler," the one leaning against the car said.

"*Snake* handler, maybe," their leader said. "That girl is a trip."

"We're her PPS—"

"Her what?" Rory cocked his head.

"Personal Protection Security, and she made us all stay outside."

"Like dogs," another added.

"The Winston girl's not easy to manage," one of them asked, "is she?"

"She is not." Rory shook his head.

"We heard her giving you the what-for back there."

"I hear you're giving her the bone," another chuckled. "You got *aspirations*."

"You boys hear a lot," Rory grinned. He tossed his head, popping his neck. "You hear much about the intruder here? A guy dressed like you all?"

He had struck a nerve. The laughter stopped, and the other two moved in closer, joining the gum chewer. Rory glanced to the rooftop, assured to find his man there with a rifle scoped in on them. He knew two more were down the hill guarding the gatehouse. Should something erupt, these TransCorp thugs would never leave the property.

"What can you tell us?" one asked, his voice eager and high pitched.

"Ever find the rest of him?"

"A clean cut, right through the bone," the chewing gum man declared. "That *is* crazy."

Rory relaxed enough to gesture discreetly to wave away his sniper. These guys were more curious than anything. Big thugs, but harmless.

"I'll give you something, but you gotta tell me more about this Briggs guy, like where he's at right now."

They shuffled. One swallowed hard. It was clearly against orders.

"I could just ask," Rory shrugged, holding up a communicator.

"He's with old man Winston," one blurted.

"Wine cellar?" Rory asked.

"Told us to beat it," the squeaky one said. "The ol' boys sent everybody off."

Rory believed them. LF had taken him to the same cellar just days before.

"So?" the gum chewer asked, "this intruder?"

"You seem to have heard it all," Rory said. He started off for the cellar.

"Not so fast," one of them said. "You owe us."

Guns were now in hand. Beretta. S&W. Glock. These guys weren't even a tight unit. Rory marveled at how a well-funded outfit like TransCorp had such a ragtag detail. If he were in charge, they'd all have interchangeable iron. They would be trained to keep their mouths shut.

"Holsters or headaches, your choice, boys," Rory said, turning back to them. The sniper flashed Rory a question with a mirror reflecting the setting sun. Rory shook his head slowly. "No."

They looked at each other. Then they studied Rory, his hands held open at his sides. They were doing the math. Rory was counting his odds.

"He's that scrub Winston bought from Combs," the gum chewer said finally. "I've seen his work before."

"Rat bastard 'Coat," the squeaky one sneered, holstering his gun.

"Can't trust 'em."

Rory resumed course for the wine cellar. "*Trust no one*," he said with a smirk.

It wasn't a long jog out back to the painted-over cellar door. Rory stopped outside, collecting himself, bringing his breathing to silence. The door was too old to open quietly, he feared, so he just bent low against it and pressed his ear to the door.

Winston and Briggs were having a heated conversation. Rory's first impulse was to rip the door from its hinges and dash inside. His hand was on the handle.

Muffled words, so hard to understand, but both of their distinctive voices were engaged in a harsh back and forth. Rory pulled his ear from the door and studied the woodwork. Thick, layered with paint. When he resumed listening, this time with his other ear, he picked up on their conversation.

"That's too much to ask," LF shouted.

"I don't believe I'm asking!"

Rory heard a crash and a struggle. If he opened the door, even a crack, the squeak would announce his entrance.

Panting. Grumbling. "You *will* give us the water, Winston."

"Not my ships!"

"Nah, not your ships, just the water ways. We got a lot to move."

"And my daughter?"

"Line up that lawyer," Briggs was chuckling. "The pretty boy from lunch."

"He's not a criminal attorney. Hell, he's not even—"

"Don't know, don't care," Briggs said, grunting, as if getting to his feet. "They make good footage."

"But Gary. Listen."

Rory heard shuffling drawing nearer to the door. He couldn't move until he heard more. He would be fired if he were found eavesdropping, but he could not pull his ear away. It sounded now as if LF were speaking right into Rory's ear.

"Listen!" LF said. "*You can't let them put her away.*"

"Well, we could, but what's the return on that?"

"But a smear campaign? She'll be devastated."

"Only if she gets wind that it's your idea."

"It's *not* my idea—"

"Your word against mine," Briggs said. He felt Briggs jostle the handle inside. It was time to bolt, but he could not.

"What kind of men are we, to turn against our young?" LF lamented.

"The kind who get what they want," Briggs said.

Rory wrenched himself from the conversation and the entryway and dashed away. He circled the house, crashing through the three TransCorp men and on into the mansion. He scuttled down one wing, then the other, scattering the house staff with nothing but a frown.

He found himself at Ashley's door in a knot of his own security.

"She's sleeping sir."

"Door's closed, see?"

Rory growled and turned away. He wandered through the house and gardens. Each route seemed to return him to the little alcove where the HotWire had been hanging.

Repeatedly, he stopped there, thinking of himself as the intruder hewn in two.

20 Cloud Cover

Ashley woke to the sound of surf, the soft scraping of page-slid-across-page. She opened her eyes to see her father in a halo of light, sitting in a chair nearby, studying, then turning pages. It was a very large book, nearly a meter wide, when laid open on the coffee table between them. He had on crescent reading lenses, and when she stirred, he stopped mid-turn and looked at her over the top of the frames. "Hello, Snow," he said softly with a smile.

After the tumult of the afternoon meeting, she wondered if she were dreaming. Where was the firebrand? Where was the ranting Mr. Winston?

Surely not this man who sat cross-legged in her room. He had sat in that very chair. She remembered now how he read stories to her when she was a very young girl.

"I brought you a gift," he nodded to the book. "It's the master charts for our every airship."

Though only twenty years old, the chart book had been printed on an old school, oversized plotter and then handbound in leather. The pages had yellowed and curled, not so much due to the age of it, but from its heavy use and cheap printer paper.

"Poppy, I—"

"I thought I might help you pick your ship to show the Parkers."

It was an about-face. Four hours ago, he was raving mad about TransCorp potentially boarding a ship. He had outright *forbidden* it...but now he was helping her pick the right one?

"You'll want one that is sizeable, eh? Need to impress on them just how large they can be. How about the Nimbus?" Ashley was about to comment when he said, "No, no. You're right. It's just too, too much. Yes."

The Nimbus was one of their concept ships, one that dwarfed all the others by miles. It could carry an aircraft carrier, and it could reach altitudes none of the rest of the Winston Weeklies could even approach. She sat up in her chair and looked over at the two-page spread that illustrated the Nimbus in gloriously handcrafted script and illustrations that complemented the engineering graphics. She knew it was his handiwork, and it made that book a priceless treasure that had never left the library's vault.

"The *Incus*...but she's a bit stodgy, perhaps." LF turned to the page depicting the *Incus*, toward the very front of the book. "Still, she was first, and I see you've kept her in good repair."

"It was Mother, really," Ashley had to admit. "I was...off on other things."

"Yes, yes." He looked up from his book. "Earning your PhD."

"And a reputation, and not a good one."

LF nodded, turned his attention back to the book. He studied and turned. Studied and turned. It was as soothing as the sea stroking a sandy shore. *No Murus. Not the Murus.*

"In the old days, I used to get a lot of hype out of launching a Cataractagenitus. You could take them up in one of those."

"I've forgotten," she yawned, "what is a Cataragen... whatever again?"

"The Cataractagenitus were the first to launch from water. Proto-ships that staged the first demonstration of surface tension and aether's lift all-in-one."

Ashley sat up and tossed her head. Her hair danced around her face, helping to wake her. She was thinking of her medical terminology class, of all she knew of Latin. "Cataract. Genesis," she mused. "Made of waterfalls."

"Yes," LF beamed. "You remember."

"I do...just a little."

"Ah, you were little, then, too, weren't you?"

He turned his attention back to the page, caressed it with his palm, then continued. "I do think I would have a harder time with TransCorp on such a ship."

"Why is that?"

"Too many trade secrets, all-too-obvious." He sighed, "Ah, we were literally 'building the ship as we flew it,' in those days."

"So... otherwise...it sounds like you're *encouraging* me to take them up now?" she asked at last.

"My wishes don't matter, Snow." He took off his reading glasses and looked at her as if for the first time. "My, how you've grown." A warm smile filled his every feature. "You've become the woman I have always seen inside you. You've grown into this all so quickly, Ashley, and so well. My baby girl, running the water works. I am proud of you."

"It's...that's all I want in the world, Poppy."

"We may not agree on tactics, but I believe you know what you're doing." He tittered, "Besides...one thing about you has never changed: when you have a goal, there is no stopping you from reaching it."

She did not think of it as that so much as she had a point to prove to Sarah Dawn Parker. Her airships were as innocuous as clouds themselves. They were immune to the dealings of any corporation, any war or warlord, anyone.

Ashley sat on the floor beside his chair. He put a hand on her shoulder, and they looked through the book some more. It was a magical moment, as if she were on Santa's lap, like nothing could ever come between her and her daddy. Her man. *No Murus. Not the Murus.*

"Mirrors?" she said, feeling a little dreamy.

"What's that?" LF asked. "Did you say, 'no murus'?"

"Yeah, yes. Yes, I did," Ashley said. "Okay then, if not a Murus, how do you feel about a Calvus?" she asked. The Calvus class ships were barren, 'bald' in Latin. These were vessels void of any ornamentation or ostentatious design. They had been engineered by LF but constructed long after he had left. They were as close as any in the fleet to being a barge. "I don't think there are any trade secrets aboard one of those...at least not in plain sight."

LF studied the page. Ashley saw the disappointment in his expression. "Such an inelegant thing," he said. "Nothing to be proud of."

They were all something to be proud of. So many ships in the air, doing so much good for the planet. Millions of livelihoods enhanced by them. Millions of lives saved. It gave Ashley a lump in her throat.

He turned past them perfunctorily. He skipped several pages altogether. He seemed preoccupied and depressed.

"I'm taking Rory's daughter up with us," Ashley said, floating the idea past him.

"That's nice, dear," he said, consumed now with an elaborate map in the centerfold of the book.

"I'm going to show her a good light show," she smiled, already imagining the look on Calissa's face.

"You'll want to go high, then. A good Stratus." LF nodded and ran his finger over the map. "And you'll want to catch the sun just right."

She sat up and ran her hand over the page, too, settling over the Pacific Ocean. "One of these then?"

"I didn't teach you how to chart," he said with surprise. "Where did you learn that?"

"That fall I was onboard," she said. "When you left me on an airship while you drifted off to work somewhere."

"You didn't complain at the time."

"I felt like Peter Pan," she said, a flood of memories pouring over her. A ten-year-old girl playing pirates and hide-and-seek and moonwalking with grown men. Four salty sailors who were so loyal to her, so true to her. She had four fathers that fall. She pried herself from the tidepool of nostalgia and got to her feet.

"Are you going to share at least?" LF asked. "Won't you tell me where you'll be?"

"We're boarding the *Arcus*, there," she pointed, then declared: "And you're coming with us."

"I cannot. I can't bear to see it."

"Daddy, they're just corporate buffoons," Ashley said. "They're not going to ruin your precious airship. TransCorp isn't the bogey man it's always said to be."

"I will not be along for it," LF said with finality.

She remembered what Grandmother had said of his stubborn streak and did not argue.

"The *Arcus* is a good choice. A very good choice," LF nodded, and returned to the chartbook. "Better than a Stratus. Yes."

"At least it's no Murus," she mumbled, relieved at her decision, yet not entirely sure why.

"Yes," LF smiled up at her. "Yes, indeed."

21 Jump

The glistening craft, the Whipstitch, was waiting at the Winston's private airfield. A man not five feet tall was grinning at them as they pulled up in the limousine. Rory was glad to see Mac again. He was glad to see the plane too, Mac's pride and joy, nearing complete restoration.

"Honolulu by dawn, eh?" the self-proclaimed 'jet jockey,' said, stroking his chin. "That's eight hours in the air."

"It's asking a lot," Rory said. "I can spell you."

"She can fly auto, that's not it," Mac said. He looked at his watch. "How do you plan to board the airship after that? You could lose an hour there."

"Some tethered gondola thing," Rory shrugged. "That's another detail I'm not privy to."

"Gondola!" Mac snickered. "Might as well climb up hand over hand. That'll take forever. And if the flight don't make you sick, a swinging gondola will toss your cookies."

"So..." Rory raised his eyebrows. "What do you recommend?"

"Don't have 'em tie that Weekly down. I'll drop you up there."

"You'll...you will *drop us on the airship*?" Zana said. "I believe I will sit this one out. Perhaps I can run interference on the island."

Rory might not believe it from any other pilot, but he knew Conan Macintyre was true to his word. He had flown Rory between thunderstorms and tornadoes, landing with only instrumentation on a highway between corn fields in pitch blackness.

"Tell me what you need," Rory said. "I'll make it so."

"Can't land up there, so we'll be needing parachutes. I assume you want two apiece?"

"Two apiece?" Rory asked, his surprise ever-increasing.

"Sure," Mac laughed, "One to get on the airship, the other to get back off."

At dusk, they were airborne. Rory stood at the cockpit threshold, making small talk with Mac. He turned to survey the commotion in the cabin section, finding Ashley ranting at the man seated by Calissa.

He was just part of the guard detail, six men, four of them from Franklin. This one, Knowles, was not from Franklin, but from Mitchum's men. He had stood out in drills and carried himself well. Plus, Rory knew, the guy had four kids and two wives. He would not be flirting with Calissa.

Knowles was loyal to his post, and even as Ashley was bringing every kind of threat down on him, he sat with his arms crossed, resolutely looking ahead. Calissa was clearly embarrassed. She had her nose in a book, but she kept looking up when Ashley would fire off particularly colorful threats.

The rest of Rory's security detail was reclining in the posh leather seats. They knew to rest up for the mission to come. The other passengers included two TransCorp security guards, two executives, and Ms. Parker herself.

Finally, Ashley caught Rory's attention and waved him over.

"What is it?" he asked.

"Your meathead here won't give up his chair to a lady," Ashley said with a stamp of her foot. "I want to sit with Cal."

"Knowles, you're relieved." Rory said.

Knowles popped up from the seat and wriggled past Ashley. He was visibly relieved. "Yessir. Thank you, sir."

"This means," Rory said in his most firm tone, pointing a finger at Ashley's nose, "that if anything happens to my little girl, it's on your head. Got it?" Then he smiled and sat in a free seat, facing them. The girls leaned toward each other, beaming at him as if for a photo.

"Sticking it on an airship! This will be a first, even for me," Ashley said. She snuggled into the seat and buckled up.

"I've flown with Mac before," Calissa said, "but...I've never parachuted, ever!"

"Not to worry," Rory said. "You'll tandem jump with Knowles. All these guys have years of experience, and all in more tough landings than this one."

"They've never landed like this," Ashley said. "It's a whole new world up there."

"They're paratroopers," Rory smirked. "I think they can handle it."

He and Knowles had the greatest responsibilities, Sarah Parker and Calissa. Rory knew Knowles had all the chops he had invented for the rest of his team. Rory had done the impossible. At least that's the way he sold Ashley on these men. He had sifted through his men, finding several with ample experience. Each civilian was matched with one of his men by approximate size and weight. Each of his men had made hundreds of jumps. That was the story, and he was sticking to it. They all were.

Ashley, of course, insisted on doing it herself. She had expected his arguments, producing her certifications and even drumming up one of her instructors to vouch for her at the airport. Though he did not budge on that evidence and testimonial, he quickly resigned himself once she described some of her jumps.

It was a long flight. Ashley and Calissa never stopped in their banter, though everyone else in the cabin at least caught a nap.

Mac told Rory they were an hour out. It was time to go over the plan.

Mac went first, sharing the logistics of flying his plane in synchrony, "in the envelope," as he called it. "Get too close, and we're all just a bug in the Weekly's grill. Too far out, and you all just land in the drink."

"You're forgetting about the storm front," Ashley said, standing.

"Oh, yeah, and the turbulence," Mac admitted, "but you don't worry about that. Rory's got it figured, right?"

"Air-to-air..." he said, "pulling off that landing is a stunt in itself, but doing it in the winds we'll face...that takes a pro. All my boys are pros."

They were nodding their heads with him, but they looked a little pale. Thinking of the powerful storm that always roiled at the cutting edge of a Winston Weekly made Rory feel a few flutters himself.

"At least," he said, "we got a target that's thirty miles long, a mile wide."

"And," Ashley chipped in, "it's spongy on top, like an old-time waterbed."

Rory did not tell the passengers about the fact that Mac's plane wasn't really set up for parachuting. There were no regulation handlebars, no booster seat, nothing outside but the sleek fuselage. This was a jet, so should the jumpers not literally spring away from the craft, odds were as good as any they would smear down the plane and into the turbines.

Then there was always the lightning.

They were hunched in the baggage compartment in the Whipstitch's underbelly. The door sheared off as soon as it was jimmied loose. The change in pressure and the blast of cold air took his breath away. For a moment, Rory thought he had made his last stupid move. They were all going to die.

Then he felt something like warm water rising up his body, encircling him, enveloping him from harm. He did not feel the wind and soon, he did not feel the nausea, and then, even the fear left him. He found himself laughing aloud, as if he were on a joy ride at an amusement park.

He turned to look at Ashley as best he could, with Ms. Parker strapped to his chest.

She winked, then pulled down her brass aviator goggles.

It would be the most fun he had ever had jumping from a perfectly good airplane to almost certain death.

22 Higher

She could see that the plan wasn't going well when she jumped. Torrents of rain and wind were tossing people everywhere. She wiped at her goggles, not believing what she saw. One of TransCorp's executives and the guard strapped to him were plummeting fast. Their chute had been whipped shut and wrapped around the two like a burial shroud. Despite the ship's size, another pair dropped wide and missed it entirely. Someone else had dropped their spare chute bundle, and she watched it land on the Weekly, far from the mark.

She knew Rory by his size, and Sarah by the red jumpsuit. She kept her focus on them and adjusted her cords to follow. Calissa's guard was pretty good too, banking out over the main storm and using currents from it to pull ahead of even Rory. The first guard to make contact with the airship was bouncing with his executive. They were like children in a bounce house. The next hit the rubbery ship and slid across, precipitously close to the tail edge.

Ashley touched down and released her carabiners, then rushed to help the others. Rory had Sarah laying down, clutching at cables that crisscrossed the ship every yard or so. Calissa was standing free, her hand a visor at her forehead. She was surveying the scene behind the Weekly.

Ashley smiled and sighed. She turned her full attention to the view too, as she strode up to Calissa's side. Rory was making his way over, now that others were gathering around Sarah.

"Not bad, huh?" Ashley yelled to Calissa.

To both the left and right, off the tail of the ship, a huge band of iridescence lit up the sky. Radiant, multi-colored strips of refracted light glowed horizontally along the tail. They did not arch like a traditional rainbow, however, and so the Winstons had dubbed them "Rainbands."

She could not tell if it was the rain or if Calissa was crying, but she was obviously awestruck. Rory put his arm around Calissa. Ashley did the same from the other side. Together they admired the Rainband as the winds whipped around them. They watched as the bands of light wavered like the Northern Lights. Colors changed to include pinks and purples, but a stark white stripe dominated in the background.

They watched it, hearts filling with beauty and wonder, until the color faded out and all that was left was the sharp white stripe.

"And now," Ashley shouted, "turn around."

When they did, they were greeted with the most spectacular sunrise radiating through the storm front. The massive thunderhead was painted with reds and oranges and all in between. As the sun rose higher, the clouds resumed their angry purples and dark blues.

Ashley led them to a structure that blended in with the sweeping front of the airship. Though the size of a bus, the pilothouse was an aerodynamic bump made of windows and brass. The doorway was on a mechanical screw, which Ashley turned only enough to pop the seal and let them in. Ashley ushered them in with one hand but hung on to the wheel with the other. She kept her feet tucked in under the furring cables so she would not be swept away.

Once inside, she could hear again. Everyone was talking at the same time. They were like children immersed in a kaleidoscopic storm. Calissa ran to her, crying in joy, and hugged Ashley tightly. "Thank you, thank you, thank you!"

"I thought you might like it," Ashley replied. She was beaming with the rest of them. They were giddy with the sensory overload, with overcoming death, and with her Affectation.

It had taken her hours of pouring over charted courses of the Weeklies to approximate just the right vessel at just the right time and direction. This was the only airship in the hemisphere that was such a perfect theater for the Rainbands and sunrise phenomena pilots simply called "Dayglow." Ashley was so happy it had all paid off for Calissa's enjoyment.

The pilot turned his attention from the window and smiled at Ashley. The crew roster reported Sam Barlow to be on navigation, but this could not be him.

"That you, Lassie?" the man chuckled.

"Sam Barlow?" she asked.

"None other!" He held out his arms to her, and she rushed in for a hug. His hair was long and curly, and he had put on fifty pounds, but she knew his voice and his hug. She snuggled into him with a sigh.

"Don't look so aback," he said at last, cooing at her. "It's been some years."

Ashley had forgotten her manners. She turned to the parachute party and said, "This is my godfather, first pilot of the first Airship *Incus*."

As they exchanged greetings and names, Ashley took a quick inventory. All totaled, six had not made it to the pilothouse. The man who had been tethered to Calissa was one of the last of her crew remaining. All the other guards were Rory's stock from Franklin.

"TRANSCorp, did ya say?" Sam was roaring at Sarah's executive assistant. "*By what authority* are you here, you despicable—"

"My authority," Ashley interjected.

"Your authority, girlie?" Sam laughed.

"That's right," Rory put himself between them. "Miss Winston here owns Winston Water Works."

Sam Barlow laughed and laughed. "Ahh, that's a good one," he said finally, wiping tears from his eyes. "I think I'd know that change in power, don't you now?"

Ashley looked at all the astonished faces. She felt her face burning red. She wondered if it showed through her ScanTats. Various people tried to offer him an explanation, and he just laughed them all away.

"I read my tapes!" he shouted at last, fed up with it all. "I would know, I would. I keep current." He gestured at the floor, which was covered knee deep in telegraph ribbon.

A polite knock sounded on an interior teak door. People stood aside as another man, dressed in a similar uniform, stepped into the cabin. He was tall and lean and clean cut. He had an elaborate ScanTat over one eye and socket. "Apologies," he said, directly to Ashley, then to Sarah. "I lost track of the hour."

"You missed Dayglow," Ashley said with some surprise.

"Pettijohn, they say here little Ashley's in charge. Can you believe it?"

Ashley looked twice at the tall man. It really *was* Sylvester Pettijohn. "Sly?" she asked. "Is that you?"

"It is, of course, Miss Winston. One moment." He approached Sam Barlow and whispered something in his ear.

Sam's demeanor changed. "Applesauce!" he exclaimed. "It's time for my applesauce!"

Ashley and the others watched as Sam waddled through the door and down the stairs.

"I am so, so sorry," Pettijohn said, looking long after his shipmate. "Old Sam's not himself."

"Sly, I....we..."

"Oh, I know, Miss Winston. Got it on the Crackle over the islands." He pointed to his temple. "Won't get good signal anywhere out here when we're at speed, I hope you know."

Surprise after surprise had her reeling. First, to see Sam Barlow, then to learn he was infirm. Sly Pettijohn implanted! "I need to sit down," she sighed. Rory was at her side and held her up.

"Ashley," he said to her softly, "are you alright?"

The screw in the outside door squeaked as it was spun from outside, then two more men entered. It was Rory's magician/surgeon, dragging in an older executive who was obviously injured.

"Lost my man when we skipped," he explained, panting. "Found him dangling off the back in the rainbows."

The injured man peeled off his helmet and lining and panted, "I thought I was dead. No chute. No hope. Spexarth here saved my ass."

"So I could end it," Sly said from across the room.

Ashley turned her attention back to him. He had his weapon drawn and pointed at Sarah's man. The cabin then bristled with weapons drawn, most of them pointed at Pettijohn.

"Do I know you?" the weary TransCorp man asked, barely able to hold up his head.

"Deacon Parker, you bloody bastard! As acting captain of the *Arcus*, I order you off the ship without a chute."

"Ashley," Sarah asked, "what's the meaning of this?"

"I... I don't know," she said, astonished all-the-more. "Sly?"

"Parker here is a TransCorp officer. Condemned to death!"

"Sly, stand down," Ashley said, fighting off the wooziness. "The war's been over for years."

"You can't be serious, letting this scum aboard our boat!" Sly said, but then he made a mistake, if even casually, for he pointed the gun in Ashley's general direction. He was a wiry man who put up a good fight, but Rory's men quickly overpowered him and dashed him to the deck. "Miss Winston," he pleaded from the pile of bodies.

"Take his weapon and restrain him. The old pilot too," Rory ordered.

"That wouldn't be wise," Ashley said. "Who'll fly the *Arcus* then?"

"Uh... another crewman?" Sarah spoke up.

"The other two are sleeping," Ashley said. "Six-hour shifts. Six on, six off. Days are different aloft."

"Apparently everything up here's a little different," Sarah said, waggling her head.

"You mean to tell me," Deacon Parker said, straightening to stand, "this giant airship has a crew of four?! Four?"

"LF is nothing if not thrifty," one of the Franklin men muttered.

"I think I can man the helm," Ashley offered. Her head was swimming, and she worried it might Affect the rest of the team. She wanted some distance between them. Things were not going as planned. The crew's rudder was stuck in the past. They scarcely recognized her or her authority.

"You?" Deacon Parker sneered. "What do you know about steering an airship, young lady?"

"Rory, toss him in a cabin below," Ashley said. "I'll take Sly and a couple of your boys to the helm. He can remind me," she made a face at Parker, "in case I've forgotten anything."

Flying a Winston Weekly was like skating, they had taught her when she was just a little girl. It might have made sense to her but was poorly received by others. She *was* just a little girl then, and she had no reason not to believe the good-natured men around her. The ship simply pushed off gravity by a generous exposure of aether. When reaching its apex, the aether was recanted, and the ship would then plummet forward at such a graceful swoon no one would notice it on a vessel so large. That was how it moved, like breathing, exhale aether and soar, inhale and dive, in a never-ending cycle. Propelled by Transpiration.

After only a few years in the air, they learned the temperature and pressure changes that afforded a Weekly to transpire of its own at certain altitudes. An airship was as close to a perpetual motion machine as anyone had ever gotten.

In the helm, however, all of that general knowledge did Ashley absolutely no good. The cramped quarters were covered with piping and valves, gauges and dials. Some were in the most unusual places, like a very worn valve at her feet, and another dial that did not seem to correspond with anything at all.

"You'll take to it again," Sylvester Pettijohn said kindly. This time, he stood behind her, directing her hand and attention at each movement. Rory's men had improvised a straitjacket of one of the flight suits, and Sly was restrained, but his confidence was winning them all over.

Ashley thought it was something like playing the pipe organ, only even more complex. She knew why the crew only worked in six-hour shifts, and she knew why they cross-trained for both posts. Keeping the *Arcus* aloft was muscle movement, yet another dance, and within the hour, she fell into the rhythm of her childhood.

Back then she had sat on his lap, and Sly Pettijohn had rattled off the gauges and valves like some kind of rap song. She would point and he would twist or pull a valve or sometimes just tap the gauge in acknowledgement. Now she was grown, and he had grown old, and yet there was that closeness again as they guided the massive ship through the heavens.

Once in a while, a course correction would sound through the brass pipes that ran from the pilothouse to the helm. She was comforted to hear Sam's voice again. He gently stated course corrections, just as he had done when she was little. "Oh, Ashley," he would croon, "we're a little high on the aft," or "give her wing on the port a little there."

Only once in the six-hour shift had Sam Barlow gotten agitated. Something about TransCorp had again set him off. Pettijohn echoed the sentiment when he heard it through the brass. Otherwise, it was a fantastic flight, though it took all her energy in the end.

She slept through the next two shifts on a cabin cot not much bigger than a surfboard.

23 Moonwalk

Knowles and Pettijohn loved the cards. Rory had sat in with them on a hand now and then. Other men would come and go, but whenever Spexarth joined them, Rory cashed out to watch the young man work the table. He could have been earning good money in Vegas doing close magic. Once in a while, Spexarth would get Rory's attention, deal a little slower, and tip his head questioningly...but those were too well-played in most cases. The only times Rory could see the slight was after Spexarth had taught it to him in their berth. Otherwise, Rory would miss the trick every time.

Spexarth had a gift.

"Nothing to brag about, really," he had said in the bunks. "Magic comes easy to a pickpocket living on the streets." He elaborated, telling the horrors of his childhood and the resolve it had forged in him.

The TransCorp executives stayed together, minding their own business. The tension was most evident in the Mess, with the two factions eating at separate tables. One time, when they had tried to work in the galley together, a fight had broken out, and one of Rory's men ended up with a fork deeply embedded in the back of his hand.

Rory was disappointed. He thought he had chosen well. He handpicked Franklin militia who were too young to be 'Coats, and too wise to jump on the bandwagon against TransCorp.

He had not, however, anticipated Sly Pettijohn, a man who would not let the war go. "I know the fighting's done," he told the militia men over chili, "but that don't mean the war's over. *It'll never be over.*"

Neither had Rory known Deacon Parker was to join them, one of Sarah Dawn Parker's loud-mouthed uncles. That man had the rare ability to make *anyone* angry. All four of the crew, and now almost all the parachute party, found him insufferable. Pettijohn's suggestion to chuck Parker "off the ship without a chute" was in constant circulation.

Rory had been touring the aether tank room when he noticed a longer than usual transpiration cycle. Something wasn't right. He squeezed and ducked through the narrow halls and found his way to the helm. He forced his way in and demanded an explanation.

"Captain's orders," a uniformed man said with a shrug, pointing to the brass funnel of the voice tube on the dash.

Rory cleared his throat. He flipped open the cover of the brass funnel, about the size of his palm, and spoke into it: "This is Rory Reed. By whose orders are we stopping?"

"Mine." It was Ashley's smooth voice. "We're going on a moonwalk, if you care to join us topside."

Ashley had the crew of the *Arcus* bring the airship much higher and then bring her to a full stop. It was riding the current of the tropopause, she explained, a very particular band of the atmosphere. Sarah, Calissa, and a couple of ever-present guards all listened to her mini-lecture on the Bridge. Weather did not climb to that altitude, she said, so the air would be dry and visibility ideal. She went on about the magnetosphere and geomagnetic storms, but Rory was fixed on the others in the room. His baby girl was about to go topside, and he did not know the guard detail all that well. One was an officer of the Franklin militia, a woman Kelli Chase had vouched for named Vivian Rice. The other two were also Franklin militia. He knew Chavez well and had selected him for the mission. The other Franklin man had drawn the lucky straw of just having been on duty yesterday outside Ashley's room. Rory only knew him as Mark someone, a skinny, cheery kid.

The excursion was coming together. Sarah's people joined the ranks: two TransCorp executives, one a young woman and one an older man. Rory sized him up as another uncle, perhaps. The woman, however, stood out to him, as she had since meeting her on the tarmac. Katrina Covarrubius, from International Relations, Ashley had told him on introducing them.

They all were wearing flight suits, adorned with flashlights, coils of rope, even respirators. He glanced out the windows at the night sky, streaked occasionally with a bolt of lightning.

They were unscrewing the watertight door, one like separating every portion of a sub he had ever been on. People were remarking at the release of pressure as the seal let loose. Rory gritted his teeth to pop his ears. The TransCorp executives were fussing with their respirators.

"You won't need those," Ashley said. "Just a precaution."

Rory grasped the shoulder of the guard he did not know. "I'll be taking your place," he said.

"Sir?" the freckled young man seemed stunned, disappointed.

"I want to see this with my daughter," Rory said. "Take an extra shift off."

"Yessir," the man said with a half-smile.

"Stay out of trouble, and don't lose all your money to Spexarth, if you can help it."

"Oh, no sir," he said, beaming now as he stood aside for the rest of the party.

Ashley was studying some apparatus tied to her wrist. It was an instrument to measure sunspots, she had told them.

Meanwhile, the rest of the party was exploring the surface of the airship. In this half-light, without the bluster of the storm that normally tore at the front, the ship looked to Rory like an enormous black balloon, strapped in a crisscrossed pattern with thick braided steel cables. The yard-square lumps between the cables swelled with aether. The skin of the ship looked, and even felt, like the rubber sole of a tennis shoe. Rory marveled that this giant vessel—this blimp—could manage so much power of the storms and sky.

Nearby, the TransCorp uncle, a heavyset man, was jumping on the ship as if it were a trampoline, laughing and smiling like a little boy. Chaz Parker, the oldest of the uncles. Rory monitored him, knowing that altitude sickness, *especially at this altitude*, could sneak up on an old man quickly.

Sarah was asking lots of technical questions. She and the other TransCorp executive were listening intently to Ashley's answers. The scale of the ship was in part to generate storm fronts, yes, but it was also to provide a failsafe. Such a vast wingspan allowed for a lot of lift, Ashley told them, more than ample. Should as much as half of it be damaged or destroyed, the vessel would still glide to a gentle landing.

"Gentle?" the woman from TransCorp asked. "Like in Texas?"

"That was an exception," Ashley said. "That ship had been weaponized."

"Weaponized...how?" Sarah asked.

"Flying too low for too long. It turns one of these into an electromagnet. Leaves behind nothing but scorched earth." Ashley paused to look again at her instrument. "We have measures against that, too, of course, but Lance Mitchum's team sabotaged it all."

"And now," Sarah asked, "you have failsafes for the failsafes?"

"Redundancies," Ashley nodded.

"Yes, of course," Sarah said, thoughtfully.

"Come on," Ashley said, unsheathing a large knife from her flight suit. "I'll show you all why it does no good to shoot at an airship."

They were thirty yards from the Bridge, bounce-walking in synchrony. Rory had to admit it was a little fun, but the knife had his attention. What if Ashley tripped? What if she lost her balance? It was setting off his internal radar when he heard someone call his name behind them.

"Reed!" the man said again, agitated, waving his arms. "Trouble. Fight breaking out!"

Rory rushed as quickly as he could over the surging of the *Arcus*. Knowles led him through the passages toward the helm, then they took a sharp left into the Mess. There was a brawl underway. He roared at them to stop, but they did not listen. Rory dove into the thick of it and wrenched people apart. More than once, he had to slug some sense into his men.

"What is this?" Rory yelled. "What is going on here?"

"The dealer's dirty," Deacon Parker yelled back, adjusting his collar. "Can't trust this Winston crew, not even at cards!"

Sly bolted at Deacon, struggling to get free from those who held him back. "You'll die on this ship if I can't get you off it, you stinking scum." He was so incensed, he spit and frothed at his words. "You'll die!"

Rory waved, and a couple of men pulled Sly back from the core of tangled fighters. Here, in the center, fists were still flying. Someone clocked Rory with an elbow, and he snapped.

In seconds, the floor was strewn with the men who had not backed up against the walls. Spexarth was unconscious and bloodied. Others were nursing wounds. A TransCorp man, however, kept grappling with one of Rory's militia, a man who was not relenting.

"You show him, Cox!" someone cheered behind Rory.

It was his custom to let fights work themselves out, but that was not often within the tight confines of a ship and never at 70,000 feet in the sky. He grabbed Cox and held him up by the collar, surprised to find he was the freckle-faced guard from the Bridge. "Cox, is it? I said to stay out of trouble," Rory growled, tossing him to the side.

Then every one of them was thrown against one wall.

Then the opposite wall.

Then the lights went out.

Rory could not get his footing. The floor was at a sharp angle. He grasped at everything he could to pull himself through the doorway and then struggled up the hall. He pulled at pipes and seams and wiring and anything else that gave him leverage to get back to the Bridge. As he fought his way into the room, he saw nothing but stars out the vast windshield. The bow of the ship was pointed straight up.

The screw was too slow, so he dove, feet first, through a back window. His fall confirmed the *Arcus* was at full tilt. Far below, he saw clouds and the break of dawn over the ocean. He was in free fall with the glass shards, and he scrambled and pawed until he snagged one cable crisscrossing the ship's outer hull. Catching hold of it nearly snapped his wrist, but Rory held on and pressed himself to the rubbery surface. He latched on with his other hand, higher up, and began pulling himself, hand over hand, back toward the Bridge.

In the next instant, he felt weightless, but he did not let go. He was aloft, swinging by the cables, then slammed hard again into the ship. It knocked the breath out of him, but he shook it off and tried to get his bearings.

The boat had leveled out, but now the winds and rain had returned.

They had lost altitude.

He clambered to his feet and ran with no regard for the ship's tilting. He did not care if his bouncing run would spring him off into space. He growled and barreled right into the storm front. He had only one goal: get to the girls.

Save Calissa and Ashley.

In the slushy gray, a clutch of people was gathered ahead. Of the original seven, Rory found only these four crouched in a tight circle around a fifth person who was down. The TransCorp man, Chaz Parker, had his respirator on, and yet his eyes alone conveyed his shock. Rain sprayed them, but through it, Rory recognized the body at their feet: Sarah Dawn Parker. The splash of dark blood stood out even on her red jumpsuit. She had been gutted and her throat cut wide.

"Chavez!" Rory yelled over the maelstrom, "take Cal inside!"

He perked up immediately and sought her out from the others. "C'mon!" Chavez shouted to Calissa.

Rory saw her face then and knew she was in shock. "Just take her—Hell, carry her if you have to!"

Calissa. Chavez. Sarah. Old man Parker. He grabbed Viv by the shoulder. "Where's Ashley?"

"Threw us everywhere." Viv called back, "I don't know."

He was nearly knocked down by the wind and rain. He searched frantically for her, spotting her at last getting to her feet some distance away.

"Get them inside," Rory ordered Viv.

Parker and Viv struggled to get Sarah up, resorting to carrying her as best they could.

"Ashley!" Rory called, closing the gap.

It was not, however, Ashley. It was the other TransCorp woman.

"Where's Ashley?" he asked when he reached her.

"She fell. That way." The woman pointed to the tail of the vessel. "I don't know if she—"

Rory was already running and tumbling in that direction. When he could get his footing, he would scan for her through the pouring rain. "Ashley!" he yelled again and again.

When he did find her, she was clinging to the last cable on the tailpiece. He untangled her arm and helped her to her feet. Together, they made it back toward the Bridge.

24 Suspect

As the screw was run in behind them, Ashley still felt a blast of wind and rain coming in. The window was out. "Somebody cover that," she shouted. Ashley gestured toward it but recoiled at the sharp pain in her arm.

"I think I broke it," she winced. Then she noticed the blood on her arm and hands and much more blood on the floor of the Bridge. "I'm bleeding!"

"Not just *your* blood, Winston," Chaz Parker said. He had blood all over his chest, up his arms to the elbows.

Two men emerged from the cabins below and passed between them. They went about closing off the window hole with a tabletop from below decks.

"What?" Ashley scanned the faces...unfriendly faces. "*Whose* blood?"

"You're going to be okay," Rory said in his comforting baritone. "A couple people got hurt from the—when the ship tipped."

Calissa burst up the stairs, rushing toward her and Rory, but she stopped and screamed at her, "You! How *could* you?!"

Her outburst uncorked the rest of them, and they spat accusations at her, one and all.

"What happened to you?"

"Killer! I saw you kill her!"

"Miss Winston, no!"

Rory pulled her close and strong-armed his way through them. He kept his free arm over her shoulder, protecting her head. "Calissa, come with us. Now!"

He plowed down the stairs, pressing others out of the way, and then he wedged the two women inside the first door he came to.

"Get *away* from me!" Calissa screamed.

Rory shut the door behind them. They were in the ship's galley. He immediately recoiled from the thick stripe of blood where they had dragged in Sarah's *body*. It was laid out on the buffet table. Blood dripped to the floor.

Both women followed his gaze. Calissa screamed at the sight of the corpse.

Rory was gagging, fighting back his urge to vomit.

Pounding at the door behind him brought him to attention. "Go away," Rory roared. "I got this."

Ashley curled up on herself and leaned against the wall.

Rory swept up Calissa in his arms and murmured to her, "It's okay, baby. You're okay."

It did no good at all. Through the sobbing and moaning, even Ashley could piece the words Calissa cried. She punched his chest with each word. She thought Ashley had killed Sarah.

Everyone seemed to think so.

"Cal, honey, you know better—"

"I SAW it, Daddy. I saw her do it," she cried.

She pushed off her father and shrieked at Ashley, "Oh my god, Ashley! Why?"

Rory pressed her into a chair and turned to Ashley. "We'll sort this out," he said. "I promise."

Ashley could not believe it, any of it. She looked at Calissa, so angry, so disgusted with her. She looked at Rory, only to see a confusion in him she had never registered before. She glanced at Sarah Dawn, and she could not believe her eyes.

"I *saw* you do it!" Calissa screamed.

Rory sat with Ashley in a mechanical room. The crew had designated this as the makeshift brig, and the door was secured from the outside. Rory had requested a change of clothes, some bandages, and bedding. Chavez slipped in a bottle of cheap whiskey. "Anesthetic," he had said to her, "for the arm."

The instant the door shut again, even as they were winding chains through the screws outside, Ashley made her case. "You know it wasn't me. You know it."

"I do know," Rory said, pulling her jumpsuit off her shoulders. He was tending to her arm. "It couldn't have been you."

"She was my friend...sort of."

"You'd never kill anyone—" They looked each other in the eye, knowing better, "—not in cold blood like that. Not without a good reason."

"I don't even know what happened!" she said, wincing at the pain when he examined her forearm.

"That's not the right thing to say—"

"I know, I know...I'm telling *you*, Rory." she said, exasperated. "I'm not testifying."

"I'm just saying..." he was distracted, it seemed, by his inspection. "That must hurt," he said, running a finger along a deep gash in her arm.

"I don't even know how I got that," she shook her head.

"Same as this." Rory showed her his palms with angry abrasions coursing across them the same width as those on her arm. "Cables, I'd bet."

"You believe me, right?"

"Of course, I do, Ash." Rory turned to the whiskey and unscrewed the cap. He splashed some over her arm, and she almost Affected him on impulse. It got into his palms, and he recoiled from it. "Ah!"

He gently dabbed at her wounds, then took her wrist and hand and elbow through a range of motions. Finally, he sat back. "I don't think it's broken."

"Why is everyone pointing fingers at me?" Ashley asked, finally letting the feelings flow. It was terrible—horrible—what had happened to Sarah. That they blamed her turned her wrong-side out. "Why *me*?"

"Ashley...it was your knife," Rory whispered. "And... you really did have—"

"We had *what*? Words? A rivalry?" She could not help her anger now, welling up and out in torrents as strong as the storm outside. "I wouldn't kill her for it."

"Help me figure it out, okay? Calissa swears up and down she saw you do it. So does the uncle who was out there."

"Chaz Parker? That fat ass? He couldn't identify his own toes." Ashley snarled at the thought of him being her accuser. "Surely no one would take *his* word for it!"

"I don't even know the guy," Rory said. "But it gets worse."

"How in the hell could it get any worse?"

"Viv Rice claims—"

"Who?"

"One of mine," Rory said. "Franklin militia. She saw the whole thing."

Ashley swiped away the bandages he was trying to put on her and scrambled to her feet. "This is bullshit, Rory!"

She yelled it so loud the men in the hall unfastened the chains and looked in on them. "Everything alright, Mr. Reed?"

"Fine," he said. "Leave us alone."

The door shut; the chains dragged again.

"Maybe it was an accid-"

"YOU TOO?" she shrieked.

"No, no... no, I... I'm just trying to piece it together." Rory cursed and swatted at the shelves. Cleaning agents and brushes were dashed to the floor. "Three eyewitnesses who all have some credibility. *My own daughter.*"

"In the dark," she said.

"But *was* it? By the time I got out there—"

"By then, the ship was righted, and the sun was coming up."

"Ashley, I got there as soon as I—" Rory did not continue. She could see he was thinking, in his own infuriating, eccentric way. Counting. Finally, he said, cautiously, "Ashley, you've been a little...out of it since you zapped the both of us."

"What's that supposed to be? An excuse?"

"No, no... just trying to explain—"

"Some kind of alibi?"

"No. Look. You just said yourself that *you don't know what happened.*"

"You know what," she said, feeling the flare of Affectation again, "just get out."

"Ashley... maybe you're experiencing side effects—"

"Now!" she gritted her teeth, fighting it off. "Before I hurt you."

25 Fallen

Their studious attention, haircuts, and postures suggested the card playing men in the Mess were monks. They had been quiet for some time, fingering their cards, eyeing one another.

"People lose the most when they're unfocused, wouldn't you say?" Rory asked, examining his hand.

"I'd remind you it's not acceptable to count cards," Spexarth chided.

"I would never," Rory said flatly.

They looked at each other across the table.

"Okay. Okay. Shuffle and deal again. I promise this time. No counting."

Spexarth deftly handled the cards while Rory continued. "I mean, at a casino, with all the drinks, all the lights, all the show girls...I get distracted."

"None of that here, but you've not won a hand yet," Spexarth grinned, dealing out cards.

"Your head's not in it," Chavez said, picking up his hand.

"Exactly. Know why?"

Neither man knew why. They both shook their heads.

"My head's not in it. You're right. I'm not winning because I'm not focused." Rory sat back. "I'm not focused because I'm not objective. I'm too distracted."

"I have a feeling you're no longer talking about cards."

"Listen. Whenever I let up, even the littlest bit, everything goes to hell. I mean, get this: six months and Ashley's safe as a babe in a blanket. *Six months*. Then I bring Cal with me and lighten up for a birthday party. And what happens?"

"Was that the night—"

"A car bomb happens. Next day, like I didn't learn my lesson, what happens when I'm off philosophizing with LF Winston? A scud missile nearly kills Ashley *and* her gram."

"That could be circumstance," Spexarth said. "It's your turn."

"Oh, I can go on." Rory tossed down a card and continued. "I take the night off for a dinner party, and we end up with half a spy in the yard. I go on a jaunt up here where I don't belong, and Sarah Parker gets cut."

"I would guess you belong wherever Miss Winston is," Chavez said.

"The point is, when I'm out of focus, I'm putting her in harm's way."

"So, focus," Spexarth said, winking at him like he did when revealing his sleight of hand.

"Maybe having her in the brig is just what I need for a bit. Clears my head."

"Who are you kidding? She's all you think about," Chavez said.

"I don't know. I think about a lot of things. I anticipate a lot of problems. I should be relieved when ninety-nine percent of my worries wash out. But when there's something I *didn't* expect, something I never thought of, that just kicks me in the teeth. I can't have it."

"Three kings," Spexarth said, sweeping the cards his way. "I'll agree with you on one thing. You're off your game when you're distracted."

"Not quite, slick," Rory smiled, revealing cards he'd pawed. "I have two kings right here."

"You're catching on," Spexarth beamed. "Good for you."

Under both TransCorp law and general maritime law, murder was punishable by death. Rory knew that. He didn't need Kyle DuPree to tell him that. Corporate law was even more swift and merciless in its dealings. It would come down to *who owned the vessel*, and that was all Rory had for solace: Ashley would not condemn herself.

If they could just make it back to land, where the preponderance of evidence wasn't dripping from tables and staining the halls, maybe she would have a chance. On land, they could do blood work. Maybe the blood all over Ashley was her own, and *only* her own. A medical examiner could review the wounds and angles of entry and possibly determine that Ashley could not have gored the Parker girl.

If Rory could just reach his friends below, Astar and Zana—possibly even the Family—could intervene somehow. Hovering as they were, thousands of miles from any landmass, so many miles from even the surface...hope was fading.

He sat on his cot, only half-listening to the men around him. It had been two days, and they were still abuzz with it all. The Franklin militia were constantly being barraged with questions about her behavior months ago, about the Dance of Death as the dark web had dubbed it. A person could find anything on the Interface, and no amount of sanitizing from CommCorp could scrub it all. The Franklin militia defended her actions then. Even Viv, who claimed to have seen the grizzly knifing, argued that Ashley had acted righteously in Franklin.

Time passed, and only Chavez sat beside him. He had something to say. Rory just gave him a nod, and Chavez was out with it: "I've been thinking about it. I've been replaying the whole thing, over and over. Talking to everyone. Walking the scene when the rains allow—now, there's a damned problem, Rory. Any amount of trace evidence is just washed away. Just like that."

"Just like that," Rory said.

"Viv still swears she saw it all. Twenty feet away, positive ID."

"I know. I know."

"But I've been thinking, too, see...and I've got a timeline that raises questions."

Rory looked Chavez over. "What questions?"

"We've been onboard three days and the only problem this ship has had was when? Exactly when the murder happened."

"Uh-huh. So?"

"So, I think everyone's looking in the wrong place, boss. I think there had to be an *inside man,* somebody working with the killer, someone who tipped the ship at just the right time."

"How's that help Ashley? There's three wit—"

"We find the inside man, and we find the motive, and then we find the partner in crime."

"There's only four men who could fly this thing," Rory said, sitting up.

"And at least two of them are batshit crazy," Chavez smiled.

The acting captain, and therefore the magistrate of the *Arcus*, rotated every six hours. Besides that, all four men were suspected of being accessories to murder, and thus, none of them could sit on the bench. The corporate hierarchy firmly established Ashley Winston as owner of the ship, making her the ultimate authority on all that transpired thereon. As she was the chief suspect in the murder, however, she was disqualified from the role. The Franklin delegation was riddled with favoritism. The Parkers and staff had a vested interest in Ashley's persecution, both from revenge and greed.

The man with the gavel, a meat tenderizer in fact, was the self-appointed, presiding judge, Rory Ray Reed. He had perhaps the greatest motivation to see Ashley Winston found innocent. Rory knew the entire exercise was one of futility.

He knew how things worked conventionally...on land...in justice of scale. It all came down to money. The story would leak, the media would be purchased, and the crime would be forgotten. The offense against the Parkers would have to be settled in some other way, also out of court and regardless of honesty, innocence, or legality. Most likely, LF Winston would forfeit a fortune to see his daughter freed.

Or would he? That was scratching at the back of Rory's mind too: *what if LF did not want his daughter freed? What if he wanted his fleet and his power returned to him? What had he been talking about in the wine cellar with Parker? Was this the "besmirching" he had mentioned?*

After shift change, the bailiff, Martin Chavez, led the third suspect to the bench, a mess hall table. He was an average-looking sort who took his seat across from Rory, quietly and calmly.

"You're the one they call Cook. Is that right? That your name?" Rory began.

"Not my name at all. It's what I do...or did...before your bunch came onboard. I've cooked for these fellows, going on twenty years."

"Doesn't anyone ever get off this boat?" one of the Parkers jeered.

"We consider it our duty," Cook said, narrowing his eyes at the gallery.

"For the record," Rory said, "what is your given name?"

"Pruitt. Lucifer Pruitt."

There was a stir in the mess hall. Someone snickered, and another said aloud, "Lucifer, huh? There's your man."

Cook glared at him, then sighed and looked back at Rory. "It has been a challenge."

"What has?" Rory asked.

"The name. The Christians used to beat me up all the time."

More laughter from the audience. This time Rory turned on them, and they all fell silent. He was aware the whole thing was just short of a laughingstock, but he only had another twelve hours until the ship would hook up with the San Francisco gondola umbilical. Just two more shifts.

"So... did you know the deceased?"

"No, sir."

"Do you know the accused, Ashley Winston?"

Cook smiled warmly at the mention of her name. "Of course."

"Have you any reason to foster any ill will toward the Winstons?"

"No, sir."

"The Parkers?"

"Who again are the Parkers?" Cook asked.

One of them coughed in the audience.

"The Parkers are the family with primary holdings in TransCorp."

Rory expected the same radicalism he had heard from Sly, but it did not come. "Why, no, sir. I would say that we of the *Arcus* stay aloft for good reason, to not mind the affairs of man."

Rory's eyebrow twitched. *We of the Arcus...the affairs of man.*

He shuffled his papers but decided to work without his notes.

"I understand that you each take turns at the Helm and the Bridge."

"Yes, sir."

"Of the four of you, who would you venture is the best at flying this majestic ship?"

Cook looked down and to his left. His chin rested on his collar for a moment. "Why would you ask such a thing?"

"Curious," Rory said, tossing it out off-handedly.

Cook looked out through the audience and gradually scanned back to Rory.

"You needn't worry," Rory said. "The others aren't in the room."

Cook smiled then, revealing his terrible teeth. In the late 1900s, methamphetamine addiction had left many with such dental damnation. Rory tried not to nod, but he was becoming surer of himself.

Finally Cook said, "I am."

"You are the best at flying this machine?"

"Yes."

"Tell me about it," Rory said.

"*Aw, c'mon,*" Deacon Parker exclaimed. "Get to it, man."

Rory was climbing to his feet, but Parker raised his palms and ducked his head in apology. "Sorry, sorry. I just want to get to the punchline here, Reed."

Rory took a deep breath and sat back down. He composed himself while Cook looked on. Rory closed his eyes and counted to ten, then resumed where he left off. "Can you describe for me just what that's like, flying the *Arcus*? How does it feel?"

"It feels..." Now Cook closed *his* eyes. As he thought about flying his ship, Lucifer Pruitt's entire demeanor changed to one of tranquil bliss. "It feels alive. Flying with the *Arcus* is my mission in life. Redemption for my worldly ways."

He opened his eyes, looking only at Rory now, and Rory let Cook know he was open to it, that he wanted to hear more. He simply nodded, his eyebrows raised in interest.

Cook continued, "I fly with her half my life up here, and I never want to land. I'm a kindred spirit with her. I can coax more out of her than any man, living or dead."

"Is that so?"

"Oh yes," he said. "Have you ever seen a condor ride the thermals? I can take the *Arcus* in those circles. Have you ever seen a Kingfisher plunge from on high, pluck a fish from the water? I have brought the *Arcus*, this mighty ship, to soar and then plunge just like that. I can skim the tip of her across the sea and bring her back up near 90 degrees. All of this *without* the pilot on the Bridge, sir, for I know the *Arcus*. I know her like no other."

Rory was almost there.

"I bet you couldn't stand her on her tail from a full stop, now could you?"

Cook opened his eyes at the challenge. "I could. I have. Find *any* other living man that can do such a thing with such a ship as mine!"

"I've heard that LF Winston could," Rory said with a casual shrug.

"Bah! He an' Sam might have done some stunts with that ol' *Incus*, but Sam's a loon and LF—well God rest his soul and be gone with him—he may'a built the *Arcus*, but he'd never fly her. No, but she'll be untethered from the corporations now. You can take my word!"

"You want your girl free from the corporations, then?" Rory said, in the same style and tenor Cook had fallen into. He mimicked the brogue of it.

"*She is free*, finally." He leaned in and continued, conspiratorially, "With that lass swinging at the yardarm, there'll be no one left to wag the title at us. The *Arcus* will be mine."

"Lucifer Pruitt," Rory said firmly, "you've been duped, sir. LF Winston is alive and well in Springfield, Texas. Check your Crackle, come California, if you doubt me!"

Cook twisted furiously toward the crowd in the mess hall. "*You lying vixen*!"

TransCorp's International Relations officer, Katrina Covarrubius, jumped from her seat and fought through the others for the door. Rory's hunch was spot-on. He had expected the worst, had felt it coming on, and it coldcocked them all like a tidal wave. Her Affectation was ruthless and cruel—and raw emotion. Rory and those throughout the room screamed and cried out in mortal fear.

He had prepared for this. Of all present, Rory Reed had likely been Affected more times than any other. He had no immunity, but he had learned that if he could *anticipate* an Affectation, he could sometimes see his way through it.

He screamed. He wept. He gnashed his teeth and moaned, but he also drew a pistol with a tranquilizer dart, aimed it at her, and popped her in the thigh before she could clear the doorway.

26 Hoodwinked

She knew shift changes by the subtlest differences in the helmsman's style. There had been four changes, maybe five, since she had been detained. She hadn't slept for the first twelve hours, too shaken by all the accusations. She wasn't sure how much she might have slept since, but based on shift changes and her waning and waxing appetite, she thought she had it down to the hour. By her reckoning, it would be the morning of the third day of her imprisonment. Nearing the end.

To pass the time, she read. She read every service manual in the room, every label and warning sign. Then she read again every note slipped in with her provisions from her admirers. Once in a while, Ashley tried to work the hanky. "Mirror, Mirror, on the wall..." she chided, then asked serious questions of it. Was Sarah really gone? Had everyone lost their minds? Would she be going home anytime soon?

The embroidered patterns did not respond.

> Hours passed, and she tried again, this time not voicing her questions aloud. Nothing.

She tried just *thinking around* some topics, hoping it would take the bait and engage with her, but the handkerchief was not making conversation.

Then she tried another round of test questions, mocking the magic. What time was it? What was her favorite color? How many fingers was she holding up?

Ashley chortled at herself. A grown woman talking to an old rag! She was amazed at her own immaturity. She was questioning her sanity.

Another shift change, and shortly after, a commotion in the halls! She stood to face the door, stuffing the hanky back in her pocket. If she was going to be thrown overboard for a crime she did not commit, she was going to go with pride. She stuck out her chin and crossed her arms.

Nothing came of it. No lynch mob. Not even a knock at the door.

Time passed, and she curled up on the bedding pile and wept. She knew she was innocent, so what was wrong with the rest of them? All she could figure was altitude sickness. Then why did it not strike her too? Or had it? Rory Reed had not lost his bearings. He seemed to believe her, or at least he *wanted to believe her*, she thought.

She felt broken and powerless. She kept returning to that moment in the pantry, after breakfast, when she had been the victim of her own Affectation. Ashley had been Affecting animals, then people, since she was a little girl. What could have happened?

She woke to the sound of the door chains unwinding.

People streamed into her room, filling it quickly. Those who would make eye contact with her smiled sheepishly, then looked away. It was no lynch mob. These were not angry men and women hellbent on revenge. Even the Parkers came into the room looking apologetic. The last two to squeeze inside were Calissa, who was a hot mess, and Rory.

"We're all sorry, Ashley," Rory began, then a chorus of others drowned him out with their own regrets. When he found the opportunity, he continued, "It was Covarrubius. She snowed us all."

"Katrina Covarrubius?" Ashley couldn't make sense of it.

Several in the room nodded. Captain Pettijohn stepped forward and asked for forgiveness. "Aided an' abetted by my own crewman," he added. "Cook."

Ashley was astonished. "You're sure?"

"Not a doubt in my mind," Deacon Parker said, "that man is a lunatic."

"Guilty as sin," said another in the crowd.

She looked at Rory, trying to pry more from his eyes. He nodded at Calissa, who was pouring tears down the front of his shirt.

Ashley picked up on it and stepped closer, placing her hand on the girl's shoulder.

"I'm so, so sorry," Calissa blurted. "She looked *just like you*."

"Hoodwinked us all, somehow," Viv said.

Ashley shook her head slowly, a frown pinching her features. Katrina looked nothing like her, nothing at all. She was Mediterranean or Hispanic. She wore her dark hair in a knot. She was taller, thinner.

"You know...like you did in Franklin," Rory said. Caution tempered his words: "Remember when you tricked us?"

Slowly, it sank in.

Katrina Covarrubius was Family.

"We tie off at six, Miss," Spexarth advised.

"Meaning?" Ashley called out to him over the sound of the showerhead.

"Less than an hour," he said. He accompanied Viv on detail now, stationed outside the single stall shower. The space was not very private, just a knee-length sheer curtain drawn between them. The stall was a retrofit, an afterthought twenty years ago that had afforded privacy enough for a four-man crew. Ashley found it a little awkward to bathe and dry and dress in the cramped quarters.

"I want to see her," Ashley said, squeezing water from her hair.

"Not advised," Viv said firmly. "She's cagey. She won't go down without a fight."

Ashley half-smiled. In the hours that had passed since they set her free, she had thought of little other than giving Katrina Covarrubias a good beating. Slaughter her friend! Set her up for murder! "You like a good fight, don't you, Spexarth?"

"Pardon?"

She felt the tingle of her own Affectation, but the suggestion was merely to take a risk, and she was all about that, already.

"A girl fight," Ashley continued. "You salty dogs would probably place bets on it about now, wouldn't you?"

She heard him chuckle outside.

"Where do you think you're going?" Viv said, her voice trailing off. "Men!" she said, eventually.

"I need to see her. You understand, don't you? A little payback before things get too civilized down there?" Ashley slid the curtain open.

"Reed said to keep you away from her. Said it directly."

"I thought you worked for Cap'n Chase."

"I do," she said, her back straightening.

"And Cap'n Chase...who's she serve?"

Viv got a twist in her brow. She was struggling against an Affectation and working through the reasoning of it all.

"Guess I serve you, above all, Princess."

"That's exactly that," Ashley said with a nod. "Show me the way."

Viv took a few steps, then halted. She faced Ashley again, anger rising in the flush of her neck and into her face. "That's how you do it, isn't it? You mess with our minds."

"It's not like that," Ashley started, then she noticed Viv's hand on the butt of her pistol. "Okay, okay, it is like that."

Viv narrowed her eyes. "How do we know who to trust?"

"What do you mean?" Ashley tried to look casual. She ruffled through her things, pulling the kerchief from her pocket to tie back her hair.

"Everything equal, if both you an' her are gypsies, maybe you're the one fooling us."

"Everything's *not* equal though, is it? She's TransCorp." Ashley shook out the handkerchief, and was about to twist it, when she noticed the squiggling writing on it taking shape. "I'm...I'm..."

"What?" Viv said.

"'*Go to the trouble*,'" Ashley read the words aloud. She looked at Viv quizzically and asked, "Go to the trouble?"

Viv read the words herself and shrugged back at Ashley.

Ashley took the hanky by the corners and twisted it quickly, then tied her hair. "Pick your battles, Vivian Rice. You with me or against me?"

"So, 'we going to find some trouble?'" Viv asked in a husky voice. "Gonna kick some—"

"You say tomato, I say tomahto," Ashley smiled, slipping on her shoes. "Where did Spexy run off to? Where can we find Kat Covarrubius? Don't you think we'd best 'go to the trouble,' before Rory comes back around?"

Muscle memory is vital in any sport or repetitive activity. Soldiers train hard to fight easily. Reasoning takes too long. Responding is too slow. A good soldier simply *is* a good soldier. Rory Reed had been drilling his squad for months now to know right from wrong...and he was right.

Ashley knew her mistake as soon as she'd said it. Viv might serve the Princess. She might follow Cap'n Chase. But she obeyed—blindly and wholly obeyed—Rory Reed. She pointed her pistol in Ashley's face.

"Ahh," Ashley rolled her eyes. "Soldiers!"

"You can stand down, Viv," Rory said, entering the room.

"How are you always around?" Ashley asked. "Always, but never when I want you."

Viv holstered her gun and left the room in a hurry.

"Spexarth filled me in," Rory said.

She growled and stomped her foot.

"You don't want to mix it up with Covarrubias," Rory said. "We're almost home free."

"But we're not. There's a lot to work out yet."

"I get the feeling this is all a big setup. Someone high up went to all the trouble of putting you in the crosshairs."

"Yeah, someone went to a *lot* of trouble—" Ashley stopped. "That's it!" She slapped him on the bicep. "I have to, Rory. Now I have to *go to the trouble*."

"What are you talking about?"

"I gotta *go to the trouble* of hearing her out. I have to go the distance. Give her a shake."

"The woman who impersonated you and killed your friend?"

"Yeah," Ashley said, as if it made perfect sense, "the hanky said so."

27 Aether

One convenient feature of the aether that kept the *Arcus* afloat was that it was also an excellent pain killer, anesthesia, and an intoxicant, all in varied doses. The crew of any airship knew these features and partook of the gas when appropriate. Aether's closest chemical cousin was halogenated diethyl ether, which was both a weaker, and yet still flammable, substance.

Rory had heard all this and a tiresome headful more from Spexarth, the would-be surgeon. Even in his limited time aboard the *Arcus*, Spexarth had interviewed the crew members and had concluded that prolonged exposure to these fumes that kept them airborne might also have left them a little infirm.

Rory did not care if the aether left Covarrubius brain dead. It was keeping her under control. His goal was to keep her sedated until they were on land and she could be contained...or at least until he was miles away from her Affectations. He suspected she would not think fondly of his tranquilizer dart.

And yet now they were guiding Covarrubias back to semi-consciousness. The trick, Rory warned Spexarth over and over, was that she could *not* be fully revived, for then she would be the most dangerous person aboard ship. The whole thing was an unnecessary risk, but it was Ashley's boat, Ashley's Family, and by all rights, Ashley's call. And Ashley had insisted.

Spexarth reassured Rory that he knew what he was doing. He had dabbled, he claimed, with lots of mind-altering substances. That did not make him any more trusting of young Spexarth's judgment.

She was strapped securely to the cot they had moved to the Aether Tankroom. Even if fully awake, she would not likely have gotten free, but Rory's imagination went wild with other scenarios for a half-drunk, angry, Family member.

"She's powerful," Rory said again. "Don't forget when Cook called her out."

"Right. Right," Spexarth nodded, watching the drip he had shut nearly completely down. He had reconfigured a respiration helmet with an aether drip, one that they had adjusted from time to time to keep Covarrubias under control. "At this rate, she should just be moderately coherent."

"Can she answer questions?"

Spexarth shrugged. "Yeah, sure. I dunno how much I'd trust her answers, though. She'll be sleepy-drunk."

"And if you back her off that?"

"She'll fill her helmet with vomit, for one thing, and she could be more of a threat than you're looking for." Spexarth tapped the drip with his forefinger. "I know I wouldn't leave Miss Winston alone in here with her, should she get too lucid."

Rory had not been idle on the *Arcus*, either. He knew Ashley was right, that the ship could be torn to shreds and it would still simply drift to earth. It was *also* true, he had learned, that if transpiration were disrupted, the careful exchange of atmosphere and aether, it could cause what Sly had called a "precipitous and catastrophic event." Translation: they would drop like a rock.

It did not make Rory any more comfortable to know that in the 30 square miles of this vessel, the one vulnerable mechanism controlling transpiration was only a few feet away. This was a risk he took, for the Aether Tankroom was the most isolated cabin on the ship, and should she come to, he wanted to minimize the risk to the rest of the passengers. He gambled that if she were to wake and overpower him, she might at least have only limited knowledge of the ship's propulsion. Maybe.

They were rushing it. Crew members insisted they would connect to the San Francisco umbilical within the hour. They laughed aloud when Rory asked if they could just take up a holding pattern. Even Sam Barlow knew that was ludicrous. The *Arcus* took nearly a week to make a controlled circle, and they had to answer to CorpCharts, weather forecasts, and 3dub.

With the clock ticking and the Princess insistent, Rory had pulled the helmet off Covarrubias and patted her cheeks.

"Don't slap her," Spexarth warned. "You want her dead before you get any answers? Because if you kink her windpipe, even a little, she could asphyxiate. I had her immobilized just right. Please," he said with a firmness that surprised and impressed Rory, "let me do my job."

Instead of a slap in the face, Spexarth ordered in some ice from the prow of the *Arcus*. He wrapped it in cloth and applied it gently to the woman's forehead. "She'll have a hell of a headache," he said, "no matter how we bring her around."

When the ice had little effect, they reversed exhaust ductwork and charged the room with the thin, cold outside air.

When that failed, they each took an arm over the shoulder and actually coaxed her to put one foot in front of the other. Walk it off.

As soon as she could mumble and shuffle, Rory insisted she be restrained again, and Spexarth agreed. The helmet was again secured. Her vitals were monitored, as well as her drip.

"Let's bring her on up," Rory said. He rapped on the door of the Tankroom and waited as the series of locks and chains were removed. When the screw had released, Rory commanded his men to bring Ashley down.

When she entered, Rory was again moved by her beauty, her radiance, her smile. Ashley had let her hair down and put on her HairPin, the glittering tiara. She had somehow made an oversized flight suit fit like something from a Paris runway. She came into the room as casually as she might her own, but when she did, the greasy old Tankroom seemed as regal as the Princess herself.

"Won't work," Covarrubias slurred.

Rory switched his attention to the captive, then back to Ashley. She was no longer glowing, and the Tankroom was once again a mundane mechanical space.

"What was that?" Spexarth asked.

"Nothing. You can go," Rory said. "I told the others to put some distance between us and them. You'll be safer above decks."

Ashley waved him away. He stood, but Steven Spexarth didn't rush off.

"I'd like to stay, all the same," he said, studying his patient. "She might need tending."

Ashley smiled a little. "Don't trust us?"

"Oh...no ma'am. It's not that." Rory had not seen him act so awkwardly. "I just... Well, you don't know the aether too well."

Rory said, "It might get dicey in here—"

"Ah, let him stay," Ashley interrupted. "Can't you see he's tripping?"

"He's—?"

"Won't matter what we say, if she's got her hooks in him."

"She's barely there," Rory scoffed. "I doubt she's..." he wriggled his fingers by his head.

"What are you talking about?" Spexarth asked.

"Ashley here thinks you're a little...spellbound."

"Good word," Covarrubias mumbled. "Bad idea."

Spexarth looked anxiously at her, then at Rory and Ashley.

Rory took a seat on one side of the cot. "Why's it a bad idea?"

Ashley was scrutinizing Covarrubias.

Spexarth slid into a seat opposite Rory, checked the drip, then held his fingers on her wrist again. "Steady," he said.

"Because," she chuckled in the helmet. The glass steamed. "Works both ways."

"What the hell is she talking about?" Rory asked Ashley.

"I dunno," she replied. She stepped closer. "Can you take that thing off?"

Rory looked at Spexarth. They both shrugged.

"Maybe for a bit," Spexarth replied, as much a question as an answer.

They worked it free. Spexarth folded a cold wet cloth and put it behind her neck.

Ashley nudged Rory, and he yielded his seat to her.

"You could go," she said to Rory with a half-smile. "I know you trust me."

"I don't trust you as far as I could throw you," Rory said, folding his arms. "Better get on with the questions."

Ashley pulled in toward Covarrubias. "Why?"

"Why not?" she smiled.

Ashley growled. Rory put a hand on her shoulder.

"Why did you do it? Why'd you kill Sarah Dawn Parker?" Ashley said in measured tones.

"Did not," Covarrubias chided in a drunken half-smile. "You did."

"Her answers may not be...clear," Spexarth said.

Rory patted Ashley's shoulder, then asked, "Katrina, what do you mean by that? That Ashley killed Ms. Parker?"

Covarrubias swung her eyes around to look at Rory. "Everyone says so. Saw it for themselves."

Rory caught Ashley giving a sidelong glance at Spexarth. She adjusted in her seat and asked, "How did that happen, that people saw that?"

Covarrubias was blowing bubbles with her spittle. Spexarth wiped at her mouth.

"I was falling off the back of the boat, Katrina...so I wasn't even there." Ashley nodded, affirming her position. "So. Then. You did it, didn't you?"

"Did what?" she smiled, feigning innocence.

"You killed Sarah."

Rory leaned down a little and said, "You made it look like Ashley did it."

"No. Yes. I don't know." Covarrubias bobbed her head within the constraints Spexarth had constructed from a tool belt and a helmet liner. He was holding her hand, and with his other hand, feeling her pulse again.

Rory looked at his watch. This was going nowhere fast. He up-nodded to Spexarth and took off on another angle. "I trust you, Katrina. You won't, you know, put a spell on me, right?"

"You mean," she said with a beatific smile, "like this?"

He had a plan to cover her face with a rag soaked in aether, if it came to that, but she had been so helpless that he had not even bothered to prepare one.

Now it was too late.

He was instantly on full alert. His eyes seemed to take in every detail. His sinuses tingled. He could smell the aether. Taste his own tongue. The others were likewise Affected, glancing like cats this way, then that, as if they all had unfettered senses.

Heightened senses and awareness. He could hear the breathing of the *Arcus*, the transpiration, the hissing of the aether coursing in and out with the atmosphere. He could hear the raging storm outside. He was calculating, estimating risk, and predicting problems.

Rory had a wash of epiphanies come over him, some that seemed obvious, others that seemed like prophecy. He had certain hunches and felt he knew the culprit behind the bombing, the missile, even the murder. Oh, and he was hungry. And he had not slept since...Tuesday. Yes, Spexarth would be good on his team. Yes, Zana was certain to be waiting at the umbilical. Why wouldn't he tell Ashley how he felt, tell the world how he felt? He could see the threat of procrastinating and the broken promises of unfulfilled ambition. It was a moment of clarity like he had never known.

Seventeen minutes to tie off.

Ashley's pulse had steadied under his touch.

Spexarth was madly in love with Katrina, and he did not yet know it.

Then he understood what she had done and why.

"*Works both ways*," he said.

"Yes," Covarrubias said. "Sharp, for such a big lug."

28 Rescue

She knew an Affectation when she felt one. Grandmother had practiced with her and the others of the Family. Some were biological. Others diabolical. Most were emotional...but this one, Katrina Covarrubias' Affectation, was enormously powerful. Simple.

Clarity.

With that insight, Ashley freaked.

If Kat was clear, not sedated, that meant risk!

Ashley about popped off her own Affectation, something debilitating, but she wanted to spare the others on the ship...and herself.

She was afraid of hurting herself.

She knew her weakness.

She knew, also, in a wave of clarity, the *cause* of her weakness!

She laid her hands on Spexarth and gave him a jolt, as direct and white hot as a defibrillator.

Katrina was struggling with the improvised straps that held down her arms and barely saw it coming. Spexarth popped the helmet on her and gave the aether a twist.

Katrina was holding her breath.

Rory was double checking her restraints.

The glass was steamed over as Katrina screamed. Ashley could not see her face, only hear her agony.

"Back it off!" Ashley said. "Two twists."

Spexarth did, then looked at her curiously. "How'd you know that?"

"I saw you do it earlier. I remembered. I—" she turned toward Rory.

"*How did you know, mister*?" She was elated. Rory had figured it out for her, basically handed it to her, the solution to the mystery of her ailing Affectations.

"She said it first," Rory smiled. "Took me a while to get it. When she's drugged, she zaps herself when she zaps others."

"Works both ways," Ashley mused.

"And so, when she popped us all with the sensory caffeine—"

"It worked on her, too, and she was almost free," Ashley said. She stood then and embraced Rory. "And that's why I was broken!"

"What?" Spexarth asked, struggling to catch up.

"You weren't drugged," Rory said, "not exactly."

"I was drunk. Now that I think about it, the same thing has happened before, but I didn't know it because I was soothing someone, and myself."

"Guys!" Spexarth was on his feet now too.

"All I told you was to *act*," Ashley said to him, "and you did. You saved our lives."

"How did you do that? How does *she* do that?" Spexarth was alarmed, like everyone was when they'd been Affected and figured it out. "Telepathy?"

"Long story, kid," Rory said. "The point is, you're safe now and—"

"I want in, Reed," Spexarth said firmly. "I want on the team...*whatever* you guys are."

Ashley shrugged at Rory. "Side effects?"

"You're being a little blunt...a little...out of character, aren't you there, Steve?"

"Don't matter." Spexarth said firmly. "Take me on, or I'll rat you all out."

Rory nodded thoughtfully. "Well, I am one man short."

Spexarth stuck out his hand. "Shake on it," he commanded Rory.

"That's some moxie you popped him with," Rory said to Ashley, then smiled and shook Spexarth's hand. "You're in. Keep you fat and happy."

"What?" Spexarth asked, tilting his head.

"Old man talk," Ashley smiled. She turned back to Katrina, hands on her hips. "Now, what will we do with her?"

"You got your... spells... and I got the aether. And he's got the muscle." Spexarth shrugged. "I say we get some answers."

"I like this one," Ashley said. "Let's keep him."

They had managed to keep Katrina in a carefully balanced limbo between consciousness and clarity. They no longer needed the helmet, just a trace of aether spritzing the recirculator that hissed by Katrina's face. Ashley felt she could almost do it without the aether, but there was no point in getting sloppy. The aether was just helping speed things along, and they were out of time.

She asked about Sarah again, and they saw a side of Katrina that was unnerving. "Yeah, I did it, and I did you."

"You *did* me... your camouflage? Impersonated me?"

Katrina nodded vigorously. "It's what I'm good at. Mind games. Mimicking."

Ashley found her boastful tone distasteful. "Where... where did you learn that?"

"Mastered it, wouldn't you say?"

"Who taught you?" Rory asked firmly.

"The Father," she said, her eyes welling with tears.

"Your father?"

Rory jumped in. "A priest, well that's something, heh-heh, isn't it, Ashley? I didn't even know there were any of you in the church."

"Is it your father who... asked you to trick us then?" Ashley continued.

Katrina was fighting the words. She closed her eyes and tears streamed from them. "The Father, yes."

"And he's the one who asked you to kill the Parker girl?" Rory probed.

Katrina's jaw muscles rippled as she gnashed her teeth shut. She growled in some internal battle. Ashley tried a blend of Affectations: *honesty, clarity, comfort.*

Spexarth placed a hand on her forehead. "She's burning up."

When he was changing her cold compress behind her neck, she had gained composure and said, "He made me do it." Though her head remained immobilized, her eyes forcibly reached out to Spexarth. Pleading. Confession. There was fear and anger in her trembling voice. "He *made* me!"

"What do you figure our altitude is, coming into San Francisco?" Rory asked, from out of the blue. She squinted at him questioningly. "And our speed?"

"What time is it?" she asked.

"Five-fifty," Spexarth said, consulting his watch.

"Fifty-one," Rory said.

She did a quick calculation. "We're at 20,000 feet. Maybe moving 100 knots... why?"

"I got a plan," Rory said, "Right out of LF's playbook."

When she spent that Fall on the *Incus* as a little girl, her greatest joy was playing hide and seek with the crewmen. Both the *Incus* and the *Arcus* had a centralized fuselage, giving the core of the ship the look of a butterfly's abdomen. Ashley loved running the length of it, out through the exhaust, then going topside, even in the storms, and sneaking back into the pilothouse. Once, she had even rigged a rope that had allowed her to swing under the ship and pop up in a trapdoor behind those seeking her.

She had never imagined she would do something so crazy as an adult, but here she was. The four of them were crouched in an exhaust flange, hunkered down to resist the worst of the weather raging past them. She was only yards from where Rory had saved her days before, but now she had a chute, and he had a plan.

"Let me hear it again," Rory yelled to Spexarth.

"The TransCorp chick killed them both, dead to rights. Miss Parker and Miss Winston." He wiped rain from his eyes and yelled to Katrina, "Sorry."

"The rest?" Rory prodded.

"I caught her tossing Miss Winston out the vent. Damn near got me, fired at me even, but she slipped. Lost them both overboard."

"There's a chute, or there was anyway, snagged on the left wing," Ashley improvised. "If you get in a pinch, join us."

"That was to be my escape," Katrina admitted.

"Sometime I'd like to hear the rest of that," Rory said, "but our ride's waiting."

"See you," Ashley said to Spexarth.

"Goodbye," Spexarth said, so obviously and primarily to Katrina.

"Stick to the plan!" Rory yelled.

The three kicked off and counted it down.

Their chutes deployed, and they drifted after Rory Reed.

She wondered, as they descended, how he had arranged a ride.

The seas were rough in the Rainmaker's wake, and the skiff sent to retrieve them could barely handle the waves. Three men were on deck, waving them in frantically. A fourth was piloting the boat.

When the boat spun about, Ashley was shocked to see Zana throwing them a line.

"We must hurry," Zana called to Rory as he lumbered aboard. "Ship-to-ship is calling for your arrest."

"All over HeadSpace too," a heavily bearded man added as he helped Katrina up.

Ashley pulled herself up and led Katrina to a seat. "We've got you," she said.

Rory swept back a mop of wet hair and settled in beside them. "How do you like me now?"

The roar of the boat made it too hard to talk. On the way to a yacht nearby, Ashley collected her thoughts. She liked him pretty damn much. She was starting to even like his plan and told him as much.

"There's a bit of a problem with both you and LF being legally dead," he said, "if they buy it."

"Maybe we can work things out sooner than later." Ashley patted Katrina's knee. "After all, we have personal testimonial."

"In my line of work, that's not very solid," Rory said.

"Especially when the witness is also the chief suspect and already confessed to the killing," Katrina added.

Ashley and Rory looked shocked.

She shrugged, "I was in law."

"You're perking right up," Rory said. His gaze settled on her. It gave Ashley reason for concern. They were fresh out of aether. What would happen if Katrina tried to pop them off with another Affectation?

"I want to know something," Katrina said, studying Rory closely. "Why did you save me?"

Ashley had a dozen answers for her. He was a softie. He thought she had redeeming qualities. He was curious about Affectations. He hated TransCorp and wanted to continue messing with them...

"Because you're innocent," he said, looking away.

"How is that?" Ashley asked, astonished. She thought, from the way he ignored her, that he hadn't heard her. "How is she possibly innocent?"

"When someone acts under duress, no matter how heinous their actions, how can they be held responsible?" Rory said curtly. He rose then to greet the yacht.

"Well," Ashley said, "I don't think that'll hold up in court."

"Exactly," Rory said, without turning back to her.

She wondered just what he might be talking about, but she knew it was not only Katrina.

29 Trap

.. / .... .- ...- . / .-. . - ..- .-. -. . -..

“What is that?” Ashley said. Rory woke to feel her jostling him. He hadn’t slept so soundly in recent memory.

.. / .... .- ...- . / .-. . - ..- .-. -. . -..

“Recognize that?” Zana said, also in his cabin. It was disorienting. Rory did not even know if he was dressed for company.

.. / .... .- ...- . / .-. . - ..- .-. -. . -..

Then he *did* recognize it. “*I have returned*,” he said.

“What?” Ashley asked, looking back and forth between them.

“That is what I thought, as well,” Zana nodded.

Just then, Calissa pushed into the room. “Dad, did you...” she looked at Ashley, shrugged a little, then continued, “Did you...get a message?”

.. / .... .- ...- . / .-. . - ..- .-. -. . -..

“There it is again,” Ashley said. “It’s coming through the speakers. Is it Morse Code?”

“Yes, it is,” Zana said. “As Rory said, the message is clear—”

“*I have returned*,” Calissa repeated thoughtfully, rubbing her jaw. “Over the *speakers* too?”

They had been at sea for a month, lying low. That had been no great inconvenience, for the yacht was ample and not wanting in any accessory. After a touch-and-go escape, they had disappeared into the mix of others out on pleasure cruises. Rory had made special arrangements to retrieve Calissa in Tijuana, and she had just been aboard for a few days.

.. / .... .- ...- . / .-. . - ..- .-. -. . -..

The message was curious, of course, in its content, but even more in the methods of delivery. It would not be on CommCorp's channels, yet it was broadcast all over the ship. It was not even on Zana's portable ham radio unit. It was, however, simulcast on the Clench embedded in Zana, Calissa, and Rory's jawbones.

The next message, just minutes later, was a series of numbers: 14.0875° S, 75.7626° W.

The second time it was transmitted, Rory was ready with a pen. He scrawled it down, as did the ship's captain. They compared and confirmed they had it right, then the third time it was issued, they smiled and nodded. 14.0875° S, 75.7626° W.

"What was all that, those numbers?" Ashley asked. "Is that a contact number?"

Calissa and Ashley both looked over the numbers they had jotted on the map in the cabin. "14.0875° S, 75.7626° W," Calissa read aloud. "Is that, like, coordinates?"

The captain and one of his hands were already pulling it up on an old-fashioned monitor. The ship's hand said something in Spanish. "Yes, in Peru," the captain said, shaking his head.

"So, someone has come back, and they're now in Peru?" Ashley was puzzled.

"Might not be related," Rory offered. He had to admit, it was confusing.

Rory had a quick conference with the crew. They were two days from Peru, and they would lose another day or two traveling inland to the designated location.

"And a Weekly passes through," Zana offered, studying another book, "just as we make land."

The Weekly would make for rough waters on its leading edge, but good cover in its wake. The same general strategy had afforded them the escape from San Francisco. To follow the storm, however, would slow them for yet another full day. "Could we push it," Rory asked, "and get ashore *ahead* of the storm, well-ahead?"

The crew consulted their charts. They conferred with Zana and his book of airship itineraries. Finally, the captain stated his conclusion in Spanish.

"It is not advised," Zana interpreted, nodding at the captain, then boring in on Rory: "He says the *Alba* can do it, but only with disregard for stealth."

"So, a quick in and out," Rory suggested. "A night landing, maybe?"

"You forget these are troubled waters." Zana said.

"I thought you could get us out in front of the Weekly," Rory asked the captain.

Before the captain could speak, Zana replied, insistently, "Yes, but it is not the storm. There is a great deal of *flotsam* along the shore."

"Flotsam?" Calissa asked. "Trash?"

"Pirata," the captain said.

"Brigands," Zana said. When Rory didn't quite catch his drift, Zana sighed and said outright, "Pirates. We must pass through pirates."

"No," Katrina said.

"I've been through worse," Rory countered.

"You don't even know what this is about, do you?" Ashley asked. "Why would we go trotting off after a random signal?"

"Through a storm and through pirates," Calissa added.

"Rapido," the captain threw in.

"Zana?" Rory asked, clamping a hand on his shoulder.

"It could only be Astar," he said. "And she could only be in trouble to have sent this, like this."

"Returned from where?" Ashley asked. "Astar wasn't.... *Peru*? Astar's from Peru?"

Rory smiled. "She wouldn't say, 'meet ya there.' They're cryptic, even on private channels."

"She is cryptic even with me, even at the best of times," Zana smiled. "I miss her dearly... but we cannot afford to be discovered. We cannot endanger the Princess."

"Pfft. Your wife's in trouble and you're worried we'll be spotted?" Ashley asked. "I say we go and now."

Rory shrugged. "This time it's not your boat, Ash. Not your call."

"What do you—"

"Zana's name is on the registry for this little boat. If the captain and the owner say we sit this one out, well..."

"Your wife?" the captain asked. "If it is your wife, then we go!"

He did not wait for Zana or anyone else. The captain spun on his heels and barked orders to his men.

"Ah..." Zana smiled in resignation. "So, it is."

"Maybe she's not in trouble," Calissa said. "Probably she's just missing you."

The *Alba* was not made for this, and yet it was. Sliced through waters at full sail, making the most of the crosswinds already pulled in by the Weekly's maneuvers. Rory spent his time at the prow, for it cleared his head. The winds through his hair pulled stray ideas right out of him, and he could focus more clearly.

The farther he was from Ashley Winston, the clearer his head.

Pirates and storms be damned.

Somehow, their Clench had been compromised. He did not want to even give voice to the idea around Zana, but it was not unlikely Astar had been taken in and her Clench removed. He only hoped it was done so surgically.

So. Who?

His mind kept returning to the idea that all of this was somehow an inside job. Infiltrating the Estate. Trying to kill Ashley... then failing that, framing her. Who would stand to gain from that? Any of the other corporations. It was possible, Rory thought, that there might again be alliances building between them, that any number of them had targeted both 3dub and TransCorp at the same time. Making it look like Ashley killed Sarah Parker would sew things up nicely for, say, CommCorp.

They were made fugitives simply by the accusations and his decision to run. They could be apprehended by any branch of law enforcement, for no doubt, there was an astronomical reward for bringing in the team that brutally murdered Sarah Dawn Parker. That was just being hinted at on public CommCorp channels Zana could tune from the ocean. It would be commonly known among law enforcement and security firms on shore worldwide.

It would take another resource, however, to compromise the Clench. Such a measure was beyond the law. To even find Astar and breach her defenses would have been beyond the law. Getting into the Lair would not be impossible for 'hired help,' Rory knew, for he had spent the last decade doing similar things. Leading the prey into a most certain trap would have been within the scope of hired help. Performing an Extraction on an elderly woman—messy field work that punched his gut—it was just the sort of thing Contract help might do for a price.

He was going to have to think like that again in order to outwit them.

30 Shore Leave

The crew of the *Alba* was the best Ashley had ever sailed with, and she had been in a dozen regattas. They kept the yacht cutting across the waters ahead of the storm, despite the storm, for hours on end. Everyone else was hunkered down in the cabins, but through the driving rain and powerful wind, Ashley was enjoying herself. She clutched rails and rigging, switched footing, fought to keep the sopping wet hair from her eyes. They were at full tilt, riding the razor's edge of every wave.

She knew they were also riding a fine line of avoiding detection and making good time. More than once, the ship tacked and turned about when another ship would be called out to the helmsman's attention.

Ashley even got into it, pointing and crying out "MIRA," when she would spy a ship heading their way or cresting waves just ahead.

For all the good she might have done, for all the trouble they had evaded, two scrappy ships were not far behind, following their every move. The *Alba* had a league on them, but when it was time to come ashore, Ashley knew there would be trouble.

Zana had warned that the trouble might not be at sea at all, but hidden in the trees of the shoreline. It was a common maneuver to press a ship into shallow waters and then fire on it from the coast. She turned her attention to the tree line, little more than a blur as they shot along parallel to it.

It was getting too dark to make out much of anything. It was prematurely, preternaturally dark. It was the heaviness of the Weekly bearing down on them more than the setting sun.

The ship took another sharp twist, then pounded hard to carve directly through the waves. Up one, down another. Full jolt from the prow against the tide. A flash of lightning surprised her—not from the brightness, more from what it revealed: the shore was *very* close.

The sailors were shouting at one another in quick Spanish commands. It sounded urgent.

Ashley fought her way down into the hull, pounding on the door of each cabin. "Land!"

The captain pressed past her just as Zana was opening his cabin door. They spoke a tense mix of Spanish and English, and Ashley got the message. They had few choices, and the best was to jump ship and swim for shore. They would be lucky if the *Alba* were to escape intact.

Ashley heard distant gunfire, and something else that could have been a cannon or thunder. None of them had the chance to worry much about the *Alba*. Bullets were peppering the beach and the water around them. She thought she could hear them whistle past her.

"Down," she heard Rory, and she fell to her knees and dog paddled. The surrounding water did not feel like much protection, but she realized Rory's wisdom. With just their heads bobbing above the surface, they were tougher targets.

"Where do we go?" Katrina asked, baffled by it all.

"This way," Calissa said, pulling her in tow. "Follow dad."

Zana dropped back from Rory's side and waded up to Ashley. "There is a niche. We may hide." She followed his lead without question.

By the time they all were in the shelter of a shore hollow, the gunshots had fallen away. It was dark, and they were invisible. Hopefully, Ashley thought, they had been given up for dead.

They stayed there, crouched in the cold water, for what felt like forever. No one was talking. Ashley knew Rory would be lost to her, that he would be consumed with calculating and scheming until all this was over. Calissa was hugging her, and that alone made it more bearable.

The Winston Weekly was only a mile wide, and even if the storm front that led it was another five or ten miles, a normal passing would be under an hour. This one, however, was on a coastal pattern, as Zana had shown them in the manifest. It was leaning laterally, and thus the full wingspan of the airship was gliding overhead.

When it passed, the shore was awash with sunset, though the sun itself was dropping below the horizon. Zana led them over some rocky terrain, then through a wooded area. The route was little more than a fisherman's trail, narrow, and as it grew darker, nearly impossible to see.

They stopped for a bit when Calissa turned her ankle. They stopped again when Zana and Rory conferred over their course ahead. Between stops, they were on a hard march, and Ashley knew why. They were being hunted.

The stops had grown more and more frequent, the hiking less forced, and then finally they stopped to rest in an area of the wood that was so dense there seemed no trail at all could pass through it. Ashley longed for a campfire, but she knew it was not to be. They could not reveal their location. In the deep of night, in damp clothes, she shuddered off a chill.

Zana and Rory took watch in different directions. Katrina was sleeping against a tree. Calissa was sitting on a boulder, peeling off her shoe and sock to look over her ankle. Talking still seemed a bad idea, but then so did stopping to rest.

Ashley approached Zana and cleared her throat. "What do you think?"

"I think this is folly," he said without turning to her. "We have no idea who pursues us."

Ashley couldn't disagree.

"We have followed the coast, but I cannot tell if we have passed the promontory that was to direct us inland. It is too cloudy for the stars. It will be daylight soon, and we have no compass, no GPS."

Just then, Katrina yelled at the top of her lungs and darted into the wooded darkness.

"And we have her to deal with," he groaned and took off in pursuit.

Ashley could not see them at all, but she heard scrambling footsteps. It sounded as if Katrina had collided with a tree, fell, but then was running again. She could hear Zana too but only his breathing as he shot after Katrina.

"What do we do?" Calissa said, now at her side. "Go help?"

"Load your hoo-doo." It was Rory's voice, dark and detached, an ominous deep tone in the night. "We're gonna—"

A bright flash, then an explosion. She thought she saw someone tossed against a tree, but it was too blinding to tell for certain. Ashley and Calissa were on the ground, and Rory was hunched over them.

"What was that?" Calissa whispered.

"Shh," Rory warned.

They waited for more. Gunshots. Explosions. Someone to attack.

Nothing happened for an eternity, then someone was coming toward them in the dark. Ashley was disoriented, but it seemed the approaching steps came from the blast site.

"Mine?" Rory murmured, the question in his baritone.

"Trip wired," Zana answered. "I have since found more."

The four of them huddled tight. Ashley felt the warmth and protection of the bodies pressed all around her. She sighed a gentle Affectation, a subtle one she hoped, one that might just give them a little comfort.

"Katrina?" Rory asked. He raised his head from their huddle to keep a watch out.

"I cannot say," Zana said. "She seems not to have moved... or my hearing is not yet back."

"Can't we go get her?" Ashley asked. "We can't just leave her out there to die."

"Or to escape," Rory said. "Or to attack us."

"Surely she wouldn't," Calissa said. "I get a feeling she's not a threat."

"That stupid stunt she just pulled is threat enough," Rory grumbled. "Everyone for miles heard that."

"If we were to go to her, we might end up in her condition," Zana said.

So, they waited the rest of the night, weapons at the ready, for an enemy that never came. When it was just bright enough to see, the four of them stepped out into the woods to find Katrina. It reminded Ashley of when she herself was hunted not a year before. "Don't let her touch you," she warned softly. "She can Affect you the most if she touches you."

Zana stepped over to Calissa quickly and guided her around a trip wire she had not seen. He pointed it out to Ashley, but he never spoke a word. Ashley could just make out Rory's form ahead, but he was moving silently and fluidly through the trees.

They found Katrina folded over like a rag doll. Zana gave her a quick once over, then nodded to Rory. "She remains unconscious. Both good and bad."

"How so?" Ashley asked.

"Because," Rory said, hefting Katrina into his arms. "She's not feeling the pain yet, and she's not causing us any problems like this."

"But bad," Zana continued, "for when she wakes, she will know pain even the morphine cannot quell."

"And she might uncork us all," Rory said.

And she slowed them down.

Ashley felt for Rory. He was a powerful man, but carrying Katrina was a challenge. He had to tire of weaving through trees, twisting to thread her legs and then her head, squeezing through tight growths of underbrush. Ashley herself was exhausted. Zana was helping Calissa limp ahead, but he remained sure footed and strong.

Eventually the trees thinned, and they waded through chest high grasses and new growth. Then the vegetation thinned until they were in sand.

Ashley looked ahead, surprised it was all sand. "What is this place?" she asked.

Rory had not stopped to take in the view. She quickly caught up to him and walked along at his side. "Are we crossing a desert? Is that the plan now?"

Sweat was pouring down his face. Exertion turned to amusement in his eyes. "You got a better idea?"

"Isn't there a road or something... easier... to your coordinates?"

"*Sometimes the easiest way is the hard way*," Rory said.

Sometimes, Ashley thought, she wasn't sure when he was quoting something and when he was just making conversation. "What's that supposed to mean?" she asked.

"If we skirt the desert or follow the shore, we're taking the easy way, sure, and there're roads—paved roads—that direction..."

"But?"

"...but there are also landmines and pirates and a host of other people who would like to bring you in for bounty."

"Making that the hard way," she said.

"Yeah. All things considered. I'd take this little hike through the desert any day."

She mulled it over a while as they traipsed through ankle deep sand. It was going to be a long hike in this, and her deck shoes were already filled with sand. When they had gone so far that she could just make out the tree line behind them, she said, "What about being sighted? We're kind of out in the open."

"Already thought of that," he smiled at her around Katrina's shoulder.

"What do you mean?"

"Look at our clothes."

She had not really paid any attention, thinking these were just what clothes the crew had available on the *Alba*. Now it was surprisingly obvious. They were all wearing muted tones of tan and sand. They were dressed in clothes that would disappear in the desert. These were clothes he had picked and purchased and stowed aboard the ship on their last stop. Rory had worked this all out, right down to their clothes. He had it planned all along.

"Don't you ever get tired of planning things out?" she asked.

He looked at her, astonished. "No."

The walking continued. Once when she turned to look, she discovered Zana was propping Calissa on his shoulder like a crutch. She looked so worn down.

A large bird glided by, and Ashley had another idea. "What about that, Rory Reed?"

"Birds?"

"Surveillance," she clarified. "Remember the heat sensors, the satellites, and all your conspiracy theories?"

"When you stare into the sun too long, what do you see, Princess?" Zana said from behind.

"What?"

"It's too hot," Rory said. "The heat of the sand blinds any heat sensors... until nightfall."

"So, you're saying you planned that too? That we'd land like we did, where we did, and when we did, so we'd cross this desert in the heat of the day?"

"Give or take," Rory admitted. "Didn't plan on the mines but didn't doubt they'd be there. Can't really plan around pirates."

"But the rest?"

"Might have been luck," he smirked.

"Might have," Ashley said.

Late afternoon, and there still seemed no end to it. Ashley had done some distance events in the salt flats, even survivalist runs for elite athletes. She knew what dehydration felt like. She had experienced the salt and sand co-mingling in the corners of her eyes and lips before. She had lived in Dubai for a while and had gone on some excursions in the Empty Quarter where temperatures could reach 120 degrees Fahrenheit. All of that, however, had been her plans, her adventures, on itineraries. Usually there were nearby jeeps and jugs of water and Sherpas to haul her luggage.

She decided his plan was the worst plan she had ever been a part of.

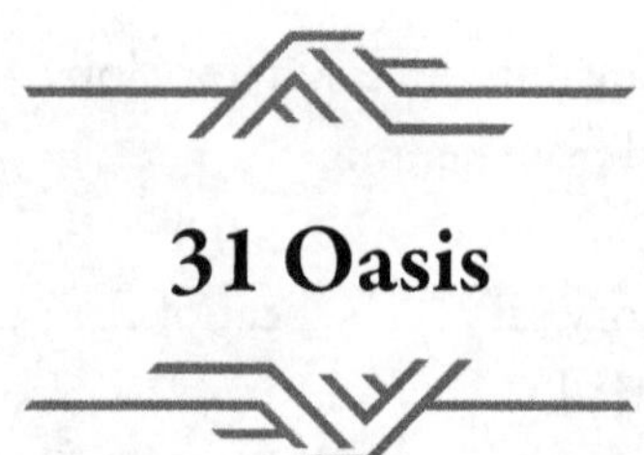

31 Oasis

Zana was the best field medic Rory had ever known. Though he had never served any flag, and never studied medicine at a University, Zana was excellent at what Rory called 'medicinal improvisation.' Once, Zana Amin saved the lives of four men, all with a piece of plastic tubing. When A-Z had visited Rory in a horrible prison, Zana had used a zipper to saw off a man's foot that suffered a life-threatening infection. "You're a regular MacGyver, M.D., Z," Rory had said on multiple occasions, though the reference to the old-time television show was lost on Zana.

So, he knew he had little reason to be concerned for Katrina, the woman he carried. Zana had said she was badly concussed and that it was complicated by the morphine. He said to keep her head elevated, and he crafted a sling that kept her head resting on Rory's shoulder.

"She would fare better at rest," Zana had said. "Immobilized."

"Wouldn't we all?" Ashley said.

"We stay on the move," Rory insisted.

"But Dad," Calissa groaned, "we've been at it for hours."

Rory was feeling it. He had been carrying Katrina the entire time, and though she was trim, she was muscular and heavy... and dead weight. The heat was getting to Calissa. Ashley wasn't speaking to him, but he did not think this desert was doing her any good either.

"Ask your father how much farther," Ashley said again.

At his last estimate, Zana had told them they were about four miles inland, eight miles yet to go due east to Huacachina. Rory now measured them at 8 miles, nearly there. He knew the last two miles would be the worst, fighting the sensation of 'so close, yet so far away.' He knew when the oasis materialized from the heat waves that it would be hard for them not to break out in a full run.

Zana was filling the dead air now. "A legend of Huacachina that I favor claims a young Inca princess was walking in the desert, brushing her hair and admiring her reflection in a mirror when she spotted a hunter watching her. Frightened by the man, she dropped the mirror, which then shattered and transformed into a lagoon. The princess then dove into the water to hide, but when she later emerged, she found she had been transformed into a mermaid and that the tunic she had left behind was now transformed into the dunes around the lake. According to the legend, she can be heard singing at night when there is a full moon."

Rory knew what he was doing, distracting them, distracting himself. Zana had been with Astar for over thirty years, and their bond was as close to magic as Rory had ever known—until recently. The husband and wife were closer than twins, the way they seemed to always be in each other's heads, working as a team.

The time apart seemed only to hone their connectivity. Usually, they could stay in contact by ham radio or HeadGear when they needed it. In the darkest times, they had sent a simple "143" back and forth by Clench. Not on this trip, however. This tour had to be absolutely clandestine. Their lives depended on it. It had been more secretive and had lasted longer than any Rory had asked of the couple—it had been thirty-three days of silence, then the mysterious "I have returned."

Zana continued, ever the tour guide. "This was one of your family's greatest contributions to preservation in the Americas. You know this, Ashley Winston?"

"I... no. I guess I didn't."

"Yes, it was Walter Winston, the water baron, who purchased Huacachina and miles around it. At the time, agriculture and the city of Ica were drawing down on the groundwater that stocked the lake. The Weekly we came in on was your father's first in South America. LF Winston made a trade. Dependable, free water, but in exchange, Ica regulates visitors to Huacachina."

"I thought you said it was a tourist town," Calissa said.

"Oh yes, and it still is."

"But, if they regulate—"

"Commerce has taken care of this. College students and day travelers from Ica were replaced with wealthy people in search of healing."

"He ran them out of town?" Calissa asked.

"To Walter Winston's disgust, the community had fallen to drunken backpackers and dune surfers. He began a campaign of de-popularizing Huacachina for that crowd, then revived earlier beliefs of the therapeutic values, the healing waters, of the lake."

"So, Winston bought it, then cleaned it up the way he wanted it?" Rory asked.

"To his thinking, he restored it, rescued it from people who did not truly appreciate it."

"Sounds like more snobbery," Rory grumbled.

"He hired archeologists and historians, unearthed the history of the place from before the Spaniards invaded it in the 1500s," Zana countered. "Brought back the pre-colonial pride and stories."

"So. My grandfather wasn't such a bad guy, see?" Ashley said.

"I'm sure this story ends with 'for a tidy profit' somewhere here," Rory said.

"Not exactly. The water table was preserved. The history was preserved. The pride was restored. Then Huacachina gradually was forgotten even as a spa."

"So, it's abandoned now or what?" Calissa asked.

"It is a quiet place, I am told. A mysterious place. It is said LF Winston honored his agreement with Ica and the surrounding lands. In perpetuity... and now again as he lives. I believe he subsidizes the families who still live and work here to serve the trickle of guests."

To Rory, it sounded as if the Winston family had just bought entire villages and lakes for their own pleasure. It did not sit right with him.

Katrina spasmed and nearly jumped from Rory's arms.

"I feel it too," Ashley said, taking Calissa's hand.

"Daddy?"

"Shh," Rory whispered. "Z, you think she needs another shot?"

Zana shook his head absently. His attention was now fixed ahead on the blue ripples in the distant dunes. "We have a visual," he said.

"Okay, we're going to do this like I've been saying," Rory began, but the three of them sprinted away. "Because... because it could be a trap," he said now to himself and the doped-up woman smiling at him.

At least they had the good sense to take cover behind the last crest of the sand dunes. They were peering over it when Rory finally caught up. He was pouring sweat and pulling air hard. When he went to his knees, he spilled Katrina onto the ground.

She groaned loudly. Rory tried to hush her.

The others huddled around tight.

"Huacachina looks just like I was saying, no?" Zana said, tending to Katrina.

"Nothing at all out of sorts?" Rory looked at them one by one.

"Sleepy village, big lake, nothing much," Ashley said. She was already creeping back to the crest to study Huacachina more. "But I do like that lake."

Rory bent down closer to Katrina. She was muttering something. He thought she was agitated, but as they pulled the sling away entirely, he found her to be smiling broadly in a way he had not yet seen in her.

Morphine and shell shock. What should he expect from her?

"There is bleeding from her ear," Zana said with concern.

Calissa was crouched with them still, but she was patting Rory's shoulder. He was a raw mix of many emotions, on edge and annoyed. "What?"

She directed his attention to Ashley, who was now laying with her back to the dune. She, too, was smiling a big, wide smile, holding brass binoculars in her hand absently. "You're not going to believe it," Ashley said, her head shaking back and forth. "Guys, come look."

Rory crept over to her. Nothing looked out of the ordinary.

"The water," she said.

Rory took the binoculars and looked down on the town. He saw nothing at first, scanning from one edge of the oasis to the other. On a scan of the closest shore, however, he noted something that did not quite fit in. He adjusted the lenses. "What? A paddle boat?"

"Closer," Ashley said, her hand on his wrist to guide him. "In front of it."

Near the dock was a cabana, and outside the cabana stood Astar Amin, waving a scarf.

Rory bristled then at the sound of a pump shotgun loading the chamber.

Behind them.

"Freeze," a woman said gruffly. Rory thought it might be Katrina.

"I think we got 'em, don't you?" a familiar male voice asked.

"You must be getting rusty, Reed," the woman chided.

Somehow, *someone* had materialized from the sands, sneaked up behind them, and had them pinned. Rory turned with Ashley, both of them speechless.

A man and woman—both wearing broad-brimmed hats and swimwear, both bristling with weapons—stood not ten feet behind them.

The man was unmistakable... lean and lanky, wearing an American flag Speedo and flip-flops. He had a terrible scar across his stomach. His crazy blonde hair could not be contained under his beachcomber hat. "I'd say we're just the superior soldiers here, Kelli."

"I think you're right, peaches," she said, planting a peck on his cheek. They threw down their weapons and shared a passionate kiss. Her straw hat fell off her head, and when they separated, Rory's jaw dropped. Kelli Chase was looking fantastic—though out of character—barefoot in a red bikini.

"Astar's ready to jump your decrepit bones, Zana," Alex said with a wink. "Let's get back to camp. My beer's getting warm."

And just like that, Alex had returned.

Ashley and Calissa were wading into the lake, splashing each other.

Rory carried Katrina down to their encampment. He placed her gently on a cot Astar set in the shade. "Good to see you," Rory said to her, but Astar was already rushing into Zana's arms. Their reunion was quiet and dignified. They held each other's faces and stared into each other's eyes.

"Get a room," Alex laughed as he passed them. "Go nuzzle or whatever."

Rory grabbed him by the arm and pulled Alex out of earshot.

"Hey, hey now," Alex said, getting his footing. "Didn't you miss me?"

"Where the hell have you been?"

"What's it matter? I'm here now, buddy. Gang's all here," he smiled slyly, "and did you see? We worked it out. Me and Kelli."

"Yeah, yeah, that's great," Rory said. Alex was sunburnt and swaying. The beer cans around their cabana told the story. "Do you know the mess we're in?"

"Of course, I do, Rory. A Stetson never lies."

"You brought *that* out here?"

"Easy. Easy. It's back at Mac's plane."

"You flew in?"

"Of course. Airport's not 20 miles from here, in Ica. Why'd you walk?"

"We were trying to be discreet." Rory gritted his teeth.

"But you got the message."

"We're here, aren't we?"

Alex eyed him closely. "But... you don't know *why* we're here?"

Rory shrugged. "Because it's isolated?"

"All you got was the location?" Alex asked. "Not the reason?"

"You mean, 'I have returned.' That reason?"

"Oh, brother, do we need to talk!"

Back at the cot, Katrina was struggling with Calissa.

Zana rushed to her side, trying to pin her down and prep another syringe.

"The poor child," Astar said, gently stroking the hair from Katrina's face. "How long has she been in this condition?"

"A month, as I have told you," Zana said, "but Astar, she must remain this way."

"Drugged? A month drugged!"

"Yes." Zana sighed. "You will understand..."

"What have you given her?" Astar asked.

"She had to be subdued on the airship *Arcus*. They used aether."

"Aether?" Astar's eyes were bulging. "She had just as well be drinking jet fuel."

"It was the only way," Rory said, returning to them.

"And it was only until we could give her morphine on the *Alba*."

"Morphine!" Kelli shook her head.

"It's a long story," Ashley said.

"She would be in great pain now, if not for the morphine," Zana said. "It may have saved her life."

"Zana...what...?" Astar was baffled.

"We were pursued by pirates," Zana said. "One of their bombs exploded near her."

"I think it was just a Flash-Bang," Rory said. "But it knocked her off her feet."

"She was barely on her feet," Ashley murmured to Kelli. "*Lots* of morphine."

Rory frowned at her.

"It gave her a concussion, I am certain," Zana said. "But it could have been worse."

"How possibly, then? Aether. Morphine. A bomb!"

"She moved with the punches, didn't she?" Alex asked confidently.

"Drunk fall," Calissa confirmed.

"What?" Rory asked. What did she know about such things?

"Drunks can fall and not be hurt," she continued. "They can sway and swagger like an inflatable tube man. They're known to dodge a punch, even dodge a bullet. Nothing luckier than a drunk."

"That's ridiculous," Rory said.

"Actually, that is a fact," Zana nodded.

"Alcohol *does* inhibit certain stress-related chemicals released when a person suffers a major injury," Ashley noted.

"Yet she has *not* been drinking. She would not." Astar said firmly.

"Why's that?" Alex asked.

Astar pulled gently at a necklace, showing them an amulet Katrina wore. "Her faith forbids it."

"So, she can't drink, but she can gut Ashley's friend?" Alex asked.

Rory glared at him.

"I would not think so, by her faith." Astar continued to look on at her, adding softly, "She may be another desperate soul."

"We're all desperate souls," Rory said, "aren't we?"

"Zoom in..." Alex exclaimed, skipping to get in Rory's face. He held his fingers out to frame what he was seeing, like a camera. "Zoom in... and, cut to commercial."

"*What's wrong with you*?" Rory brushed him aside.

"You, big guy," Alex said. "You're all pent up and pouty! Aren't you glad to see us?"

"Relieved," Ashley said. She squeezed Kelli's hand.

"You know I am, Alex," Rory said finally, pulling his friend in for a bear hug. "I was starting to think—"

"And that's where you're always getting into trouble," Alex smiled, offering Rory a beer. When he refused it, Alex tossed aside his own can and popped open the fresh one, then flopped down on the sand by his girl.

Rory had trouble accepting it. He had feared the worst for Astar. He had given up on Alex. In a million years, he had not expected Alex and Kelli to spark it off, but they did look good together. Rory looked them all over. Two beautiful women, then the spikey haired madman. All three of them toasting him with their cans of beer. Nearby, Calissa, his precious girl, was tending to Katrina, the semi-conscious psychopath. Zana and Astar were walking off together toward the lake.

This was going to be fine... at least for a while.

Ashley patted the sand at her side.

Rory hesitated.

Someone needed to stand guard.

Someone needed to scout the town.

"Sit, or I'll sit you down," Ashley commanded. She wiggled her fingers in a mock threat.

He lowered himself to sit beside her. Everyone was exchanging smiles except for him. He could not let it go. "Why here, again?" Rory asked, "Why this pond?"

Alex looked at him quizzically, then studied Ashley. "You really don't know then?"

"Alex," Rory said, "I have no clue."

"I figure we're in for a full-on family reunion," he said. "Old man Winston's due here any day now."

Kelli nodded toward the lake. "He's sure that's some kind of holy water."

32 Married!

Ashley knew the rumors about her family, how wealth had gone to their heads in the worst of eccentricities. Before CommCorp had been pacified, Ashley could remember vids and entire channels dedicated to the Winstons. She largely avoided them. Sometimes, when friends had teased her or when something seemed a little too plausible to let go, she would delve into it all. It was fascinating to study, even had it been about some family other than her own. That it was her grandfather and father who had done these things made it even more compelling.

Zana's desert stories had brought much of it to mind. Now that her father was on his way to Huacachina, Ashley was reeling with memories and stories. Somehow none of it seemed possible, while all of it was fact.

She knew her grandfather was obsessive. From his first purchase to his final dealings, Walter Winston was single-minded in his obsession with water. He had purchased entire aquifers and waterfalls, rivers and deltas, mountain caps and glaciers. That he had bought up this little oasis was not even a stretch of the imagination.

But that he had *gone out of his way* to restore the area—that was surprising to Ashley. What she knew of Walter Winston would suggest he looked out only for his interests in water. Battles between townships over water rights and rivers had been common under his devil-may-care acquisition years.

She was aware of times he had rerouted shipping lanes and the boundaries of international waters, all for his own needs. He had created a global outcry for running deep sea exploration in the Marianas Trench and other ocean canyons. He had favored his search for caches of deep fresh water over the preservation of sea life. The case marked a turning point, for Winston Water Works came out victorious, and thereafter, governments came to answer to corporations more and more often. History books marked it as the "rise of the big five," and claimed 3dub would have the global water monopoly to rule them all.

Ashley was puzzled. As she sat in the sand, sipping a cold drink and listening to Alex banter with Kelli, she could not come to terms with this Huacachina lake. She looked at it constantly, as if some answer might come floating to the surface for her. Both her grandfather and then her father had behaved strangely around this tiny spot of water. Walter Winston had developed a conscience and preserved the place. LF Winston had deviated from his typical altruism to isolate Huacachina, hoarding it for himself.

Zana and Astar invited her and Rory for a stroll down the horseshoe boardwalk around the lake. Before Rory would agree, he pried more specifics from Alex as best as he could. LF Winston would drift in under the cover of darkness. Rory looked at his watch, then at the sun, and nodded.

"You should forfeit the watch," Astar said as they set out.

"You would live longer and happier," Zana seconded.

Rory mumbled dismissively.

They had just rounded an old, colonial-looking hotel and restaurant when Zana stopped and asked, "So, are you going to share your burden with us, Rory Reed?"

Astar gestured toward an outside table. It gave them a good view of the lake, yet it was in the shade of palms and the restaurant's veranda. "Now let us sit and talk," Astar smiled.

Rory removed his sunglasses and held pressure on the bridge of his nose. He sat like that even as the waitress took drink orders. Zana ordered for him.

Finally, Ashley rubbed his bicep. "What is it?"

"LF Winston." He looked up at them, then sat his full height and took a deep breath. "The locals. The young ones think he's a wacko. The older ones think he's a saint. I can't work it out."

"Why do we need to work this out?" Astar chuckled. "He is just a man."

"Arguably the most powerful man on earth," Rory said, "and he's coming here. And he believes it, that Ashley jumped from the *Arcus* because she was guilty of murder."

"More likely, they have thought you lost at sea," Zana said. "Our escape was undetected."

"In any case, it will be a surprise to him, and I need to see that look on his face to know his true heart."

"Good luck with that," Ashley said. "I don't know that anyone has him figured out."

"*A true heart thrives behind the mind's eye*," Rory said.

"There you go again." Ashley took a drink.

"You do not trust in her father, then?" Astar asked, "The great LF Winston?"

"And then I can't figure this: what brings him here, to Huacachina?"

"Maybe," Zana said, "he believes his own stories, that the waters truly heal."

"Ah, yes," Astar said. "In the news, he has seemed so devastated by his loss. He may come here to renew."

Zana was nodding with her.

"That wouldn't bring Alex out of the shadows, and it wouldn't move him to get us on site either," Rory said.

"What *does* Alex say?" Ashley asked.

"He is all jazzed about how he found out about LF's Huacachina visit. Tells me more about electronic footprints and Interface algorithms and digital hygiene and—not much about your dad's reason to come down here."

"I have spent more time with him of late," Astar offered. "I believe Alex has us all here to witness something."

"But why?" Rory asked. He held up his hands and panned the area. "What's to see?"

"In his Stetson, he was speaking to someone about a 'sea change.' Maybe that is it? I do not know."

"Alex must think it's safe, whatever the old man's going to do here. He's brought together everyone who means anything to him."

"Including his betrothed," Astar smiled.

"Wait. Wait." Rory couldn't take it. "Married? Alex is getting *married*?"

"I wanted to be the one to tell you," she said.

"No offense, Astar, but shouldn't Alex be the one—"

"Ashley, look at him. Would you want this to be the face to meet your life's best news?"

"So.... you two wanted to take the edge off of it?" Ashley surmised.

"That's not like Alex," Rory said, downing his drink in one swallow. "Married?"

"You see?" Astar said, talking around him. "Rory has his own belief system that is unshakable."

"He must see some things to believe them," Zana added.

"Not the most imaginative," Ashley smiled.

"Waitress! Miss!" Rory called out, "I'll have another. A double."

After his third round, when he hailed the waitress, Ashley asked if he really needed another, adding, "Whatever happened to that finely honed attentiveness, the one that keeps us all alive."

"It's all too odd," Rory said. "Too odd."

"This is when he becomes repetitive," Zana explained to Ashley. "You will enjoy it."

"It's odd that they got together. It's odd that he didn't tell me already. It's way past odd they're getting married. *Married*!"

"I see what you mean." Ashley winked at Zana.

"And I don't repeat myself," Rory growled.

"What is so odd about it? He wouldn't leave her alone after Franklin," Ashley said. "He was asking to move in with her."

"Odd that he didn't tell me that, either."

"It is not so odd that Captain Chase changed her mind, is it?" Zana asked. "After all, he can be very persistent."

"Very charming," Astar said.

"But he's... Alex." Rory made a goofy gesture.

"Yes," Ashley said with a laugh, "charming. Like that. Impulsive, too."

"Waitress! Where's my drink?" Rory shouted.

"We have already closed out the ticket," Zana said.

"My drink?"

"I hear they used to surf down the dunes outside of town," Ashley said. "Maybe we should go do that?"

All three of them looked at her as if she had suggested they wrestle alligators.

"I mean," she continued, "it sounded fun. Like sledding, I think."

"Your dad's coming in on an airship, and you want to go play in the sand?" Rory shook his head.

"Yeah, maybe it'll be just the thing. Lighten the mood." Ashley bounced in her seat a little at the thought of it. "Maybe Alex will tell you about Kelli then?"

"Sand surfing?" Rory mused. "Sand surfing sounds about his style."

"Sounds like something for you four," Astar said. "We will prepare a welcoming party."

"I can only imagine," Rory said. Then in a falsetto he imitated Ashley: "'Hi daddy! Your little snowflake is covered in sweat and sand, but hey, hi!'"

33 Count on it

Rory was familiar with the pace of places like this. It took over five minutes for him to suspect something. Mary, his waitress, had been gone for five minutes. There were only two other tables with guests at this early hour, a little after 4, a little before happy hour. Then again, as they loved to say in Huacachina, every hour was happy hour, twenty-four hours a day. Rory shrugged. "When in Rome..." he started to say aloud, then he started to wonder why Rome got the honor, got named in this little idiom.

Sand surfing. It seemed like an oxymoron. It seemed like the worst, least believable combination of words since "lead balloon."

Then all he could think about was Levi Finn Winston. Michael Finnegan. Begin again.

"When in Rome..." he smiled this time and said it aloud. "I bet that has to do with the Roman empire."

"What?" Ashley cocked her head. He liked it when she did that. He liked it so much he wanted to say something else to get that same expression, maybe amplified.

"Sand surfing! Why not surf surfing? Did you know some of the best surfing in the world is less than an hour's drive from here?"

There it was. Her head turned sharply, that cute scrunch of her nose and eyes. She turned her attention back to A-Z, which gave him time to mull over the Roman empire. Empires in general. They were good, for they brought modernization, right? Roads, sanitation, protection of a military. Yet empires were bad. Bad because they led to standardization. Standardized tests. A test of his patience.

"Where is Mary?" he said. It had been well over five minutes. The other patrons were looking at him, as if sharing his concern. "Mary, Mary, quite contrary. Where's my drink?"

"Would you please?" Ashley smiled at him. "We already closed the ticket."

"Mary. Marry. Married man," Rory said, then stopped himself. "Hey! Are you in my head again?"

"I am not in your head," Ashley said, patting his arm. He liked it when she did that.

"Were you in my head in the pantry?"

"What?" Ashley looked surprised at the innocuous question. "No, Rory!"

"Maybe I was in your head then, 'cuz that was some heady stuff." He thought he had said it aloud, but it didn't get a laugh. Not even a head tilt.

Rory sat back again and tried to do the math on blood alcohol percentages.

"What sea changes might your father bring, Princess?" Zana was saying.

Ashley was thinking it over.

"Think he's being literal?" Rory offered. "You guys own—what—half the ocean or something?"

"3dub has been into oceanography since I can remember," Ashley said. "I don't think he's talking about a sea change like that, though. Do you Astar?"

He was probably at about .06%... scarcely legally drunk, even had they been in Utah. Just 0.05 grams (50 milligrams) of alcohol for his every 100 milliliters of blood.

"—-said this would fix everything," Astar was saying.

"That's where we run into trouble, isn't it?" Rory said. "Always trying to fix everything. Always gets me into trouble. How about you, Zana? Wouldn't you agree?"

He stammered and looked at his wife. She looked at Ashley, and Ashley looked at him. "What are you talking about now?"

"Fixing things." It was obvious.

She nodded slowly. A frown pinched her brow.

"The Roman empire went in and put a Christian veneer over everything. Your family empire buys up whole villages, like this one, and cleans them up the way they want them."

It was quiet at the table then. Rory was sure everyone was absorbing what he was saying, so he stood and continued to pontificate: "Now, don't get me wrong. I like standardization, I do. I like good roads and I'm a fan of the ol' Pax Romana. However, maybe we shouldn't clean up everything. Take rain, for example. Now don't get me wrong, I like knowing when it's going to rain. Right as rain. Check your watch by it. I do like that... but does everyone?" He leaned down to them and whispered, "What about the aboriginals? Messes up their whole religion, am I right? Messes up all manner of religion. You don't need to pray for rain or sacrifice anything anymore. You don't need a rain dance. It's gonna rain, just as scheduled in the Weekly's manifest."

The rest of them stood now and looked apologetic to the other patrons of the restaurant. "Please excuse us," Astar said, bowing a little to them.

"Drinks are on me!" Rory said, then, reconsidering, pointed to Ashley. "Her. Drinks are on her. She already owns your whole lake."

"Rory," Ashley said firmly. "Let's play the silent game."

"The silent game? Never heard of it. What's the—"

"We're going to go around the lake, right out here on the boardwalk, and we're going to time people on how long we can stay quiet. Do you want to go first?"

He winked and nodded. That had to be the easiest game in the world. He thought, probably, a monk could beat him at it, maybe, with their oath of silence, but it wouldn't be a walk in the park, or rather, a walk around the lake.

They rounded past another restaurant. Then some shops. Rory asked eagerly, "Are we starting yet?"

Ashley took his hand and pulled his wrist to her attention. "Ready?" she was studying his watch now, waiting like he was for the second hand to reach the top. "Now go!"

He walked with them, listening but not joining into Ashley and Astar's conversation. He thought they might be trying to get him to lose, for their talk went from Alex and Kelli to LF's visit, all of which he had a lot to say about. He did not budge, however, and remained resolutely silent.

He only had to beat Zana now. The other two had not lasted five minutes.

"If he follows his old pattern of big reveals," Zana said, "I believe we—"

"I WIN," Rory said. "You guys suck at this."

"I believe," Astar said to Ashley, "another lap around the lake might be in order."

Rory took off at an easy jog.

They couldn't beat him at the silent game, and they could not compete with him in a lap around the lake. "Run, run, fast as you can," he sang out to them. "Can't catch me, I'm the gingerbread man!"

34 Sand and Surf

The good people of Huacachina were happy to take them up to choice sand dunes with slopes descending six hundred yards and more. They had made great time rounding up the old gear from the tourism days, snowboards and sand-proof HeadGear to capture and share the action. They packed it all in a lime and red jeep, tricked out with light bars and loudspeakers. Rory insisted they lead-box all that HeadGear and take it back to the village, but he did join Alex in wearing a helmet-mounted drink dispenser.

Ashley listened closely to the advice from their guide, a Peruvian in her sixties who had never heard of sunscreen. The woman went by 'Cha Cha,' and Ashley did not even ask for the details. She seemed all too familiar with the men and a little strange, overall. "Shirts!" she gestured. "Boys—no shirts."

Alex and Rory shrugged. Alex popped off his jugo helmet and stripped off his shirt. Rory, however, fought to get his over his helmet and ultimately just tore it away. Ashley was counting his scars, so many bullet hole puckers and long gashes.

"Reed's spent time on the rack," Kelli said. "Damn!"

"What?"

"Weight rack. Guy's ripped."

"Oh," Ashley smiled. "I hadn't noticed."

Alex had heard. He pranced over and gave Kelli a quick peck. "All the muscles in the world won't help him beat me down there!"

"Chews," Cha Cha ordered. "Everybody, chews!"

When Ashley kicked her shoes off, she savored the warm sand between her toes. Rory did not seem a fan. He was shaking off his feet with each step, like a cat walking in puddles.

Their other guide was a man who looked to be an original settler of Huacachina, right down to his loincloth. Cha Cha shouted to him, "Hector! Show them."

He had been rubbing the bottom of the boards with something, but he hopped to his feet and spun the board in his hands, a showman. He placed the board on the sand perpendicular to the slope and looked at them with a toothless smile. He shook his head woefully, 'no,' and then set it right with the slope and tapped it with his toe. The board slid away. He mimed panic as he watched it descend.

He turned back to them and shrugged. Hector would have been a great clown, Ashley thought, and his instruction was good, in its own way. Don't let your board down unattended, she learned. Good start.

He took a second board from the jeep and was mocking and modeling Cha Cha's instructions just out of her line of sight. Put your feet in the straps. (He put them facing each other). Lean back. (He fell back completely, his board in the air.) Hop a little to get started down the slope. Hector hopped in circles, jumped up and down, but he did not descend. Then he took one foot from the board and was examining it as if it were the problem, and then, standing on just one foot, he shot away down the slope, waving his arms and scrambling. He crawled back after just a few yards, but his board was lost to the bottom of the run.

Cha Cha feigned anger. She rattled off a colorful rebuke in Spanish that would make a sailor blush.

Ashley giggled. It was an old routine, one Cha Cha and Hector had likely done a thousand times, thirty years ago.

"First timers go feets first, on the butt," Cha Cha recommended. Hector sat on yet another board to demonstrate. He held his hand above his eyes, surveying ahead, eager for the action, then frustrated it did not move.

"If you feel mas macho," she looked at Rory, "go on the belly, with your head first."

"Oh, hell no," Rory said, nearly shaking his jugo helmet off.

Alex snatched a board from the Jeep. "Or if you have really big balls, just do this!" And in an instant, he was rocketing down the dune like it was his daily transportation.

"Skateboarder," Kelli explained. She grabbed a board and dutifully sat down and waited. "Gimme a push, Ash. I gotta catch—" Hector had shoved her off before she could even finish.

It took both Hector and Cha Cha to launch the big guy. He was lying on his back, laughing as he descended. Ashley took a running dive at her board, and headfirst, sped down the slope. It was hot and fast and, at times, the board slapped her chest so hard it took her breath away. She eclipsed Rory, then put out her hands to drag in the sand and slow up for him.

He was easy to find; just listen for the uproarious laughter. It made her laugh too. She had never heard him having so much fun. He tried to talk as they zipped down the dune together, but all she could hear was, "Fun! Fun!"

At the end of the slope, they slowed to a stop. Alex and Kelli were under a makeshift canopy, laughing at Rory. As he pried off his helmet, sand coursed free. He shook out his hair and brushed at the sand sticking to his sweaty skin. "What," he said, "I don't like sand."

The Jeep pulled up, and Hector bailed out to load their boards for another run. On the way back to the top, Cha Cha was goading them. "Jew can do better. Fasser. I have seen it."

Challenge accepted. Ashley put just her front foot in the strap and used her other to launch and kick more speed from her board. Alex was right behind, then beside her. "That's it, desert Princess!" And then somehow, from a crouch or a kick, he sped ahead of her.

Ashley loved the feel of the wind and the heat of the sun. Her hair furled back behind her, and she crouched low, gaining a little more speed. It was not as fast as snowboarding, but it was crazy fun. She took a knee and made her profile even lower, like an animal on the prowl. She pawed hands full of sand to go even faster. Now aerodynamic and propelled, she was catching Alex. She squinted to fight the sand blasting from his board and kicks. She pulled up neck and neck with him, smiled over at him, then stroked ahead to beat him to the end.

They gave each other a high five. They had made great time.

Rory was high on the dune but coming down fast too. He was not standing, and as he neared, Ashley was impressed to see he had gone headfirst. His eyes and mouth were sandy, but this time he did not seem to care. He just spit aside the sand and laughed. Kelli was catching on too.

Each time, Cha Cha pushed more from them. Hector would pantomime techniques; she narrated. One time, he broke into a hula dance during their instruction, then tumbled down the dune when missing his footing. Even in his prat fall, Hector was a professional goof—his tumbles were epic, head over heels, cartwheels, and somersaults that rivaled Ashley's floor routines.

"Drink," Cha Cha gestured to a cooler beside the Jeep. "I go get pendejo."

"I can't believe people don't do this anymore!" Kelli said. "This is awesome!"

"Good times," Alex added. "I could do this all night."

"But you can't beat me," Ashley beamed. "None of ya can."

"You haven't seen the best of me yet," Rory said. "I'm going to really surf this next time. On my feet."

"We should put some money on it," Alex suggested. "Stay on your feet, an' I pay you a hundred bucks."

They bantered about for only a few minutes, then the Jeep was back. Their hosts were eager to join in the wagering. "I can beat everyone," Cha Cha said, and it kicked up a good laugh.

"Let's say it's America versus Peru," Alex said.

"You against us," Ashley clarified with gestures.

The two Peruvians looked frightened by the challenge but accepted. "Fife hundred," Cha Cha said.

"Done." Kelli shook her hand.

Cha Cha extracted a very special board from the Jeep: a raggedy, thin thing that looked like it was made from bark. She made a grand show of it, passing it before each of their faces. "My rocket sled," she said, "is your doooooom."

The six of them were soon tipping their boards on the edge of the dune. Rory counted it down. "Three. Two. One."

Ashley felt her muscles tense. She had a fleeting idea to hit them all with an Affectation, then Rory shouted "GO!" and surfing was her only thought.

An instant into the descent, Rory went tumbling, his moves rivaling Hector's earlier stunt. She laughed but kept pushing more from her board.

Alex was coaching Kelli, even during this competition round. Ashley looked farther back and saw the Peruvians at the crest.

"LISTO?" Cha Cha asked.

Really? Ashley thought. A head start.

Then she realized why.

Cha Cha and Hector were good! They were cutting and banking, sometimes catching air, and then using the spring in their boards to eke out more forward momentum.

Alex had seen it too, and with permission, he tipped Kelli into their path. They both jumped over her and closed rank.

Alex got serious then, catching up with Ashley immediately. "C'mon, Ash. Let's do this!"

Both of them were doing all they could now. Alex was leaning forward and low, streamlined and streaking fast. Ashley took her position again and practically did a breaststroke in the sand. It was exhilarating!

Then, to their surprise, Hector flew between them, backwards on his board, shrugging and smiling at them. Ashley looked behind, and Cha Cha was out of the contest, helping Kelli get righted, but she took a second to thumb her nose at the racers.

They had been snookered, but Ashley didn't care. She figured she could scrounge up five hundred dollars. It had been worth it.

35 Reverie

A shower had never felt better. Rory tried to wash away every grain of sand, marveling at how much swirled around the drain at his feet. It had been fun, sand surfing, but he thought he might just rather stay in the shower than gear up for the arrival of LF Winston.

The sun had set hours ago, and from his balcony room, Huacachina looked like a wonderland of golden lamps and candles. A light breeze from the east waved the curtains in his room. In the distance, he heard Alex laughing.

Could Rory, a man who killed others for a living, have a best friend? It was a conundrum that had circled around him for years. Could he have *any* friends? Could he have a life? A daughter? A love? When the Contracts turned on them, would he obey or risk it all?

Hadn't he settled that? He was no longer an Extractor. He was a Franklin militia leader. He was Ashley Winston's bodyguard.

Rory shook his head. Water drips whipped away. He turned from the view. It was more than a matter of Contract or loyalty, love or loss.

In times of battle, when Rory first served TransCorp's One World, he was the most decorated man for his service. In the Turncoats, he felt he served an even greater good, revealing TransCorp's lies.

But when the CorpseCorp conscripted him into service, he knew there was no Just War, no higher calling. It was money for blood, and he had no alternative than to serve. It disgusted him, and it made him physically ill. He was the Corp's top Extractor and Assassin, but it made him sick every single time. They would harm his wife and his daughter. It was a matter of fact, not an idle threat. They would kill innocents if he did not comply. At the very least—and yet in ways, the very worst—they would expose him for the horrors he had committed.

They had owned him in this way, and they were too large and too powerful for him to overcome.

Similar offers had been extended to everyone he had known in the Turncoats. He had seen them, here and there over the years, on operations like he would be on, sometimes given his same directives, his same Contract.

Closing the Contract and doing it best became Rory's priority. He thought then that if he were the best, he might curry favor, and if he could rise to what Alex called "scary good," they might leave him alone for fear of his vengeance.

The problem, however, was that he never knew who cut Contracts in the CorpseCorp. He only knew his handlers, men and women who would approach him with new work and large rewards. He had gone through several handlers. He thought the Corp liked it that way, preventing him from becoming familiar and learning too much.

So, times would change, and handlers would change. He did not get close to them. It made it easier—though it was never easy—when he had the chance to interrogate one once in a while. He had even closed Contracts *on his own handlers*, when assigned, and that would give him a complicated mix of joy and sorrow, pleasure and guilt... and always the sickness.

As his fortunes grew from wet work well done, Rory learned he could afford to have Contracts placed on others, and his first targets were his handlers. Then some *other* man or woman in his same situation, some other assassin, would close the Contract, and a month or more reprieve would follow while the Corp found a new handler for Rory. In those months, Rory would have his morning coffee with Calissa and then just stroll the streets and visit libraries and cafes without the haunting guilt and nausea.

In this way, he came to understand how Contracting felt less like murder, more simply like work. It felt better, killing once-removed, through the guise of paperwork. It was just a job, only a Contract. People behind those Contracts he closed could be anyone, but they had to be people without conscience. People wanting others ended outside the course of law.

More than a few handlers had disappeared from the Corp's complicated systems, many of them not the target of a Contract, but discreetly removed by their own best Extractor, *Rory Orman*.

It was his trade name; only one person in the Corp had ever known his real name was Rory Reed. That man, Stan Combs, was a true sadist if ever there were one, working in strange circles in and out of the Corporation, continuing as Rory's handler for years.

He had been the only handler to learn of Rory's peculiar tic, his kryptonite, and he had squeezed and twisted at Rory's conscience for years. He had taken pleasure in Rory's pain and illness. Rory was certain it was Combs who had driven his wife to madness. He had threatened Rory's family, however, one too many times by kidnapping Calissa, and he had ultimately and summarily been dealt with in the Franklin, Texas melee.

Perhaps the CorpseCorp had let him go long ago. Perhaps there never was such an entity, and Stan Combs had been behind it all along, despite what he said. Perhaps he had earned his freedom, finally, by eliminating someone so despicable even the CorpseCorp was indebted to him. Whatever it was, he had been relieved of duty now for half a year, and he had never felt so free.

In that way, Rory seemed to have gotten to his answer. He had developed a relationship with his Mark, his contractual target, of all the women of the 5 billion on the planet. The irony would never be lost on him. He had *not* closed the Contract that Combs told him was on Ashley Winston. Instead, he had to admit, he had fallen in love with her.

He was also decades deep into relationships with Astar, Zana, and Alex too. His daughter could now walk the streets safely and attend college and live the life of any other kid in the country.

Rory was still harboring a heavy heart. LF Winston was coming, and he had designs for something big—Winston-level big. Rory and his team were at this secret oasis to intercept the most wealthy and powerful man in history. What could they do but stand by and watch? Who were they to pass judgment on this man's plans?

Something nagged at him, however, that just maybe, the few of them in this pivotal moment might be the only ones who could ensure the right outcome, whatever it might be. The machinations of even the most benevolent man might need a counterbalance, a course correction. Rory had seen Winston's dreams dashed before. He had tangibly felt Winston's pain... but in that, he had also felt something too close to vengeance to forget.

Rory was sampling that emotion, tasting and feeling it, trying his best to figure it out. What was it LF Winston was planning next?

Lightning on the horizon stirred Rory from his dark reverie.

It was time to find out.

It was five of midnight when the people of Huacachina fell entirely silent with the blackout. All the singing and dancing and partying stopped abruptly, leaving only an ominous rumble that made ears tickle and itch. Electricity to the city was suddenly cut off, and with it, any HeadGear transmissions and all recording devices. It was as if an EMP blast had radiated over the town. Only candles and lanterns illuminated Huacachina in an eerie, prehistoric glow.

The townspeople seemed to expect it, but Rory had not. He stumbled around the hotel without even a flashlight. He checked in on Calissa and Katrina, then Zana and Astar, finally Alex and Kelli. They were all in their rooms, on their balconies, watching the black on black of the descending airship in the night sky. It absorbed stars as it came to hover overhead.

From a rooftop patio that overlooked the hotel entrance, he saw Ashley, surrounded by locals with lanterns, heading down the boardwalk. Rory jumped to the ground and caught up quickly.

She smiled at him. He thought he knew her well enough by now to gauge this as her nervous smile. She had put on her heavy makeup, concealing her ScanTats, and she had done something to her hair that gave it a silky glow. She was barefoot, wearing a satin gown not unlike the robes LF had worn.

Rory felt under-prepared and overdressed.

The rumbling of the airship created a rumble he could feel in his teeth and soul. It had descended to the point Rory felt it would crush the palm trees.

Then he noticed it was not hovering but drifting in. He could not make out details of its hull, but he could at least mark the passing of seams and rivets in the black. It was small, by Winston standards, spanning just the width of the village, a mile wide rather than horizon to horizon.

Rory thought it must be all engine, for the rumbling turned now to a shuddering groan that drowned out all else. He wanted to talk to Ashley, to go over the plan again, but there was no talking, no point in even yelling in each other's ears, with the thunderous overhead vibrations.

In the near distance, Rory heard a sliding sound, and soon this sound came to muffle out the rumble, and then it didn't seem to move at all. The airship had drifted into the dunes and landed.

It was utterly silent now, and Rory joined Ashley's little party as it hurried to the vessel. When they drew near to the back of the airship, Rory stole off into the shadows to watch the exchange.

A slice of light opened to be a rectangular door, and Estate security guards poured out onto the sand. Behind them, again in his robes, stood LF Winston, radiant light framing him in the doorway.

LF shielded his eyes while trying to get a better look at the welcoming party, then he nearly stumbled out of his ship to approach it. "Snow? Snow, could it be...?"

Familiar silhouettes of Franklin militia and Mitchum mercenaries surrounded them, but from Rory's vantage point, he could still watch them interact. "Yeah, it's me, Poppy," Ashley said with a smile.

He threw himself through the layers of welcoming people and security to embrace his daughter fully. "Oh, Snowflake! Oh, my god. I'm so happy!"

"Me too," she said through the hug. "Me too."

Then he remembered himself, and he pulled away to look at his men. "Zip it up, please," he commanded, and the security personnel went in all directions. They were inspecting the people who had come to witness the landing. They were checking every window and door, exchanging curt language with Huacachina residents.

Rory felt like a ghost, for no one seemed to notice him standing by the airship entrance, back in the shadows. When he did emerge, after the tearful hugging was through, he found his own men pointing guns at him.

"It's alright," LF said softly. "He's with us."

"Mr. Winston," Rory began. "I am so glad to see—"

"Rory Reed! I should have suspected you, too, would be with my Snowflake." He chuckled. "Once again, we are meant to be here and now together."

"Yessir," Rory said. He never knew quite what to say in LF's presence. Nothing seemed adequate.

"However did you know to come to—*you know, it doesn't matter*. It was inevitable. You are *meant* to be here. You and your friends," he said now to Ashley, "are meant to be at ground zero."

"Ground zero? What's going on? Why here?"

"Ah, walk with me," he commanded the whole entourage. Then he sang an eerie verse Rory did not quite know: "*Come with me, and you'll be, in a world of pure imagination.*"

If Rory's radar had not been flashing before, it was now. Something seemed especially not right about the old man. He seemed more spirit than man, and in the glow of candles, draped in his white robes, barefoot, he seemed even more spectral. He seemed more spiritually powerful and sure of himself than he had at the Estate. He seemed outright otherworldly.

A steam powered vehicle popped and sputtered out of the airship. It sounded more like a percolator than transportation, but it chugged along behind them. It was a peculiar vehicle, a steam truck, mostly a deck moving on bulldozer tracks. Rory saw a pile of canvas layered and stacked on it, weighing it down.

"That would be the hose, then," LF said without even looking back.

"Hose?" Rory squinted to see it better in the candlelight. "A giant hose?"

"Yes. Oh yes. We could walk inside of it when it's all fired up."

LF led them onward, rounding the boardwalk, heading toward a mission-style church that faced the water. It was obvious to Rory that LF knew his way around. Without ceremony, without waiting for a priest or a key, the townspeople swung open the doors, and the group went inside.

From the steps of the church, Rory could look back at the steam truck and better study the hose. It was a pile of folded hose, easily twenty feet tall, teetering on the truck bed. A huge metal flange, the size of a poker table, was attached to one end of the hose. The men quickly untied the flange and pulled it and a length of hose up the church steps and inside. Rory could hear pews being dragged around on the stone floor inside.

"Ashley, what—"

"I have no idea," she said, spellbound by it all.

Rory chanced a look inside. At the front of the church, panels were being removed from the pulpit, revealing a dark recess underneath. He took Ashley's hand and pulled her past guards and hose handlers and on into the front of the church.

"Reed!" someone said as he passed. It was Chavez.

"What the hell's all this?" Rory asked as softly as he could. "What's going on?"

Chavez looked ahead and behind, then said, "This hose? It's to load the *Murus*."

"The *Murus*!" Ashley exclaimed. She pivoted back as if to look outside at the airship.

"Yes," Chavez said.

"Load it with what?" Rory asked.

"Isn't it plain to see?" Chavez said with a sardonic grin. "With holy water."

36 Murus

The instant she heard the name of the airship, the spell was broken.

"You... you *tricked* me!"

She recalled again the night at the Estate and the strange way the *Murus* was always on the tip of her tongue, yet never worth reconsidering.

"That's right, Ashley," LF said. "The one ship you would have never taken those Parkers on, the one ship you dismissed, is parked here tonight."

"But..."

"I couldn't have our work interrupted," LF smiled from the altar, his arms spread wide.

"Your work?" Rory asked.

"Yes, yes." LF nodded to the men with the giant hose, and they went inside the hole inside the pulpit. "To harvest the Deep Water. To share the Deep Water."

His life's work had been sharing water, so why should this be so different? Ashley wondered, why so special, so secretive?

She looked quizzically at Rory.

He shrugged.

LF picked up on this, and he continued as he descended the pulpit stairs. "The *Auteum Murus*, I have christened her, for she will both build and tear down the walls we believe."

"Sometimes," Rory rumbled, low and quiet just to her, "he's got to be harder to understand than you say that I am."

Someone shouted something in Spanish from the hole. LF nodded to a man nearby him, and commands were barked up and down the length of the hose in rapid fire transfers of several languages. Ashley noticed someone was speaking in muted tones to Rory, interpreting.

"Mr. Chavez?" she said. "What is happening?"

He kept busy but spoke out of the corner of his mouth. "We're about to pull from the aquifer under the lake. Filling up a bladder in the airship."

Ashley frowned at this, puzzled. She approached LF, himself busily overseeing the arrangement of the hose. "Poppy?"

LF turned and smiled at her. "Yes?"

"What's it all about? The *Murus*? The water?"

He patted her shoulder and spoke to her like she was five again. "Poppy's taking water to the clouds."

"Why?" Rory asked, standing so closely behind Ashley she could feel the heat off of him.

"To share, of course," LF said.

"Your clouds already make rain, right?" Ashley shrugged.

"Not like this," LF said with a wink.

She watched him hustle down the hose, outside, and toward the *Murus*. He patted the hose lovingly as he went.

"What was all that?" Rory asked Chavez. "*Auteum Murus, for she will both build and tear down the walls we believe.*"

"Winston believes this water's going to change the world," Chavez said. "Gonna be a big wake up call."

She did not know why, in fact it seemed an illogical leap of reason, yet she had to ask. "Is it... is it some kind of poison?"

"Just the opposite," one of the others said. "It's going to bring us all together."

Rory looked like someone had kicked him. "One World," he said sourly.

"Heard this one before," Ashley groaned.

"I dunno," Chavez said. "He may have got it right this time."

Ashley wandered outside, a little put off by how the many men and women tending to the hose just ignored her. No fanfare that they were reunited with their Princess. No 'pardon me, Miss Winston.' Everyone seemed to be on a mission, and a hurried one at that.

She followed the course of the hose, walking in the ruts left by the steam truck. Rory, she knew, was just a pace behind her, always watching out for her. Even if the others had completely forgotten who she was, Rory was faithfully following, literally in her footsteps.

"He tricked me," Ashley said over her shoulder.

She ducked around a man draped in long chains he was carrying toward the church.

"How so?" Rory asked.

"About the *Murus*."

"The *Auteum Murus*," he said. "The Church Wall."

"Pfft," she said. "Brush up on your Latin. Could mean anything along those lines... like he said, a belief wall, a barrier... who knows?"

"How'd he trick you?"

"He zonked me," she said, smiling as she used one of his words for an Affectation.

"Why?" Rory asked. "How?"

She stopped and turned to him. "I don't really know. It's like he could misdirect me from that ship to think about anything else, and I *knew* he was doing it... yet I still believed him. Trusted him."

In the lantern light, his features looked more carved from stone than ever. He reminded her of Rodin's "The Thinker" as he mulled over what she had said. He rubbed his chin.

"I don't do that, do I?" she asked him.

"Do what?"

"Maybe... absently... like, *persuade* people?"

"Umm, how would I know? If you didn't even know it was happening, and you can Affect people like you can—how am I supposed to know?"

"You don't think I, like, 'get in your head' like that, do you?"

His expression reminded her of Kyle, then, of that night he had doubted his feelings having ever been fully his own. She felt that now too. So many things: backfire hoodoo from too much drinking, being half-afraid of what Katrina might do if she were fully revived, and now, realizing her own father had tricked her... manipulated her.

"Because," she continued, putting a palm on his chest. "I wouldn't. I know where I'm not wanted."

A curious expression came over him, as if he were about to ask her if she were Affecting him right then and there. Then he said, his eyes glittering in the black, "It might be something very special, a natural high... a new kind of intimacy. I might like it."

"You're saying you'd *invite* me into your head? After all this time of warning me to leave you alone, you'd *ask* me into your thoughts?"

He smiled sheepishly. "Would you think less of me if I said it sorta felt good when you zapped me in the pantry?"

"Whoa, whoa, whoa!" Alex said, stepping between them. His breath was sodden with beer. "No *zapping in the panties* on this man's watch."

"You're drunk," Rory said.

"I'm just happy," Alex replied. "Amused."

"Oh?" Ashley said, gently pushing him out of the way.

"Oh?" he mimicked. "Oh yeah, oh."

"He is drunk," Kelli said, now joining them.

"You two lovebirds are carrying on like there's not a giant freaking airship parked over there about to suck this mudhole dry," Alex laughed. "Like you haven't even noticed!"

"Not Huacachina," one local corrected, "*under* her. We take the water from below."

"Whatever," Alex said. "So... what gives? Where's the old man?"

"I am right here, lad," LF said.

Ashley's head was swimming. Everyone seemed to be popping up in their lantern light with something to say. LF seemed to have just appeared from thin air again, as he was apt to do.

A commotion was surging up and down the line. Again, people were shouting to one another, something about preparation.

"Ah!" LF said with a smile. "This is going to be something."

He was animated again, and he was starting away. Rory put out his arm like a turnstile bar. "What's happening now, sir?"

"Well," he was full of mirth and excitement, "have you ever seen where lightning strikes on a sandy beach? Yes?" He asked in one direction, "No?" he asked in the other. People were nodding or shaking their heads, but he seemed not to care, continuing, "Ever seen fulgurite? Of course you have, perhaps in a museum or for sale. You know, Zeus marks!"

Ashley had seen what he was babbling about, sand that was turned to glass when struck by lightning. It made wild, root-like shapes in the wake of the lightning bolt. They had some at the Estate. One priceless stretch of it measured nearly ten feet.

"Or... or have you been around glass blowing much?"

None of them responded beyond confused nods of agreement.

"In moments, the *Murus* is going to sear the sand dunes, and I am thinking, perhaps, to leave fulgurite markings there when we leave."

"Leave? But you just got here!" Ashley protested.

"Come with us," he said with a buoyancy in his step. He moved aside Rory's arm and continued toward the church again.

Rory shrugged at her.

Kelli was wagging her head. "Believers," she said. "Always the ones to watch out for."

"Yeah," Alex agreed, absently.

"Ash," Rory said with a tip of his head. "What's he mean exactly about searing the sand?"

"I... I don't know," she said. "Maybe we should stick with him though?"

As they ascended the steps, the hose crew moved quickly past them and into the church. It looked to Ashley as if the entire town were crowding inside now. She found her father again on the pulpit. He smiled down at them benevolently.

"What's going on here?" Ashley asked over the excited conversations around her.

LF spoke loudly and slowly, as if he expected someone to be transcribing his speech. "The airship *Auteum Murus* is going to be my tanker. She will take on millions of gallons of water and yet still take wing in the morning."

"What kind of pump can pull that much water," Rory asked, "in such a short amount of time?"

"I'm no hydrologist," Alex said, "but that's not possible. You cannot pull that much water—"

"By igniting the exhaust from the airship's transpiration, we will create a massive heat sync, and that will create a vacuum which will pull at approximately 1,000 cfm through this line."

"What?" Rory asked. "You're using fire to pull water?"

"That's good, my boy. Seems too easy, doesn't it? But the *Murus* will vent such a hot aether mix that it will make the sky around it weep. Burn the sand into glass. It's yet another added value of our aether, you know."

"Has this ever been done before?" Alex asked, soberer than she had seen him since he had arrived.

"Nope," LF chirped. "That's why this is so exciting, yes?"

The sound of the airship's arrival was a whisper compared to the roar of the flame-throwing front of the ship as the Transpiration was lit aflame. LF was correct; it was exciting. The fireball that rolled and built up as high as a thunderhead also lit the night afire too. It was a terrible and powerful sight.

Ashley and Rory huddled in the church's entry, taking it all in, holding each other. She knew the aether was not immediately flammable, but she also knew it could be vented like this and made into a powerful blast of flame. She had seen it once in the sky during an exhibition of a Nimbus, but she had never seen it on land.

"Takes a lot of heat energy to pull this much water," LF said over the roaring sound, slapping the fat canvas tube. "You should see the manifold."

"The what?" Rory asked, leaning toward him.

"The manifold," LF said. "Like a mantle for your little gas lantern there. Of course, we don't know if it will last long enough."

"And if it doesn't?" Ashley asked, dreading, and yet fully expecting, his answer.

"We all die," Alex interjected. "Am I right?"

LF tipped his head left and right. "Aww, I wouldn't know about that, but I certainly hope not."

As the fire roared and the hose surged and burbled, many of the people who had helped with the set up drifted off to their homes.

LF's crew made themselves at home, too, turning lawn chairs and chaise loungers to face the *Murus*, then flopping down in them for the show.

Alex and Kelli had returned to the hotel.

LF was wandering up and down the surging hose, fascinated at his fireball water pump.

Ashley was wondering more now about the *Murus*. It was named after the meteorological phenomenon known as a wall cloud, an impressive display. Wall clouds, like all the giant airships in LF's fleet, could span horizons in ominous dark, low-lying bands. Had LF ever decided to use his vessels for transportation, as Sarah Parker had proposed, a *Murus* model airship would have been the workhorse. She had no doubt a *Murus* could hoist an entire armored cavalry up and over mountains, then around the world, should the need ever arise.

In his phase of showmanship, not a year before he disappeared, LF had staged a number of demonstrations like that. The showstopper had been when a *Nimbus* would rise off the sea and pull a half a dozen aircraft carriers up with it.

As the *Murus* was filling with what they had called Deep Water, Ashley was confident it could take flight, even when full.

What she did not know was simply *why*.

Rory was muttering into her hair. "Gallon of water's about eight pounds," he said to himself. "Six feet in diameter's about...." she heard him mumble.

"Two million gallons," LF said in passing. "She'll top off at two million gallons."

37 Melding

Rory had been to many hot-air balloon launches, and the roar of a hundred of their propane burners could not begin to rival the off gassing of the *Murus* and the fire she breathed. He had witnessed carpet bombing that had not sent up such plumes of flame and clouds of condensation. It truly was an incredible sight.

Like so many things he had encountered since meeting Ashley Winston, this was yet another over-the-top experience he would not forget. He was happy to be able to share it with Ashley, and yet he hoped Calissa was watching it from the hotel, too.

Huacachina was illuminated as bright as day. Rory wondered what the people of neighboring Ica would be told to think, most likely, with content LF would provide CommCorp. Surely this plume of flame would attract their attention. Rory wondered if satellites were picking it up in space.

After an hour, he was ready to rest, knowing that something big was on the horizon with LF back, with the *Murus* being loaded as it was. Chavez was not talking much. None of his men were. They seemed unusually reserved. Fearful.

He strolled back to the hotel with Ashley on his arm. "Someday you have to tell me what it's been like growing up with a guy like that," he said.

"Like what?"

"Larger than life."

Ashley shrugged. "It wasn't a life, really. He was always too big for the room, you know?"

Rory could feel that. Wherever LF Winston went, the world seemed to struggle to encompass him. Especially of late. He thought LF was fulfilling his own prophecies, becoming who he had painted himself to be. He was living his own legend.

"Is there something to that?" he asked aloud. "To living up to your own legend?"

Ashley pondered as they walked along the boardwalk together. She started to respond, then restarted again and again. Finally, she was out with it: "You've heard of a self-made man? I think Poppy's creating himself in his own image, if you know what I mean."

Rory nodded. "*So God created man in His own image, in the image of God He created him.*"

"Exactly. So, you see the paradox, right?"

"So, he's a god."

"He's *seen* as a god, and he's *created* what is seen from what was imagined and forecast... from his own imagination."

"It's too early in the morning for me," Rory scoffed. "You're saying he's locked into his own press? He's stepping up to live the life his PR team cooked up."

"Except he had no PR team. He's doomed—determined—whatever you want to call it... to be the LF people expect him to be. And those expectations are his own hyperbole."

"Maybe he should have shot for something a little less exaggerated."

"When he was dead—missing—when he was *thought* dead, his legend just grew. I think that's the bigger problem now, from what Grandmother says."

"He's been eulogized for so long, and now that he's back, he has big shoes to fill."

"There you have it," she smiled at him.

For the first time, Rory realized he had come to think of the tattooed face as the real Ashley. This one, coated in makeup that made her look much tamer, but no less beautiful, just wasn't her.

"So then," he said, shaking off a flight of fancy, "what's this next big thing of his? How's Levi Finn Winston going to rock the world again?"

"You heard him. He's taking water to the people."

"That's kinda anti-climactic after all he's done. Aether. Airships. Averting hurricanes."

"Yeah, yeah. Typhoon Tycoon. Rainmaker," she continued, "hard to top... but this... " she waved at the fireball, "he says that this will be his Magnum Opus."

"Doesn't make sense." Rory said. "He created a way to give water to people *without* hauling it. Why backpedal now?"

They walked on, past the loudest area where shouting and fire would have drowned out their conversation. They were making the loop around Huacachina.

"Maybe there's something to the water," Rory said after a while. "What's Deep Water, anyway?"

"I don't know."

"You're the professor," he said.

"I don't know that it's all that scientific."

"They said it's from an aquifer below the lake, right? You think it could be... different?"

Ashley shrugged. "Different how?"

Rory looked around, then behind them. He half-expected LF to pop up and correct him, but he ventured anyway. "Deep Water. Holy water. Healing waters... bringing us all together—you heard that, too, didn't you?"

"Yeah, so...?"

"And you heard Zana's big history lesson on the place?"

"Yes, and?"

"So," he said, "what if it is... medicinal or something? What if the water's packing some kind of punch?"

They made another lap around the town, avoiding the giant hose and roaring airship and most of the people who were still awestruck by it all. It was their fourth pass when she shared another sobering thought.

"What if he's losing it?"

"Losing it? Like his mind?"

"What if Poppy's popped? I mean, maybe bringing him back to 3dub was just too much."

"He can still command a room," Rory said. "He's still a great leader. Just look around." He gestured toward the hose team.

"Rory, this is just... strange."

He couldn't argue that.

"I can't tell you how much I've missed him, how I've longed day and night just to ask him how he likes my leadership... how he likes me behind his desk. But now..."

"But now...?"

"It's not the time, what with all this." She scoffed. "It's never the time. Never been the time."

"I'd agree with you. He's been a little obsessed since we found him, but—"

"Rory, he's been ridiculed before for things that turned out to be miraculous. He's been beaten down by rival corporations and chased away. He's been made of strong stuff, but I worry about this one." She gestured at the flaming *Murus*. "This 'water to the people' thing is insane. When it comes to nothing, what will that do to him?"

"He'll regroup and reinvent and show them all again."

"Will he? Or will he fold up and lose it completely—if he hasn't already?" She sighed hard and heavy.

"Ashley, I don't know. That day back at the Estate, he seemed to know what he was doing. He seemed—"

"He zonked you, I'd bet." She looked back over the bizarre scene, squinting as if she were looking for him out there, patting the hose or doing a jig. "All I ever wanted was to have him back in my life, maybe to run 3dub together." She swallowed hard. "Now, here he is on some last crusade."

"The best you can do is to be there for him if it fails, then invite him back into the office, maybe. It'll all work out, Ashley." Even in saying it, he doubted it. He doubted she could miss that in his tone.

They walked on without words. It was as if the thunderous Murus was LF booming and bursting with confidence and pride, compelling them to believe in him.

It was an increasingly tough sell.

They were back at the hotel, standing on the veranda. It was so late at night it was early morning. She was especially talkative now, and Rory did not want it to end. Everything seemed so ethereal to him, from the strange lighting of the sky to the heady feelings he was again experiencing. He had not really felt quite like this since his prom date, decades ago. It was a golden-glowing night he did not want to end.

"Let's do it," Rory said abruptly. He was standing toe to toe with her, holding both of her hands. The fireball was in the distance, yet close enough they could feel some heat from it.

"Rory Reed!" she smiled. "Aren't you being a little direct?"

"No, no..." He was shocked and flustered. "I.... uh... I meant, let's do your mind meld, or whatever you want to call it."

"My what?"

Rory shook her hands gently. "I'm saying, let's do it. Let's experiment. Just for a while yet tonight, why don't I come *over* to your place, then you come *into* mine... inside my head?"

"You keep saying that, but I can't—"

"You can experiment with that thing your dad does, if you want."

"I like your first idea better, to just share, if we can, a sensation or something."

"You've said it before, that it's more like suggesting something biological or emotional, right?" Rory grinned. "Refresh me, maybe. How about that?"

"Right here, on the steps?"

"C'mon," Rory said, and led her to her suite.

The power was still out, but now the room was illuminated by the golden fireball. It seemed especially cozy and warm. Giant curtains and cloth draped on the bed frame were all painted yellow-orange by the glow. Rory liked the vibe.

"Let's have a toast," she said.

"I thought you were laying off the sauce for a while, especially after you popped your own cork."

Ashley sat on the bed and crossed her legs. The satin that clung to her looked to be dipped in gold. The hem slinked up mid-calf. He had seen her naked twice, but she had never looked more alluring than just then.

"I thought maybe I'd bewitch us both," she said. "Put us both in the mix."

Bewitching had never sounded so good to him. "I'll be your bartender. Just point."

She directed him to a mini fridge. He opened it and turned to her. "Really?"

"Bring it all," Ashley said.

He scooped a dozen little liquor bottles into his shirt, dumped them on the bed, and sat next to her.

They sat on the bed together, fighting the little labels and corks and screw tops, then clinked their bottles in a toast, "To the mind meld, then," she said with a shrug and a smile.

"To sharing my head," Rory said. "Come on in."

Ashley downed her bottle, opened another, and downed it as well. They sat in silence for a while, then made small talk about the fireball for a while. Then Rory pulled her down onto the bed with him, and they found themselves kissing.

"We ought to do this right," Rory said, coming up for air.

"Right, right," she said.

He massaged her temples, then spread his fingers to touchpoints on her neck at her jawline, her temples, and her cheekbones. "You do it, too," he said.

Ashley's fingers had been tangled in his hair, but she moved to approximate his own placement of fingertips. She aligned her index fingers along the shaved stripes at his temples.

She was looking into his eyes with a curious smile. "Now what?"

"Now, repeat after me," Rory said. "My mind, your mind; our thoughts to divine."

"My mind, your mind; our thoughts to divine," she whispered. She added, "Now close your eyes."

Their lips were just inches apart. Rory wanted to kiss her again, but as that thought came to him, others flowed into his head. It was as if her voice was inside his head, in a stream of consciousness very different from his own. His thoughts were calculus; hers were a symphony.

He opened his eyes to take her in, and she opened hers as well. They gazed into each other's eyes and souls. There was no boundary between them, no looking from one person into the other. They were sharing a mind kiss more intimate than anything Rory had ever known.

"Deep," his voice commented.

Deeper? She thought the question.

Please, Rory longed for more. He thought he should be more cautious, though then he didn't care. She had already quelled his conscience.

He closed their eyes, and she brought them together. It started as a butterfly kiss, then an Eskimo kiss, and then they were gently brushing lips and tongues and spirits together. Time and gravity didn't matter in this cone of silence, this blanket fort of bliss. Their hearts synched up to beat in unison. Their breathing was one. They were one.

This is new.
Whole.
One.
Safe.
Together in this stolen moment
We dwell
And dwell on what's ours.
While we have it all
We cannot wait.
Time will call us out
When we wake to be two
Tomorrow
Yet we can revel in us now.

38 Una Mente

"How do you feel?" Rory whispered in her ear.

It was dawn, and she was wrapped in his arms. She sighed, then admitted, "I feel... terrified."

He seemed surprised. "Terrified? How about, I don't know, 'cuddly,' maybe?"

Ashley extracted herself from the bed and smoothed out her gown. "Rory, I've never done that before. Never. Not with anyone. Ever."

"Me either," he said, enjoying a luxurious stretch. "But I'm not terrified."

"It's hard to explain... I... we just discovered a level of Affectations that I never dreamed of." She tried to keep her voice down, but this was difficult. "It wasn't just *pushing buttons in your gray matter to Affect your autonomous functions.*"

"Oh, I know," he said, sitting up. "There were lots of—"

"It wasn't just me implanting ideas. Like Poppy did to me. Like I did to Kyle and—well, it just wasn't like that. It was like a *gateway*, like a back and forth."

"Sharing," Rory nodded. "We shared something there."

"I wasn't in control of it," she felt her energy discharging. "I couldn't have stopped it even if I had wanted to."

"And that's bad because?"

"What if it were... *adversarial*, Rory? What if I were trying to Affect someone and he or she fired back?"

He shrugged. "Guess you could test that out on Katrina."

"Did you miss the part about me not being in charge?"

"You weren't in charge because we both agreed to sink into it. I'd like to think our connection was, I dunno... special." Rory sounded a little hurt by her line of reasoning. "I'm not asking you to have another mind meld like that with her. I don't think you could anyway, right?"

"Because it takes two consenting adults, you're saying?"

"That, and we'd have to dry Katrina out," Rory said. "She might not be too cooperative."

"She might run right over me," she said. Looking in the mirror, she asked, "Got a brush? I look awful."

Rory got up and rummaged through the bathroom, emerging with a brush and a shrug. "Ashley, everyone who knows you can do the Affectations is scared of you. Even Grandmother said you were—what was that again?"

"She said she'd shudder at the thought of me being provoked." Ashley nodded.

"There. So, what are you afraid of?"

"If Grandmother's afraid, then I'm afraid." She was brushing out her hair, but in the corner of her eye, she spied him changing clothes. She tried to look busy and continued, "Rory, if anyone could understand, I thought it would be you. It's all about control."

"Control... like focus."

"Yeah," she said. "I mean, you are great at that. You have a memory like no one I know, and you said you can slow down time with your focus, right?"

"I guess. I can dial in pretty good." He paused, adding in a different tone, "Usually."

"What if you couldn't, though? What if someone was sharing a mind meld, like we did last night, and you *couldn't* control it? If they tripped triggers in your head, maybe they'd make you go insane. Maybe they'd get trapped in your head accidentally? You see how dangerous it is?"

"If someone's going to get trapped in my head, or me in their head, I'd choose you."

"That's sweet and all, but what if it was a permanent reversal? Traded consciences?"

"Ash, this is a lot of what-ifs." He was standing behind her now. Their reflections were framed in the mirror like a portrait of newlyweds. "I think we need to just take it for what it is and keep it to ourselves, maybe."

"I'd like that a lot better," she said. "No more talk of experimenting with Kat, then?"

"Deal... but I'd like *us* to experiment again, eh?"

She turned around and hugged him. "Deal," she said and squeezed him tighter.

They strolled downstairs and into the hotel restaurant. It was in full swing with several locals dining, as well as two tables of Winston's security. Mixed right in with them, she spotted Alex and Kelli.

"Missed the big sendoff," Alex said, standing to greet them. He was smiling ear-to-ear. "Must've been... distracted."

"Big sendoff—you mean—" She darted to the doorway and dashed outside.

"Not again!" Rory shouted behind her in the restaurant.

The rumbling was gone.

The fireball was gone.

The *Murus* was gone.

LF—gone?

"Out of his damned mind," she said.

"Alex said it left hours ago," Rory said as he came out with her. "Something about ideal conditions for launch."

She clenched her fists and roared, "I *hate* him! Leaves me for 10 years. Leaves me for dead in the ocean—hardly bats an eye! Now he does it again? Just like that!"

"Maybe he's got a deadline—"

"Maybe he's just an asshole, Rory!" she stomped back into the restaurant. "Nobody thought it would be a good idea to tell me? To wake me?" she called out to them. "Not one of you?"

Several people shrugged. Others looked down at their tables, ashamed. Alex came around the table toward her, munching on a strip of bacon. "He'll be back," he said. "Said he was just going to run a few tests."

"I've heard that before!" she said, fighting back tears.

"But really. That big hose is still out there. His crew's right here." He turned to wave a hand in their direction. "The guy's coming back."

"Did he say when?" Rory asked.

Alex shrugged, chewed. "I think he said something about a cycle..." He turned to Kelli and said, "Isn't that it? That he'd be back next cycle?"

"Rotation," Kelli said from her seat. "I think it's like a Weekly move? Maybe he's falling into a pattern?"

"So, a week," Rory said, putting a hand on her shoulder.

She wrenched free from him to drop into a chair. "Coffee!" She called out, "I need some coffee."

Rory sat across from her. His eyes were on her, wary.

Alex and Kelli joined the table. Alex had brought over his plate. Food was piled high and falling off the edges. He had a beer in his other hand.

"Order the Salchicha Huachana," Alex suggested as he forked up some sausage and eggs. "Can't go wrong."

"*Run a few tests*," she repeated.

"That's what he said," Alex confirmed.

She ran her finger along the grout on the tile-surfaced table. "Tests on what? All that water?"

Alex shrugged. Kelli, too.

"Chavez!" Rory called over his shoulder. "C'mere."

The Franklin militia member snapped to attention and rushed over. "Yessir."

"Why don't you pull up a chair, Martin, and fill us in," Kelli suggested, making room for him at the table between herself and Rory.

Chavez took the seat, glanced around the table at the four of them, then set his eyes on Kelli. "I don't know much, Cap. Just what I hear on the *Murus*."

"More than we know," Rory shrugged. His eyes smiled disarmingly.

"What's going on with these experiments? This Deep Water?" Ashley asked.

Chavez's eye snapped open a little wider, as if the question were a challenge. "Miss Winston, I really—"

"Just what you heard, roundabout," Kelli nodded slowly, reassuringly.

He took a deep breath, but before he could speak, the waitress was at the table serving Ashley a cup of coffee. She asked the others at the table, then shouted out orders to another server who came back with empty cups for Rory and Chavez.

"He was telling the ship's pilot he was going to release the water somehow up high, like in the jet stream or something."

Ashley tipped her head at this. It didn't sound right. He had proposed the delivery of water decades ago, before he learned the ships alone could affect weather patterns. "So, he's dumping it out way the hell up there?"

Chavez shrugged.

"All of it, all at once?"

"Didn't hear, one way or the other, ma'am," Chavez said, then took a drink of coffee.

"You heard more, though," Rory surmised. Ashley knew him to be a great observer, a student of character. He had peeled back a number of people's reservations in the time she'd known him.

"Not about that exactly."

"About the distribution, then?" Ashley asked.

"He went on about tankers, some." Chavez looked at Rory, then Kelli.

"Tankers?" Rory asked.

"Like those air-to-air ones," he said, nodding. "You know, for bombers and long-distance airplanes, so they didn't have to land."

"Just how did he go on?" Ashley asked.

Chavez looked very uncomfortable.

Rory was picking up on it too. She could see it in the way he used his body language to be friendlier, mirroring Chavez. He chuckled, thoughtfully. "Those are some amazing pilots, huh? I don't know how they do it."

Chavez nodded. Breathed again. "Yes. Amazing."

"So, the *Murus* is the air-to-air tanker for...?" Kelli was pulling at a thread.

"Cap, I dunno. I think the Rainmakers."

"Well, there ya go," Alex said, unable to be quiet any longer. "Old man's going to pour water from his tanker to another airship. Big deal. Make the transfer and be back in a week."

Chavez shook his head slowly, his eyes still on Captain Kelli Chase.

"What is it, Chavez?" she asked.

"I don't understand it myself," he said. "Mr. Winston, he said he was getting it to all his ships, all at the same time."

Ashley snorted. "That's not possible. They're all over the world. Even the fastest *Cirrus* couldn't get coverage like that."

"How many *Murus* models are there?" Rory asked.

"I... I'm not even sure. Maybe twenty?" she said.

"So, what if all twenty were loaded?"

"Still couldn't load the others all at once. There's just too many, too far apart."

"No, no..." Chavez was trying to be polite. She could hear it in his tone. Kelli started to say something, but Ashley put up a hand. Eventually Chavez filled the silence. "This is what I don't understand. None of us could understand when he talked about it. I think he's planning to dump all that Deep Water all at once, to all the ships. Like that." Chavez snapped his fingers.

"Just like that, eh?" Alex asked.

Chavez nodded, a worried look on his face.

Both servers were back with food, but one was having a hard time doing her job. Clearly agitated, she finally set her platter down on a nearby table. "The Deep Waters," she said, struggling with her English, "Nuestro padre will pours the waters, *todos mundos*."

"On all the dead?" Alex interpreted.

"No... all the world over," Chavez said, looking at her. He asked something in Spanish. She returned in a quick sentence or two, animated, smiling.

"What is it?" Rory asked them both. "What happens when the water is all over the world?"

"That's what I was saying, Reed," Chavez said. "And she just confirmed it."

"The One World thing again," Rory growled. "Uno Mundo or something?"

"No, *una mente*" the other server set a plate in front of Rory and further corrected, "One Mind," she spoke in clear and perfect English. "He will make us of One Mind."

39 Daughters

"Sort of stretches the definition of 'morning coffee,' doesn't it?" Rory asked.

Calissa looked at the sky, set up a makeshift sundial with a couple of Peruvian bread sticks. "Close enough. Besides, we could do worse."

They were sitting on her patio, shore side, the breeze wafting in the cool, late morning air. Her suite was split level, one of the best at the hotel. He wanted her to have it for the multiple escape routes, which he had drilled her on upon arrival. Upper balcony, out to the sand. Back entry for stealth. Patio doors to be in the open most immediately.

She sipped her coffee. He did the same. It gave him a moment to appreciate her. Beautiful. Brilliant. Lethal. She was his dream kid, all grown up. Her hair was tied up in a red kerchief. She was wearing a simple Peruvian shirt she'd bought at a gift store in Ica. Forty years ago, she could have been any rich kid from town over to Huacachina on a weekend jaunt. His mind was moving to think about that, about how the Winstons had bought out the town and diverted most of the tourists away—but he forced himself back to the present. "*Be here now.*"

"I know that one. *Your life requires your mindful presence in order to live it,*" Calissa completed Akiroq Brost's quote. "What are you thinking about, Dad?"

"The past," he looked around the lake, "and your future."

"I'm thinking how this coffee is so good!" she smiled.

"Think it's because we're close to Colombia?"

"It is Peruvian," she smiled. "It's called Misha."

"Yeah," he said, savoring a swallow. "Who knew?"

"Zana said coffee is one of Peru's top exports."

Rory nodded, looking at his cup, at the reflection of the sky in the dark coffee.

"So... you like it?"

"Yeah, sure." Rory shrugged. This was a game, too. Since he first taught her to think through coffee flavors, they had experimented with so many. He was no coffee snob, preferring good old Folger's to about anything, but the game gave him a chance to teach Calissa focus. He needed that focus now. He knew she could see that.

"It's like that stuff we had from Africa, from Uncle Alex, that Elephant coffee," she blurted with a giggle.

He spit it back in the cup. "Got anything else?"

"Daddy, it's the most expensive coffee in the country!"

"What did this stuff run through? A bird?"

"Raccoon, actually. A Coati."

Rory sloshed it around in his cup. At least she had his full attention.

"You never finished telling me about Mr. Winston and what happened last night."

"Let's talk about you first." Rory sat his cup down and put his elbows on the little table between them.

"I'm fine. How often's a girl like me gonna get to see a place like this?"

"I should have taken you with me more often," he mused.

"I'm not feeling deprived," she said.

"Ashley..." Rory took a deep breath and let it out slowly. Only a five count. "Ashley hates her dad. Feels he left her out—"

"You're comparing your parenting style to his?"

"I don't know... it's just that... Calissa, I just want the best for you. You know that, don't you?"

"Duh. Of course, I do."

"Lately, though..." He wanted to get up and walk, but he kept himself perched on the patio chair. "I mean, take the coffee hour. I've missed our coffee more in the last few months than I did in the last ten years."

"First of all, you're not doing good at the 'now,' Dad," she chided him.

He grunted in confirmation.

"And second," she patted his hand, "I think you're just finding your own way. Experiencing things for the first time."

"Funny," he said. She was turning his own parent talk back at him.

"Seriously though. I get it," Calissa said, then tossed in, "When's the last time you were in love?"

"I'm not... it's just..." Rory was grappling for something. Anything.

"C'mon Dad. Who else can you talk to about it? Alex?"

"I don't need to talk about it." He was in freefall. "Let's just talk about you."

"We are talking about me, remember? How we're growing apart?"

Finally, he grabbed onto his guilt. "I left you on the *Arcus* with no explanation. A *month* without our coffee hour. Just a little morse code to keep me sane."

"The ship was probably safer than running with you," Calissa shrugged. "Besides, the closer I get to your work, the more amazed I am that we *ever* had coffee hour. Dad, you do great."

"We didn't even get to talk about the Rainbow Ride. I had to hear about it on your VidBlog."

"You actually watch those?"

He nodded. "Whenever I can. Sometimes over and over."

"But you hate being Jacked." She was truly surprised, then she remembered something and asked, "All of them? You watch all of them?"

"Want me to quote something from one?"

"Oh gawd, no." She was clearly embarrassed. "So, you saw the ones about the Princess?"

Rory smiled a little. They were playful posts in which she told her audience that her father was dating a celebrity. She never said who, as per his orders, and she never shared footage, but she was so giddy in those posts that he had watched them more than any others of late.

"I didn't mean it on there when I said I was jealous," she said, alarmed. "I was just, you know, just kidding around."

He took on her airs and started quoting her Vidblog: "*When he's not with her, she's all he talks about.*"

"Really?" she chuckled. "You're going to do that?"

"*She doesn't fit the wicked stepmom role, but she is—*"

"Okay, okay. You watched them, already!" She was blushing now. Rory smiled.

They sat for a while, enjoying the morning.

"But we're okay?" Rory asked finally. "You don't feel—"

"I feel so happy for you, Dad!" Calissa stopped pouring another cup of coffee in mid-stream. She sat the carafe down. "I've wanted this for you our whole lives!"

He nodded. Then he smiled, confessing, "She is really great."

"Why's she hate on her dad so much? I get the faking-his-own-death thing, but I thought she was getting over that."

"He has a bad habit of ditching out on her," Rory said. "He took off again this morning without even a goodbye."

"He spoke to me," a voice behind them said.

Rory whirled, gun drawn. It was Katrina, in night clothes, leaning against the patio door. He glanced at Calissa, who was not alarmed at all.

"She's a great roommate," Calissa said, smiling at Katrina. "Sleeps a lot."

"Cal, she's... you can't just—"

"I am under control," Katrina said softly. "May I join you?"

Rory put his pistol in his lap. He was worried Calissa might be Affected. He was trying to sense if it was happening to himself. Still, he nodded to an empty chair folded by the railing. "Sure," he said.

"Coffee?" Calissa asked.

Katrina shook her head no as she sat down. "I practice Clean Life."

Rory was flustered. He felt another wash of guilt. Practitioners of Clean Life were like the Muslim version of Christian Scientists, if not a little more strict. He felt terrible they had kept her sedated so long.

Then again, he was going over the contents of their room in his head, thinking through which drawer might hold her next syringe.

"I would take a glass of water," she said, "if you please."

Calissa left to retrieve the water.

Rory studied the woman at his side. She was bleary-eyed and leaning a little on her elbow, squinting at the sun on the water. She could have passed for any tourist with a hangover.

He knew her to be part of the Family, powerful enough to dupe everyone on the airship. He knew, too, that she had military training, and that she was a tightly wound bundle of muscle and sinew. She was formidable.

From a month with her at sea, Rory knew she was strong-willed. Keeping the balance of sedation and lucidity was difficult, even for Zana to maintain. Clear enough to eat and go to the toilet, out enough to keep from zapping them all.

Calissa had been lax in the medications, obviously, for here she sat, making conversation.

"She must not know," Katrina rasped a whisper, "what I had to do on the airship."

"She knows," Rory said.

"And yet... and yet she—"

"Here's your water, Kat. No ice." Calissa sat down a glass and rejoined them. "What is it about South America and ice?"

Rory was on full alert. A fast smash of the glass, and it was a lethal weapon. The iron patio chairs, too, could be weapons. She could strangle Calissa with the IV hose that dangled from her arm.

He liked keeping his handgun nearby, and he could feel the other one in his ankle holster.

"Thank you," Katrina said, then took a sip and closed her eyes. She swallowed, then looked at Rory. "He spoke to me before he left this morning."

"I never saw him," Calissa said. She rolled her eyes ever-so-slightly. She sent a Clench suggesting Katrina wasn't all there.

"He was here before the power returned. He came and went through this doorway. He whispered in my ear."

"What did he say?" Rory asked.

"He said he would return to a different world," she said, then sipped and savored another drink of water. "He said this is not goodbye. He said to welcome the Obsolescence."

"Wait, wait, wait," Calissa said. "What's Obsolescence?"

Rory half-wondered about that, too. He had been the world over, dealing with every manner of cult-leader language, justifying every kind of horror. He had dispatched his share of 'gods' and prophets in his work. This sounded like more spooky talk. It never ended well. Something else bothered him even more.

"I don't get that guy. Talks to the whole restaurant. Comes by here and says this 'not-goodbye' to you and not to his own daughter?" Rory rumbled.

Calissa was shaking her head adamantly, but the question was already out there, and now, the answer:

"I *am* his own daughter," Katrina said.

40 Friends

"Not one ship, you're telling me?"

She could read Kyle better than anyone. Even from half a world away, strained through the limitations of HeadGear, depriving her of all his body language, she knew he was telling her the truth. "That's right. He's turned the tables, Ashley. He dropped a terabyte of proof on CommCorp's doorstep that verified he was who he claims to be. DNA. Dental records. Affidavits. Even a testimonial from you—"

"I never—"

"That's why I bring it up. I know Shine when I see it, but the public didn't."

"*The Truth is What's Told*," she recited CommCorp's cut line.

"Exactly," he said.

"So, he's collaborating with the fab four at CommCorp? They made the Deep Fake of me saluting dear old dad?" The whole idea of it infuriated her. CommCorp had kept her on the run for years with their sensationalism. They had made her a fugitive time and again. Their broadcasts had brought her in before. Now she was accused of murder, and she was wanted internationally. The crime purportedly had happened in a belt of the atmosphere akin to international waters. Anything was fair game.

"He's not exactly collaborating. More like *commandeering* CommCorp."

"What do you mean?"

"He all but bought them out."

"What? Why didn't he, you know, *completely* buy them out? Corporate Takeover. Pennies on the dollar, like he was talking about."

"Appearances, Ashley..." He was squinting, looking around inside his HeadGear. "Are you sure this line is secure?"

"Stetson to Stetson," she said. "*Above the law...*"

"Beyond the law," he completed the phrase. They both wore the most elite communication hardware available. His had mysteriously shown up at his office by private courier. Hers was actually Alex's, which he had readily loaned her in exchange for some gossip on Rory.

"Okay, okay... well... here's the news you missed," he said. "In the last month, he's sent disruption notices globally. Some recall on his ships, he claimed, nothing big, just a retrofit or inspection—stories varied. They're all back on course now, but it was odd, missing a rain, you know?"

She tried to keep the curiosity off her face, but then, he knew her about as well as she did him.

"Weird, huh?" he said.

"What else?" she prompted. Through the veil of the Stetson, she could see past the projection of Kyle to the airfield outside the *Whipstitch*. Faithful Franklin militia was stationed around the plane, which gave her at least some comfort. Regardless, she did not want to stay on the line too long. Not even on a Stetson.

"You *don't* trust this line either, do you?"

"Sure, I do," she said. "It's just... busy here."

He examined her face a bit, then continued, "One Rainmaker, the undulating one... I dunno the names—"

"*Undulatus*," she said.

"Yeah, that one. They claim it crash landed. The story is terrorists again. How many terrorists does CommCorp think there are these days? Anyway, that happened. 3dub says it's the first ever, well, since the one in Texas, anyway. Is that true?"

She bit her lips together. A shipwreck would be devastating news. Like LF was always saying, the public is fickle. Why hadn't he bought that story out? "I thought he had CommCorp under his thumb?"

"I know, right? Doesn't add up."

Ashley nodded. "There's no reason he would run that story, is there? Where did the *Undulatus* go down?"

"That's another thing. Crash landed. At night. At sea. All hands aboard." He was giving her the eye again, sizing her up. "It sounds flakey, doesn't it?"

"Yeah," she had to admit it did.

"Not as strange as the other one," he said. His face was projecting a little closer up, the Stetson software recognizing the importance of what he was saying now, "A *Murus* just up and disappeared. No one's even offering a story on it."

"Really?"

"Really. Puts me in a spot, being on LF's legal team. You can imagine."

"I barely can," Ashley said. She smiled to deflect, then asked, "When was it last seen?"

"Disruption alerts started a week ago when it drifted out of pattern. It fell off schedule, then it fell off everything. Radar. Satellite. All Comms."

"A ghost ship," she murmured.

"They already beat you to that. CommCorp's been beaming out every kind of speculation, and the banners are all 'Ghost Ship' this and 'Ghost Ship' that." Kyle let out a deep sigh. "I guess it sounds better in the HeadGear than *Murus* or whatever. *Better sound sells.*"

"How could a ship just go ghost?" she asked.

"You know more about them than I do," Kyle said. "I'm ground interference."

"Right," she said, lost in thought.

"Ash, wherever you are this time, just know you have full company resources." Kyle smiled, his eyes veering off screen. He was attending to something else, maybe her balance sheet. Maybe sports scores. Just like in person, he was obsessed with his Interface feeds. "You don't have to rough it this time. Everything's yours. He insisted on it."

"Is that right?" She was reviewing what she knew.

"Well... everything but the ships."

Of the early airships, an *Undulus* had first kicked up a storm. They were discovered to be best at Transpiration in flight, able to glide up and down as gracefully as a Manta Ray, and not all that different in appearance either. They were a popular Rainmaker, and it troubled her that an *Undulus* had taken a dive... or had it? She knew the missing *Murus* was now lugging around millions of gallons of Peruvian water. Maybe that *Undulus* was on a similar mission. Maybe it was due at Huacachina any day now.

Mac confirmed nothing was on the charts or screens. He told Ashley there was no sign of anything out of the ordinary in the fleet, not anywhere even in distant range. They talked a while about how a ship could escape detection. His stories were engaging, everything from dazzle boats in World War 2 to Stealth bombers, but none of it applied to an airship. The boys brought them some great local food and some beers, and Ashley spent another leisurely hour visiting about Mac's travels and covert operations. This was the kind of friends Rory kept, and she was getting comfortable with them.

Finally, she figured that any traces on the Stetson might have cooled, and she went back to the private cabin to make another call. She flopped back in the leather chair and let the Stetson's correcting gear gently pull her in. It felt like she was once again easing into an isolation bath.

Carl was worried. From the moment he accepted the call, he was frantic. "You shouldn't be on here," he said, "Mrs. Smith."

"Relax Carl. It's a Stetson."

"I'm on university-issued HeadGear. Did you forget?"

She read the peripheral signatures on his projection. "That's my old piece, Carl."

He looked sheepish, shrugged. "Well. Yeah. I forgot."

Her discards were still better than most military grade HeadGear. That unit, if she remembered right, was still worth an apartment in the city or a fleet of Transports. It was no Stetson, but it was a nice model.

"Carl. I know it's not your field, but riddle me this: how could an airship disappear?"

"You mean the *Murus*?"

"The *Undulatus*, actually," she clarified.

"That's what I suspected," he said with a curt nod of his head. "We're not caring about the *Murus*, sight unseen." Even his voice carried air quotes. "Instead, we're talking about the *Undulatus*. Downed at sea by terrorists."

She nodded her head. He was shrewd, carrying on both conversations with her at once. "That's the one."

"The other one remains a mystery," he said. His eyes were sharply on her next move.

She shook her head ever-so-subtly, 'no,' then she said, "I hear LF's at large, too?"

His eyes nearly exploded in surprise. It took him a bit to collect himself. He chuckled as best he could, "Ol' LF. *International* man of mystery."

"Sipping his Peruvian coffee and hiding with the Aboriginals again, I bet." It was all she could tell him.

"So, the *Undulatus*..." he was thinking it over. "What would happen if you, say, deflated an airship? Maybe displaced the aether with water, entirely."

"Well... I don't know that the superstructure could take much water pressure, but an *Undulatus could* roll with the waves, at least on the surface."

"That's my bet," he said, nodding emphatically. "Those *terrorists* sunk her, and she's waving away underwater. Lost at sea."

"I suppose you're going to tell me she went down in the Bermuda Triangle or something," she scoffed. Then, when she heard nothing from Carl, she did a double take. He was nodding, serious. "Because that would be silly," she said, and read his cautious shake of the head.

"Terrorists. Outlaws. If I knew one, I'd tell them to lie low. Especially one wanted for the murder of a corporation darling like Sarah Dawn Parker." He was reading the edges of their transmission for any interference. Always cautious. Always a conspiracy nut. That's why he and Rory had hit it off.

"I hear you," she replied. "So that's still in the Interface, eh?"

"Everywhere. All the time. Her uncles act like they'll stop at nothing to avenge—"

"Good act, then," she winked. "And the suspect?"

"Good as dead, should she ever poke her head up."

They spent a good minute of Interface just looking at each other, letting any scanning roll on through, just in case their signal was being swept, even over the security protocols. A minute of Stetson Interface was worth about one hundred dollars, but it was worth waiting it out. Especially to Carl. She would grant him that.

"You remember that Mr. Gault we knew back in college?" She broke the silence. She couldn't help herself from sharing this bit of news. If Carl had liked Rory, he had become best friends with Alex immediately.

"Yeah. Another ghost, eh?"

"He's back," she smiled. "And he can't keep from getting Jacked now and again."

"Huh." Carl smiled back. He would be looking out for Alex.

"Carl," she said as an afterthought, "do me a favor and stay out of the rain."

His expression was one of genuine curiosity when the screen faded to clear.

It would give him something to explore. Maybe, should LF pass over Springfield soon, he would heed her advice. She could only hope so.

She sat in the leather chair, trying to clear her head. Why would they sink an *Undulatus*, and why in the Bermuda Triangle? She couldn't think of a reason that made any sense. She hated it when things got this way. Complicated. Curious. Rory would tell her it was '*always darkest just before dawn*,' or something cryptic like that, trying to reassure her it would all work out.

The biggest puzzle was not the airships, nor her father's bizarre behavior. It was Kyle DuPree, her best buddy since she could remember. "Everything's at your disposal," he had said, urging "don't rough it." Was he *intentionally* trying to get her caught?

Tricking her into spending on the grid so he could reel her in as he had done before for Delores? It did not sit well with her, and she was going to get it worked out. She needed a neutral party she could trust.

"Mac!" she called out. He came to the door and knocked as he entered. He had a pistol at the ready. That was taking some getting used to, as well. Everyone was armed in her new world. "Mac, I need you to ask around. There's a guy you dropped on the *Arcus*. See if you can find me the Spexarth kid. Steve Spexarth."

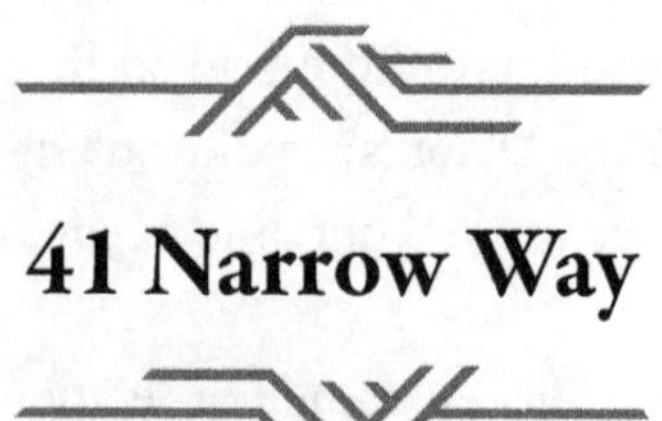

41 Narrow Way

"Where exactly are we going?" Rory asked.

"A familiar place," Astar said with a smile. She looped an arm through his and guided him down the boardwalk.

"You really think she'll be okay?" Rory looked back to the hotel, up toward Calissa's balcony.

"Katrina is resting once again," Zana said.

"Resting!" Astar said. "Such a terrible thing to do to her."

"It is the only safe way," Zana said firmly.

Rory was not convinced. For all he knew, Katrina might have been Affecting Zana this entire time, convincing him to reduce the sedative day by day.

Then again, he was also second guessing his own better judgment. Astar and Calissa both were sure Katrina was no harm... didn't he trust them? "And what about her claiming she's another Winston?" Rory asked.

"Rich men have been known to... pollinate freely," Astar shrugged. "What difference is it?"

"Not this man," Zana said. "Mr. Winston is cut from another cloth."

"You say this because he is of the Family?"

"I agree with you Zana," Rory said. "LF's an odd one, but I think he'd be faithful."

"He would be faithful, for he is a man of incredible faith."

"Speaking of faith..." Rory mused.

They had led Rory up the steps of the church and now went inside. Though the hose had been extracted, the church was otherwise still a mess. Pews were scattered about. The altar had yet to be reassembled. Panels of it were propped here and there, unceremoniously. The gaping hole in the front exhaled cold air as they approached it.

"Ah! When you said familiar..." Rory chuckled.

"Yes, it will be like home," Astar said, leading him in.

The tunnel walls were dug by hand with chopping movements forever reflected in the texture chiseled into the stone. The floor and stairs were also stone, but the surface of the stairs was worn smooth. So many had passed up and down these stairs over centuries, each step was indented from the erosion of footsteps. Millions of footsteps.

"The church was first a Spanish mission, and that was placed over a simpler building. You might call it a well house," Zana began. "In other cultures, the water and the cistern we approach had other names and values."

"These stored produce," Astar gestured at shelves along a stretch of the tunnel. "I would suspect they preserved a great deal of it, when the original peoples lived here."

They each had a bright flashlight. Zana carried other flashlights on his belt, should these fail. He also wore a bandolier and utility belt with various other tools for caving. The Amins were expert spelunkers. Rory had utter confidence in them. They were also crack archeologists, and he was finding this tour to be fascinating.

"When boxed up," Zana waved a hand all about, "as she has been with the church atop her, this cavern could have mustered."

"Mustered?"

"Mildewed," Astar said with a scrinch of her nose.

"That it did not tells us there is another entrance."

"At the very least, another vent."

"When did you guys check this out?"

"I began my study when we had the coordinates from Mr. Winston," Astar said.

"We came through here first when you slept. Again, during the transfer of water."

"Such a terrible thing," Astar said with a cluck of her tongue. "Or so it seemed."

"What do you mean?" Rory asked, trying to make out her features better.

"Look around. They have sullied this place with their hardware. Dragged that big hose through here. They have scarred the walls, the stairway... everything."

"We were fearful that this underground lake would be entirely drained," Zana said with some bitterness in his words. "Thankfully, as you will see, it is full again."

"We have plumbed it and have not found the bottom, in fact."

Rory pointed his flashlight closer to her face, "You're kidding."

"We lost the anchor on the end of our string, so we do not truly know," Zana smiled.

"Lost your—how long was your string?"

"Two hundred feet," Astar said softly. "And it was not exactly lost to us, Zana. You must be honest with Rory Reed."

Zana sighed, and it bounced down the stone tunnel. "She believes it was taken."

"What was taken?" Rory asked, confused.

"I was holding the string when it was jerked," Astar said. "Something lives here, Rory, and it bit the weight from my string."

He held back his laugh. Nothing was living in a freshwater aquifer hundreds of feet beneath a desert. Nothing that would have bitten at a weighted string.

"Ah, and here we leave our shoes," Zana said, running his flashlight over the landing they were now on. Here the stairs ended in a twelve-by-twelve foot landing, the middle of which was polished and smooth, again from so much traffic over so many years.

"Why would we leave our shoes?" Rory asked. He panned his light around and noted the remains of some wooden structures, possibly more shelves. They had been run over rough-shod by the hose team, it was clear. He spotted what looked like the soles of sandals wedged in the woodpile. "Why did *they* leave *their* shoes?" he rephrased the question, pointing out the sandals.

"It is a mystery," Astar said, "but so much is mysterious, isn't it?"

She had kicked off her shoes and bent down to unlace his boots.

"I got it," Rory said, sitting down to take off his boots and socks. Astar and Zana sat with him, both smiling.

"What?" he asked, noticing them still smiling kindly at him.

"Time changes things," Zana began.

"Every. Thing." Astar nodded. "These stones around us, the lake below us, and the one above us, as well."

"Imagine what the changes here have been," Zana said. "What this cavern has hosted!"

"How old do you think it is?" Rory asked, pulling off his sock and stuffing it in his boot. "If the Spanish built a church up there in, say, the 1500's... and it was old then?"

"Yes," Astar smiled. "It was old then."

"Perhaps a thousand years or more," Zana speculated. "In the Andes, over ten thousand years ago, there were people in abundance, living with nature."

"You're saying this hole's ten thousand years old?"

"It is possible," Zana said.

Rory panned around the landing with his flashlight. There were no cave paintings. There were no carvings. He wondered how much of this tunnel was natural, how much hand made.

"Change is good, yes?" Astar asked, abruptly.

"Sure," Rory said. "I guess."

"Think of how long people have come to the Huacachina. Now it has changed to belong to one man, Mr. Winston," she continued.

"Think of how long then that we have been acquainted," Zana said, himself changing the subject on a turn. "A good while. And we have done good work."

"You're not retiring on me, are you?" Rory said, shining his flashlight on one face, then the other.

"Now think of your daughter, of lovely Calissa. She is changing too."

"That's a fact!" Rory said. He wanted to unload on them, but they had no children. It was always awkward when he shared his child-rearing woes. They had heard it all over the years:

"No way I can send her to school. I about died when she got on that bus."

"I'm not ready for this every month, guys."

"Boyfriends! How am I supposed to deal with these boys all the time?"

"She's teething. She's got to be teething. Do teenagers cut teeth?"

"She cried, and it made me cry. Me. It's too much."

"And now, think of yourself, Rory Reed," Astar said. She put a hand on his forearm. "You have changed, too."

"What makes you think so?"

"You have no master," Zana said. "You are your own man now. No attached strings."

"You may now choose your own way, as you have with us these years... or maybe to settle down."

"Maybe to settle down with Miss Winston," Zana said.

"Hold on," he could hear his voice echo. "What are you getting at?"

"We could also find another way, perhaps, if you did so," Astar said, patiently.

"So, we all hang it up?" Rory could hardly speak. "Just like that?"

He swiped away a swath of dust from the smooth stone floor. They shared how they were all getting older, of how many times the four of them had been wounded or imprisoned or left for dead. It was a difficult life. There were few causes left that were pure or decent or even... profitable.

"Even profit has lost its luster," Zana said.

"We are all now independently wealthy," Astar said. "Even should you *not* marry the Princess."

He had rebuttals. Rebukes. Reversals. He had all sorts of things to say, but he knew it would do no good. He knew this conversation was just a courtesy. He had known this day would come, but the timing seemed odd. The location seemed odd. There was something more to it.

So, he waited them out.

"If you agree, then," Zana said, "there is but one last battle to be waged."

"But this is our *last* one, Rory Reed. It has already taken too much from us. Too many days apart. Too much bliss lost to the work."

"It is a very powerful opportunity, this one, but if you wish, we could all walk away without risk."

"We could let the world spin," Astar said. "Zana and I can live the rest of our days comfortably in Springfield and enjoy our home in the Lair."

"And the rest of the world may, as you are fond of saying, piss itself."

"Piss off, you mean," Rory said. "You're saying we can just let things take their course. Walk away from whatever's going on with LF Winston. Forget the woman—maybe his daughter—we have drugged in Calissa's suite? Ignore whatever this whole Obsolescence thing is all about?"

"Yes," Astar said. "The four of us—although now there is Calissa..."

"...and Captain Chase," Zana added. "And the Princess..."

"Mm," Astar smiled again. "So perhaps the *seven* of us. We all could leave tomorrow and be better off for it."

"Or...?" Rory was growing weary. He wanted them to get to their big reveal. He knew from their tone there was something to this 'last battle,' and he wanted to know what it was.

"Or, we may continue down to unsettling things that you cannot let pass."

"I might let 'em pass, Z," he said defensively. "I can let a lot pass."

"What lies below will decide your future. There will be no other way for a man of your nature," she said.

"*Astar and I* could walk away," Zana nodded in agreement. "You will not."

"What makes you so sure," he smiled, as if it were a joke, knowing it was not, all the same.

"We have known you these many years and watched you always do the right thing. Not always the legal thing. Not often the easy thing. But always the right thing."

"Always," Astar agreed.

Rory sighed. He counted everything within the glow of the flashlights. He took his heart rate. He replayed everything they had been telling him about himself, and he knew it to be true. *Walking away is walking off. Off the cliff. Off the thin line of conscience and deceit. Stay the course.*

"Walk away, or face this last job. That's it then?"

"It is how we see it, yes."

"And we are very wise," Astar smiled, "You have said so yourself."

He stood, gathering up his boots. "Let's go topside, then, and find some tequila. Let some other martyr deal with the demons down there."

A-Z stood slowly, silently. Their shoulders were slumped. Their expressions numb. Even their flashlights were aimlessly directed at the ground.

"I'm kidding!" he laughed. "If it's that big a deal, let's slay some dragons. Who knows? Maybe I'll end up with the Princess, and we'll all live happily ever after."

The mood was suddenly a celebration. Astar hugged Rory tightly. Zana cackled merrily.

Rory started down the stairs, whistling merrily.

They did not follow.

"What now?" he said, turning back to face them.

"Did you not see the inscription?" Zana asked.

Rory climbed back to the landing and looked where Zana's flashlight pointed. It was a petroglyph he could barely make out. "What's that?"

"As best as we can discern," Astar said, "it warns that is the way of the unclean."

"The unwashed."

"Generally, the impure," she continued. "There is a better way."

"Less stairs, too," Zana smiled, then directed Rory across the landing to a fissure he had not even noticed in all his idle study of the space.

"What's this path, then?" Rory looked for markings, and finding none, offered, "The way of the too stupid to call it quits?"

"It is the way of the believer," Astar said.

"The narrow way," Zana said, his smile now fading. "The hard way."

"But... you just said less stairs."

"Sometimes even a path such as this will pose its own problems."

"Greater problems," Zana said. "But it will be worth it."

"For the worthy," Astar said.

"Where's it say all that?" Rory scoffed, but he led the way through the fissure and down a narrow trail. "I want to meet the guy who said all that."

"You already have," Zana said.

42 Sisters

Ashley was a little jealous. *The kid had a nice set up.* Calissa's suite was second only to her own. Both were split level, both opened to private rooftop decks, but Ashley's had a private pool (and a pool boy on request) and generally a better view.

When she had knocked, Calissa shouted, "Just bring it to the balcony, por favor!"

Ashley passed through a large room with tile floors and a nice cowhide couch set. She passed through the master bedroom, raising an eyebrow at the empty bed—Katrina's bed. When she brushed aside the sheers to the balcony, she was shocked to see Katrina sitting across from Calissa, the two of them engaged in a card game.

"Oh!" Calissa said and immediately began to apologize, "I ordered room service and I—"

"It's good," Ashley said, not taking her eyes off Katrina.

"She's okay. Dad said so."

"Dad said so..." Ashley trailed off.

"I am now under control," Katrina said. "Self-control."

"Run out of morphine?" Ashley asked Calissa.

"No, really. Kat's okay," Calissa said, patting the seat of a chair at the table. "Join us."

Ashley had been waiting a long time to have another go at Katrina Covarrubias. She sat between them, watching as they played their hands out.

"Kat's like... a whiz at cards," Calissa smiled at Ashley, making introductions. Then she turned to Katrina, "And Ashley... Ashley's the most fearless woman I know."

"So then, the drugs were not your doing?" Katrina asked Ashley pointedly. "You did not take the cowardly way?"

"No," she replied. "Zana said it was for your head. He's the best doctor I've had."

"He is no doctor," Katrina said. "He is a warrior."

Ashley shrugged. He had patched her up more than once. "He knows his stuff anyway."

Katrina scoffed. "I am tired of cards," she said.

"How is your head?" Ashley asked. "*Clear*?"

"The headache is gone."

"She had a concussion, don't you think?" Calissa asked Ashley, then said to Katrina, "Ashley's got a PhD in medicine. Brain surgery."

"Biochemistry, from MIT," Katrina said, as she tapped the card deck into the box. "Additional work in oceanic biomimicry, settling into work in the gulf for Johns Hopkins."

"I'd say you're cleared up," Ashley raised an eyebrow.

"I have my wits back about me."

"How do you know so much about me, but I know nothing of you?"

"You know nothing of most things until they matter," Katrina said.

Ashley wondered when everyone had found time to take up philosophy. Katrina sounded too much like Rory. She was talking in parries and foils.

Katrina seemed to sense the tension. She shrugged, "My story is not so remarkable."

"She told me that she made big global deals with TransCorp," Calissa said. "She speaks seven languages."

"Four," Katrina said. "I can read more."

"What's International Relations, anyway?" Ashley asked, recalling the title.

"Just what Calissa has said. I brokered deals here and there."

"What kind of deals?" Calissa asked.

"Purchased thoroughfares. Leveraged eminent domain. Traded coin for causeways."

"Deal with a lot of *Contracts*?" Ashley asked directly.

"Oh yes, it was constant interpretation of contracts, negotiating—" she stopped, looked at Ashley more closely. "What are you suggesting?"

"You know...Contracts."

"I do *not* know."

"Contracts for CorpseCorp?"

"Room Service!" a voice shouted from inside. A man carrying a platter of fresh cut fruit and frothy drinks sashayed on the balcony. He was all smiles and flair, swooping and stooping to deck out the entire table with Peruvian delights. With each plate he announced in his best English, "Mangos. Papayas. These you call elderberries."

Ashley was feeling edgy. She even found herself distrusting the waiter. She felt like Rory must constantly feel, assessing the man before her for any sign of a sham. Were his shoes right? *He was barefoot*. Was his accent right? *How would she know?* It seemed like a supercharged moment with a balcony full of electric tension and her job was Rory's job now: protect Calissa.

Then the man was gone, and Katrina and Calissa were enjoying the gala of colorful food and drink before them. "Ahh, that's so good! Ashley, you have to try this fruit. I don't know what it is, but yum!"

"That is guavas," Katrina said with a smile. "And this is a dragon fruit."

"They're chilled. Refreshing!"

Ashley surveyed the colorful drinks in frosty glasses. They looked like various flavors of fruit smoothies and juices. "Cal, are these *just* fruit drinks? Not alcohol?"

"That's what I ordered, no booze," she said, picking up a pink frothy drink and taking a gulp. She wiped her lips with the back of her hand. "That's soooo good."

Ashley was still studying Katrina, but it seemed now that Katrina had lost interest in her, focused entirely on the treats before them.

"You should have some, too," Katrina said to her. "These are the best mangoes in the world."

She shrugged, then picked up a sliver and sampled it. The flavor was stunning, so much more potent than any store-bought fruit she knew. Though Ashley had access to the freshest foods that could be purchased, nothing she knew rivaled the fruits before her. She was digging in like the others, letting her inhibitions and her distrust cool.

The three marveled at the spread, tasting, sharing, talking about each morsel as they munched at it. Ashley savored the cool fruit flavors. She had two glasses of a dark juice Katrina thought was made from the guanábana, or soursop. "Tastes like pineapple strawberry."

"With some lemon or something citrusy," Calissa added, and the three clinked their glasses in a toast to the drink.

"HEY," they heard from below. Calissa stood and looked over the railing to the patio below. Ashley looked past her. It was Spexarth, detained by guards out front. "Where's Miss Winston?"

"Come on up, Steve," Ashley called down to him. "Meet me in the hall."

"Who is that?" Calissa asked.

"*That* man is more of a doctor," Katrina explained. Her eyes had grown large, perhaps alarmed.

Ashley tipped her head, curious.

Katrina continued, again controlled, "He watched over me on the airship."

"That's Spexarth," Ashley said, on her way to fetch him. "He helped us escape the *Arcus*. He's helping Rory."

"How did you get your hands on this?" Ashley asked him in amazement.

"Reed said he wanted some intel, so I just lifted it."

She was holding a ragged, leather-bound journal spread open between her palms. They were sitting on a back stairway in the shade, where they'd been talking now for half an hour.

"You know the value of this?"

"I don't know. Probably bring a fair amount?"

"What I saw of what's in here could leave you set for life, if you got it in the hands of the right people." Ashley shook her head, marveling.

"I think giving it to you is putting it in the hands of the right people. Even over Reed."

It looked to be the last of the Lost Journals, as family historians had called them, journals her father had kept throughout his career. Some were known to have been burned. Others were treasured by collectors. None were discovered from the last decade. Now this one, the current one, was in her hands. The last few pages ended in frantic babble and illustrations she couldn't begin to understand. A dozen or more pages had been torn from the end.

"Where's the rest of it?" she asked.

"This is how I got it."

"Did you read it?"

He looked out over the dunes in the distance, then looked her square in the eye. His pupils were pinpricks of honesty. "I did. Not all of it, but I thought, you know, if it fell out of my possession before I could get it to you, then that'd be a loss."

She nodded thoughtfully. "And?"

"And... well... hell, Miss Winston. I was curious. Can't blame a guy."

"I don't blame you a bit. I can hardly wait to read it myself."

"There are spoilers I should probably tell you about now. Might make for tough bedtime reading later, if I don't."

"Are you saying I'm not going to like what I read?"

He was looking at the journal as if addressing it. "I can't say I cared for it. Didn't even believe parts of it... but I do now."

"Okay, so spill! What's inside?" She started flipping through it again.

He gently closed the journal by pressing her hand. "Let's get a drink first."

Ashley rose with him and accompanied him to a shoreside cabana with a makeshift bar. He ordered something powerful and vile, but she had another juice. She thought of Calissa up above, and the threat of Katrina coursed back into her. She would want to keep a clear head. Stay sober. No backfiring Affectations.

Spexarth had on sunglasses now, which was a disappointment. She liked his ice gray eyes and his young, high-spirited expressions. The sunglasses made him look like any other tourist. They were good quality sun blockers. They also blocked his expressions from view, and that was the greater disappointment. She liked Spexy, and she wanted to really get his full take on things.

He had come in on the *Murus* and had a lot of questions about Huacachina. They talked on and on about the airship and the fireball. The server brought him a second round before he returned the conversation to the journal. "Mostly it's about 'making amends,' as he calls it."

"Late in life, old man lamentations," she surmised. She expected as much.

He held out his hand, and she passed him the journal. He flipped through, turning the book this way, then that, examining illustrations in particular. "Check this out," he said, spreading it open and sliding it across the table. "Recognize it?"

It was certainly his workmanship. She recognized the same artful hand as in the giant master charts LF had shared again with her recently. This illustration between them, however, was bizarre.

"He's lost his damn mind," she said, but she could not look away.

"If I'm not wrong, that's the *Murus*." Spexarth nodded to himself. "That's proof positive for me that this thing's legit. Even if I don't like it."

"Don't like what? That he's planning to turn the airships into a sprinkler system?"

"May I?" Spexarth asked, then thumbed through the book to a page of text, again in LF's flowing script.

He offered it to her, but she pushed it back. "You read it." She was knotting up. She couldn't help herself. They held the last fragments of her father's genius between them, and it seemed as ragged as the cover. He *was* going crazy, she was sure of it now, and he wasn't even saying goodbye.

Steve Spexarth cleared his throat and read:

"The Air-mada will sweep over highly developed and heavily populated areas first and foremost. This will take a week or more, but they will never see it coming. Yes, there will be unrest from disturbed flight paths, but they will be too soon swept away to think much of it. In a month, virtually every population center of any scale will have been exposed.... he goes on, but you get the drift."

"What is he doing?" Ashley asked herself aloud. Afterall, what would Spexarth know about it... but then..." What has he been doing since we left you on the *Arcus*?"

"He was there, in San Fran, when we tied off," Spexarth began. She heard caution in his voice. "He was frantic when your story was told. LF had to hear it from me, the whole thing about the fight in the airship. About how you died. Demanded details... Not really dad-sad, if you know what I mean? He wasn't weepy. He was—"

"Anxious?" she offered.

"Yeah. Like so full of questions. So busy trying to put it all together. Yeah. Anxious."

"He's always been like that when he's on the job. Not surprised he was back to his old self. The retired hippy act just hasn't been very convincing."

Spexarth removed his sunglasses. He took a long drink.

Ashley saw it. "You didn't find it convincing, either?"

"When you're in the background, you see things, but people don't see you," Spexarth said. "I'm just one of the guys, Miss Winston. Nobody paid me any mind."

"And you saw things?"

"Maybe." He was fidgeting with his sunglasses, then the journal again.

"Steve, what did you see?"

"It didn't add up. The Parkers... LF... No one was all that worked up. They fell into business talk with their lawyers before the *Arcus* was anchored. Succession. Reinstatement." He shrugged and looked at her, "If you don't mind my saying, if you were my girl, I would have been doubled over in grief. They'd have to take me out on a stretcher. But these guys... it's just cold. Just business."

"But publicly, there's been lots of brouhaha about it all. I've been told the Interface was on fire about Sarah's murder. The uncles were devastated, calling for a manhunt. My dad was destroyed, they said."

"Maybe on the Jackchat. Maybe around the cameras and out and about," he nodded. "But I hang out with the drivers and doormen. I drink leftover tea with the tea service staff."

"And?"

"And it sucks," he said. There was more, Ashley knew there was a lot more to unpack in that. Spexarth was more uncomfortable now than at any time she had seen him. He asked the wait staff for a cigar and another round. He made himself look busy rifling through the journal until his drink and smoke arrived. Ashley waited him out. He clipped his cigar. Licked it. Fired it up like he was a death row inmate enjoying his last wish.

"I haven't even told Reed this, remember that. I'm just shooting from the hip. You guys will make more sense of it than I can."

"Let's hear it, Steve. I'm a big girl." She cast out a slim Affectation in his serotonin receptors.

"I think, maybe, they had a plan. I hate to say it, but what if the Parkers had you framed? What if they're all shitting themselves because you *and* Katrina are both missing? They *acted* like they were buying my story—I mean it's the only story anyone has to hang anything on, so I can see why they're believing me—but I think they wanted to tuck you in prison, and I think Katrina's just collateral damage."

"But without either of our bodies, they weren't confident," she nodded.

He nodded back. It was a bitter pill, even considering that this could be the truth, but she found Spexarth straining to share it all, even though it was difficult, even with the Affectation. *He was not lying.*

It sent her through a tailspin. LF had to be involved. How had he been so kind at the Estate? So concerned for her well-being? So angry about the Parkers and TransCorp? Was it all an act? How had LF been so sweet and wispy and spiritual, just the night before? Ashley could not rectify what she was hearing with what she had experienced.

Then again, she wouldn't put anything past the Parkers. Maybe they had forced it on him? Promised him something in return for the *Arcus* murder? She had been told her whole life how devious and underhanded they were—even though she had not experienced this from Sarah, even though she had just begun to doubt TransCorp was anything like she had heard. Now every bad thing she had been told seemed to be slapping her in the face. Could they have ordered a Contract on their own niece like that?

"It's old LF, 'you ask me." He wagged the journal in front of her, spoke quickly now. "*He planned an assassination*. Says so right here. It got all botched up—best laid plans and all that—but he planned *his own assassination*, planned to be killed by a girl he raised just for this one thing. His daughter. Your half-sister." Spexarth patted the book with his hand. "It's all here. Katrina's your sister."

"That's ludicrous... What? Why?" she stood abruptly. She could not read that journal, now or ever. Her father was a lunatic. She shoved it back at him. "Why would he—"

"Botched. I don't know how or why, but he was working it all out in here, and his ultimate and public execution would have cinched it up, according to him."

"Are you saying Katrina was supposed to kill *him* on the *Arcus*, not Sarah? Not me?"

Spexarth puffed on the cigar and shrugged. "Count yourself lucky, I guess."

"Lucky?" she asked. She chuckled through the tears.

"He's still alive, so you can ask him yourself," Spexarth held up a finger with each point. "You're still alive. He seems content that you're alive, happy even, maybe. And... and you have a sister."

"But she's a killing machine," Ashley countered. "My father's a suicidal, megalomaniac unleashing something weird all over the world, and I'm legally dead."

Spexarth held the journal to his chest and folded his arms over it. He looked off in the distance again. A few minutes passed. The cigar grew shorter.

"Mac didn't even know I had this," he said, pointing his chin at the ragged book on his chest. "He said I was supposed to pay you a visit, your orders. I almost forgot. What did you need?"

Ashley was eager to process everything with Rory, maybe even with A-Z and Spexarth, maybe even with Alex and Kelli, altogether. She needed council. Perspective. None of them would give her the long throw, however. No one had the history she needed. No one else was such a company insider. "I need you to bring me someone from Texas, from inside 3dub. It's gotta be on the downlow, and I need him just as soon as possible. Can you do that?"

"Of course."

"Bring me our family attorney," she said, standing. "Kyle DuPree."

"Anything you want, Princess."

43 Deep

Zana had been honest; there were less stairs. This route was natural, and Rory found himself navigating an irregular footpath strewn with cracks and stones. They had not gone far when Zana patted his shoulder. "I have been here. Want me to lead?"

Rory was at once deflated (he wanted to discover!) but at the same time renewed (this truly was a trail of some sort). "I'm fine up here," he said over his shoulder.

"Here then," Zana extended a headlight to him. "It will free your hands."

Rory was glad they were with him, and he knew that even though he was in front, they were leading. He was okay with that. He also knew the Amins were the type who abhorred a conversational or educational vacuum, and it wasn't long until they began explaining what they knew of the place.

The sand above suggested there would be a layer of sandstone. Often this is deep, miles deep. Here, however, that ended with the landing. "Had we taken the stairs," Zana continued, "we would easily see polished stone, perhaps with tiny pinholes the water seeped through, as this was an aquifer. In this path, there is no polish save that from generations—eons—of water. The deeper we go, the more evidences of water."

"Yes, the more porous the stone, as well," Astar said.

"Why two paths?" Rory asked.

"This is scarcely a trail, as you have said. We think this was the original direction, the path of finding. The other came later, for the masses."

"Why didn't they just all use this route, make it more domestic?"

They did not answer his question. Instead, they had an enraptured conversation on the pleasures of following through caves and faults. They exchanged memories of narrow passages and close calls, belly crawls, keyholes, and maze caves.

"In all, Rory Reed, it is the journey which makes this the better way."

"Always," Astar affirmed.

"But why two passages?"

"Ah, someone sometime came to tire of this climbing and twisting"

"Likely a leader who needed to keep his people busy."

"Or *her* people," Astar said. "'Make a short, straight route," Astar imitated an Inca queen. "'I do not care the cost.'"

"Why did you say this was the path of the believer?" Rory asked.

"It is more difficult and deceptive. In the end, it will make a believer of you."

"*At the end*," Zana said. "Surely by then."

Rory continued in front, wondering what the early travelers here had been thinking. They would have carried torches, he suspected. Seeking salt, he supposed, or shelter. Maybe some had ventured here for the sake of exploration, like A-Z would have done a millennia ago.

"In this wide cavern, follow the cairns." Zana's voice was now an echo. The walls had, indeed, given way to a wide cave. His light could not reach the edges before long, but it did reveal a stack of rocks he navigated to, and then just at the edge of lamplight, the next stack.

"Are these your handiwork?" Rory pointed his toe at a cairn as they passed it.

"Oh no," Astar said. He could hear her smile in the reply. "Before our time."

"Just seems they're about a lamplight's range apart."

"Listen to our junior archeologist!" Zana said. He clapped Rory's shoulder. They were walking three abreast now across the wide, flat plain.

"They are beyond candle or torch, yes, but at the fringes of what one might see with a kerosene lamp."

"We could guess then; these rocks may have been put here at the turn of the 20th century."

"You should watch your head, for the ceiling lowers ahead."

Rory was not looking forward to crouching, and he was even less eager to crawl. He would if he must, if it came to it. Something was down here the Amins wanted him to see.

"We have descended a good way," Astar said, encouragingly.

"Here we will begin to feel it," Zana added. "I will lead."

"So, it's more steep?"

"And less like a mountain hike."

"More like a water slide," Astar chuckled. "Without the water."

Rory ducked through a keyhole and quickly learned what they were talking about. For a long, long time, they were scooting on their bottoms, crab walking. He was amazed at their agility for their age, in these awkward passages. Even under greater exertion the two continued to explain. "We are descending a flume, a pipe if you will. The water was fast here. Fought hard here."

"Going up or coming down?" Rory wondered aloud.

"Ah, again, he is asking the good questions!" Astar said.

"Up," Zana said. "Water was pushing up."

"Otherwise, this would be an entirely easier way," she added. "It is as if we are fighting the current, if you can imagine. All the erosion is from below." She directed his attention to a nearby outcropping that was more smooth underneath, a little less polished on the top as they passed it.

At long last they stopped to stand in a massive cavern. Their lights could barely find the walls, and Rory could not see the roof of it at all. He was wandering around, surprised to find sand again underfoot. It looked just like the sand from the desert far above.

In the distance, he saw a glow, and Rory diverted his headlamp, looking then from the edge of his vision to confirm it. He had heard of moonpools and of light penetrating miles below from a network of cracks and fissures... but this seemed unnaturally bright. "Guys," he said, "is that something?"

"You are very good at this," Zana said, joining him as they headed toward it.

"He is a natural," Astar beamed.

The sand became firmer, then was silt. Then they were trekking in ankle-deep water. The blue light reflected on the water, illuminating the cavern walls as they closed in on it. Rory came to see the blue light was at a narrowing place, and here he heard flowing water. The cavern was reduced to a chamber that seemed to end at the blue light, the light at the end of a very long tunnel. This was surely the end of their travels.

He was surprised, however, when drawing near. The bright blue light was not a distant light source down a tunnel. Astar held her arm out in front of him, "Do not pass through," she said, and he realized then something beyond his understanding or belief. It was more like a light source or an illuminated mirror than it was another passage. It was like someone had hung a big glowing mirror on the cave wall.

"What is this?" he asked in a hushed tone.

"Wait until your eyes adjust," Zana said. "Do not look only at the light."

Rory looked at the surface of the water they stood in. It reflected the glow, and that stretched the entire way they had just come. It was something like an underground stream, a shallow, wide river, maybe. He turned his attention back toward the glowing panel, noting that the base of it was in the water, that the stream was flowing right into the light, then disappearing into it. He tipped his head in wonderment but followed the direction of A-Z's lamps to examine the wall the magic mirror was suspended upon.

He could see that the walls had been immersed in water. He could just make out what may have been a waterline, almost a ridge, some thirty feet overhead. Above that, the stone was different, not as smooth.

"Yes, you see it," Zana said, also craning his neck to trace the line with his headlamp projection. "We believe that is the normal depth of this river."

"What's that?" Rory asked, pointing both his headlamp and finger to an artificial looking part of the stone wall. It was above the waterline, centered over the blue light mirror...a large, smooth wall that reminded him of a chalkboard, though it was made from the native stone. "It looks...like it's been sandblasted out of the cave wall or something."

"Let us take a closer look," Astar said, gesturing to a makeshift ladder. It was easy for him to have missed it, having been drawn to the light and not noticing the rest of the chamber. A crack possibly twenty feet to the left of the blue light hosted decaying rungs as thick as his arm. Astar scurried up the ladder, then Zana.

"Come, Rory Reed. Come up and get your answers," Astar called from a landing above.

He put his hands on the waterlogged rungs and pulled himself up the ladder. He needed some answers. His head was not able to keep up. How long had this ladder been submerged here? How was it still intact? How had anyone put it here, and why?

"Now we are at a place where men have spent more time," Zana said once Rory was standing with them. The landing was substantial, disappearing into the black beyond, ending at the edge of the chamber wall that hosted the river, now just a trickle below illuminated by the blue glow. Scattered across the landing were remnants of wooden structures, some of it looked to have been furniture. The floor was littered with other things that did not hold his attention, papers, trash, scraps of cloth.

"We believe there was once a natural outcropping that directed the river's flow here to this wall for a great while."

"Over lifetimes," Zana said. "It has smoothed the stone. But that is not the most interesting thing."

"It is the words here," Astar said.

"Words?" Rory asked.

Zana sparked up a phosphorous light that nearly blinded Rory. A-Z were ghostly, paled from the phosphorescent glow. When his eyes adjusted, the upper part of the chamber where they were perched shuddered gray-white in the light. The smooth wall was fully illuminated now. It looked like an alley wall that had been scrawled on for generations. Characters and symbols danced in the eerie fluttering lamplight. Shapes of animals, ancient petroglyphs, seemed animated.

"Wow," was all Rory could say.

"Yes, and all of this came long after the water receded, after it quit splashing there on the wall."

"We are not linguists," Astar said. "Much of what we have read, we may have read into it. It tells the story of a source of healing, deep below, the source of this river, we think."

"We followed the river back to the pool Astar spoke of, which we have been probing."

"The one with the serpent that ate my anchor," Astar sprung on her toes as she talked. "It is written right there, of the water dragon." She was aiming her headlamp and a flashlight at a serpentine symbol.

"Bah!" Zana's voice echoed. "Not all in myth and fairy tale is true, Astar."

"Another time, Zanantho Amin!" she said firmly. Then composing her smile, she continued, "So you see, Rory Reed, this is quite a find!"

"A healing source?" He questioned. "A dragon?"

Something within him winced a little, as if Ashley were there, giving him a little zap. Hadn't he just joked about slaying dragons, not an hour ago at the stairs?

"Every culture has the stories of magic elixirs, healing waters. Fountains of Youth," Zana said flatly. "Obviously we have stumbled onto one of those stories."

"You may doubt some of it. We may, again, have been liberal in our interpretations. However, the English is clear enough."

"English?" Rory squinted at her, then the wall again. He walked as close as the landing allowed, still twenty feet or more away. He wished for a good, strong halogen flood lamp. As he studied the wall, shielding his eyes from the light Zana held, he could see it now, superimposed over all the other languages etched in stone.

"*No turning back,*" he read aloud. It looked as if it were written in chalk. Scratched into the wall with some sharp object, time after time. The most recent layer was painted in what could only be blood.

"There is more, here," Astar pulled something from a pile of clothes on the cave floor. "It was tossed all about. I hid it for safekeeping."

She handed him a crumpled collection of handwritten pages. Rory held them up to the light. The writing was in an elaborate and distinctive script. He had seen it before. It was the same as the flowing, stylized logo of *Winston Water Works* recognized the world over. It was LF Winston's handwriting!

Time stood still as Rory flipped pages. "What's it all mean?"

He read through quickly, hearing LF's voice in all the jumble of words.

I will make amends for all our wrongdoing. The hardship will be worth it.

Worthwhile for the worthy.

I will rectify the world's greed and set straight the suffering.

Though difficult, this path is the righteous one.

At last, the world will know peace.

Though it could not be possible, Rory felt the same Affectation as he had in the Winston's wine cellar that night LF had shared with him. He felt the sorrow, the betrayal... and something new in these words. Hope.

"Many of the stories here are predictions," Zana pointed back to the graffiti wall.

"Prophesies," Astar said. "They tell of a time to come when the healing will leave from here."

"Not *leave*," Zana said, noting Rory's expression. "Go from here. Be shared out."

"*Rain down upon the earth*," Rory recalled from the pages in his hand. He looked down at the blue white glowing stream. "*This* water?"

"Yes," Zana nodded. "All of this," he gestured again at the wall, "*forecasts* it."

"Forecasts," Rory mulled it over. "Forecast calls for rain, then?"

"This is what Levi Finn Winston must believe," Astar said. "He believes in the prophecy."

Rory frowned and pawed through the loose pages again. "He thinks he is fulfilling a prophecy? With his Rainmakers?"

"Vainglorious, no?" Zana said.

"No, maybe not!" Rory turned his full attention to the wall. Beneath the English, he could make out some Spanish, and beneath that, in larger, faded symbols, wide-winged birds with flaming tails. Always to their right, no matter where they were on the wall, Rory noted streaks and stripes coursing down... like rain. And the rain was flooding lots and lots of circles. Layers and layers of circles all crowding down thick at the slab's waterline. Circles... figures of two-dimensional faces that all looked so contented. They all looked the same, all the faces from all the generations of illustrations. They were all happy.

"One mind," he said softly.

"LF Winston has loaded his airship with this water, as we know," Astar said, "and it replenishes at the source, at the dragon's pool."

"A spring," Zana said. "It is water replenished from the mountains. The spring is overflowing, but this—" he pointed below to the chamber with the stream, "this is no longer the cistern it was."

"Stealing the water is a sacrilege," Astar said. "In this, the Winstons cannot be forgiven. They no more own this than they do the sky."

"He sucked it dry," Rory said. "But he might be coming back for more?"

"All for his ridiculous fantasy," Zana said. "All of this, sullied and lost."

"But the water's coming back up, right?" Rory asked, still piecing it all together.

"It might have," Astar said.

"In its natural state," Zana added. "We believe there was a natural exit, a drain hole. Perhaps the water recirculated. Perhaps it went somewhere else entirely."

"Now, it goes through that!" Astar spat the words. "And we know not where from there."

"Through that..." Rory was reeling with ideas. If water was flowing through it to some other location... could it be a portal? He had seen whole battalions deployed through TransCorp's big portals, and they had flashed light with every man, woman and weapon that passed through. He had not seen a *continuous* port before. Maybe with the steady flow of water it would glow constantly.

"How? Could it be a portal?" Rory asked aloud now, interrupting his own illogical thinking. He looked from Astar to Zana. "There's nothing there, just a glowing hole in the wall."

"It is as we have told you. There are other ports, illegal, rogue ports."

"Priceless, dangerous ports that TransCorp would stop at nothing to eliminate."

The three of them stood on the lip of the landing, looking down at the glowing light as it absorbed the underground stream.

"The stairs. The tube. They're upstream from here?" Rory asked, finally.

"Yes, the siphoning was done at the spring," Zana said.

"Is it hard to get up here from there?"

"We have just taken the way, though much of it is usually underwater." Astar said.

"How did people get up here, then?"

"I led us past the chimney that leads here."

"Oh, I do not like the chimney climbs," Astar said.

Before they could reminisce, Rory pressed on, "So LF knew the 'narrow way,' and the chimney... but who else? Who put that portal down there? And *after* the *Murus* sucked it dry? *After* LF left on his airship?"

"I do not know the nature of these Hot Wires," Zana ventured, "but maybe, at great personal peril, Mr. Winston himself could have brought it in at the depths, at the drain, and ignited it there."

"A seventy-year-old man swam in, fought the current, turned on a portal, and climbed out alive?" Rory asked.

"He might be a fine specimen for his age," Zana said, defensively. "I could do it."

"Oh yes, you are such a superman," Astar said sarcastically.

"Escaping against the current would be challenging. Opening such a large exit would have created a mighty whirlpool."

"The water would have been freezing cold too." Astar shook her head. "With no wetsuit, how could he have survived?"

"What if he *didn't* go against the current? What if he went with the flow?" Rory asked. "Did anyone see him board the *Murus* this morning?"

"We were asleep," Zana said.

"Only a very few went back aboard," Astar said with curiosity and excitement in her voice. "Most of his crew remain in Huacachina."

"And we were here before even the narrow way was dry. There would have been only a slim chance we would have missed someone on their way out this morning."

"That is right. We were here before breakfast."

Rory was eyeing the glowing blue light. "No turning back," he rumbled softly.

"You are not thinking of going through that foul thing!" Astar exclaimed.

"Got a better idea?" he asked, handing her the journal pages.

"You do not know that this may dump water off an airship, casting you to the heavens."

"What a way to go," Rory smiled. It was not his way. He would never leap before looking at every angle. He was a man who knew the known and calculated the risk. He had a daughter to take care of.

Still, he pressed Astar's buttons. "You said this was our last adventure. Right?"

"You are an imbecile," she huffed.

"Maybe all seven of us should make the leap?" he continued. "We're all in this together."

"A child," she scoffed.

"Our choices are few," Zana said. Rory thought he was only half-kidding by his tone. "We cannot wait for another airship, for with that thing in operation, another ship may never come."

"We will not go through that portal," Astar stated flatly. "We will fly after Mr. Winston with McIntyre, on the *Whipstitch*," she said decisively. "I will fly the plane myself, if I must."

"But love," Zana said, "We don't know where to go."

By that reasoning, the unreasonable seemed the only way. He wondered if Zana truly meant it, but the phosphorus light was fading, and he could not see Zana's face well-enough to read his features.

"I think I know where to go," Alex said, waltzing in from the dark edges of the landing.

"How do you keep doing that?!" Rory asked. He holstered his gun, not even realizing he had drawn it.

"Took the chimney," he said, thumbing over his shoulder. "And I'm good in the dark."

44 Truce

Ashley's rooms were a comfort. Giant windows welcomed a gentle breeze that ruffled the sheers. The canopy bed looked fit for the queen of the desert. She curled up in bed, inhaling Rory's cologne still lingering on the pillow. This was the place they'd had their mind meld, and she longed to be so close to him again. It was getting late, and he was still not around. She wished she could have an out of body experience and somehow wend her way to him, wherever he was.

She pictured Rory and Calissa back at his apartment, laughing over morning coffee. Then she saw him playing catch with her. Then the three of them were racing along city streets, Calissa at the wheel. Ashley was lucid dreaming now. She reimagined Rory at the wheel, herself at his side. Calissa was not in the picture. Ashley put her in the back seat, chattering on and on. They were on the *Arcus* then, the three of them again admiring the Rainbands. Calissa brushed them both aside and dived off the tail of the airship without a word.

She woke abruptly, and Calissa was looming over her bed. The teen swung a heavy floor lamp at her, just missing her head! Ashley struggled with the sheets and was unable to miss the second strike. The heavy wooden lamp struck hard against her collar bone.

This was no dream. Calissa pulled the lamp back to hit her again, but Ashley sprung to her feet on the far side of the bed. "What are you doing?!"

Calissa jumped onto the bed and swung wildly again with the lamp. It crashed against the headboard, giving Ashley just an instant to Affect her.

The girl's legs collapsed, and the lamp fell free. Calissa flopped to the floor and hit her head hard on the tile. Then, to Ashley's amazement, it was Katrina, not Calissa, growling, shaking off the Affectation.

Ashley had little time to spin up another Affectation. It caused Katrina to wretch, a harsh series of heaves, and vomit spewed from her. In a split second between the contractions, Katrina hit her back with an Affectation of her own: confusion.

Ashley could not keep her balance. She felt the vertigo wash over her, then she did not even know up from down until she crashed into a bedpost. She was picking herself up when Katrina kicked her hard in the ribs.

Ashley was furious. She cast a violent Affectation into Katrina, one causing her to scream and cry. Katrina shrieked and tried to hide her eyes.

"Serves you right, bitch!" Ashley said, getting more firmly to her feet. She palmed both sides of Katrina's head and squeezed, boring into her with a fierce headache. If she kept it up, Katrina would suffer severe cerebral edema.

Katrina's nails dug into Ashley's forearms. "Truce!" she screamed. "Truce!"

Ashley glared at the woman's eyes. Was she serious?

Then Katrina was LF Winston begging for his life.

Then she was Rory, commanding her to stop.

Ashley did not want to kill her, did not want to inflict permanent brain damage, but this fight felt so good. She had so much power over the murderer. She squeezed with all her might but did not press the Affectation harder. Then, with the tiniest faltering, Katrina had a break, and she was herself again, and then she lashed at Ashley with a blinding Affectation.

Ashley tripped, letting go of her victim, unable to even get a grip on her again.

But she heard more fumbling around, too.

Stumbling.

Katrina was also blinded. The damage to her brain had caused her Affectation to backfire. *Works both ways when one is not right in the head,* Ashley realized again.

She felt around frantically, listening to Katrina growl and pant, then they collided in blind fury and punched and clawed at each other. They fell over a low object—a coffee table?—and Katrina took the brunt of their fall to the floor.

Still, she had Ashley by the hair, and she was slamming her head against the tiles. Ashley couldn't eke out an Affectation and feared if she did that it would backfire. The blindness was all the more disorienting, and the compounded Affectations were unrelenting. She felt herself struggling to keep her wits about her, to stay conscious. The pain was excruciating. Her collar. Her ribs. Now her head.

Both of them gasped for air, sweating and bleeding and grappling for advantage.

Ultimately, they ended up in a violent and powerful tangle of limbs, a wrestling death match that deteriorated into aimless, blind grunting and twisting. They were equally matched in this deadlock, and they held each other tightly, just waiting for the other to make another move. Countering that move. Pressing another tactic.

Then they were both exhausted and could hardly even flex against one another.

"Truce," Ashley offered past the arm that choked her. "For real?"

"Truce," Katrina agreed.

Seconds passed as they gauged each other's sincerity. They gradually relaxed their grips, in turn. Breathing eventually returned to normal. Ashley could see starbursts, then shapes, and then her sight faded back into focus. They untangled and scooted a few yards apart.

Ashley licked the blood from her top lip. She was shocked at what she had done. Katrina's black hair had been pulled out by the fistful and was mixed in the blood between them on the tile floor. Her face was already swelling on the left cheekbone. Vessels in Katrina's eyes had burst, leaving them red. Tears streamed down her face with the blood from a head wound.

The room was a wreck. One of the bedposts was cockeyed. The coffee table was destroyed. The curtains and canopy had been torn down. A chair was toppled.

"You fight like a girl," Katrina snarled and spat blood.

"You fight like an animal," Ashley sneered. "No skill at all."

"You gave up first," Katrina said.

"You said 'truce' first."

Katrina scoffed, then chuckled.

Ashley chuckled, too.

The two of them laughed and laughed.

They laughed uproariously, as if under Affectation, unable to catch their breaths. Tears welled from Ashley's eyes with all the laughing. Her stomach cramped from all the laughing. Still, neither woman could stop.

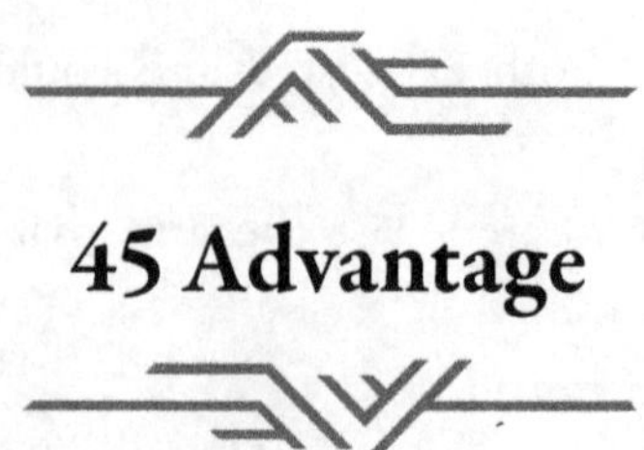

45 Advantage

"The age-old question is, do we think, or do we act, am I right?" Alex smiled at them.

"There is nothing wrong with *thought out action*," Astar argued.

"Astar, hang on to your knickers, doll: I agree with you!" He chuckled and continued, "We all know, Alex Gault is a man of action," he said of himself. "However, Rory, have you thought of the children?"

"What children?" Rory blinked hard.

"Why, our children, pal! We've never been so close to making all our dreams come true." He feigned punching Rory in the arm. "The love of my life is waiting for me back at the hotel. Yours is too. We've never had it so good."

"Alex, I don't think you're quite caught up on—"

"Lest we forget, I *brought* you here... all of you," Alex said, pacing now. "What was it I told you on the plane, Astar?"

"I believe you said that this was some End of The World shit, if I were—"

"Exactly. And Rory, who's known you longer than me? Nobody. When I got a snootful of Winston's big scheme, I knew it was right up your alley. And I was right, wasn't I?" He was at the edge of the landing, gesturing wildly at the wall of words, "If this doesn't scream 'One World,' I dunno what does!"

"Alex," Zana said firmly, "the time to be coy is past. We are here, and we are committed to this. As the wall says, it seems there is no returning."

"You said you knew where we should go next?" Rory asked.

"How could you possibly know where this leads?" Astar exclaimed, pointing at the portal.

"Oh. I have no idea where that goes," he waved it off. "But I've found the *Undulatus*."

"I didn't know it was lost," Rory said.

"You really do need to Jack in more, guys. I don't know how you ever keep up. The deal is, nobody could find it. Downed in the ocean—of all places, all the conjecture—the Interface claims it crashed in the Bermuda Triangle!"

"I do not see how a wrecked airship is any help in finding Mr. Winston," Zana said.

"Or in finding where the water is going," Astar added.

"I found her, that's the main thing, and you're not going to believe the rest."

"I seldom do," Rory sighed.

"Everyone was looking where CommCorp reported. No one was thinking for themselves. They were thinking the *Undulatus* was an airplane or a rocket or something. They were thinking straight."

The three waited. Finally, Rory asked, "And yet?"

"That was their problem: thinking straight. An airship is not a rocket. An airship is alive, man, breathing in and out, riding thermals, tacking this way, that way." He simulated the motions, cutting across the landing to the left, the right, the left again. "Like a sailboat, not a damn tugboat."

"Okay..." Rory said.

"So, who do you know who never thinks straight? Me, right?"

Astar chuckled, "Yes, of course."

"So, I did a little calculus. I'm not a meteorologist, but I can follow a front. I can take it all into consideration. If I were a bird, like a condor, where would I have gone—that's what I asked myself. How would I get there? That's what I wondered. You can ask Kelli, I was swooping around her place in Franklin, getting into the spirit—"

"Alex. What's the point here?"

"So, I found the *Undulatus*. She's hidden in a huge tropical storm a thousand miles from Bermuda. Those CommCorp clowns didn't have a clue."

Alex strutted now, burning off energy as he spoke. "I think they just picked the Bermuda Triangle because it sounded good, and because, frankly, who cares about one Rainmaker—well, I guess the route it flew might be getting a little dry, but honestly—"

"Alex!"

"Right. Anyway, it gets better."

Rory sighed. Always with the drama. "What else?"

"Guys, *every freaking airship* has been over that *exact spot* in the last week. All of them, over a hundred of them, just happen to fly through the same impenetrable storm within seven days of another?"

Rory was impressed.

Astar and Zana looked perplexed.

"We didn't get to do a proper intervention out here. Hell, we didn't even really know what he was up to. But I can tell you this: 3dub's got a base out there in that storm, and I'd bet my fiancé that's where you'll find LF Winston and the *Murus* and your answers."

For maintenance training, generally for rucking, and training Calissa how to outmaneuver an adversary over a long stretch, Rory had depended on a conversational pace. Mild exertion but never so much that a conversation couldn't be held. Alex was capitalizing on this pace, talking the entire time.

Before their return trip in the narrow way, Alex recommended they leave that portal just as it was. To dismantle it, he said, would tip their hand. LF would know they were onto him.

Then, the whole way back up, Alex carried on and on, offering details on his formula for finding the *Undulatus*, telling them how he theorized 3dub must have suspended a storm in place—it had not moved in weeks, best he could tell—for this massive rendezvous site. He talked about how impressive LF's planning had to have been, and how challenging it would have been to work all the vessels off course. "Guy must have a lot of charisma," he said over his shoulder in a fissure. "Got a lot of loyalty out of those ship captains."

Rory was dwelling on that very thing. They all had to be in on it, all totaled, 400 crewmembers. If what he had seen on the Arcus was any indication, they were lifers, having served under LF Winston before he had disappeared and fallen from grace. To sustain that commitment from so many for so long was remarkable, an indication of brilliant leadership... or more evidence of the cult-like following he suspected.

"...we were welcome here, anyway. Isn't that right, Astar?"

"Yes—"

"Yes, even though it was clear we weren't locals, and we weren't quite *with* the old man, either. They just welcomed us in, acted like we belonged here."

"Alex!" Rory called to him from the back of the line. "Alex. Did they seem a little complacent to you?"

"Complacent? I dunno. Place seemed like a vacant tourist trap. They're happy to have some guests, maybe."

"It is as if they knew of last night's plan well in advance," Zana noted. "The *Murus* crew, even your men, Rory, seemed ready to rally everyone to the task."

"The locals were like, have a beer and enjoy the show, yeah. Then most of them threw in and helped with the hose thing," Alex said. "Like it was nothing out of the ordinary."

"Or that they had trained for it," Rory said. "And they could care less who witnessed the whole thing, no matter how strange or spectacular it was."

Alex went on to share how Huacachina was like a black hole when it came to CommCorp's coverage. There hadn't been a blip on the Interface about the place in years. He thought there was some kind of geofence around it and Ica too. In terms of coverage, it was as if the area was quarantined. He talked about how when he first lifted the coordinates, he thought they were a mistake, for the area had seemed so unremarkable. "Winston took them right out of the public eye," he said, "as if the place never existed."

"Hence the carefree attitude," Astar said. "They bring in a *Murus* and burn brightly all the night with it and never worry about detection."

"Brazen," Zana said.

The conversation turned to Kelli Chase. Alex extolled her virtues for a good fifteen minutes. He sounded like a lovesick teen to Rory, but it made him smile.

"Know what's better than the sex?"

Rory and A-Z all groaned in protest, but he continued. "Wrestling. I kid you not. That girl is double tough. I never had a girlfriend who could pin me, beat me at arm wrestling, leg wrestling, you name it. She's a beast."

"Beauty and the Beast," Zana smirked.

"You know that's right," Alex said. He spoke on and on about her, how she was a dynamic leader in Franklin, well-respected and commanding the respect of her citizenry. At Astar's prompting, Alex went in to how he finally won her hand. As Rory expected, it was unconventional.

"The way to a man's heart is his stomach," Alex said. "But to a woman's? It is to be of use. She had no use for me when she was trying to rally everyone in the town clean up. Too busy for love."

"That is tragic," Astar said. "I believe she spent far too much of her life this way."

"I fixed that," Alex replied. He told them how he resolved their rolling black outs, how he ultimately got Franklin wired like a true suburb, not the skirts. Still, she ignored him, scarcely giving him the time of day for his efforts.

So, he sabotaged his own work.

She would come to call on him for help, time after time. She had seen the benefits of bringing her town into a better standard of living, and the pride in Franklin was reaching new heights. Then, when her attention returned to community building and city infrastructure, another blackout would follow. Ultimately, she caught him disabling the grid, and putting two and two together, Kelli realized resisting him would do little good. They arrived at an agreement, and she came to trust him when the lights stayed on consistently.

"Still sticks with candles herself, though. I think she doesn't want to depend on my help. That's another thing I love about her. Independent as hell."

When they finally reached the landing that hosted the stairs down to the springs, Rory had them huddle up. "Guys, this one's getting dicey. I'm running out of people to trust. I'm not sure of much, outside of the three of you."

"We are, as always, in it with you to the quick," Astar said.

"In it to win it, pal," Alex said.

Zana nodded, but he looked at the floor more than at Rory.

"What is it, old friend?" Rory asked.

"I long for a simpler time, that is all."

"When good and evil were black and white?" Rory asked.

"Yes, and when it was just the four of us without a care. If we were to be found out, even executed, that was the extent of it. Now... I am glad this is our last mission, that you will grant us this graceful exit."

"It was a terrible burden to carry the town of Franklin on our conscience," Astar added.

"And now, it feels, the world," Zana said.

"If only we knew the consequences would not be too heavy to bear," Astar said. Her eyes panned over Alex, then continued. "All that is to come would be more tolerable."

Rory sighed. "We'll pull through, and we'll pull the whole world along with us, if it comes to that."

The Amins' flashlight beams bobbed as they nodded vigorously.

Rory glanced at Alex, who was surprisingly quiet. "You good?"

"Sure, sure," he said with a shrug.

"Let's pack it in for the day, then," Rory said, starting up the stairs to the church.

"Hey," Alex said, "why don't I show you the dragon pool?"

"It is a sight," Astar said, "but I do not recommend swimming in it."

"More with your fabled dragon," Zana said. "Let it go, Astar."

"I will take my monster to our room," Astar said, pulling at Zana's arm. "He is tired and hungry, and we have seen the pool."

The two trudged up the stairs, arguing in another language. Rory smiled as they climbed the stairs. By the top, he knew, they would surface to be the kind and cool A-Z the rest of the world knew them to be. That was all the longer their arguments ever lasted, and they never held grudges. He wondered idly if he and Ashley had such chemistry.

Even if they did not, she could boil his brains with an Affectation should he get too far out of line.

46 I Have Never

"I have never... eaten caviar," Katrina said.

Ashley put down another finger. She only held up two now. "That's hardly fair, knowing how I grew up. I still know nothing about you."

She felt Katrina's shoulder shrug against her. "This is how you learn."

They were lying on the floor, side by side, staring up at the ceiling fan, a cabana fan with broad blades that circled slowly. Rory would be counting the revolutions, Ashley thought, and she felt a pang of missing him again.

"I have never..." Ashley was having trouble with the game. It seemed there was very little she had not done. "...never been to Panama."

"Panama!" Katrina exclaimed. "How did you know I have been there?"

"Typical TransCorp land grab, I figure," Ashley said. "You tried to buy the canal, didn't you?"

"Yet you already owned it through some proxy," Katrina said.

"Yeah," Ashley said. "Put down a finger."

"I still have three to your two."

"How long have you known I was your sister?"

"All of my life," Katrina said. "When did you learn?"

"Today," Ashley said. "Spexarth told me."

"Really?" Katrina propped herself on an elbow. "And how did he know this?"

"He read about you in our dad's journal."

Katrina flopped on her back again and let out an exasperated sigh.

"Does that bother you?"

"Who knows what that man has written about me? It may not be a word of truth," Katrina said. "And now the journal is being read like gospel...and by *him*!"

"I dunno," Ashley said. She worked at a loose tooth with her tongue.

It was quiet between them for a while.

"I have never been chipped," Katrina said at last.

"Neither have I," Ashley said.

"Really? That is good," Katrina said. "That surprises me."

"I'm full of surprises," Ashley replied. "And... I have never made my bed."

Katrina put down a finger. "That does not surprise me."

There was no Affectation between them. Ashley wasn't kidding herself, either. There was no long-lost sisterhood, either. The woman next to her had still killed Sarah Parker, and that was unforgivable. She had started a fight, too, and that had not ended well for either of them.

Still, it was something to be equally matched. To feel the end of a hard-fought battle and not be full of regret or loss. The giddiness was a first for her.

"I have never been in love," Katrina said softly.

Ashley hesitated, then begrudgingly put down her index finger. She waved her middle finger in Katrina's face. Trying to lighten the mood, she said, "How is that possible? Were you raised in a *convent* or something?"

"An orphanage, and then an all-girls school. And then when I thought I was in love, I learned it was forbidden."

"Forbidden?" Ashley turned her head to look at Katrina.

"I was not allowed to love him," Katrina said faintly, her eyes fixed on the fan.

"But you *did* love him. You were in love!" Ashley said. "You're cheating."

"Unrequited love is not being in love. It is hell."

Ashley thought that over. The more thought she gave it, the more she felt for Katrina. Finally, she felt she had an experience just as solemn and sincere, and she said, "I have never really known my father."

"You expect me to put down a finger?"

"He's been out of my life most of my life," Ashley said. She tried to prop her elbow, but her collar hurt too much. She sat up.

Katrina sat up too. "Being around him is not knowing him."

"You know him better than I do," Ashley said.

"Consider yourself fortunate in this," Katrina scoffed and put down a finger.

It was two to one.

"What was it like, being around him?" Ashley asked. "I mean, I only knew him when I was a kid, and even then, he was... larger than life."

"Yes," she said thoughtfully, "he is larger than life."

"Even when he was in hiding?"

"He told me of the beginning, when he was taken in by the orphanage. When he was our groundskeeper. Those times, maybe, he was small... but when I was on holiday from school, and when I would travel with him through college—he was fantastic."

The way she said it made Ashley ache. She knew the eccentric and anxious LF Winston but not a *fantastic* one. She wondered what that man had been like. Clever. Evading the law with some fanciful maneuver. Thumbing his nose at convention.

"I have never known my mother," Katrina said, and struggled to her feet, knowing she had won. "She died giving birth to me."

Ashley got up, too, wincing in pain. She was still somewhat woozy. "Game and match," she admitted. "Now tell me the rest of your story."

"As I have said, there is nothing of interest to tell. Besides, you lost, so I owe you nothing."

"I think you owe me an explanation, at least," Ashley said. "Why did you attack me?"

"I have been told to." She sat at the foot of the bed. She seemed to struggle with her balance too. Katrina looked away. "I have been forced to. I am sorry."

"But you're not chipped. You have free will. Who could make you do anything?"

"I have been programmed," she said, wiping a tear. "It is a terrible thing, Ashley, when you are doing something against your own will and you are well-aware, yet helpless."

"You're about the least helpless person I've ever known."

"I may fight—"

"You fought off the drugs for weeks on end. Who has that kind of willpower?"

"I do this to have some control. I fear I would do worse if I succumbed to the drugs, or to sleep, or to anything that would leave me to my programming."

"I have to ask," Ashley said, "just what are you programmed to do? Kill me?"

"It is bigger than that," she said. "I am to *unstop TransCorp in any and every way.* The programming that you have relieved me from, if even for this little while," she gestured at the back of her head, "is unequivocal. It is broad and open to interpretation, but when obstacles present themselves to the successes of TransCorp, I cannot do anything short of clearing them."

"*TransCorp*?" Ashley wasn't following.

"Yes," Katrina said, leveling her eyes at Ashley.

"What of dad, old LF Winston, then?"

"I am not certain, but I believe the programming is his handiwork." She smiled bitterly then and pulled a blood-matted patch of hair away from her temple, revealing the scar. "And I cheated. *I am chipped.* The programming is not just behavioral. I think I could beat that. It is bio-electric. The pain is unbearable when I resist. When you did that to my head, when my head was swimming, I was relieved. But... I fear I will again resort to attempts on your life. I cannot do otherwise."

"Well," she said grimly, "we'll just have to short you out, is all."

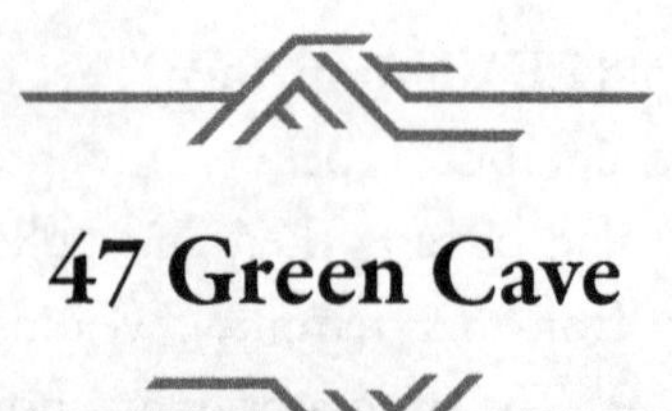

47 Green Cave

"If you turn your light off here, you'll see you don't really need it," Alex said, just ahead in the dark.

Rory fumbled with his headlamp, shut it off, and then his flashlight, too. To his amazement, the tunnel walls and stairs were luminescent. Everything took on a milky green glow. "Is... is it all like this?"

"Nah, just the closer we get to the pool," Alex was a negative space now, a shadow moving in the green. "And it's just up ahead."

Rory followed along, keeping his sights on Alex's shape. As his eyes adjusted, he could make out more detail, and finally, he could see well from the glow alone. In a few hundred yards, they rounded another bend, and then they were in a chamber that felt humid. He could just see the surface of the water lapping against the stairs that leveled out into a shoreline.

"Dragon or not, this place feels... mystical, don't you think?" his voice startled Rory from his awe. He had no idea how long they had moved through the tunnels in silence. No idea. It surprised him that he'd been ignorant of his internal clock, that he had not even been counting stairs.

"Magical!" Rory said.

"Sit with me," Alex said, situating himself on a rock outcropping that was smoothed from generations of people sitting just as he was now.

Rory joined him, and together they looked at the emerald water.

"You believe in magic, Rory?"

"Didn't use to."

"But then...?"

"Ashley Elizabeth Winston," Rory said, his baritone reverberating in the cave.

"I know, right? Love is magical."

"That's not what I mean, and you know it. Before I met her, I would have doubted anyone had supernatural powers. Now I take her Affectations for granted."

"To say nothing of the magic hanky," Alex added.

"That too," Rory nodded. "Why'd you ask? Are you going to tell me Astar's dragon is down there?"

"That would be something," Alex said, suddenly solemn. "I think this is bigger."

"Bigger than a dragon?"

Alex nodded, glanced at Rory, and groaned. "Know why I like tech?"

"The money?"

"No."

"The women?"

"No. No. Just listen," Alex said. "I like tech because it's magical, but it's also practical. There is no supernatural in tech, but it seems like it, eh?"

"Sometimes, yeah."

"I think it's like that with the Family, by the way. Not technical, but not magical either. Maybe biological. *That's it.* They have a biological advantage. Something that lets them do more with their minds."

"Glad we could come here to work that through, Alex." Rory smiled.

"In the same way the Family can do that, what if other people have distinct technological advantages? You know, new tech nobody's even thought of yet."

"I'd say if no one has thought of it, then they can't have the tech, can they?"

Alex cleared his throat, changed his tone, and tried another question. "What if I could tell you that everything you suspect about that water is true?"

"I'd ask you how you think you know what I suspect."

"Just play along for a minute."

"Okay, I guess I could believe you knew what I suspected because you were at the restaurant when Chavez and the waitress went on about the water."

Alex just listened. It was so out of character. Rory worried his friend had bumped his head in the caves, but he continued, "And I know you're good at getting the drop on people. You could have heard me visiting with A-Z about the whole thing back at the port."

"You also suspect it might not seem such a terrible thing that maybe Winston's finally figured out how to bring about One World."

"Again, Chavez said that... and LF was carrying on, himself, how that water will *build up and tear down walls*. You could have been in earshot anytime."

"Right. Right."

"And, well, you know me better than anyone, Alex. You'd know what I think about that water. You'd know I'm not all butterflies and unicorns about corporate technology, but I'm a Turncoat, underneath it all, so... yeah, I'm still a holdout for One World, one day."

"So that's what you suspect, and maybe I did hear all that, infer some of that, but how do I *know* if that's all true?"

"Huh." Rory shook his head. "I don't know, Alex. Maybe you tapped some secure files at the Estate or something. Read up on it. Followed the science."

"Nope."

"LF told you?"

"No."

"Experiments?"

They both chuckled dryly. Alex was always one to experiment with any substance, from licking frogs to doing acid. Maybe he had gone swimming in this dragon pool?

"The only way I could confirm your suspicions was if I'd seen the result of dropping that water and lived to tell about it."

"Uh... the result hasn't happened yet."

"Exactly," Alex said, bracing himself. He physically pulled away from Rory, as if expecting to be swatted to the floor.

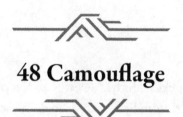

48 Camouflage

Katrina had left with apologies and forewarning, but one thing she could assure Ashley of, by no manner of imagination or interpretation, was Calissa a threat to TransCorp. She had no reason to worry that Katrina would harm her.

That wasn't much assurance. What threat had TransCorp's CEO posed to the company?

She struggled to her feet, wincing at the pain in her ribs. She still suffered from some vertigo. Ashley wondered if she had taken too many hits to the head. When she tried to prop herself on a door frame, pain blasted from her collarbone. She was in no shape to get help, but what if she didn't? Katrina could be driven to kill them all if prodded by her implant.

"Rory Reed, where are you?" she said aloud to an empty room.

She glanced at her nightstand, knowing it was a futile idea. While standard-issue everywhere she ever stayed, there wasn't even a utility model of HeadGear here. The whole town was offline. Even if HeadGear had worked in Huacachina, she could not have reached him.

The piously unplugged were sometimes aggravatingly inaccessible.

Ashley hobbled to her windows overlooking the village. Across the little lake, some partiers from Ica were singing in the bar. A few people were out for a stroll. Lights were coming on in preparation for an evening of relaxed revelry. She wondered if she called out from her balcony, would someone come to her aid?

Then it dawned on her that no one had so much as opened the door to check on her during the fight with Katrina. Rory's security people had not gotten lax, had they? There was always someone stationed at her quarters, protecting the Princess.

"Could have at least shot me up with a pain killing over-ride," Ashley grumbled, thinking of the rush Katrina had been in. Even had it backfired or affected both of them, it would have boosted their synaptic norepinephrine, numbed them both some.

Opening the door, her worst fears were confirmed. A man was down in the hall. Urine had pooled at his waist, and he smelled terrible. "Scared the shit out of you, didn't she?" Ashley said, crouching carefully at his side. His pulse was strong, and at just her touch, without the slightest Affectation, his eyes fluttered open.

"Miss Winston!" he said in surprise. He sat up and looked up and down the hall. He gingerly poked at the back of his head, likely where he had hit it when falling. His eyes fell to his pants, and realizing his mess, he cursed. More surprise. "I was... she just..."

"It's okay," she said as she emitted a touch of calming through her hand on his shoulder. "Slow down and tell me what happened."

"Conard came by. Left his post here to tell me he was going for a swim. A swim!" he shook his head. "By the time I got to station, it sounded... busy... in your room."

"Busy?" Ashley frowned.

The man was fumbling with his words. "Yes, ma'am. And we've been told if you're in quarters to leave you alone."

"Busy how?"

He was fully blushing now and unable to look her in the eyes. "Well... I thought it was foreplay. You know, roughhousing."

Ashley raised an eyebrow, wondering if Kat had put that idea in his head, or if he, too, had hit his head a little too hard. "Foreplay?"

"Yes'm. Then, next thing I knew, that rehab girl was busting out at me, and I blacked out."

"What's your name?"

"Kip. Name's Kip, but please, Miss, don't report me. Nothing like this has—"

"Kip, I think there's something in the water here. You probably blacked out from a virus; don't you think? Not at all your fault."

"Virus? Yeah, yeah, that must have been it."

"You go clean up now, and don't say anything of this to anyone."

"Oh, you can bet I won't say a word, Miss Winston, and thank you. Cap'n Chase would send me packing for less... and I'd hate to think what Mr. Reed would do."

"Not your fault," she said again. "Run along."

As he rose, he rediscovered his soiled pants, and he ducked away so very embarrassed that Ashley felt bad for him.

She stepped around his puddle and made her way across to Calissa's room. She hesitated before knocking, wondering if she might find Katrina again in there, only with her edema receding, perhaps in worse spirits.

Ashley wasn't up for another round with Katrina, but she wasn't willing to risk Calissa either.

She held her breath and fought the pain, moving as quickly as she could down the stairs. In the foyer, a contingent of Rory's men was loitering around. When they saw her, they jumped to attention. "Kip come through here?" she asked.

"No ma'am."

"Miss Winston, you alright?"

"I need you boys to come with me. *Quiet-like.* We may have a hostage situation upstairs. Miss Reed's room."

Only two of the four accompanied her. The other two darted around the front of the building. One of the men with her was familiar, someone from the Estate. He handed her a pistol. "Do not use lethal force," Ashley commanded, grunting with the pain. "But if you do hit her, you're just going to make her more dangerous. She has to be knocked out cold."

They popped in the door. The others had scaled the stairs inside the suite. All of them converged on Calissa at once.

She was standing, hands on hips, in the middle of the room—shocked but not screaming. Just shocked.

"Is it Kat?" she asked. "Did she get away?"

The men were swarming the rooms. Calling clear, room by room.

"Calissa," Ashley rattled through her memories, then asked, "Where did we meet?"

"Where did we...?" Ashley leveled a pistol at her, and Calissa blurted, "Dad's. The panic room."

She lowered her gun. It was a camo test that might work. So long as Katrina did not know intimate details, past history... she could only fake it so well. This was the true Calissa.

Katrina was nowhere to be found.

She tried not to get any blood on the cowhide sofa. The living room was not as comfortable as the bedroom, but Ashley didn't want the reminders: broken mirror, cockeyed bed frame, smashed table...

Zana was tending to her. It was getting to be routine. "At least there is little blood loss this time," he said cheerily. "However, I would trade stitches for broken bones."

"Broken? What's broken?"

"I believe you have at least one broken rib. Your collar, too, could be fractured, but without an x-ray, it is impossible to be certain."

"And my skull?" She tried to smile, but her lip was split, and it just made her spasm in pain. "It feels cracked like a walnut."

"You have a lump. Another here." He pressed at her scalp, noting times she jerked with the pressure. "Here, too?"

"Yow. Yes."

"No problems with dizziness, nausea, focus?"

"Nothing much."

"I am sure you know the lumps are better than indentations. If the lumps do not go down, we may have trouble. I do not think you are concussed, but it would be best to rest and relax. Keep with the ice packs."

"I feel like I need ice packs all over," she groaned.

"Katrina did this?" Zana sounded surprised. "All of this?"

"She's a brawler. All out, but no sense to it."

"You have impressed me with your training," Zana said with a smile.

"I pick up things well," she said.

He wrapped another ice pack in a pillowcase and laid it against her ribs. "I would not move from this spot."

She knew that Zana knew better than to ask that of her. She noted the careful way he had couched it, telling her what to do by sharing what *he would do* in her situation.

"Where's Rory?" she asked.

"We left him at the church," Astar said from nearby. "He will be along."

"As soon as he learns of your injury, he will be here. I am sure of it," Zana said.

"What took you guys so long?" Ashley asked. "I thought it was just a peek at the underground pool."

They looked at each other, as if conferring.

"What? What is it?"

"Will you be able to fly in the morning?" Astar asked.

"Fly? Leave? I thought we were giving it a week... to see if the *Murus* returns."

"We will be flying to the Atlantic," Zana said. "To a private island."

"Do you know of this place?" Astar whispered. "Is it a dock for the airships?"

"Dock?" She was so confused. Her head ached. "They land on water."

"Underwater?" Zana asked.

She was immediately reminded of the *Undulatus*. "Did you catch some vids? Did you hear about the *Undulatus*?"

"We are going to catch up on the plane," Astar said. "But we have heard enough."

"Is Rory going?"

"Of course," Astar patted her gently. "I believe we all are."

"I better—ugh—" the pain cut her short.

"You had better rest. We can do your bidding. What did you want to do?" Zana asked.

"I was going to talk to Calissa and Kelli."

"We already have," Zana said.

"Are you sure it was Kelli?" Ashley asked.

Zana looked quizzically at her. "Yes, of course it was Kelli," he said.

"What did you give to her?" Astar whispered to Zana.

"*I'm right here*," Ashley said. "I haven't taken anything. Guys, she's doing the camouflage thing. Katrina's able to masquerade as any of us."

"Is this how you came to be accused of murdering Miss Parker?" Astar asked.

"Yes," Ashley said. "She can pose as anyone. Our only hope is backstory. Surround ourselves with people we know well, ask questions only we know of each other frequently. She can't fake history."

"We have seen you do the Affectations," Zana said, "but to trick so many? Bah!"

"I tricked the *entire town of Franklin*," Ashley said. "Besides, she was outside, on the airship, topside," Ashley argued. "And it was dark and raining."

"Yes, yes," he continued, "but that *Katrina* could do this? I still do not believe she is even of your Family. Now you say she has fooled even you?"

"I would think such a thing would take incredible energy." Astar shook her head.

"Whatever," Ashley tossed aside the ice packs, and, in spite of the stabbing pain, she forced herself up and pushed past them.

"Are you going to bed, then?" Zana called after her.

"We will take care of the lights on our way out," Astar said.

The bedroom door slammed shut.

"Whoa," they heard from the bedroom, then more loudly: "What happened here?" It was Rory. He ducked his head in the living room, giving it the once over. His face was wrought with concern. "Guys, where's Ash?"

"She..." Zana said. "Rory, she just went in there."

"Did you look in the master bath?" Astar suggested.

"I looked everywhere. I mean, I climbed the balcony to surprise her and—" he shook his head in astonishment. He eyed the ice packs and gauze pads Zana was picking up. "Is she okay?"

"I assure you, she is fine," Astar said, moving past him. "There, you see? The door is shut." She rapped on the door to the master bath. "Miss Winston, I told you he would come here straightaway. Rory is here."

When she heard nothing from within, she tried the door. "Locked?" She looked back at Zana and Rory.

The two men approached and pounded at the door. "Ashley!" Zana called out.

"Open up, Ash."

The Amins were having a hushed and hurried conference.

Rory turned on them and said, "I'm open to suggestions."

"We are not certain. Maybe her head injury is—"

"Head injury!" Rory bellowed. He whipped back to the door and fought the knob more frantically. "Ashley, open this door right now, or I'm coming in!"

"Allow me," Astar said, advancing on the door with a pin from her hair.

"It won't work," Rory said. The anxiety in his voice was thick.

She picked at it and shook the knob for a long while.

"Rory," Zana said with a sigh. "If she has hit her head falling, the toilet or sink..."

"Get back, Astar," Rory rumbled, and threw himself at the door, shoulder first.

"Oh, ow! Ow! Ow!" Ashley cried and crumpled to the floor. "Took the act too far. Oh damn, that hurts!"

Zana and Astar stood over her, wide eyed and slack jawed. She could barely make out their features through the tears in her eyes.

"That—that is incredible." Astar said reverently. "I have known him for many, many years, and I could swear you were him!"

"Try the door," Ashley gritted her teeth, pointed at the bathroom with a cock of her head.

Astar stepped over Ashley and cautiously grasped the knob. She turned it freely, and the door opened. "How is this?"

"I told you it would not work, remember? I told you, and you believed it."

"Remarkable," Zana said.

"Don't trust what you see. Ask something personal," Ashley said, then slumped down to the tile, losing consciousness.

49 Harbinger

"What is *with* you? What are you afraid of?" Rory asked.

"You're not a little freaked?"

"You say you saw the water work, so tell me how the test went? Where was it done?"

"Ugh!" Alex palmed his forehead. "Not where, Rory, *when*."

"Okay, when did you see it? And how did it go?" Rory shrugged. "Is Winston on the right track? Does it, somehow, make for One World?"

"Have you noticed I'm never in one place too long? I get restless. Get the wanderlust."

"Yeah, so?"

"So where do you think I take off to?"

"I dunno. I never get postcards or anything." Rory smiled at him.

"Funny." Alex sounded exasperated.

"So," Rory prodded, "you saw the test dump... when?"

Alex hopped to his feet and paced back and forth in the narrow lane between the bench and the pool. "I was gone *for six months*. After Kelli gave me the stiff arm, I had to get some space, some time away."

"Get your head on straight."

"Figure some things out."

"And you did figure something out. You won the girl," Rory smiled. "Now we're gonna save the day. The usual drill."

Alex stopped pacing and looked at Rory.

"What?" Rory asked.

"There's nothing *usual* about this."

"Because of this?" Rory tossed a pebble in the glowing pool.

"No. Well, yes, but... no." As he spoke, Alex reminded Rory of some petroglyph, Kokopelli, with wild hair, arms waving above his head in a mad dance. "Listen. When A-Z started talking about this being their last mission, it all clicked."

"Oh, not you, too. You're quitting me, too?"

"Brother, we have *girls* now," Alex said, and Rory could see his broad smile, his teeth glowing fluorescent white in the green. "I'm in *love*, Rory."

"That *is* unusual," Rory laughed. "Usually you're just in lust."

"She has changed my life, man. I wish you could understand the size of what I'm telling you here, Rory." Alex stepped closer. "My love for Kelli Chase changes my *everything*. Changes the world!"

"I don't know what to say, Alex. You want a quote on love or something?"

"Ahh!" Alex's cry echoed in the chamber. "This is so hard!"

Rory was a patient man. He had once watched ants for an entire afternoon as they built their anthill. As they mined underground, emerging with tiny rocks, returning to dig some more, he had wondered what they were up to under there. He began to see patterns in their placement of rocks they extracted, suggesting underground routes through strata of dirt. It was not that different just then with Alex. He waited and watched, listening for it to all come together.

"You've been my best friend since high school, senior year," Alex said, his voice pleading. "We would do anything for each other, right?"

"Absolutely," Rory rumbled.

"Take a bullet for each other."

"You did for me, once, remember?"

Alex fluttered his hands as if to erase that line of reasoning.

"Telling you the truth... *this truth*... it's the hardest thing I've ever had to do... and I've put it off the whole time I've known you. That's how much your friendship means to me, Rory."

"Hey, if you gotta quit the team, it's okay. You don't have to get all emotional."

"Just listen, you big ape," Alex pulled at his hair. "I've been leading a double life—at *least* a double life. Surely you figured that out? I'm here, and I'm gone. I barely made it through school, would not have made it, without you covering for me, man. Surely, you've noticed, too, that when I'm gone... I am *gone*. Incommunicado."

"That does get a little frustrating," Rory nodded.

"But you deal. You always have. You quit asking after a while." Alex took another deep breath and continued. "You just take me as I am."

"Always will," Rory said. "Alex, I'm your best—"

"I didn't have anyone else in my life like you. You and Cal, you've been my family. You guys were accepting."

"Are you worried about Kelli accepting—"

"I want to raise a family with her. Someday, I want to be half the dad you are."

"So, drop anchor," Rory said.

"I want to. I want to sink my roots in the here and now."

"But?"

"Here goes: when I say, 'here and now,' Rory, I mean it. I mean, I'm ready to stick a flag in the timeline and stay the rest of my natural life with you, with Kelli, right now in 2054."

"Great."

"I'm ready to quit being a *Harbinger*. I am ready to quit meddling. I'm ready to just be a regular guy."

"O-kay," Rory said. "You're getting a little far afield for me, but... okay."

"*Rory, I time travel.*"

"You what?"

"I've been doing it the whole time I've known you, young and old. I could tell you things—but I don't. I don't meddle like that. I try not to meddle at all, just inform, you know? Just nudge a little now and then."

Rory's eyes ached. He felt like he had the worst sinus infection of his life. His head was about to explode. He cleared his throat to speak, but he was at a loss.

"*That's* my advantage. It's mechanical, and technological, but biological, too. I think I'm the only guy like me." Alex dropped to sit on the bench next to Rory. "I know it's crazy, man, and I know you'll have a lot of trouble with this. Why do you think I've never told you?"

"Why are you telling me now?" Rory heard his own voice, but it sounded like he was deep underwater, like his ears were plugged. He had not known a physiological change to a truth like this ever before. He grew increasingly nauseous as it all sunk in.

"I'm telling you, because this is that big. That water, that crazy LF Winston—it's *dragon-sized* big, friend. I've seen the outcome. I know what can happen from his stupid, stupid ideology." He sighed, then looked Rory square in the eye, "Even if it costs me your friendship, even if there's some goddamn Butterfly Effect, you need to know what's coming, and we need to work together through this one last show. We gotta stop it."

"Why?"

"Because I'm in love, idiot, and this is where I want to end my days. If we blow this one, I don't get my happy ever after."

Rory drummed his fingers on his knees. He was lost in thought, truly lost. He cycled back, trying to recall the chain of thoughts that had led him into this void, but he had lost the link. He had lost track of time, too, only able to recall having drummed out four minutes on his knees.

Alex had read the doubt on his face and then done something impossible: *he left*.

He had hooked something together, spun it like an electric lasso, glowing blue white. "Don't doubt me, Rory. Wait here."

Then he tossed the lasso overhead, and when it dropped, it fell empty to the ground.

Rory blinked away the blindness. He was left alone in the green cave. "Alex?"

As he recalled it all, yet again, he picked up his reasoning. A Hot Wire. He had just witnessed Alex Gault adeptly deploy a Hot Wire.

Z said TransCorp took them seriously.

Alex went through one.

He said he time traveled. Hot Wires for time travel? Hot Wires for any kind of travel? For moving water. He had seen it for himself: a four-foot oval gateway transporting this water to...?

Rory realized he had stopped his drumming, and as best as he could estimate, resumed his count and kept time like a Swiss watch.

Ten minutes had passed.

Why should anything surprise him? His girlfriend—could he call her that?—was a supernatural being. Her father and Family were, too. Portals existed. He had learned that in the last months too. His best friend... why couldn't he be a... what had he said? A Harbinger.

Rory pulled up his earliest memories of Alex. He studied the gaps. Now that he was focused on it, he noted a lot of gaps.

Alex was a joker, a fun loving, in-the-moment, flash-bang, good-time buddy. Even if he could travel time, even if he changed things like he said, how would he bear the responsibility? How could a goof like Alex be a harbinger of the future he had seen? How could he know what to share and what to withhold? One nudge in the wrong direction and the world could pivot.

The more he dwelt on it, the heavier his heart weighed down.

Seventeen minutes. He had been waiting now—for something—for seventeen minutes.

Rory was a little insulted. Did Alex actually think he would have been that shocked? How could Alex think that? To have kept it from him for decades out of fear of rejection?

"What a chickenshit," he said aloud.

Maybe, Rory thought, Alex was now producing evidence. Rory appreciated evidence. He was typically a pragmatic guy, a self-proclaimed empiricist. Once his grandfather had told him he should have grown up in Missouri, the Show Me state. That was a good quality, Rory thought, crossing his arms. It had saved them from a lot of trouble.

Rory did a double take. Something had changed in the luminescence. A thin seam of light was cutting its way to the floor. The glow of it radiated perpendicular to Rory's position. He rose to his feet and approached it, circling it to find another bright blue white portal snap into reality.

Alex walked toward him, nearly running right into him.

"Alex! How did you... I'm so glad to see you, man!"

"Brought you something," he said, extending his palm.

Rory squinted in the glow, not believing what he was being offered. "A Yoyo?"

"Your Yoyo, bozo." Alex stuffed it in Rory's hand. The portal behind him disappeared. They were left in the eerie green glow yet again.

Rory snapped on his flashlight and looked at the Yoyo closely, turned it all around in his hands. It was a blue Yomega Stealth Fire—*his* Yoyo, complete with the scratch across the pog.

"I lost this... then you gave it back to me..."

"You lost it *just now*, when I slipped it from your room in '32. I gave it back on your wedding day, June 1, 2034. Remember?"

Rory remembered the very moment. Alex was standing with him on the beach as the wedding party was approaching for the service. He had fished in his pocket and revealed the Yoyo back then, saying with his trademark goofy grin: "Something borrowed, something blue."

"But... but I lost it again when Cal was little..."

"And yet here it is," Alex said. "Just keeps coming back... you know... like a Yoyo."

"Boomerang," Rory corrected out of habit.

"Well. Hell... maybe, if you'd grown up in the Outback. Point is, you get it, right? You believe me now?"

"Alex, I don't get it. Not at all." Rory wagged his head, still marveling at the Yoyo. "I mean, how can this be here now, when it was there then...and how—"

"I know, I know. I gave up trying to figure it out."

"You don't know how it works, but you do it all the time?"

"You know how your breathing works? No, I doubt it. But you breathe all the time."

Rory paused to think, then shook his head violently. "That's the weakest argument you—my *breathing* doesn't change the course of world events, Alex."

"You get the point, though. Porting is that easy for me. Intuitive. In some ways, time porting is even easier." He shrugged his shoulders.

Rory looked at his face closely. He was looking for tells. Any indicator Alex was lying. Then he noticed something he could not believe he had missed. He shined the flashlight in Alex's face. "You... you need a shave?"

"Oh, yeah. That." Alex stroked his chin.

He had a week's growth, easily, by Rory's estimation.

"It's nothing," he shrugged it off.

Rory continued to examine his beard, his face.

"It's complicated," Alex said.

"How long were you gone? I only clocked 20 minutes, give or take."

"Give or take?" Alex said. "Are you okay?"

"How long, Alex?"

"It's not like math, not a ratio thing... I don't really know. It varies. The Yoyo caper was eleven days."

"Just now? Just now you were gone eleven days?"

"Well, think how silly that sounds, Rory: Now. Eleven days?" He smirked.

Something was bothering him, Rory could tell, but he did not pry. He waited.

"So, this time, the tradeoff was eleven days to twenty minutes. Not bad. It's been worse."

"What's the worst?"

"I don't keep track."

"Yes, you do, Alex. What's the worst it's been?"

"Years," he said, taking a seat on the bench. "You didn't even know I was gone, but I was stuck in the 1990s for *three years*. Didn't think I could ever come back."

Rory couldn't fathom it. To go back in time a decade before you were born. To know no one. He patted his friend's back. "You came back, though."

"Know the worst of that one?"

Rory's imagination was reeling out dozens of terrible things.

"Grunge," Alex said. "I never want to hear that music again!"

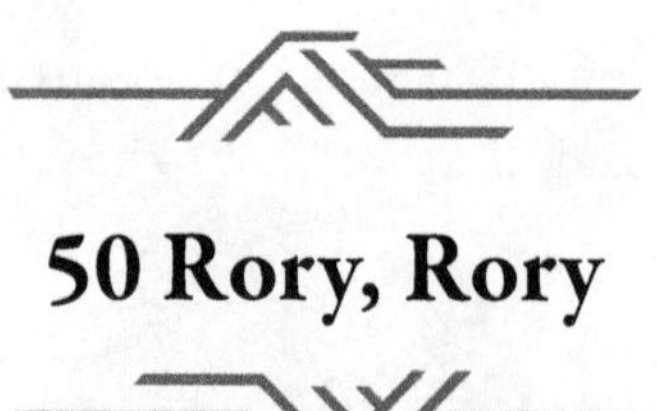

50 Rory, Rory

Zana and Astar were keeping her on her feet, and she was doing her best to walk with them. When she was coming around, she had noticed they were out of the hotel, now making their way to a new black Jeep. Rory was searching the floorboards, the visor, everywhere for a key.

"Just wire it," Ashley mumbled.

"No," he shook his head.

She looked at Astar for confirmation, but Astar ignored her.

"Zana, I—" she began, then clamped down on her words when he squeezed her ribcage with a little tug. He did look at her, his eyebrows raised. A subtle nod.

She thought they were telling her something. Maybe they were.

Cha Cha came around the side of the jeep. It had to be her personal model, for it wasn't painted in the garish colors and did not have the ridiculous lights and tires of the other vehicle. "Oh, you are back wanting to surf again?"

"No," Rory said, all but ignoring her. He seemed so preoccupied with stealing the jeep that he did not even realize it might be hers. That was his focus, sometimes blinding focus.

"I drive you," she smiled at him. "Where do you want? Ica? Maybe out to the Nazca?"

"Do you have the keys?" He turned and stood his full height; she came to his chest.

She wiggled her fingers in his face. Biometrics. Out here in the backwater village. He looked at her hand, and Ashley half-feared he was thinking of taking it from her, leaving Cha Cha behind with a stump. Instead, he shrugged and said, “You drive.”

Zana helped Ashley onto the front bench seat. Rory squeezed in on the passenger side.

“Where do we go?” Cha Cha asked as the back doors slammed shut. She pressed her fingerprint on the dash, and the vehicle fired up.

“Airport,” Rory said, looking out the window absently.

“Airport?” Astar could not bite her tongue. “What of Calissa? Kelly and Alex?”

Rory turned to face her; a confused look turned into annoyance. “I left a note, okay?”

Ashley snickered. She looked over her shoulder, but Zana was shaking his head ‘no,’ slowly. *Ride it out,* she figured.

Regardless, she was making an inventory of pain points she could use to her advantage.

It wasn’t a long ride to Ica, and Cha Cha did her best to entertain them. It must have been confusing to her, expecting Rory to be the party animal he had been on the dunes. She couldn’t even get a smile out of those in the back. She knew the way to the airport, but she wheeled up to the general gates.

“Where is the plane?” Zana asked Rory.

“We’ll catch a charter,” he said.

“Oh, you fool girl, you are so bad at this,” Astar said at last, swatting Rory on the back. “Pull around to the hangar with the silver jet,” she commanded Cha Cha. “Pull inside, please.”

The Jeep wheeled around Mac’s plane and into the hangar.

Zana and Astar were out of the vehicle before it stopped. They split up and made a quick sweep of the building. Rory got out and gestured for Ashley to follow. "Tip her," Ashley directed Rory.

"I cannot," Rory said with a shrug.

"Here," Zana said, passing some cash through the driver's window. "Tell no one you were with us?"

"I don'no even who you are," Cha Cha said.

Zana handed her another bill. "Be gone now."

The tires chirped as the black Jeep sped away.

"What the hell?" Ashley asked the three of them.

"We are to help her get away," Astar said.

"My guise has limitations," Rory said—in Kat's voice now. "With surveillance, with binoculars, they would see the real me, but in passing, even through the terminal, I am Rory. Think of me as Rory."

"Why are we helping her get away?" Ashley winced in pain. She was exerting herself too much, and she knew it.

"I believe we can pull her plug," Zana said. "I studied those men in Franklin, the Terminals, and between us, we know a good deal of behavioral management."

"But... why?" Ashley stomped her foot. "She killed Sarah. She tried to kill me!"

"If they can do as they say, I will be a threat to no one," Rory said in the woman's voice. "Perhaps I can even avenge Miss Parker."

"You trust her?" Ashley asked Astar.

"She told us of her sorrows, of how she worked as friends with the Parker girl, and how then she was forced to kill her," Astar said.

Rory nodded, then looked away. He pressed his knuckle to his mouth in an uncharacteristically feminine gesture. Fighting back tears. Perhaps, Ashley bristled, fighting back an Affectation?

"Are you willing to be put under again until we can get you corrected?" Ashley asked.

Rory's eyes had teared up. The real Rory would not easily give in to being sedated. Katrina had suffered through it already far too long. "Yes, we have already spoken of this, too," she nodded to Zana. "He is prepared to give me better... better *medicine*."

Ashley shook her head, so unsure. It was so risky. Looking at Rory, she wondered what the real Rory would do. She wondered again just where he was. What could possibly be keeping him?

"And you, too, sister. You are here to keep me honest, as they say. You would know if I were to try anything with my thinking."

Ashley sighed. The Amins knew what they were doing. She was having such a difficult time of trusting Katrina. She felt around for a lingering whiff of an Affectation. There was nothing.

"Ah!" Astar smiled. "I have just learned he is coming. And Alex and Kelli are along."

"And Calissa?" Ashley asked.

"Of course," Astar smiled. "Always Calissa."

Bringing Calissa again into this meant Rory trusted the plan, so they waited. They sat in the hangar, the cool night air wafting through. She wanted to doze but vigilantly watched over Katrina/Rory. Something was scratching at the back of her mind, a question, but it was overshadowed by Katrina's presence. It would be hours later before she would remember to question how Astar had heard Rory was on his way.

"There was a TV commercial once," Mac said to Ashley. She was serving as his co-pilot, though she had never flown his plane. "I was just a kid. Some luxury car. They were trying to sell it as a smooth ride, you know."

"I barely remember TV commercials," she confessed.

"Yeah... well... that's too bad, Miss Winston, just a shame—but I digress." He smiled at her, continuing, "A jewelry guy's in the back seat, got the little eye glass thing on..."

"A jeweler's loupe," she said.

"Yeah... and he's cutting this priceless diamond as the car's going down the highway, smooth as glass." Mac laughed. "Only thing more convincing was a parody of that I saw, where they were doing a circumcision in that car, same conditions. More at stake. Get it?"

She smiled, along with his laughter. She understood his point. She understood his anxiety, too. Ashley had flown with Mac, and she knew the plane was remarkable. The pilot was remarkable.

But was it so graceful, and was Mac so skilled, that the surgery taking place in the next compartment would be flawless? *Brain* surgery.

"It'll be just fine, Mac." Ashley rubbed his shoulder. "You're the best pilot in the sky."

"Don't kid a kidder," he said. "And don't do your hoo-doo either. I got this."

Once aboard the plane, Katrina had let go of her Rory camouflage. It brought a gasp of amazement from Astar, even though she was aware of the situation. It was the right thing to do, sparing the rest of them from the confusion. By the time they boarded, Katrina was strapped down to a makeshift bed near the back of the cabin. Zana had an IV started before everyone had their seats. The Amins were measuring and marking for an incision before the plane had taken wing.

"What's the rush, anyway," Ashley asked Mac. "Why didn't they just do the operation in Ica, you know, at a hospital?"

"Orders," Mac said. "Rory wanted us airborne. I never ask anymore, Miss Winston. I just fly the plane."

"We have to get to the mid-Atlantic, as soon as possible," Rory said from behind them. He smiled at her startled expression. Even though he annoyed her, popping up like that, she did like that smile.

"See?" Mac said. "Now you know as much as me."

"You're about to learn a whole lot more, MacIntyre," Rory said, squeezing into the cabin and drawing the door shut behind him. "Think you can keep it steady while I blow your mind?"

Mac did not answer right away. Composing himself, he smiled at Rory and Ashley, then laughed it off. "Go for it. Nothing's going to surprise me, and nothing's gonna jostle my bird."

51 Secrets

"Alex dug deep," Rory began. He looked at Mac. "You know how he knew there was action in Ica?"

"I don't ask, I just fly," he nodded at Ashley.

"He told you, though, didn't he? Alex cracked LF Winston's code somehow, weaseled right into their comms."

"He did say he could take over an airship if he wanted to. That's some computering, I'd say," Mac whistled.

"Alex figured out where the airships are landing."

"Landing?" Ashley scoffed. "What are you talking about?"

"Alex did the math. Every last ship in your fleet has been flying in and out of a storm at exactly the same coordinates, one after another."

"That's impossible," Mac said. "Kid told me they were landing in the same area, but it isn't under a storm. That would be rough. Even for an airship. Storms don't sit in the same spot, either."

"All our ships are flying coordinated routes, Rory. You know that. *Right as Rain*, remember?"

"Jack in and tell me that again," he gestured to the Stetson. "They've *all* veered off course... all about the same time as the *Murus* was headed down to Peru," Rory said. He turned his shoulders and crouched against the wall, trying to get a little more comfortable. "Alex figured it out, Ashley, and I choose to believe him."

"Believe what, exactly?" she asked.

He cleared his throat, then continued. "I think the *Murus* is just a test, maybe even a distraction. The real work is being done out at sea."

"What?"

"I think your ships are going there to tank up, just like the *Murus* did. Then, like you heard him say in Huacachina, he's going to share it worldwide."

"So, it's all happening," she mumbled.

"What?" Mac asked. "What's all happening?"

"Spexarth stole my dad's journal," she said.

"He did what? How?" Rory hit his head when he stood suddenly.

"He read a passage to me," she said, holding herself now, as if she were freezing. "Oh, ow!"

"Your ribs, Miss Winston?"

"Collarbone," she groaned.

"Shouldn't that be in a sling?" Mac asked.

"*What about the journal*?" Rory asked.

"I can't remember it all, but I got the gist of it. Said he was going to expose the biggest cities first." She caught her breath as she sat up straighter. "What do you think he means, 'expose' the cities?"

"There's something in that water, some contaminant, and he thinks it's going to change the world." Rory grumbled at the tight quarters, then continued, "Usually, I'd chalk it up to a rich nut job, a cult leader, maybe someone with more money than smarts, just spinning off into space like Bezos and Branson and Musk—but this time LF has the resources, *all the resources*, and he's... methodical. I think he's been at this for years."

"I don't see how spraying some water is any different from making it rain his usual way," Mac said with a shrug of his shoulders, careful not to disturb the yoke.

"I don't know either, but I know someone who does. He's seen the test results," Rory said, careful with his words now. "It isn't pretty."

"Maybe. Maybe it's a little messy, but *in a good way*," Ashley said as positively as she could.

"You sound like Calissa," Rory smiled.

"Winston Water Works *has* made the world a better place," Mac said. "Why would the world's greatest do-gooder do any different now?"

"You sound like a commercial," Ashley winked at him.

"Sometimes good people do bad things," Rory said, "sometimes even for noble causes."

"What are you talking about, chief?" Mac asked.

"I'm talking about history. Ancient history, now." Rory let himself feel it, just the tiniest bit. "We fought for freedom," he sighed. "We were sure we were right... but we went about it all wrong. I want to get to LF before he does something he'll regret."

"If they've been filling up airships for weeks, we may be too late," Mac said.

Ashley was looking at Rory with fear in her eyes. "Hearing you say it... you remind me so much of him. He really does believe in what he's doing."

It was an unlikely looking surgical theater, but Zana had worked in worse conditions. Ashley was across from Astar, and together they served as the anesthesiologists. Calissa stood at the tray of instruments, sometimes sponging, sometimes just watching intently.

Alex was on the Stetson, also stationed at Katrina's bedside. He was pulling information to relay to Zana as he worked. "Okay, now this says to apply pressure. Looks like a lot of pressure. This guy's got some jar-looking thing, open-ended, one end pressing all around the incision equally." He looked past his display and asked Kelli and Calissa—"What do we have? Something about two inches across—"

"Does it have to be open on both ends?" Kelli asked.

Alex was gesturing, like he might have had to on a cheap HeadGear. He was advancing vids quickly; Rory saw the varied scenes flashing on Alex's face. "Yes, it does. This guy's having a hell of a time reaching around in there. Ours could even be like a funnel. Two inches diameter though, on the end against the wound, that sounds important."

"Does it have to be glass?" Calissa asked.

"It should be sterile," Zana offered, his attention on his patient's temple.

"Got a 3d printer onboard?" Alex asked Mac.

"What?" Mac was surprised at the idea. "No, of course not."

"Do we *need* this printer, or a tool it might make?" Astar asked.

"What we need is to hurry," Zana said.

Rory was not getting into their tight huddle around Katrina's head. He had seen enough field surgery to last a lifetime. Always improvisational, less refined than it should be. Always an emergency. This time, it was an Extraction of sorts, and he was regretfully, intimately familiar with those. He dropped into a big leather chair with a drink and waited until he was needed. If they hailed him, it meant Katrina's life was already forfeit, for his methods of Extraction were crude, messy, fatal wet work.

"Kelli, give me your pea shooter," Alex said suddenly. "Somebody, get me a bottle."

"What are you thinking?" Astar exclaimed. "You cannot shoot that thing off in here!"

"We're at 52,000 feet, Gault, don't be stupid," Mac called from the cockpit.

"Gimme a minute," he said, working at the weapon. His back was to them all as he jimmied this and pried at that. Rory was standing now, curious.

He turned back to them, flushed and grinning. He held up the modified weapon.

"My gun!" Kelli said. "What have you done—"

"I can fix it later, kitten," Alex said. "I need that bottle."

Calissa followed his gesture to it, then handed him an empty wine bottle. He sat it on an arm of a chair, fired up the plasma cutter, and sliced off both ends of the bottle effortlessly.

"It's a little warm, might need to be rinsed out when it cools, but it should do the trick on the compression you need."

Everyone looked at him, dumbfounded.

"What?" Alex asked. "We gotta make do."

An hour later, Katrina was sleeping in the back quarters. Ashley was staying with her to monitor her drip and otherwise keep her Affectations under watch. Zana was smiling broadly, again examining the compression tool Alex had made. "This could be your retirement, friend. Surely there is a market for improvised surgical devices."

The others were tired, retiring to chairs throughout the cabin.

"You guys have to hear this," Alex had tuned in a channel on the Stetson and switched the broadcast over the airplane's sound system. "It's at the tail end of a press conference." As he turned it up, Rory recognized the voice of LF Winston.

"That is an excellent question, thank you. For the first time in over two decades, we brought our ships down for retrofitting. They are now even safer than ever, and all positioned for maximum yield."

Someone on the broadcast asked a question beyond the range of the microphones. "Yes, yes, that remains our basic premise. Water is the essential element. Our water is distributed by natural water cycle basics any child could recount. With these ships, and these cyclic showers, we have afforded a higher standard of living than the world has ever known."

"Yes," he answered another question out of the mic's range. "We provided modest enhancements to every ship. I cannot disclose the details, but know this: the changes we are making in distribution will affect mankind for generations. Current plans will bring an era of enrichment. We have the whole world's interests at heart, and the new waters we distribute will bring this world together in unity. My dreams of no one going hungry are at hand. No hunger. No thirst. No confusion."

The questions were flying now, and LF cleared his throat. "You. Yes... yes, what is your question?"

"You said, 'new water,' did you not? What exactly does that mean? Additives? Purification?"

More questions erupted. LF took his time in calming them down.

On the *Whipstitch,* as people often do when listening to a disembodied voice, they looked to the speakers in the plane's ceiling. In the pause between questions, they were looking at one another now, all of them puzzled.

Alex's eyebrows were raised. He was asking Rory with his expression whether to sever the signal.

Rory shook his head slightly. Let it go.

"Again, thank you for asking," LF said finally. "In a manner of speaking, the new water we will all be sharing will be the most pure spring water man has ever known."

"...rainwater?" someone asked at the press conference.

"True. Rainwater is an undistilled delight, and it has been my great joy to share this with the world, to irrigate even the most remote regions," he paused. "*This* water, this Deep Water, brings with it a purity of intentions by design."

Questions were being shouted from every quarter, but LF's voice drowned them out. "I bring you peace of mind, solutions to your every problem, water to your woes. You'll thank me later." The press conference hosts were back on the channel, processing his words.

Alex rolled his eyes and cut the broadcast. "What's it mean if *I* even think the guy's losing it?" Alex said, and several chuckled.

"Sounds kinda awesome to me," Calissa smiled.

"Really?" Kelli jeered. "Kinda pie in the sky, don't you think?"

"It does sound pretty good," Rory said.

"Pretty familiar, anyway, right 'Coat?" Kelli said.

They shared a fist bump.

"It is a tired ideology," Zana offered. "It is hard to believe this fresh rain will change anything."

Those were his words, but his face was struggling to hide some deeper emotion. Rory could see Zana's poorly masked concern. He gave some thought to his own expression, trying to smile, as if Zana had just made a joke. No one picked up on his smile, save Alex.

"Hard to believe," Kelli said, a twinkle in her eye, "but what if it worked?"

"Believers," Alex scoffed. He bore into her with the rest of his commentary: "Captain Chase, are you sure Winston wasn't in on your merry little band out to save the world? Now that would have been some backing. Might have changed the course of history then, eh? You might actually have won!"

"Get dredged, Alex," she said. She saluted him with an unsavory gesture and left to join Ashley in the back cabin.

The rest were shocked at the exchange.

"Mac," Rory rumbled, "we need some privacy."

"Running out of room on my ship," he said. "Take the cockpit, but *don't touch anything*."

When they entered, Alex was repulsed by a yawning stretch of easy listening saxophone. "Ugh, this has gotta go," he said, scanning the dash. He flipped switches until he finally switched the music off and sighed.

"That goes for messing with my Kenny G!" Mac said from the cabin.

Rory shut the door. "What is it?"

"I think it's a band from—"

"What's got into you?"

"Dredged, that's a nautical term, right?"

"Alex!"

"You think I pissed her off again?"

"You pissed me off," Rory glowered.

Alex was panning over the twinkling dashboard, collecting his thoughts. "I kid, you know that. You two get all blustery and proud about your days in the Turncoats. Well, it's not my battle, the whole One World thing, the whole Turncoat thing... but it is my war."

"Meaning?"

"Meaning... remember what you said earlier, 'people do bad things for noble causes?' Well, it's like that."

"Like what?" Rory

"I evoke time continuum confidentiality."

"That's not even a thing," Rory growled.

"Point is, I can't tell you everything, even if I wanted to."

"Why wouldn't you want to?"

"Rory, here's the deal, and I don't even know how it works, okay... time is on some kind of turntable. This time, the needle drops here, another time, there."

Rory shook his head, wrestling with it all. "What?"

"I can tell you this: things are different than I remembered they would be."

"Different. How?"

"It's shaping up to be a future I don't recall. It's different because Winston's a lot more... orchestrated. This time, he's got it all together. It's accelerated."

"So, you don't know where this is going any more than the rest of us?"

"It's like that saying, 'history repeats itself,' you know, where we ought to be informed by our past mistakes... only I ought to be informed by the way this has played out... but it *hasn't* played out like this." He shrugged. "Not knowing sucks."

Rory had a plan. He smiled a little at the prospects.

"What? I hate it when you get that look. Always means trouble."

"We need a playbook," Rory said.

"A what?"

"A playbook. LF's journal. Ashley has his journal." Rory continued, "Maybe it will give us an angle that you can't. It might explain—"

"Are you talking about the Lost Journals?" He was excited at the idea.

"I don't know, man. She said she had a journal where he was writing about all this. I say we bring her in on this."

"You're kidding, right?" Alex asked.

"Who's got more stake in this than her?"

"When you say bring her in on 'this,' are you talking about *all* of this?"

"I'm an honest guy, Alex," Rory chuckled. "No good at secrets."

"Your whole life's a secret," Alex argued. "But to get a hold of that journal... can't you just borrow it or something?"

"We're trying to stop LF Winston from brainwashing the world, and you're worried about Ashley knowing you're a time traveler. You're the big picture guy, Alex. In the big picture, what's it matter if she knows?"

"That would double the number who've ever known. I don't like it."

"Who knows LF better than his own daughter? We need that inside angle."

"I dunno. Some people aren't mature enough to handle it. I haven't even told Kelli—"

"Maybe you should. Sometimes it's better to not go it alone."

"Listen to yourself," Alex said.

"Besides, when I said I'm no good at secrets... well... sometimes Ash and I share thoughts... at least once we did." Rory couldn't quite explain it, but this confession was embarrassing.

"You *shared* thoughts?"

"Alex. We've read the cave wall. You know the future," Rory continued, "She's read his journal. She's his daughter. She knows him."

"So does Kat," he said.

"So, bring them all in on it?"

A sharp knock, then Mac opened the door. "You already did, stooges." He flicked a switch on the audio panel. "You left the comms on."

The entire conversation had been piped throughout the plane.

Alex turned to Kelli immediately, "Pumpkin spice, I—"

"I can't wait to hear *all* of your secrets!" she sneered, then gave him an exaggerated pout, "when I'm more mature."

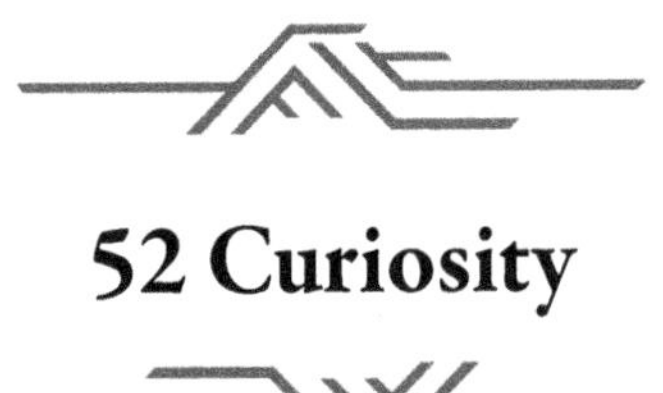

52 Curiosity

She had heard the whole thing over the speakers in the bedroom, but Ashley wasn't taking it as hard as some others. Though some of the shouting in the next room caught her interest, she hoped to avoid it and stayed at her post.

Even that, the act of not acting, made Ashley question herself. She had been looking after Katrina for hours now, and she wondered if this curious inertia was some faint Affectation from her half-sister. She dismissed the idea again and again, but she came back to it, too, for she had no better explanation.

Kelli threw open the door, still engaged in a heated conversation with Alex. "Oh. No. Of course not. The *Princesses* are in here," she gnashed it out.

Alex offered, "We could take her out to the—"

"No," Kelli whirled back on Alex. "We will not move around a woman recovering from *brain surgery,* so we can have a little talk."

"Okay, so we do this out there, or with these two," Alex said. "Your choice."

"Well, I suppose *they're mature enough* to hear anything you have to say," Kelli sneered. "Shut the door."

"Really," Ashley said, "I could step out. She doesn't need much—"

"Leave us alone with her? No way," Kelli said.

"Fine," Alex said, closing the door. "Sit down."

"I will *not* sit down," Kelli said. She crossed her arms and glared at him. Then, on her own terms, Cap'n Chase sat on the edge of the bed, careful not to disturb Katrina's feet.

"First of all, love, you're the last person I would ever want to hurt."

"Are your lips moving? Ashley, are his lips moving? Because if they are, they're making lying noises. Lies. Lies. Lies."

"Secondly, I never lied to you," Alex said patiently.

"You don't think so?" she said. "Hiding something this... this *crazy* is deceitful. You're living a lie."

"I'm living my best lie," Alex said, trying to coax a smile. "I'm choosing to take my stand right here, in *this* now, with you, Kelli."

"For all I know, you did some damn time loop around me until you could manipulate me into loving you."

"So, you do still love me, then?" he said, stepping closer.

"Did you?" she snarled. "Did you manipulate me?"

"If you mean, was I annoyingly persistent? Yes. Otherwise, no, of course not. I wouldn't even know how to do that."

"Haven't you seen the movies?" Ashley asked. "You try your hand, say, offer her roses, then learn she likes daisies, so then you go back in time, and then you offer her the daisies."

"Yeah!" Kelli pointed at Ashley. "That."

"You just course correct until you get it right," Ashley said.

"That's clever and all," he chuckled, "but it doesn't work that way. You're the most important person in my whole world, my whole life and timeline, Kelli Jo Chase, but I couldn't spend my time traveling that frivolously."

"Frivolously!" she said. "So now I'm not even worth that? Big waste of your time travel budget or whatever?"

"You don't understand. Hell, I don't understand. I just know I have a finite number of these." He shook a thumb-sized bottle, and the contents tinkled inside like glass beads. "When they're gone, I'm through traveling. Period. So, no, I would not go back and forth sorting out daisies and roses."

"You still know too much," she said, wiping at the tears angrily. "You probably get a big laugh out of me, don't you? See right through me, huh? You know if this is going to work out, and even when I'm pissed, like now. You know if we have kids, what their names are, what our life's going—"

"No, I don't, Kelli. I have no clue. This is a first for me, and I am not going to look ahead. I don't want to know. I want to cherish it all as it happens, in the now, babe." He went down on one knee, and he held her hand in his. "Kelli, I'd never laugh at you. I'd never manipulate you. For one thing, you'd kick my ass."

"I would too. I will. If I ever—"

"You won't," he said with conviction, "and I'm not saying that because I've seen the future. I'm saying that because you won't have a reason to. I promise."

Ashley had never seen Alex Gault be so sincere. She felt a little awkward sitting in the same room with them at this tender moment.

"What do you promise?" Kelli brushed back her hair with her free hand, then clasped his. She sniffed.

"I promise I will never abuse our timeline for my advantage. I won't move ahead or go back to... *course correct.* I won't spring forward to get past a rough spot, and I won't fall back just to live in the past. Kelli, *I want every minute of real time in this time with you.* I'm hanging up my guns. We're all getting out of the business." Alex glanced over at Ashley with a sheepish grin. "You'll have to ask Rory, Ashley. That's too much information."

"Hanging up your guns?" Kelli tipped her head a little. "I like your guns."

"They are nice, aren't they?" Alex twisted so he could admire the holster on his hip. He wore his big, nickel-plated pistols cowboy-style. Then he seemed to remember his vows and turned his attention wholly back to Kelli. "I'm hanging up *these* guns, the time travel Tic-Tacs. I'm done."

He put the bottle in her hands.

Hours had passed. Conversations out in the cabin had moved on from surprised to inquisitive, and from there to eager and speculative. To Ashley, it had all grown boring. Rory wasn't speaking to her. He acted angry that she let Spexarth take the journal, something about wanting some perspective and that now it was lost to him. Alex and Kelli had left her alone with Katrina, and as time had passed, she had given a lot of thought to the current circumstance.

Kat might not recover. It was the undergirding that allowed for the surgery in the first place. If she lived, she might be free of the implant. If she didn't, well, there was Sarah's murder to account for. Both the implant and life in prison seemed equal recompense. Death by scalpel seemed a generous end.

Zana was no brain surgeon, however. Should Kat live, but never be whole again—that was a terrible prospect. It posed dangers, too. If she had brain damage, would she be in charge of her Affectations, or would she use them like a child, wildly and freely?

Ashley was giving thoughts to attempting a mind meld with Katrina. Too many vague answers and too much mystery was haunting around her. Maybe she could get inside and not only learn Kat's past, but maybe she could ease her present, too. If there was brain damage, could an inside, shared Affectation address the harm if not restore her entirely?

What if members of the Family wanted to work in mental health? In recovery centers? It opened up a whole host of opportunities. Drug-free anesthesiology had its appeal. The Family could be involved in all aspects of medicine, she thought. Caring for trauma victims—providing immediate pain relief and mental comfort, as she had done herself at the car bombing—would be a priceless talent to offer. Why weren't people with her gift well-known public servants?

A glance at Kat answered the question amply. Family couldn't roam the earth doing overt Affectations. They would be rounded up in detention centers at the first indication. She had felt the vitriol from Stan Combs and his hatred of her kind. If the world knew Family were, say, manipulating International Relations, trust would crumble. If CommCorp found out about mental camouflage, warning that no one could be trusted to be who they appeared to be—Ashley couldn't imagine the result.

If the military or the underworld were populated with Family, even now, it could be a different and dangerous world. Better to keep this priceless gift a private venture.

Unusual people found safety in the vague, unknown recesses of ignorance: Alex. Katrina. The Family. Ashley revisited how many people were aware of her craft. Too many.

She leaned in closer, thinking how she had already Affected Katrina Covarrubias more than anyone she had ever known... except Kyle, maybe. She had already been in Rory's head, and she knew how to do it now. Curiosity was curling around her, drawing her closer and closer to Kat.

"Even on closer inspection," Zana said behind her, "I believe she will remain the same."

Ashley jumped back in her chair. "Yeah. Sure. I... I was just..."

"I don't believe she does this on purpose."

"Does what?" Ashley stood and smoothed out her clothes. She stretched.

Zana waited until he had her full attention. "You know very well what, Princess."

"You mean... you think... just now?"

He nodded. "I believe she radiates it."

He closed the door and gestured her closer. "It was my greatest concern in removing the implant that this charm of hers might be diminished. Selfish, I know," he chuckled. "Do you think less of me that I like to be around it?"

Ashley was on an unfamiliar footing with Zana.

"I liken it to the scent of a neighbor's flower garden. The flower cannot control its scent," he looked at Katrina, "and though we may be attracted to it, we would never take the flower from our neighbor."

Ashley squinted her eyes. She felt her nose crinkle as she tried to sort it out. Was he saying he was lured into Katrina's Affectation? If he was, what about the rest of them? Zana was a meditative, reflective gentleman who was more in touch with himself than the rest of them. *He* was feeling drawn in? Spexarth had a thing for Katrina. Alex had tended to her. Rory had carried her across a desert! Astar was always defending her.

"We would not even walk among the garden flowers... would we?"

She thought she got it now.

He was as subtle as a neon sign: Keep Out.

"I say this only after I heard you shared thoughts with Rory," Zana said, pointing up at the speaker system. "That had to be unsettling."

"It was... we were... maybe it was like what you and Astar feel? So close we could complete each other's thoughts."

"Yes, like any married couple, there are times," he said, adjusting Katrina's bandages. "I would not want such times with just anyone."

"No. It's too deep."

"Katrina has had a bond like this, you know."

"With Rory?"

"With the card player. Steve. She told me about it when we were at sea."

"Steve..." Ashley said, then jumped to her feet. "Steve Spexarth! Zana, I gotta get a hold of him. He's probably on his way back to Peru, and we're not even there."

"It is an odd hour to Interface," Zana said, but she was already out the door and looking for the Stetson.

Maybe she could redirect him to Alex's proposed landing site: the Azores, west of Portugal.

53 Dark Horizon

They that wait upon the Lord shall renew their strength. Rory liked that passage from Isaiah. It was his favorite meditation on patience, but it didn't quite apply. They were not waiting on the Lord, so far as he knew. They were waiting for guests by order of a hanky.

Two days ago, on their descent to the island of Flores, it had last communicated to Ashley again. As the wheels touched down, the ink quit swirling, leaving the words "Wait for us."

Interpretations were argued.

Calissa read it as an enthusiastic plea, as in, "Hey, wait for us to catch up and join you!"

Mac was practical. "It means wait here, maybe for reinforcements? Refueling?"

"Wait—as in don't go on to whatever's under that storm?" Kelli asked, looking to Alex for answers. He simply shrugged.

"Wait on the plane? Wait on the island? Ashley, how are we to understand so little?" Astar had asked, perplexed.

There was waiting, and there was waiting. Rory had his own ideas. One could prepare while waiting. One could strategize.

And so, over the last 48 hours, he had done exactly that. He excused himself from the others, claiming he just wanted to plan a day trip to Corvo, the very western little island in the Azores archipelago. "Some R&R," he told them, "and whale spotting. Maybe we'll swim with the dolphins out there."

It gave him an opportunity to visit with the charters, the crews in the one seedy bar, and he had secured a ship for their trip to Corvo and far further west. The ship he hired, the *Obsidian*, was contracted for a four-day run to Bermuda and back, so Rory could keep the records obscured.

He had no idea what to expect, so he prepared for the tropical depression they were going to approach. He had extra provisions, clothing, and blankets. He secured a cache of weapons that would make even a Franklin militia blush.

All the while, he played the innocent tourist, working in a bicycle ride with Zana and Astar, a tour of volcanic lakes with Ashley and Katrina, and having his morning coffee each day with Calissa. He even worked in a launch around the islands to catch a rainbow with her, managing at least to keep their tradition.

On every outing, in every instance, he reserved himself from too much distraction. The place was beautiful, he knew, but the mission was coming to a head. He would not let his guard down, and he would not let them know what he was up to. He would not appreciate their heckling.

"Lighten up," was one phrase he had no tolerance for now.

Rory had left Alex and Kelli to themselves, but on the second night, Alex insisted they take in a sunrise run. It had, by any measure, been a great idea and a very scenic route. They took a meandering shore-hugging trail for a good half an hour. Rory was impressed that Alex was holding up as well as he was. Conversation was getting strained from Alex's huffing and puffing, so as they passed a sign to Moinhos de Corvo, Rory recommended they take in the sights.

Three windmills were perched on the hillside overlooking the ocean. Signage explained that seven windmills had been built in the late 1800s and that only these three survived. They walked a cobblestone path to the windmill that had not been whitewashed. Rory was admiring the natural basalt stonework. It reminded him of the sandstone back in Springfield.

When Alex was sufficiently recovered, he clapped Rory on the shoulder. "Did you ever think we'd live to see such things? That sunrise. These windmills."

"I can't take my eyes off the waves," Rory said.

They admired the view. Rory clocked them at four minutes when he spoke up, "Alex, we haven't been on a run together since... since I don't know when."

Alex smiled. "Yeah, but they don't know that, do they?" he gestured toward the village where the others were still asleep.

"If they were to catch wind of this, what should we tell them we talked about?"

"The weather?" Alex pointed west, where the storm, still over 100 miles away, was roughing up the sea and sky. At the horizon, farthest from dawn, it was roiling and black and foreboding. It was their destination.

"What will we find there, Alex? Is it dangerous?"

"I don't know what's out there, honest. I've never been, and it's not in recorded history."

"But there's something out there?"

"I think LF Winston's out there, and yeah, he's up to something."

Rory looked long and hard at the distant storm. "Could there be another island, just so small it's not even charted? You think he's set up shop out there?"

"I do," Alex said. "Then again, I dunno. He's the richest man alive. He may have raised Atlantis for all I know."

Rory thought about that. He had heard stories of the showboats in the Winston fleet, and he had little doubt that they could perform some mighty feats of power. Raising an island was impossible, no matter how rich or powerful a man might be.

Still, something was happening out there.

"I'm imagining some James Bond villain's lair," Alex chuckled. "Something just incredible. Maybe an undersea docking station, a la Jules Verne."

"And LF's the villain?" Rory asked. He was trying to prod gently, knowing Alex would clam up whenever he thought he had revealed too much.

"Could be. Can't you see him monologuing while he's holding a cat? Blowing things up with a laser like that Goldfinger dude?"

"Taking over satellites and space stations," Rory chimed in with a chuckle, "or releasing a chemical agent that will make the world depend on him for a cure."

Alex's smile faded.

A dozen enormous waves came and went from the rocky shore below.

"You know how old I am, Rory?"

"You're thirty-eight and three weeks," Rory said confidently. "Oh, and happy belated birthday."

"Yeah, thanks. Guess I missed my own party, going back in time." Alex chuckled. After a bit, he said, "I don't know anymore. I don't know how old I am."

"What's that supposed to mean?"

"I told you, time is relative, the whole mixed-up thing about when you drop the needle on the timeline... the inconsistency of time passing here and there."

Rory nodded. Alex had aged a week in 20 minutes. He had spent years in other intervals of absence, none of it linear or sensible to him. "So... thirty-eight, give or take, then?"

"I've been trying to do the math, but it's daffy. I mean, I feel like me, like I'm still your age on your timeline, right? But when I'm then and there, I think I physically regress or progress or whatever."

"What?"

"I am younger or older. Not like Benjamin Button or whatever, but not like myself."

Rory let it go for a while. Then he was consumed with it. His logistical nature was annoyed. A person was born, lived, and died, day by day. It was linear. Beginning to end. His imaginative side, which he seldom acknowledged, was loving the ideas of an irregular twist to time. What if, for instance, Alex kept going back in time, farther and farther and farther.

"So, how does that work? You always get younger when you go backwards, older going forwards?"

"No." Alex said it with no mirth, no curiosity, and that told Rory this was the crux of the matter. He waited, as he was accustomed to doing, and Alex did not disappoint. "I think I'm dying, pal. Dying of old age."

"That's... that's not possible. Look at you."

"Next time you see me, I may have been gone a decade, may look the same though," he smirked. "It makes no sense. Up until recently, it didn't really matter."

"Up until Kelli?"

"I told her I wanted to grow old with her," the words caught in his throat, but he continued, "you know, like normal. Not like this."

"Ah, maybe you're just coming down with something," Rory said with a smile. "Ask Zana for some beet juice. Run with me every morning. I'll whip you into shape."

"Yeah, or maybe it's like Time Cancer or something," Alex said. "I don't know. I just know I feel something foreboding. Something fatal."

"You sound like a *gypsy* time traveler now," Rory said, elbowing him. "Getting into fortune telling too?"

"I know, I know... there's just so much left unsaid."

"You're the most talkative guy I know," Rory said, trying again to lighten the mood.

"Kelli said that not telling you all about this made me a liar. It hurt her a lot. Worse, she thinks I'm messing with y'all, like I know everything, and I'm making you guys sweat it out, like I'm some kind of sadist."

"Alex, I know it's had to be—"

"What I was trying to do was keep it simple, you know?" He picked up a rock and threw it in the water. "So yeah, I lied to you. A lot. And I'm sorry."

"You don't need to—"

"And if I were you, all of you, I'd tie the creepy Time Traveler to an anchor and pitch him out to sea." Alex cleared his throat again.

This time, Rory didn't interrupt. He waited.

"Rory, maybe I should have taken this on alone. I mean, if I got the Time Cancer, and if whatever's out there is as bad as I think, I should've never sent you the coordinates to Huacachina. I shouldn't have told you about the mystery storm out there. It's bad enough I've lied to you the whole time I've known you, but now your daughter, your girlfriend and mine—hell, even A-Z... all of you could bite it, and it's all my fault for telling you about it."

"Do you run the hanky?"

"What?" Alex looked at him in shock. "Of course not."

"Then it's not all your fault," Rory said with a smile. "The hanky gave us those coordinates too, at the same time as you did."

"You're kidding."

"I am not kidding. Ask Zana."

"Huh!" Alex said, and even his posture looked relieved.

"And, like you said before, once I caught wind of this whole thing, once I figured out Winston was going to make One World come true—you know I would have been looking for the action, with or without you."

"Yeah, but—"

"And you heard Astar and Zana. They think this is that important, like one last huzzah," Rory said. "They *chose* to be here."

Alex was quiet for a long time now. Something was still eating at him.

"I wish we could send the girls back with Mac," he said. "I'd at least feel better about that."

Rory peered off to the east. The sun was pushing back against the dark horizon. What if there *was* a villain's lair cloaked under a perpetual storm machine? What could LF be up to out there? Pumping water into his airships? What would he do to them, should they interfere? Hose them down?

Alex let out a big sigh. "Ever play video games with those boss battles?"

"Sure," Rory said. "Why?"

"Because this feels like that. Like we're going into the big one," he said, then stared at Rory. "I told you I don't like to meddle... but this is my timeline, and you're my people. I've spent maybe a hundred years doing little to nothing out of fear of messing up this timeline, this life I've lived and loved the most. This time with you guys. Every time I'm in the past, I'm walking on eggshells, you know?"

"So, you like it here," Rory said flatly, trying to pin it down.

"Yeah, I love it here," he laughed as if he'd never realized it before.

"Good. Me too."

"So, I say to hell with the futures I've seen. Whatever gets funky from me meddling in the here and now is just fine."

"Okay," Rory said, not at all sure what he was agreeing with. "So, let's meddle with something."

Alex was pacing now. "Yeah... but I still need to be careful... man I hate responsibility, you know? If I tell you what's bugging me, what's really about to happen... at least out there... at least as best I know it—"

Rory stepped in front of him, his hands raised to bring Alex down a notch or two. "Buddy, listen. Tell me as much or as little as you need to. I'm not going to accuse you of lying. I'm not judging you at all, okay? But I could surely use some intel about now. You're freaking me out, and that's never a good thing."

54 Dead Signal

Even lounging in the sun had gotten old. In the last month, Ashley had spent more time sunbathing than at any time since college. Her tan was perfect, of course, except for scar tissue that would not turn the same deep brown as the rest of her skin. She had realized that in the last year; she had more scars than ever before. She was becoming a different person.

To her left, Kelli Chase was sleeping, her straw hat pulled down over her face. Kelli had no shortage of scars, though most of hers were old, and almost all were bullet wounds. She, too, had a deep butter rum tan and a body to show it off.

To her right, Katrina was also sunning, but as usual, she seemed preoccupied with something. It could have been her managing pain. She was pretty beat up, and she had a fresh incision from Zana's handiwork. Regardless, she did not let on that anything hurt. She just sat there, being perfect in her own right. Her body was even more defined and muscular than Kelli's, and her tan blended in with her complexion flawlessly.

The three of them must have made an impression on the locals, for men kept walking up and down their street, gawking. They weren't that subtle about it. Some of them passed repeatedly. Ogling.

Ashley owed it to the off season.

The saving grace of all this sunning was that she had companions to use as sounding boards while Rory was off making his arrangements and while Kyle was who-knew-where. She asked, "Either of you getting anything on your HeadGear?"

Kelli did not respond.

Katrina sighed, "I am not allowed any appliance, as you know. And if I were, I would not waste my attention on it when at a place so very beautiful."

"Yeah... well... I have things to do. Questions to answer."

"Like what is it we're going to meet up with out there?"

"Yeah. That's a good start." Ashley stretched her arms wide, relishing the muscles flexing to her wrists and back, yet careful not to overexert her collar and ribs. "I also want to know why CommCorp is broadcasting yesterday's news over and over."

"News is never new," Kelli said, from under her hat. "Same old, same old."

Ashley turned to her. "So, are you able to get anyone?"

Kelli tipped the corner of her hat to peek out. "Who would I ping? Alex is here."

Ashley rolled her eyes. "You have a town to run. People report to you. Aren't you even the least bit worried—"

"No," Kelli said. "I'm on vacation."

She pulled the hat back over her eyes.

"Yeah. Well... I've been on vacation a month now, and—"

"You are dead," Katrina reminded her, "as am I. We have no business on the Interface."

It was true, and she knew it. They had been given up for lost at sea. Their story wasn't headline news anymore. It wasn't even *making* the news, to her surprise. Hadn't Carl said it was all the rage? What would pacify the Parkers like this? Why would they be airing old news?

"I mean, it's literally on loop, you guys."

Kelli sighed. "What is?"

"The news, everything I tune from CommCorp directly."

"Maybe we are out of range?" Katrina offered.

"Maybe there's nothing new," Kelli said again.

They continued lounging, but Ashley's mind was not lounging at all. She was curious, if not outright concerned.

An idea came to her as she sat at a roadside vendor eating a popsicle. She tried to resuscitate an old contact, so old the Interface might just barely be able to touch it. She homed in on Skip.

It was a terrible, audio-only feed, but she knew his voice. "Hey neighbor," he said.

So, he knew there was trouble. He was being vague.

"How's your trip going?" she said. When she was so anxious, it was hard to be all cloak and dagger. She felt like this was shaping up to be like a conversation with Carl, but even he had been offline.

"Trip?" he said. "Oh, I'm still back at the house."

Ashley closed her eyes, wishing his image would appear inside her eyelids since it had not on her HairPin. Why wasn't he coming over with Spexarth? "You're not coming over tonight with Steve?"

"Steve?" he asked at last.

She did not know if there was signal delay, or if it was being sieved, or if he was just composing his thoughts—but it was excruciating to wait for a reply. "Dammit, Skippy, I want to see you. Amp up."

"My other toys are down," he said.

It sounded like he only had access to this one archaic Interface appliance. What had come of his sleek glasses? Of his HomeRoom, which was his very favorite big screen Interface tool? It allowed him to have screen upon screen simultaneously on the wall of his study.

She sighed. Something wasn't right.

"Your dad now owns all the toys," Kyle said.

"What?"

"I was with him when he bought *this one*."

This one. This one... what could he be talking about? He was there for a purchase... so it was probably a big 3dub buy. A buyout? Had they bought out CommCorp? If so, why be so secretive?

The line, however wavering the connection, was still open. She wanted Kyle to talk to her on his own terms. He felt threatened by something.

She was walking the trail of volcanic rock, cresting a hill. This landscape could be a distraction, a welcome one. If only she knew what was going on. She might let go and enjoy herself, but too many mysteries were stacking up.

She was astonished when Kyle zapped into her field of vision, as clearly as if he were there, face to face. "Dad's got the map and the car. He's going to drive us all over the edge—" he cut out, his lips still moving, but the audio came and went. She couldn't quite make it out, and she hadn't time to record it. "—playing the radio full blast, and if you listen...stay out of the rain...lose your damn mind."

Ashley rocked her head. *CommCorp, Fidelity You Can Trust.* They couldn't even hold together a conversation!

Kyle was back then, his eyes boring into hers. He looked afraid, but more as if he might be afraid for her. "He bought the company. He's going to pull it off soon. I'm going to the Lair, Reed's orders. Take cover and stay with the big guy, Ash."

Then there was no glow. No static. No sound at all. It was as if she were wearing a tiara that was not at all enhanced. She fingered the controls and cursed. She sought higher ground, but she was already on the volcano lip, likely the highest point of the island.

"Kyle!" she shouted to the sky in frustration.

She was making her way back when the HairPin snapped to full power and attention again, and she was seeing her father in a closeup. Right where Kyle had left off, LF Winston was there. "Poppy! Where are you?" she said.

He was already talking. "—experiment, Snow, and I'm not sure of your safety. A storm's coming, and when it does, take shelter and—"

Again, the signal died. When it resumed, she tried again to speak, but he was still speaking. "I have launched my greatest experiment, Snow, and I'm not sure—"

Dead air.

"Poppy? I want to talk to you. I want you to rethink—"

"—respirator just for a day or two, and then again at the next Rainmaker to pass. Do this for me, honey. It's just a precaution." The visage skipped, and he had the same expression as a moment before, and she realized this message was cycling too. "I have launched my greatest experiment, Snowflake, and I'm not sure of your safety. A storm's coming, and when it does, take shelter—"

Ashley pried the HairPin off her head and threw it as far as she could. Damn CommCorp. If her father had bought out CommCorp, he had been sold a bad bill of goods. They couldn't even carry a recorded vid without screwing it up.

What was all the nonsense about staying out of the rain?

She looked to the west, where the hurricane was tethered to the horizon. "A storm's coming," she repeated from his recording.

55 Devil's Breath

Alex popped a treat into his mouth. "Know what they call these? Suprisas, you know, like surprises."

"Huh." Rory was examining one between thumb and finger. It was a small chocolate they had served after dinner, reminding him of fortune cookies.

"You can let it melt in your mouth, or you can bite into it. Either way, it's got meringue inside." He smacked his lips.

"Can we please just get back to it?" Rory asked. The entire dinner had been sprinkled with minor revelations and tourist trivia.

"Fine. Here's what I've learned," Alex said. "Recorded history is only that: history someone recorded. I mean, I think a lot happens no one thinks to jot down. Sometimes things happen that are so little at the time, no one even tracks them back to write them up later."

Rory shook his head, clearing the cobwebs. "Your perspective on history, pal... it baffles me."

"It baffles *me*, Rory. How could anyone but a time traveler really write up history?"

"So anyway, from *recorded* history..."

"Yeah, right. The storm out there hasn't made it to the books yet. I suppose there are lots of storms that come and go in a year that don't cause much damage, some probably that never even make land." Alex popped another suprisa and continued. "So, maybe it's happened before when I've been by, but then again, this could be a *first-generation anomaly*."

"A what?"

Alex shrugged. "Sometimes I name things like that. Never had anyone to share it with before, but I think that maybe, due to whatever—maybe even due to my meddling—things don't happen the same every time. If there's a new thing, like if this spinning airship out here is new, then it's a first-generation anomaly."

"At any rate, you know nothing about it?"

"Honest. Zip. Nothing more than you do, which is that it's strange and all the airships have been in there."

"But you don't trust it. You think it's trouble."

Alex chuckled. "If I let myself, I think everything's trouble."

"I think it's another tap to that Deep Water LF Winston's loaded up. I think he's loaded everything with it, from the little blimp cloud things to that CumuloNimbus from the World's Fair."

"Then what do you think happens?"

"Alex, why don't you just tell me?"

"As we have already established, there's some new ingredients. Kelli Chase. That storm. My perspective's all washed up."

"The journal's a historical artifact. You heard what Ash said was in there, right? You saw the cave drawings."

Alex nodded.

"So, confirm this. He's going to put that Deep Water in the rain. Right?"

"Aerosol release might work, too, but he's a water guy, and he's right, I think. The water will be easier to manage and have more staying power."

"What?" Rory wanted to get this right. "This contaminant is *airborne*?"

"Could be. Has been."

"Riddles!" Rory roared. He pushed away from the table and stood. "Come on."

Alex threw cash on the table and joined him.

They walked the cobblestone streets in silence.

Finally, Rory spoke. "If whatever LF's going to share is airborne, what is it then? Like a virus or something?"

"Or something."

Rory balled up his fists. He counted his steps. He counted the cobblestones between each stride. The average was seven. "Something... as in?"

"It's like a rufie."

"Date drug?"

"More like a rape drug. In Colombia, they call it the Devil's Breath."

"You gotta be kidding me. LF's going to spray the world with *Devil's Breath*." Rory groaned. "In what stretch of the imagination does that sound like a good idea?"

"In his head, at least what I read and what I could interpret from his cave under Huacachina, maybe it's not the worst idea." Alex shrugged.

"Tell me more. Tell me everything."

"It's fallen out of vogue, but in the 1900s, there was a rash of crime in which the criminal was also the owner of—"

"I swear on all that's holy, Alex, if you don't give it to me straight, I'll—"

"Chill. Really." Alex took a quick couple of steps in front, turned, and walked backwards to face Rory as they went. "This is as straight as this one gets. Devil's Breath is derived from the Borrachero shrub in South America, like I said, mostly around Colombia... but this stuff gets around, even to this day. People get a shot of this stuff, then they just do whatever they are told. There are testimonials of people emptying their ATMs, unlocking their homes, hell, even carrying out the valuables to waiting criminals."

"Riiiiiiight."

"They call it the Zombie Juice sometimes. I had to see it for myself. This one guy in Caracas had a bit stirred in his drink, and half an hour later, he was doing whatever I told him to. Dancing on tables. He'd ask anyone to dance if I pointed him to them. Gave me every penny he had on him. And the best part... the victim wakes up later totally unaware. Zero recall."

"So, it's a drug. A hallucinogenic?"

"Yeah, you'd have to see what Dr. Ashley says, but I know it's called scopolamine. She could tell you all the medical stuff."

"Side effects? You just black out a little while, and everything's back to normal?"

"Well... people felt a little... violated." Alex was stumbling over the cobblestones and his words—trying to contain himself.

Rory was more and more puzzled by his behavior.

"Like any bender, a guy wakes up with a headache, maybe a dry mouth or a little dizziness. Sometimes they can't pee. Sometimes a few lingering hallucinations. Nothing new for a trip to South America, right?"

"Why haven't I ever heard of it?" Rory asked.

Alex smiled wryly.

"What's the point of crop-dusting the planet with it?"

"Think about it, man. What if you could soak the whole wide world with a drug that makes them all follow your will? If you could somehow plant the seeds of what you wanted them to do once they were like, all zombie-fied, it would really be—"

"WAIT A MINUTE. CARACAS?" Rory reached for Alex but couldn't grasp his collar. "Who was this guy in Caracas, Alex? Was it me?"

"I'll never tell," he said, speeding ahead, dodging Rory's swipes at him again and again. He was laughing and gasping for air at the same time as they ran through the streets together.

Panting and pouring sweat, Rory rounded yet another whitewashed building. He dashed after Alex through a wrought-iron gate. He was in the private courtyard of their resort and caught his breath at the sight before him: two gorgeous women in bikinis laying out in the sun. Their tanned bodies were glistening with oil. "Excuse me," Rory mumbled. "'Skews me."

He was backing out of the courtyard when one woman lifted her sunglasses. The other lifted a hat from her face. "Hey, Reed," Kelli Chase said. She stretched lazily, her lithe body flexing, glistening.

"Hey, Reed," Alex imitated her sultry voice. He peeked around a shrub behind their chaise lounge chairs.

Rory held back a curse. He cleared his throat, but the gravel edge was still in his voice. "Let's take a walk, eh, Alex?"

Alex was smiling. Always smiling. It was so funny, was it? Drugging him just to see if it worked? *Dancing on tables*?

"Do you wish to join us?" Katrina asked. "To wait for your princess?"

He was feeling an urge to join her, rub her down with oil, and slip into a lounge chair with her. Rory recognized it for what it was, an Affectation, or at least the remnants of one. He backed up another step or two. "Nah. No. I'm good."

"You could use a shower, bub," Alex said. "You know, cool off a little?"

"We're not done with this," Rory said, but he was eager to be out of the courtyard, to get some distance from Kat's charm.

He took a few steps backward through the gate and turned to—crash full-on into a woman on the street. Her groceries tumbled around their feet.

"Really?" Ashley asked, perturbed but smiling. "Help me pick this up."

He knelt beside her, picking up fresh fruit and handing it back to her to put in her bag.

"I've been... I was just... just looking for you."

"Good," she said. "You found me."

She was wearing a delicate crocheted cover up over a bikini that invited the imagination. He tried to count cobblestones, but her feet and ankles and legs distracted him.

They stood, and she shoved the groceries into his hands. "Do you deliver?"

He nearly fumbled the bag, mumbled a vague response, and fell in behind her as she scaled a stairway to her room.

56 Waiting

Rory followed her into her kitchenette and set down the groceries. They were in tight quarters, and she liked how awkward he could be in such places. She remembered the pantry then, and from the sudden look on his face, he might have too.

"Busy day?" he asked, bolting into the dining area.

"Just more waiting," she said. Ashley put her foot up on a chair back, pulling muscles from her gymnastics days, just to lean far forward and unbuckle her sandal. It was having the desired effect. Lots of leg. Lots of muscle. He was fixating despite himself.

She smiled and did the same move with her other sandal, then stopped herself and said, "Can you fix this? The buckle's messed up."

Rory approached and worked at the sandal as if it were made of glass. He did not make eye contact with her. Rory kept his focus on her foot, but when the buckle came loose simply, his eyes traced up her leg and back to her eyes. They shared a smile, and he released her ankle. "Got a good quote on waiting?"

"*Our willingness to wait reveals the value we place on what we're waiting for*," he said.

"But we don't know what we're waiting for," she said.

"You're waiting on Kyle. Right?"

"Yes and no," she shrugged. "We've Interfaced."

"Well, we're waiting for the hanky. It's never failed you yet," Rory said.

"*Wait for us*." Ashley smirked. "We don't even know who 'us' is. What if it's a trap?"

"Now you sound like me."

"If my dad's on that island or whatever it is under that storm, I don't know if it's worth waiting. What if he's in trouble?"

"We need every advantage we can, going into that hurricane. If someone can join us and help us, someone with that kind of communication and foresight... I want to wait for them." Rory sat on the edge of the table and folded his arms. "Who do you think's sending you those messages?"

It was a good question she had spent hour upon hour processing. Clearly, they had her interests in mind, suggesting she run and evade harm or duck to miss the bomb in the bedroom. It had urged her to pursue Rory once, and it had told her to listen to Katrina.

"Who could do that?" he gestured as if he were mixing a drink with his fingers. "I mean, it's not technological, right?"

She shrugged. The ink just moved. That's all she knew. "Maybe it's new technology, or maybe it's very old."

"A-Z have never seen anything quite like it. They're calling them divining cloths. None of them they've seen or heard of were still working, let alone working overtime. They say there's never been one that sends message after message."

"It's frustrating, anyway," Ashley said.

"But it is worth waiting for."

"Maybe."

They sat at the foot of her bed making small talk. Though it wasn't easy, she was able to get him to talk about something other than the hanky, the storm, LF, and the other curiosities that had brought them this far.

Finally, they were walking about the suite, as if they were in some calculated tango. He was going off script at last, sharing tour guide insights. "This island's named after crows, you know," he said.

"Corvo?"

"Crow in Portuguese," he nodded.

"I haven't seen a crow yet," Ashley said. She thought the small talk was getting very small. She advanced on him some, but he sped up and walked around a coffee table to peer out a window. He talked about the islands being formed by volcanoes. She had heard all that on their Jeep tour, but he was now recounting it almost word for word as he absently admired the view.

Ashley had discovered Rory was getting very sensitive to her manipulations. He could feel it coming on almost every time she Affected him. They had drilled and practiced it, in case Katrina were to turn on them again. As on the *Arcus*, he wanted to feel it coming on and do something about it. Still, she risked a subtle Affectation to limber him up. She liked drunk Rory, but she wasn't trying to get him *that* loosened up, not sand surfing sloppy. She just wanted him without the inhibitions that constantly plagued him... without the nervous tics of counting and observation he hid behind. She wanted 'comfortably numb' Rory, the crooner from the closet.

"I have another quote on waiting," he offered.

"Let's hear it," she said.

"*Delay is a bitter tonic, but it increases appetite.*"

She raised her eyebrows and smiled. "I like it. Where's your appetite about now?"

He started out tenderly, only their lips touching, though they were now standing so very close together. She could feel the heat radiating off of him, even taste the salt of his sweat.

"In love, all kinds of love, we wait." Rory whispered it, eyes closed. *"If I can't be your dawn, I will be your sunset."*

"Good quote," she said, pressing her body to his. He was holding his hands up as if in surrender. It was as if he did not want to be accused of anything. If LF Winston himself entered the room, it was only a kiss, and even that was a feather kiss. She wanted more.

Ashley licked his lip, then nipped at it, and his eyes flashed open. He had been standing there, surrendering to her, his eyes closed to her, and she thought she knew why. He was attempting to control himself, like always. She was going to see about that.

Rory's eyes had changed. It was as if a switch had been flipped. He groaned in resistance, but his eyes were devouring her now, eager to dive deeply into hers.

She could see his fingers flexing in her peripheral vision, and she wanted his big hands on her. She reached out for them and pulled them to her hips, where he latched on powerfully. Ashley stood on her tiptoes, her chest sliding up his. She whispered in his ear, "Wanna go deep?"

She could feel him smile. She could feel his breath on her neck. His hands were clutching her waist now.

"Yeah," he said in a tremulously deep voice. "Deep."

Ashley slid her palms up his chest, resting them briefly on his shoulders, then collar, then caressing his neck. She had his head in her hands, her palms pressed against his scalp. She was pulling herself to his mouth, and a powerful Affectation reverberated with their kiss. She wrapped her legs around his tree trunk legs and hung there, becoming one with his mind.

Before, the mind meld had been an experimental, passive thing, just flooding warmth and understanding and unfettered thoughts. This time, it was awash with potent desire and lust. She was tapping into his most primal self, and she did not pull away.

Their kissing and groping were heightened by the mental connection they shared. Rory followed her lead and gently laid her on the bed, never extracting himself from her arms and legs and lips. His weight was on her, and he did not retreat.

He was in her head now, pushing through her vulnerabilities and discovering her desire for him too. They were entwined in a hot mess when Rory sprang back and gasped for air. He looked more fearful than she expected.

"What is it?" she whispered, but she knew from the residual of the mind meld. She knew exactly what it was. *He was afraid of her.*

"Nothing, nothing," Rory said, flopping on his back on the bed.

"We don't have to share heads," she said, leaning against him, draping a leg over his. "We can still share the bed."

His smile was all she needed. She squirmed to straddle him and pressed herself against him in a full-body kiss. There was no mind meld this time, but then, she didn't need it. There was little between them but some clothes, and she so wanted to be out of them.

Suddenly, his back stiffened, he caught his breath, and she wished fleetingly she *was* inside his head to understand why he stopped kissing.

Again.

He was pushing her off gently.

"Got a message," Rory grumbled. "Gotta go."

Ashley couldn't believe it. "Message!"

He wiped at his jaw, and she knew: his subdermal implant. It had to be important, she thought, *to interrupt this*. Rory was on his feet, doing his best to adjust his clothes and act as if everything was fine. He dropped his guard, however, when he told her, "It's Alex."

"What's wrong?"

"All he said was 'trouble,' and he never says that lightly." Rory smiled at her then, as best as he seemed able to muster. "Sorry. I was a little too forward there. I just—"

"Don't apologize," she said. "Settle it with him, and get right back!"

He was already on his way out the door when she called to him, "Anything I can help with?"

"Some CommCorp thing," he said, bounding down the stairs. "We'll handle it."

CommCorp, she thought. She already knew what was wrong with CommCorp. Their crummy network was falling apart. Couldn't hold a signal. She hopped up off her bed and went to the window to watch Rory walk away below.

57 No News

"See for yourself," Alex said, passing the Stetson to him. "CommCorp is messed up. This should be all over the News Vids by now."

They had the plane to themselves and settled into the comfort of the *Whipstitch*. Mac and Calissa had left to find more suprisas for Alex and a bite to eat for themselves.

With distaste, Rory strapped on the Stetson and let his eyes flip channels. The top stories were initially related to Portugal, due to their location, but as Rory controlled the scroll, they ran on to world news. TransCorp North was proudly porting explorers to the pole, making the adventure much less taxing and expensive. A Nobel Prize was being issued to another ChompCorp scientist for a new preservative.

Rory pulled 3dub news into focus.

There was a nice obituary on Ashley, complete with a very flattering portrait of her. He missed her, even though she was right there on Corvo with him. A caricature of LF lassoing a cloud made him smile, though he did not bother to have the caption translated. Lesser news from 3dub reported holdings, acquisitions, and some features again reflecting LF's recent press releases. Rory was skimming through them with increasing frustration.

"Nothing," Alex said. "Right?"

"That's strange," Rory rumbled. He directly searched for the *Undulatus*, finding the story about it sinking near Bermuda, but there were few stories and nothing sensational about it. He tried the same with the *Murus*, and found even less, only some vague reference to it veering off course. "What should I be seeing?"

"When the *Murus* took her test run *the last time I can recall,* she made headlines," Alex said.

"Headlines?"

"The usual slap happy crap that goes for news. 'Placido Placebo,' I remember that headline, and 'Lake Placid," he smirked. "They were all over how everyone in Austin was opening their doors to the homeless and giving away their car keys to strangers."

Rory sighed and pulled an index for recent Vids of Austin. Again, there was nothing much in the news. "Why Austin?" Rory asked as he prowled.

"I don't know," Alex said. "Maybe LF had some enemies there."

"Maybe he was shooting for Springfield," Rory said, "Or Franklin... or who knows where? How accurate can these things be?"

"Check the dark web," Alex recommended.

Again, even an hour into searching, they had no news.

"Last time, or every time, or whatever—before—you're sure the *Murus* did a test dump, and it went badly."

Alex shrugged. "Badly is relative."

Rory sighed and stripped the Stetson from his head, enjoying the farewell tones it emitted, even though he would never admit it. Being jacked into a Stetson was unlike any other HeadGear, though it was still unacceptable to him.

"I mean," Alex continued, "it technically created the whole One World vibe you guys always yearn for."

"Giving away your car is not what we were talking about back then," Rory said. "We were holding ground against TransCorp. A transportation monopoly that left you on foot if you didn't comply—that's just not right."

"I know, but—"

"Holding whole nations hostage, restricting goods and services like no embargo ever could, charging heinous—"

"I know, Rory. I know. Sharing is a beautiful thing."

"Winston might be crazy now, but think about what he accomplished while the rest of them were squeezing us."

"I know. He did a lot, and he still does with his free water and irrigation programs and all his charities to provide—"

"The Big Gulp. The Gulf. The River Runs Through It Initiative. The Suez and Panama Canals. Protecting the Poles...all his enterprises, all liberating people to share this world's water."

"Yes, I get it," Alex said firmly. "But going about it like this? Brainwashing people to be good, to share? You think that's ever worked?"

Rory was quiet.

Alex put on the Stetson and prowled some on his own.

Rory began again. "I don't think this scopolamine *brainwashes* anyone, does it? Just leaves them open to suggestion, right?"

"Right. Maybe? As best as I can tell—"

"So LF just has to make the right suggestion?"

"I dunno, Rory, that still sounds manipulative in my books."

Rory tried not to ask about the future too much, for it just made him angry. Alex had an irritating reframing technique whenever the questions leaned too far into his foreknowledge: "I don't know, Rory, what do you think?"

Alex would, however, entertain any number of speculations. Rory was pressing him on what possible reason someone other than LF might have for taking the *Murus* off the grid. "Where could someone even fly an airship that's not going to show up?" he asked.

Alex pointed out the window at the storm cloud. "That one's not on anyone's radar."

It was a valid point. He wondered, too, if the *Murus* could fly as high as the *Arcus*, or maybe even higher. To be at such a high altitude might make her harder to find. He made a mental note to ask Ashley.

"Would someone just want to hold that scopolamine for a particular situation, maybe?"

"Maybe," Alex said noncommittally.

"Could it somehow be a weapon?"

"Like converted into a Lightning's Hand?"

"Or crash landed...think how much that thing must weigh with two million gallons of water on board. It could crush about anything. Level a city."

"Eight thousand tons, roughly. It could surely make a dent."

"But you're not telling me why the *Murus* is missing?"

"Hasn't happened before, I told you." Alex shrugged. "It mellowed out Austin for a while, but it's never—"

"For a while?" Rory sat up. Suddenly, things didn't seem nearly as awful. "So, what... does scopolamine just wear off?"

"It dissipates. Evaporates. Some of it gets in Lake Travis and other groundwater, I think. Some floats around for a while, you know, trees and tires and puddles and all."

"But it goes away?"

"Yeah. Why, is that what you want now? A *temporary* One World?"

"If it's inevitable that LF is going to do this, and it mucks things up, I'd like to believe it will not be irreversible or permanent. It's like a warning shot, maybe?"

"Except here we are, and still no shot fired around the world," Alex said. "What are we waiting for?"

"Ashley's hanky, I guess," Rory said. He pivoted in his seat to address Alex more directly. "I want to know who's behind that. Always have. They're wanting us to wait, so maybe they'll have some idea how to deal with this."

"That's not like you, boss."

"How so?"

"You're waiting for help," Alex said, "from someone you don't even know. I'm not saying it's not a welcome change, but it's not like you. You're more a do-it-yourselfer."

"This one's more than blood and brawn," Rory said. "I'm out of my element."

"Just another caper, pal. Like you said, our last huzzah."

"A caper with time travelers and gypsies and zombie drugs and airships as big as the sky," Rory said. "That about sum it up?"

"Well, when you put it like that—"

"All the while, working within the straitjacket of high society, corporate empires, and rich folks nuttier than a fruitcake."

"You left out bottomless pockets and beautiful women," Alex countered, "and a crack team you can depend on."

"Oh... and a dragon. Astar thinks there's a dragon back at the green cave," Rory added. "Beat that."

"What if I *could* beat that?" Alex said, raising his eyebrows.

"Let's hear it." Rory sat back and folded his arms.

"The fate of mankind hangs in the balance. The love of your life is counting on you."

"You're just making that up about the fate of mankind."

"Am I?"

"And just ask her—Ashley Winston, doesn't count on anyone but herself."

"Annnnd there we are," Alex smiled. "Lesson learned?"

As they spoke, Rory noticed a rickety helicopter attempting a landing at the runway's end, next to the commercial hangars. "Expecting anyone?"

They watched the helicopter lurch and wobble, then bounce on its skids.

"No, and I can't believe anyone flew that rust bucket out here." Alex shook his head in astonishment.

There was a commotion as Mac and Calissa climbed through the hatch. "Did you boys see that damn thing?" Mac asked without ceremony. "That's an old Sikorsky S-92. Old as you fellas, I'm guessing."

"Is that... plywood?" Rory was studying something over the side windows.

"How's that thing—" Alex stopped.

"Do you recognize it?"

"Remember it from the future... or whatever?" Calissa asked. She had confused even herself in asking the question.

"Déjà vu," he whispered. He was watching it closely, waiting for something.

When the rotors stopped, a cloud of smoke belched from the engines.

He nodded absently then.

"What is it, Alex?"

"That chopper," he said. "I *have* seen it before."

He scrambled, found the Stetson, and worked into it. "I saw it in some footage from one of the Round Ups. That one was seized by the 'Coats."

"That'll be the day!" Mac scoffed.

"Why haven't I ever heard of that before?" Rory asked.

"Look," Alex said, flipping the visor open.

Rory watched the camera footage as it was projected there. It was obviously someone's HeadGear recording, not a trained news vid reporter. The view panned over a Smoker. TransCorp black suits were lounging everywhere, smiling at the camera. The footage was spliced twice, and the last segment was harder to see. It was grainy and filmed in low light. It showed a ragtag group of men and women sneaking onto the helipad. A violent hand-to-hand exchange quickly ended for the helicopter's guards and crew.

It was a cold start, but the rotors spun up, and the craft angled off screen. The camera operator was running now and swung the camera back on the helicopter as it did a full circle before rising up and away under heavy fire.

"How in the hell did you remember that?" Mac asked.

"The tail number, N1016-S, that's my birthday," Alex smiled. "November 10, 2016."

Rory had a pistol in hand and another tucked in his belt behind his back.

He tapped a quick Clench to the others. Stay Put.

His best friend was capable of time travel. He had come to embrace that, but he could not believe what was now just thirty yards away. It was an impossible relic from a war long lost. Yet it sat there smoking. As they drew nearer, it popped as it cooled. Some fluid was dripping from it.

It was weathered and rusted and riddled with poorly filled bullet holes. The stolen helicopter that had provided another surge of energy from the 'Coats when they should, instead, have surrendered. Rory both loved and hated the craft. It was the last campaign of the Turncoats, the old *Feldergarb*.

The door was ajar, and someone inside was crashing against it to force it open. When it did open, Steve Spexarth fell out on the tarmac, then got to his feet quickly. "Hi guys," he said. "Am I late?"

58 Dream

They called them gypsies, but Ashley's lineage did not point directly to any of the Roma peoples of Europe. She did not know her family history back prior to her grandmother, who was adopted into the Amish. What was clear enough, however, was the bloodline carried their craft.

LF Winston's bloodline.

The Family craft.

Affectations.

"A lot of good that is," she said aloud to her empty quarters. Affectations had helped her get her way in her youth, then pulled her through some tough scrapes. Lately, all the craft had caused was hardship and pain.

She winced at the memory of striking the bedpost in her fight with Katrina. Her collar bone throbbed a steady reminder of the brawl. Her loose tooth brought back the thrashing in vivid detail.

Hardship and pain.

Maybe that was Poppy's problem. The craft had taken away his mother. He had never been that good at the craft. Maybe he resented it, recoiled from it. He had turned full force to the Water Works, and the business had taken away his time. Then to have all that effort and success quashed by the other corporations...

Ashley knew him to be a sensitive man. She thought of passages of his journal, trying to remember something from it that would explain his dealings of late. Of his cryptic message on the Interface. What she could recall knotted her stomach.

Affectations! She would gladly be done with them in exchange for telepathy. She willed her mind to reach out to sea, to the strange storm looming. She felt for his presence, just certain he was out there somewhere.

Nothing. He was as opaque and remote to her now as ever.

Even as a child, she had wanted to know his mind, at least to know what he thought of her, his only daughter. She *still* wondered what he thought of her, of the way she had kept 3dub running, the way she tried to preserve his interests. She had just grown into knowing the pressures he must have had from rival corporations. It had to be soul crushing.

Somehow, through it all, he held onto the One World fantasy. Maybe it had finally broken him. She leaned against the balcony door and stared out to sea. She wished she could cradle him as he had cradled her. She wished even that they might honestly share Affectations of good will, rather than his manipulations about the *Murus*. She longed for a rewind, for a chance in which she could prove herself, even as that young girl on the *Incus*. She could have made him understand her passion for his creations. She could have been there to help him through the corporate slaughter years later.

Ashley flopped on her bed, regretting it again for the surge of pain.

What if she could rewind and relive her childhood better? If time travel were real, as Alex asserted, wouldn't it be wonderful to be back then and cherish the moments with fresh eyes? As she dwelt on it, however, the whole concept was even more confusing. What time in her life would she revisit? Those days before the launch of the *Incus*, when LF had not taken time even for a change of clothes? Those darkest days when he wept privately in his study? When and where would she intervene, and would it ever be enough? If time travel was true, and if one could pinpoint re-entry... such decisions would be agonizing.

Her mind whirled over Alex's claims. She could hardly grasp how a man could remain so chipper with such choices at hand. When she saw him next, she planned to talk all that out with him, to get a feel for what he felt. Maybe he could use a little hoo-doo, too, she smiled wanly.

She had dozed off in that haze of thinking and daydreaming. She woke, knowing something of a moment to relive. "*We Winstons*," Poppy's voice whispered from a sacred bedtime ritual she could barely recall, "*we are the music makers, Snow, the dreamers of dreams.*"

His dream, however, *this dream*, this One World, was not her own. He had called this latest venture his Magnum Opus, but as she thought more, his return from the dead might be purely for revenge. Maybe in all his loftiness he had taken a header. His generosity, his "peace, love and joy shtick" as Rory had called it, might truly be a sham.

59 Feldergarb

A dozen men scrambled out of the doors of the helicopter quickly, as if they feared it would catch fire. There were familiar faces among them, men who gave Rory fist bumps and high fives.

Chavez approached, dropped to the ground, and kissed it. "Thought we'd never see land again!"

Grimes was carrying empty canvas duffle bags. When he saw Rory's interest in them, he paused in passing to say, "Getting some fruit, some decent food."

Another man from Franklin paused to ask directions to the nearest bar.

"Who are these guys?" Alex asked when they thinned out.

"You know Chavez," Rory reminded him. "Maybe you met Gurt?"

"Why are they... here?" He seemed lost in thought. Rory thought he might be trying to make sense of this moment in its larger timeline context.

"I brought reinforcements!" Spexarth beamed.

"Why are *you* here?" Rory asked, "How'd you—"

"Oh, Miss Winston's been sending me coordinates. I figured it was a big deal going down out here."

"Where'd you get that chopper?" Rory asked, still confused himself.

"Did you know an airship's big enough to hide a helicopter on? We've been a bug on the wing of that thing all the way out here."

"Which airship?" Alex asked.

"*Undulatus*," Spexarth said. "Talk about seasick!"

"I heard that the *Undulatus* sank in the Bermuda Triangle."

"Did you?" Spexarth chuckled. He turned to watch crewmembers behind him. "News these days! Have you tuned into CommCorp lately? It's all wack. Can't trust anything you hear any more on the Interface."

Alex tipped his head to the side as he studied Spexarth and the crew, those who toiled around the helicopter. Rory could read the curiosity brewing behind Alex's sunglasses.

"Stay with the ship," Spexarth called to the pilots. "Need to be on standby."

Rory felt his neck muscles knotting up. Alex wasn't like this. The continuing pauses and reflection, matching timelines and circumstances—it was not the Alex he knew.

"So," Spexarth asked again, casually, "have you kept up? Been jacked in?"

Rory started to tell him about the disturbance, the news loop, but Alex patted him on the shoulder and spoke up, "We've been too busy with the sun and fun. No time for tech."

"Oh, well..." Spexarth looked at both of them, then offered, "There's some sweet old HeadGear onboard. A TopHat."

"You're kidding?" Alex glanced at Rory—was he asking permission? Still skeptical? He smiled broadly. Then he said to Spexarth, "I haven't seen a TopHat in ten years!"

"C'mon then. You're gonna love it." The two headed for the helicopter.

Rory was still taking in the *Feldergarb.* None of his questions were answered. Even if the helicopter had come, complete with crew, on the back of a Rainmaker, where had it been before that? How had it come into Spexarth's possession?

Grimes was at his side again, this time offering Rory a spare beer. "Never thought you'd see that old barge again, did ya?"

"*How*?" Rory marveled.

"Spexarth. Kid's a genius. He could talk paint off a wall."

"Steve Spexarth stole the *Feldergarb*?"

"Complete with crew. German pilots." Grimes said it with exaggerated humor, like a bad actor tanking his lines. "Damn, they're fun boys. Wish we would have had them back in the day."

"Grimes, I can't wrap my head around this. Catch me up."

"Living the dream," he sighed. Men were coming and going past them. Grimes was not speaking when anyone was within earshot. "Spexarth came back from San Fran with a bug up his ass. Then he hopped in with LF Winston's inner circle. Told us to..."

Rory was watching Nick Grimes closely. The old Turncoat was not himself. His eyes kept returning to the helicopter's cockpit. They were walking around the helicopter. Rory stroked it as they passed along the fuselage, still shocked he could reach out and touch the legendary *Feldergarb*. As they rounded the tail, Grimes stopped walking and started talking in earnest. "Told us to wait him out at the Estate. Last week, he landed in this thing on the helipad, and we were off without so much as a toothbrush. Three days in that damn thing, and the whole time, he was regaling us with old Turncoat shanties and pumping us up."

"Spexarth? The kid wasn't even alive—"

"I know, Reed. I know."

"So, you *didn't* ride in on the back of an airship?"

Grimes shook his head, but he was mum again. He scratched at his ear subtly, just as Spexarth and Alex were rounding the ship. Alex was wearing a tall, stovepipe top hat. Once it had been a state-of-the-art appliance. Now it was HeadGear that had seen its better days.

Rory took Grimes' cue, plastered on a smile, and tapped his beer to Nick's. They saluted by touching the shaved swath at their temples.

They toasted together, "Fat and Happy."

"I still don't get that one," Spexarth said, half to Alex, half to Rory.

They sat on a retaining wall, looking out at the early rays of sunset cresting the distant storm. Alex and Steve were in a conversation about how sunsets were more beautiful in a storm. "In any case, there's particulates," Alex was saying. "Forest fire, volcanic ash, wheat harvest, smog..."

Rory sat on the end, next to Alex. Spexarth, Chavez, and a couple of other men sat farther down the way. Grimes was undoubtedly rounding up food.

Conversation ranged from sunsets to HeadGear, from card tricks to casinos. Spexarth and Alex seemed on their way to becoming fast friends. On multiple occasions, however, Rory noticed Alex peppered their visiting with questions: *Why had they taken the helicopter to Corvo?* Miss Winston's orders. *Why did she want them there?* Reinforcements. *What had she contracted him to do for her?* Bring her Kyle DuPree, but he was unavailable. *Why not just call it in on the Interface?* Damn thing's acting up, all of CommCorp's buggy. *Why the Feldergarb?* Seemed like a good idea.

Rory nodded. Alex was a master at conversational interrogation. They would have a lot to untangle later in the privacy of the *Whipstitch*.

After an hour, most of the men had returned to the *Feldergarb* with ample stocks and provisions. Rory wondered what they had been eating all those days in the chopper. They set about loading the ship without regard for any of them.

"I almost forgot—" Spexarth said, right in the middle of a conversation. He jumped up from the wall and made a dash to the helicopter.

Alex and Rory shrugged at each other.

Steve Spexarth returned with a huge bouquet of white trumpet flowers that dangled like lolling heads. "No worse for the wear," he said, looking a little crushed that the flowers did not present themselves better. He adjusted them as he spoke. "Got these for the Princess and her court."

He tossed the bouquet to Alex and Rory. Between them, they jostled it, almost fumbling it to the ground.

"Take a whiff," Spexarth said. "I think they're amazing! Got 'em over at Isla de Flores."

Alex took a big whiff, passing them to Rory, who did the same. They smelled more like fresh cut grass than anything else Rory could put his mind to. He held them awkwardly.

"Eh. They don't look right on you. Tell you what, *I'll deliver*, if it's all the same to you two," Spexarth offered. "I know you guys got a boat to catch. Taking a ship into that hurricane, I hear. Big balls."

"Sure. Sure," Rory said.

"We got the biggest balls of them all," Alex joked.

"Probably best to leave the women here," Spexarth winked. "We'll look after them."

Spexarth took the bouquet from them and headed up the hill to the Villa.

A skinny, freckled man popped his head from the helicopter. It was Cox from the *Arcus*. Noticing Spexarth leaving, he shouted, "Wait for us, wait for us!"

...but no one had budged to follow Spexarth, nor to go anywhere else. It was like an inside joke.

Rory was shaking his head as he watched Spexarth go. He looked at Alex a beat, then just came out with it. "Steve's the new guy on the team. I brought him on to replace you."

"Him?" Alex snorted.

Then the two of them set off, arguing all the way to the dock. They were taking Rory's ship, the *Obsidian*, out to meet the storm.

60 Empire

It was dusk, and the four women sat together in the resort's empty foyer, talking and waiting. Ashley spoke of the men who had arrived by helicopter, familiar men who had been at the Estate what seemed like an eternity ago. The newly arrived were intent on finding food and returning to their aircraft. Calissa reported they didn't even stop at the bar or gawk at the sunset... or at them. This was no normal shore leave, they all noted.

Kelli had to be right—they would be exhausted too. Ashley agreed. Even nice helicopters lacked amenities, and that old bucket of bolts would just be benches and bailing wire inside.

Conversation came to focus again on the waiting, how none of them really knew who they were waiting for. Katrina was loyal to the magic handkerchief, as was Ashley herself. If the hanky said, "Wait for us," then that was the right thing to do, Katrina argued. Their Affectation 'magic,' Ashley thought, might make the two of them more likely to believe in other magic.

Neither Calissa nor Kelli could deny that the hanky had offered life-saving advice, but they were skeptical as to the sender of these messages. Calissa said if it could not be experimented upon and the results replicated, then it was just some kind of fluke. Ashley smiled at that, for she would have said the same thing at one point in her career. Kelli simply said it was a bad tactic. Leaving their fate to a magic rag was ridiculous. She said, the first time its advice ran contrary to her common sense, she was breaking ranks. She asserted, however, that waiting was, for now, all they could do.

But Ashley had grown tired of it. Waiting was a waste, no matter what Rory slathered over it. It was literally getting them nowhere to sit and visit.

She stood and spoke. "Is there nothing we can do? Nothing at all? Why can't we paddle out there and see what Poppy's up to? I mean, how bad could it be? He's filling airships with water. I mean, what's your dad been telling you, Calissa? 'Cuz he's not telling me *anything*. Kelli, I bet you're just as much in the dark. Alex has been acting odd since we left Peru."

"Have you just met him? He's always—"

"I know Kelli, but the time travel thing? I just don't know..."

"Dad said we would all push off for the storm in the morning," Calissa said hurriedly, "that the storm out there has been losing energy at dawn."

"How would he know this?" Katrina asked.

"He's observant," Ashley replied. "He'd watch for something like that."

"So, let's find the guys and gear up," Kelli said, agreeing with Ashley now. "Where's Rory doing his waiting?"

"The *Obsidian*," Calissa said. "He's chartered a ship. He's been gearing up since we got here. It's tied off down the hill from the airstrip."

Ashley did a double take. "*That's* where they are?"

When would he have found the time? How had this slipped her attention?

"Yes and no," a man's voice proclaimed, and Steve Spexarth entered the lobby with a ridiculously large bouquet of flowers.

"Spexarth?"

"Got here as soon as I could," he said, passing the bouquet around. "Slight detour to Flores for these."

"Where's Kyle?" Ashley asked, pulling a draw of the fragrant tropical flowers, then passing them on to Kelli.

"I was still looking for him when I got the remnants of your message."

"CommCorp is spotty," Ashley nodded.

"And with nothing else to go on, I thought it might be urgent, so I found that copter in a scrapyard and got here as quickly as I could."

Kelli was holding the flowers far from her face. She was fighting off a sneeze. "Allergies," she said, handing them back to Spexarth.

"Me too," he said, tossing the flowers on a table. "This'll help."

Spexarth spritzed a perfume atomizer at Kelli's nose. "That's better, isn't it?"

"Yeah. Better," Kelli said.

"You didn't ever reach Kyle?" Ashley persisted.

"Couldn't. Sorry Princess." Spexarth smiled. He didn't look particularly sorry. He looked a little too cocky for a new recruit who failed his first responsibility.

"Wait a minute," Calissa said. "What did you say about Dad and Alex?"

"The ship! Yes, they are on the *Obsidian*. However, it's no longer docked," Spexarth turned to her and sneered, "They left without you."

"They wouldn't!" Calissa was moving toward him, perturbed. Ashley thought the girl was going to shake the truth right out of him.

Spexarth directed the perfume at her as if he were bearing a flame thrower. "Nighty-night, kiddo," he said, and spritzed her twice in the face.

It didn't feel like an Affectation was in the air, but Ashley noticed Kelli and Calissa were suddenly non-responsive.

"It figures you'd be a tougher case, but it doesn't matter," Spexarth said, approaching her with his little perfume flacon. She was springing on the balls of her feet, intending to kick that bottle from his hands with a roundhouse, but she fell to the floor. She struggled to get up.

Spexarth laughed and tucked the bottle back in his pocket. "Don't even need it, eh? You huffed the Devil's Breath, babe, right from the flowers. You're all so gullible."

Ashley looked over at Katrina. Had she smelled the flowers? Been spritzed? Ashley was having trouble remembering anything. She felt drunk. In the back of her mind, she was thinking about zapping the lot of them, something that would serve her as well. *Works both ways.*

"You're all victims, you know. Corporate greed. You all got suckered in by the Princess here, and more, by her lunatic dad. Her knight in shining armor, too—now there's a gullible sap if ever I met one. *But even you*, Capt'n Chase. I admired you, you know. I feel bad that it ends like this for you."

"What ends?" Kelli slurred.

"You chose your bed, though. Sided with the rich folk in the end." He turned to Calissa and said, "I feel bad for you, too, little pussywillow. If ever there was a victim! I know you grew up humble in Delrose. I know you're more of a bystander than a bad guy, but I gotta clean this up. Can't have you girls messing with my plans. Besides, what should you expect? Your daddy's an assassin. His girlfriend's..."

A flashing light and chime went off on the appliance Spexarth was wearing on his forearm. "Ah, well... no time to monologue," he sighed, turning again to Ashley. "Your sister here's going to do mop up. I just wanted to see you one last time to say it's been a pleasure ruining your little empire."

"My empire," Ashley repeated, unable to sort it out.

"Katrina, give them something to fight about." Spexarth tapped his forehead.

"Of course," she said obediently.

The Affectation hit so hard Calissa screeched in pain. Ashley stumbled to her feet, looking for something to arm herself. Kelli had come to attention, angered that her plasma pistol was not holstered on her hip. The three women dived at each other, nails and teeth bared, colliding into a hair pulling, grunting fight.

"Oh, kick it up a notch," Spexarth grinned. "Make it primal. Make them pull each other apart like animals."

Katrina shrieked, "No. I won't do it."

Spexarth pulled his necklace from inside his shirt and fingered at an amulet he wore that matched her own. "Yes, you will," he said, challenging. Threatening. "You'll do whatever I say, won't you?"

Ashley only caught a glimpse of the bizarre scene between them. It was as if he had a remote control on that necklace. Katrina glowered at him but turned her attention back to the fight. The next Affectation was so powerful it seared Ashley's mind.

"*That's it.* And join in the fun." Spexarth handed Katrina a large knife, hilt first. "Slit some throats. Make it a bloody mess, if you want, but be at the chopper in five minutes. Got me? Five minutes."

"Five minutes," she repeated.

Spexarth laughed merrily and walked out into the night, whistling as he went.

61 3dub. 2.0

Rory was alarmed at the fuel gauge. He tapped at it, as if that might make any difference. The lights flickered in the tiny engine room. He tapped the gauge again, knowing there was no correlation. The lights stayed on. The gauge still showed empty. Hadn't he told them the trip was for Bermuda? Wouldn't a rental come fully fueled? He was sure he had checked it on his afternoon rounds.

"What's the latest?" Alex yelled from above deck.

"We better be close," Rory called back. "And it's a one-way trip." Rory climbed the ladder and twisted himself back to the deck, back into the storm. He grasped the rigging Alex was clutching. "Empty," he explained.

They had done many things, crazy things, but piloting a small craft into a hurricane was a new one. It might give them stories to tell the girls someday. Maybe.

According to Alex's interpretation of the instrument panel, something very large was dead ahead. He had lashed off the wheel to point them toward the object. He assured Rory that they could not miss it, regardless.

The *Obsidian* had been beaten and battered, tossed up and down by vast waves, and yet she was still afloat. From what Rory could tell, they were through the worst of it. They'd endured wind that took their breath away. Rain had soaked through their slickers and rubber boots. Lightning threatened to scorch them from the sea.

For Rory, the worst of it was the sound. He could close his eyes. He could meditate away the ravaging winds. Sounds, however, persisted. Wind was screaming through the rigging. Waves battering the hull. The Obsidian was groaning and creaking nearly to the breakpoint.

And then there were Alex's sea shanties.

He had felt drunk, then seasick, then collapsed in the sloshing water on deck. Alex was there, face to face with him. He was pale and only half-conscious. The two of them would drown here. Alex might already be gone.

As if reading his mind, Alex opened his eyes and said, "Hella way to go, after all this time."

"I don't leave things undone." Rory frowned at him.

"That's why I should have filled you in a long time ago," Alex said. "Guy can't do it all alone."

"What are you—"

"I always think I have the answer. *Cocky*. You know."

"Alex, if we're going to bite it here..." Rory couldn't follow his own argument. He grew quiet and tried to listen over the storm. By the look on his face, Alex was spilling his soul.

"Maybe I was waiting to get out here and shut it all down myself... maybe I waited too long. We could have nuked it, the whole damn storm and all... better ending... bitter ending."

It was too hard to hold the thought of it all intact. Too heavy.

The black of night and sky and sea swirled around him, and Rory lost consciousness.

Rory was tossed into a bulkhead. Alex careened into the mast, whacking his hip. The wind was dying. The rain had stopped, and the ship was no longer tossing in the sea.

They had struck land.

Rory stood and panned a light over the bow. It was smooth and dark ahead, waving with the tides. The running lights shined below, revealing that this was not land. It was a flexible, man-made material.

"What is this? Shoreline? A dock?"

"I don't think so," Rory said. He patted at his vest and pockets. Knife. Gun. Flashlights.

"What are we doing here?" Alex asked.

"How did we get here?" Rory asked.

"What's the last thing you remember?"

Rory shrugged.

"Ah, it's happening already," Alex groaned.

"What? What do you mean?"

"We got doped by Spexarth. He used the Devil's Breath, brother." Alex cackled then and bounced on the deck a little. "You know what that means, man? *We get another chance!* We can still save the day!"

Rory was trying to piece it all together. Taking the *Obsidian* out like they had, just the two of them, had been foolhardy. Navigating in the dead of night into a hurricane was stupid. He would never have done that spontaneously.

"Why would he do that? Send us to die at sea?"

"To get rid of us, yep," Alex said. He fished in his pockets and extracted a little tin container. "You're not going to like this, but you need it if we meet that kid again. Trust me."

Rory examined the Vicks tin. He popped the top and was immediately repulsed. He snapped the lid back on. "What is that?!"

"Menthol, and a little more."

"Flammable?"

"Maybe." Alex smiled. "You need to wax your nose with it. Inside."

"Nope." Rory shook his head, extending the tin to Alex.

"I did it, and I'm fine."

"That might be true, but..." Rory knew it was important, and he knew not to ask, but he had to. If he was putting that in his nose, he had to know, "...why?"

"Kat gave it to me, says it stops the Devil's Breath."

"Didn't work to keep us from sailing out here."

"I... uh..." Alex smiled candidly. "Okay. Okay, I didn't use it yet either."

They scooped out dollops, two fingers each, and on three, rubbed it in their nostrils. The pain was bearable, but it made Rory's eyes water, then it made him sneeze.

"Tequila snorting," Alex said, between sneezes.

"What?"

"Reminds me of snorting Tequila."

Behind them, far behind them, in fact all around them at a good distance, the storm continued to rage. Overhead, however, the spinning sky was lightening up. Disorienting. They seemed to be in the hurricane's eye. It was breezy and cool here, but nothing compared to what they had endured.

"This is unnatural," Alex said, surveying the situation. "I don't like it."

"We don't have to like it," Rory grumbled. They bounded over the railing and landed on the rubbery surface. It gave underfoot like a trampoline.

"Airship," Rory said.

"The *Undulatus*?" Alex asked at his side.

"Maybe," Rory nodded.

Sea water sloshed with rainwater. Hatch mark puddles raced through the crisscrossed strappings only to pool again in different directions. Reforming again, liquid black diamonds on the alien surface.

The two men splashed farther onto the airship. Rory's flashlight seemed powerless against the oppressive night, but the swirling clouds and distant lightning provided some illumination. They walked for a mile, by Rory's best guess. It was hard to know, with the rocking and rolling of the surface, the twisting sky above.

It was all disorienting and otherworldly.

Eventually, Rory could discern huge hills and rounded, almost bubble-like obstructions on the surface of the airship. They fought their way over a few, then discovered they could see them in silhouette, and after that, they worked around them. Something brighter was ahead, around hills and turns and bloated shapes that no longer resembled an airship's taut surface.

With no other plan in mind, Rory made his way toward the light.

"I think we're on the ghost ship," Alex said eventually.

"Agreed," Rory said. "But it didn't settle well."

"The humps. Are they pockets of aether or what?"

"Could be. Could be ripples in the wreckage."

"So weird, man," Alex said, looking all about.

Rory could not argue that. There was no better description. As they made their way over and around hills, then knee deep in valleys flooded with sea water, Rory continued to marvel at the scene. He could feel the ocean rolling underfoot, surging some, but it was tamed, crushed by the massive airship. He could see more clearly some brilliant glow ahead, and he ran through the options. He was no longer bound to logic or reason. He reviewed his memories of the surrealistic cave paintings and imagined one depicting this landscape of darkness, perhaps with a glowing sun in the center ahead. He was not holding himself back from speculating about magic or the stuff of science fiction. He smiled at himself when even thoughts of something extraterrestrial crossed his mind.

Then, rounding a hill, they were on a plain larger than the Winston Estate, nearly as large as Corvo Island. Around the edges of the plain were portals radiating their phosphorescent blue white glow. From somewhere high in the heavens, a waterfall streamed a flow of water to the airship surface, and from there, the waters snaked and divided into a dozen streams that made their way to the portals.

Nearby, a stream was flowing into a shimmering portal, then disappearing within the bright light. "Like Huacachina," Rory said, pointing.

"Only bigger," Alex marveled.

They waded across streams as they gradually circled the waterfall. Rory could hear thunder in the distance. He had almost forgotten the hurricane, but its rumble competed with the waterfall. Spray from the falls created an ethereal mist that took on the glow of the portals. At times, it was difficult to see through it, but Rory persisted. He wanted to get to the center, as close to the waterfall as he could. Nothing but the symmetry of it pushed him to it. There was no reason to go there other than curiosity. There was nothing reasonable here at all.

A turn around the waterfall led them into thicker mist and louder thunder from the waters. Alex tripped. Getting to his feet, he put something in Rory's hand. He shined his flashlight on it. "It's old comm tech," he explained, "a mobile phone."

They tripped over more and more debris. The closer they came to the waterfall, they found ever more hardware littering the landscape. It came to cover the surface, with only crooked paths for them to follow. Antiquated hardware was knee high: generations of discarded electrical devices, from tube radios to CRT monitors, from massive Jumbotrons to scattered HeadGear. Some of the machinery looked military in origin. All of it seemed so out of place. Damp. Jostling with the ocean waves. Discarded.

Rory put a hand out to stop Alex. A figure stood just ahead, seemingly *under* the waterfall. No, he was under a white umbrella. They stepped closer. Rory wiped his eyes. He was squinting in the mist, trying to confirm what he was seeing.

"Come in, come in," LF Winston said, beckoning them to him. The umbrella he stood under was actually a canopy, and glass walls extended from it to the floor. It was a glass gazebo.

It seemed like a giant upturned glass to Rory. When he reached the wall of the glass, Winston said again, "Come in out of the weather, boys." He reached through the glass and pulled Rory in by his arm. He retrieved Alex too. Then the glass wall solidified. The three of them were in a silent, transparent room, at the foot of a waterfall, surrounded by radiant Hot Wire portals, in the eye of a hurricane. They were a thousand miles from Portugal and another thousand from Bermuda, but they might as well have been in outer space.

"Do you... have you *traveled time*?" Alex said, swiping moisture from his face.

It was as good as any opening question, given the circumstances. Rory had to admit, he was thinking the same thing. Though it was the same old LF Winston he had seen just days ago in Huacachina, the man seemed more vivid and lively, like the old maverick, the Typhoon Tycoon from twenty years before.

"Time travel. That would be amazing!" LF chuckled. "Pure fantasy, but amazing!"

Rory looked beyond the liquid glass at the scene outside. It was all pure fantasy.

LF simply stood, smiling at them as they wrung out their clothes and wiped dry as best they could. LF acted as if they were standing in his foyer at home, having just come in from a rainstorm. He wasn't seeing the absurdity of the moment.

Rory felt the frustration welling up inside him. He tried to be patient. There was nothing in the glass gazebo to count. The floor was mist as thick and white as milk. The walls were clear. The ceiling was white, and it glowed independently of the portals that otherwise illuminated it. The three of them stood just a few feet out of arm's reach.

"Mr. Winston," Rory grumbled, "what is this place? What's it all about, sir?"

"Ah, we're beyond formalities, aren't we, Rory?" With a flourish and a smile, he pronounced, "Welcome to the Obsolescence."

There was that word again, Rory thought. "A ship?" he ventured.

"Hmm?" LF questioned. "Oh. Oh, no. We're *standing* on a ship, an old Undulatus. *The Undulatus*, if you're into history. Hee hee. We're standing in the nexus of the next, boys. The next Great Perhaps, perhaps."

Rory grumbled. He felt his fists clenching. Cult babble.

"Allow me," Alex grinned. "If there's anyone more at home in the gloam, it's me, pal."

Alex took a step toward Winston. "I get it. It's 3dub 2.0."

LF smiled and nodded. "Yes. Yes."

"You're porting water here," he waved to the waterfall, "from Peru."

"Who is your wise friend?" LF asked, looking past Alex to Rory.

Before Rory could answer, Alex continued. "From here, you're porting it to... where? The airships, maybe?"

"Yes. Yes." LF was admiring his portal arrangement. The glow of the portals gleamed in his eyes. "It was a volume displacement issue, initially. Limited resources, at least limited flow. *The Murus* nearly dashed my dreams, you see?"

Rory did not see at all, but Alex heartily agreed with him. "You couldn't just suck it all up to every ship, one by one?"

"No, no. Not if we were to obtain status flow," LF said, appraising Alex more closely now.

"Because you want this out *everywhere*, all the time," Alex said. "It would be... tedious to hose it all up. Even if you could get it all on one big ship, like a... a..."

"Even a Nimbus could not manage the flow," LF said. "The nexus had to be here to manage all the water. So much water." He shook his head in reflection. "And pardon the mess, but it took me so long to fit every ship for the job. No time to clean up before it began."

LF had turned from them now to look out over the debris field of electronic components that stretched indefinitely out into the dark and mist.

"Now they're all rigged and plumbed, and the fun has begun, right?" Alex said, and his feigned enthusiasm brought back the Typhoon Tycoon.

"Yes!" LF said, almost prancing around the glass gazebo now. "Yes!"

Alex managed a quick smile at Rory, then continued to stir LF up more. "So, it's all underway. No turning back."

LF's eyebrows arched high. The phrase resonated with him, clearly. "That's right, young man. Not even the sky's the limit."

"The Deep Water is as high as you can fly it."

"That is right! Any higher and it would turn to snow on the way back down."

Alex turned to Rory then and said flatly, "Exactly what I told you happened in Austin, Rory, only globally, and quickly, and..." he looked around at the portals, "from what I can tell... irreversibly."

"Because this time... it's ported?" Rory asked.

"Oh, the teleportation!" LF said, joining the two of them. "The missing link! Deep Water is potent, but every time it's ported, it's amplified in suggestive energy. A happy accident! It's glorious!"

"Suggestive energy?" Rory asked.

"It's scopolamine," Alex said, "on space-aged crack."

"What?" Rory asked again.

"The Devil's Breath," LF cackled, "down from heaven above."

Rory shook his head in wonderment. Both of them were lost in the abstract now.

"Suggestive power," Alex clarified, "that hypnogenic hoo-doo that comes out of our pool in Peru—"

"The most potent reserve on earth!" LF interjected.

"—is somehow chemically altered and made *more powerful* through these portals, then it's distributed from the airships. That's the medium. All that's missing is the message."

LF Winston seemed to remember himself then, and he grabbed Rory by the front of his vest. He fixed his rheumy wild-eyed gaze on Rory and said, "It's time for our One World, Rory! All the rest is Obsolescence."

62 German Engineering

The fight was intense between Kelli and Calissa. Ashley was resisting as best she could, trying to push an Affectation at Kat. When the fight came at her, however, Ashley tried Affecting the others, all of them, forcing it, but trying not to damage her friends.

Then the women all slumped to the floor and sighed.

They were awash with a cool, placid Affectation of peace.

Katrina nodded at Ashley. And that was the last thing she could remember.

It seemed like everyone in Corvo had come to help resuscitate them with wet cloths and smelling salts and fresh fruit and prayer. The resort staff did not complain about the blood stains or destroyed lobby furniture. They did not ask questions as to what had started the fight between the four rich mainlanders. They were some of the most accommodating people Ashley had ever inconvenienced.

Still, it annoyed her, and the syrupy fruit only compounded her nausea. Calissa's ear was sliced, and she kept swearing she had been bitten by one of them. Kelli tended her own wounds stoically, sitting apart from the chaos. She looked angry.

When they were first rousing, Katrina had explained things. Steve Spexarth had arranged the implant in her head. Like Zana had speculated, it was to detonate by remote control and kill her instantly. He had used it to command her to kill the Parker girl. He had tended to her on the *Arcus*, Katrina said, to make sure she did not talk.

Last night, he had approached them with flowers and a *mist of burundanga*, leaving them unable to resist his suggestions that they fight. This was compounded by her Affectation, one that Spexarth demanded she enact. He would have blown the implant, he threatened, had she refused. Her Affectation had compelled them to fight without reservation. He was protected from the burundanga with something as simple as a nasal block. He had surgery done that made him immune to the Devil's Breath and *almost* immune to Affectations.

What Steven Spexarth *did not know* was that Katrina had been released from the detonating implant and that she, too, had blocked her own olfactory senses with a home remedy of a menthol balm. She had to play along with the Affectation, feigned obedience to the implant, but as soon as he was gone, she recanted it and put them all to rest.

Ashley was still reeling with it all. *Steve Spexarth*? She had trusted him. She was sure he had confided in her. He had read LF's journal with her so purely, so passionately. He was one of Rory's men!

She was struggling to clear the cobwebs of her common sense and her scientific knowledge too. She knew indigenous people used drugs like Katrina described. She knew about the implant Zana had extracted. She was surprised, however, that Katrina had overcome the burundanga, like she seemed so immune to pain. It was not incredible, but it gave her a newfound respect for her half-sister.

Ashley had nothing but contempt, however, for Spexarth. How had he altered his synaptic system to develop immunity to an Affectation? She wanted to know more. She was going to find him and pry it from him... or conduct an autopsy and learn what surgery had been conducted. Either was fine with her.

The four of them had a fresh topic of conversation, at least. What was Spexarth trying to accomplish? Where had Rory and Alex gone with that boat? Surely not into the hurricane overnight?

They were soaking up coffee and teasing out every potential when Astar and Zana found them.

"We have prepared a craft," Astar said, without so much as a hello. "We can follow the helicopter and retrieve Alex and Rory."

"What kind of craft?" Kelli asked.

"Wait. Wait..." Calissa said. "That helicopter's not long gone?"

Zana had a twinkle in his eye. "Mechanical complications," he said.

Katrina looked ill.

"What is it?" Ashley asked.

"It has been much more than five minutes, yet he did not come for me. I was to return to the helicopter," she said. "He *left me* here. He thought I would die with the rest of you, perhaps by my own blade."

"I say, let them get airborne, then we shoot them out of the sky," Kelli said. "I don't care if they are in the *Feldergarb*."

Everyone was considering the option.

"I want Spexarth in one piece," Ashley said at last. "I need some answers."

"They are making preparations to fly," Astar said. "If we are to pursue, we need to go."

"I don't want to fly into a hurricane," Calissa said.

"We will follow by sea," Astar patted her shoulder. "We have found a speed yacht."

"Speed boat into a hurricane." Kelli shook her head. "You old folks should stick with antiques."

"It is a little more than a speedboat," Zana said. "She will run 60 knots and cut through the microbursts like a butter knife."

Ashley looked at him, assessing. She offered a plan. "Can you create a distraction?" she asked Calissa. "Get the chopper pilots interested in that yacht?"

The girl smiled broadly. Ashley knew she would be interested.

"And Kat, can you get us on that chopper—hide us?"

"Together we could mimic the others, sit among them even, except that—"

"Good enough," Ashley said. "Let's go."

Zana was not kidding. Somehow, the Amins had found a speed yacht, a 100 foot fire breather, complete with crew. It was jet black, and the pilot was whipping it around in the harbor, gunning it, standing it nearly on its tail.

"Fazar," Zana laughed.

"He is our nephew," Astar explained.

Nephew? Ashley had not even thought about them having an extended family.

"I stand corrected," Kelli said. "That boat might just be the way to go."

They looked from the speed yacht to the cockeyed helicopter and back.

"How fast did you say it goes?" Calissa asked, wide-eyed.

"Seventy knots in fair weather," Zana said. "We shall see in the chop."

"His antics are not to be unnoticed," Katrina warned, glaring at the yacht.

"Exactly," Astar smiled.

"Exactly," Ashley affirmed.

"Yes. He has cloaked himself in bravado."

"Meaning?" Katrina asked.

"A race," Calissa smiled.

Astar nodded. "Rory's own daughter. It is what your father would have done, yes?"

Ashley didn't like the past-tense sound of that, but she understood now. Fazar was goading the helicopter pilots with his ship. He was challenging them.

"Yeah, but... a helicopter's going to fly lots faster," Calissa said. "What's the point?"

"It would seem everyone knows this but Fazar," Zana smiled.

"Then why bother?" Calissa frowned.

"In its prime, the *Feldergarb* could cruise at—I dunno—twice what your boat there can do," Kelli said, still comparing the two craft, left and right.

"Yes, in its prime. In clear skies, not in a hurricane," Zana said.

"Winning isn't everything," Ashley offered.

"Yes, exactly," Zana said.

"What are you saying?" Katrina asked with frustration.

"*Cloaked in bravado*," Ashley repeated Astar's previous claim. "The yacht has no hope of winning, but a race gives it every excuse to take the same course."

"Steven Spexarth would not have that. He will blast that boat from the water."

"He might have at one time," Kelli said. "But the *Feldergarb* doesn't have anything mounted under her anymore, not even a 50 caliber."

"For insurance, we can keep Spexarth distracted, can't we, Kat?"

Katrina tipped her head, smiled at Ashley then, and said, "Together, disguised, we might accomplish even more."

Astar came to stand between the two, putting an arm around each, and saying, "Revenge is sweet, girls, but for the mission, we must get there, and we must know his intentions."

"So then, a two-pronged fork," Zana summed up. "We shall be on with Fazar, along with Captain Chase and Calissa. You two will be on *that thing—*" he gestured dismissively at the helicopter, "and keep them occupied."

"We must only stay out of his sight," Katrina explained as they suited up. "And for this, we wear the helmets." They were wearing black motorcycle race suits, but it was the notion of a jumpsuit uniform, and that would carry Katrina's Affectation. Even Spexarth would believe, Katrina said, unless he saw her face directly.

"You're sure of this?" Ashley asked.

"No, of course not," Katrina smiled, sliding her reflective facemask into place.

Ashley and Katrina were soon mixing among the other men, carrying spools of wire and lugging black boxes. They were roadies loading a bus for a concert, except this was no bus, and whatever was out at sea was no concert.

No one paid them any mind.

They boarded and took seats and buckled in with the others.

Still nothing.

The *Feldergarb* popped and lurched as the pilots went through preflight warm-ups.

A little man Ashley recognized but could not name tapped her helmet, "Good idea," he yelled above the noise. "At least your head will be in one piece when we crash."

Several of the surrounding men laughed at this. Ashley joined in. Katrina was distracted. Maintaining their ruse took her greatest attention.

"What's wrong, Barnes?" A man sitting across from Katrina slapped her knee. "You still air sick?"

"Get over it, already!" Nick Grimes told Barnes/Covarrubias. Ashley felt an itch of worry. Katrina wasn't the smoothest at the interpersonal. Grimes was one of her men from the Estate, too, one of Mitchum's men, and she looked away, hoping he could not possibly recognize her.

Over the loudspeaker in the cabin, the pilots were laughing, exchanging jabs and jeers in German. Ashley tried to focus on their banter. She had taken German in school and spent a winter in the Alps, but it was not coming back to her well. Something was exchanged between them about a little fish. Fast. Little. Yacht. She understood "yacht" clearly enough.

Ashley caught sight of the speed yacht once or twice as the helicopter veered and tilted. The *Feldergarb* was spinning, leaning this way and that, tossing boxes that were not well-secured. Two men unbuckled and worked on the cargo. "Dammit, Cox," one of them yelled, "learn to tie a knot!" Cox, the scrawny man attempting to help, shrugged his shoulders. He looked too cheery for the circumstances.

Her collar was killing her. Every snap of the shoulder harness was excruciating. Ashley sympathized with Barnes and his airsickness. The *Feldergarb* flew like a Tilt-a-Whirl jackhammer. She looked over at Kat more than once, but the visor obscured her face. She wondered how she was faring. Katrina was beat up, too, but there would be no admitting it.

The pilots were not concerned, even when the engines paused to cough. They were laughing and narrating the race for the rest of the men. Ashley did her best to heckle and scoff with them, though she was afraid for her life. She realized, as the death-defying flight continued, that the distraction of the race was good for morale. It even came to help her think of something—anything—other than the sputtering copter.

Spexarth, in one of the nicer co-pilot seats up front, was distracted with a HeadGear projection. He seemed disinterested in the boat below. She leaned forward once or twice to peer into his projection, but she couldn't get a good look at it from a distance. Once she unbuckled, thinking she might approach him from behind, but as she got to her feet, the helicopter bounced hard, as if it were landing suddenly. She grabbed at cargo webbing and swung off her feet.

"Ah, siddown," a man said, pulling her back into her seat with a thud. "It's just the hurricane."

Everyone laughed. Ashley understood gallows humor in that moment.

The yacht was forgotten, far behind them. A new challenge held the pilots' attention.

The Germans might have been cursing then, Ashley thought. She was. The helicopter bounced sideways like it was a skipping stone. The cabin lights flickered out.

"*Put us on top,*" Spexarth commanded.

"Was das?" a pilot shouted back.

"Park on that spinning airship," Spexarth said in exaggerated clarity. "You need visual aids or something? Land. There."

63 When it Rains

He heard something oddly out of place, yet familiar all the same. Mixed in the thunder of the storm and the rumble of the waterfall, Rory thought he heard the more steady, mechanical beat of a helicopter.

By the way he was craning his neck, Alex had heard it too. LF was oblivious to it. He was pawing through a pile of cables and hoses.

"Even if it did work," Rory continued, "it wouldn't be right."

"'Right,' like history, is determined by the righteous," LF replied without even turning to face Rory. "Destiny can be determined. It needn't be the stuff of chance."

"Determined by the individual," Rory said. "Not like this."

"I thought you of all people would understand, my boy." LF was following one particular cable now, and Alex and Rory followed along.

They had left the shelter of the glass gazebo and had wandered around in the mist for far too long. It gave Rory too much time to think and worry. If Alex was right about everything, would the menthol nose wax really save them from becoming automatons again?

He could accept that Spexarth had drugged them, probably with the flowers, and sent them on the fool's errand of floating into a hurricane, sure to meet their demise. They had followed the suggestion and did not even know it.

He had no doubt there was something to this Devil's Breath in the Deep Water of Peru. He had seen the portals flowing with the water, and he could fathom it would go from here to the other airships through a network of portals. "*Rain down upon the earth,*" he recalled from LF's journal.

He said aloud then, "*This path is the righteous one.*"

"Indeed," LF said. "Shine your lights here, will you?"

Dutifully, both Alex and Rory aimed their flashlights at a bundle of cables. LF was tracing them, fingering the one he wanted to pursue to its end. He led them around another black hillock and then directly toward the powerful waterfall.

Cables from all over the plains and debris were snaking in and out of the base of the waterfall. LF kept following his one cable, ducking right into the tumbling flood—except there was apparently another liquid glass shelter, a tunnel, for when Rory and Alex followed, they did not get more wet. The water was pounding on the ceiling of the clear structure, roaring and gushing against the glass. Alex looked at Rory, incredulity in his eyes. Rory shrugged and followed LF forward.

"Let's see this out," Winston said. "Let's change the world. Boys, I've worked for this my entire life, and Rory, as you know, my life began when the last of the 'Coats laid down their arms."

"You're doing this for the Turncoats?" Alex asked.

"I'm doing this for what's right." LF looked back at him. "For One World, for world peace at last."

"It won't work," Alex said. "It's a hella plan, but it won't work."

"It *will* work," LF said. "You'll see."

"People are gonna get it wrong."

"Preposterous!" LF said and resumed tracking the cable. "I've thought of it for years. I've refined it to a fine point. A universal truth."

"I know, I know, but you'd be better off with something like, 'Take care of your own,' than 'Be Kind.'"

LF looked at Alex with astonishment. "*Kindness* will end wars. *Kindness* could lead to the end of poverty entirely and hunger too."

"It will lead to paralysis," Alex said. "In doing no harm, we will do nothing."

"You sound too certain of yourself," LF said. "How do you know this?"

"We'll second guess ourselves," Alex continued. "Think about it...I want to feed the poor, but what will the poor do when they're no longer poor? Rise up? How is it sustainable? I guess I'd better not upset the balance—"

"That's nothing but justification," LF said. He returned to his cable tracing.

"I can't even have a good time because I should be busy being kind," Alex continued, shouting at the back of LF's head. "Enjoy myself when I could be spending my time or my money that I should be giving in kindness to others? *That won't fly*. Or this: how damn kind do I have to be? Don't have my own possessions, 'cuz others need them. Don't eat meat, because an animal would die? What about insects and plants? How can I be cruel to them, if I'm programmed—*brainwashed*—to be kind? I cannot do anything at all without risking harm to someone or something."

"That is a bastardization of the most fundamental principle—"

"*I'd rather die than cause harm*," Alex said. "I've seen it, old man. Pacified people globally passing away."

"You'll see," LF said, quickening his pace. He no longer paid attention to Alex and his barrage of questions.

The floor of the glass tunnel was entirely made up of cables, layers and layers of cables. LF persisted in tracking his one cable. Rory did not see how that could be possible, but he followed along.

They were two hundred feet or more into the tunnel when it opened up into a cavernous space that Rory guessed might be a hundred feet across. The walls, if he could think of them as walls, were cables rising from the floor into the mist. It seemed to him that the entire ceiling was composed of microphones, various types, suspended from various lengths of cable. All of it extended beyond Rory's sight up into the center of the waterfall.

"How is it all this electrical stuff isn't shorting out?" Alex asked LF.

"It's this water!" LF chuckled. "It's like it refuses to acknowledge logic."

"I'll say," Rory grumbled.

"Ah!" LF found his one cable that, like all the others, went up the wall into oblivion above. He found his one mic dangling from that cable again, from among hundreds and hundreds that hung at ceiling height. He favored one just out of reach. "Can you pull that one for me, the chrome one?"

Rory jumped up and touched a mic. "This one?" he asked.

"No. To your left, there. The older one."

Rory jumped again and wrapped his hand around a fat chrome mic from the mid-1900's. He pulled at it gently, and the mic descended to a comfortable level for LF to grasp. "Why this one?"

"I've tested them all. Every last one. This is it, my mouthpiece." He was breathing heavily now. Chuckling. "My mouth to God's ears."

Alex spun around and around, astonished.

"There's over a thousand microphones—"

"Rory!" Alex warned.

Throughout the room, clumps of mics dropped, chased down by long coils of cable that spooled on the floor. Alex pushed LF out of the way of a microphone pour, but LF held his favored mic doggedly.

Men descended and dropped to stand on every pile of mics and cables. They were the men from the *Feldergarb*, now heavily armed, pointing their weapons at Rory and Alex. The cable in LF's hands shook, and someone zipped down it.

Rory wrenched LF clear, just as Steve Spexarth dropped from it to the floor.

"I'll take that," he said smugly, prying the mic from LF's hand. Spexarth looked over the mic in his hand, then shook his head at the ceiling of microphones. "Thanks for saving me a whole lot of time, Winston."

Alex took a step forward. Mixed in the rumble of the falls, Rory registered the sound of bullets chambered, weapons cocked. "You. Back off. You too, Reed."

"What the hell are you— "

"I'm winning!" Spexarth proclaimed. "You and all your Turncoat talk didn't do shit, Reed, but I am. I'm changing the world."

"I am here to change the world, boy," LF said to him. "Give me that mic."

The cable retracted then, a tight connection to something above. "No can do, you rich old fuck."

"Excuse me?" LF was surprised, but no less intent on grabbing for the microphone.

"*Nimm mich hoch*," Spexarth said in German. "Take me up." The microphone cable grew taut, then strained, and Spexarth was pulled slowly up off the floor ten feet or more. He held onto it with both hands, his wrist looped with cable. He was pulling his mouth toward the mic.

"This is not cool," Alex said, perturbed like Rory had not seen before. "Not. Cool." Alex raged up at Spexarth, "I've waited for this moment—you're stealing my moment, you crazy..." Then he shifted, continuing his rant, "Rory, where'd you get this loon? *He's ruining everything*!"

Spexarth looked back down at them all. "Here's where I have to leave you for a public service announcement," he said. He pulled himself up more until his mouth was at the mic. He laughed as he spoke then, looking directly at Levi Finn Winston. "Eat the Rich," he said with a caustic grin. The message echoed loudly, drowning out even the waterfall: "Eat the Rich."

"Drop!" Rory yelled, and he and Alex were on the floor instantly.

LF did not follow.

He was staring up, indignant, hands on hips, watching as Spexarth was pulled up and away.

Shots fired from every direction, and Rory could no longer see LF through the spatter of blood.

"Eat the Rich," Spexarth's voice insisted, again and then again. Same snide chuckle, same tone and pace. Rory realized it was on loop, somehow recorded and replayed repeatedly.

"Get up and take it like men," one of the Franklin militia shouted. "Hang out with the rich, hang with the rich."

"Eat the Rich," one man yelled.

"Think!" Rory called back. "I'm one of you!"

"Toss me your sidearm," Alex said.

"That'd only leave me one."

"I got a hunch."

Rory sighed but obeyed. The pistol landed in a puddle by Alex's head. He retrieved it, shook the water out, then fired nine rounds in succession. The others fired back. A few shots narrowly missed Rory.

"What are you doing?" he yelled.

"Watch," Alex said, tossing the empty gun back to him.

"You're the worst shot—"

A loud burbling sound was followed by a burst of mist. The mist grew and grew in the mic room, coating the floor a foot deep in milky white fog. It was rising in a blinding haze.

"Don't breathe much," Alex said, now at Rory's ear. "It's aether mostly, I think. Might get us out of here. C'mon."

The two men scrambled and ran in the mist blindly. They crashed into a militia man and all three of them fell. It was Chavez, from Franklin. Rory helped him up and pulled him along in a fireman's carry. Chavez was already unconscious.

"Eat the Rich," Spexarth's recording continued to chant. "Eat the Rich."

It was still impossible to see, and yet shots were being fired. Curses were called out about rich people and revenge. They bumped into another man, but before he could aim at them, Rory clubbed him with his empty pistol. Rory fanned at the fog, trying to get a look at the man, but he could not. The blood that coated his hand and gun made him look away, queasy.

"Behind us! Get behind us," a familiar voice called out. Shots were directed at the voice. Random, sporadic gunshots.

He knew it was Ashley.

He could not see her, but he ran toward her voice. His every footfall tossed him up and down. He was running on the *Arcus* again in his memory, and he tried to run like that now, using the spring in his step, using his reduced gravity. "Are you alright?" he yelled.

"Over here," another woman's voice sounded in the white swirl.

"Kat?" Alex questioned. Another gunshot, this one seemed to pierce a rise in the *Undulatus* even more closely.

"Here, yes," she called. "Get in back of us. Feel for the wall and follow it."

Rory was surprised to hear her voice, and he was unsure of what to do. He was still moving, but he was not sure of his direction.

"You're pathetic!" Spexarth yelled down at them over his own recorded voice. "You're all pathetic. Running around blind. I can see you all. I can see—yaaaaaawwww."

A whump sounded to Rory's right. "Eat the Rich," Spexarth's disembodied voice repeated. "Eat the Rich."

"Who's pathetic now?" Ashley said in the distance. Rory heard meaty thumps that must have been the sound of her kicking his body over and over.

What he did not hear, he noted, was any more gunfire.

They rested with their backs against a black bubble hill. Rory thought they all looked like bleached white statues in the glow of the portals. They had made it from the mic room and the tunnel of cables. Now they were slumped here, at the foot of the waterfall, talking loudly to be heard over the incessant phrase from Spexarth's recording. "Eat the Rich," Spexarth's voice repeated over and over, without end. "Eat the Rich."

Katrina and Ashley had Affected the men in the mic room. They suffered both that and the aether that had confused Rory and Alex.

Chavez was coming to, as were other survivors.

Rory replayed the firefight in his mind. Seven men.

No one else from the helicopter had shown up. Rory thought he had heard the old bird thumping away right after Spexarth's fall. Possibly those boys up on the chopper had betrayed their leader, Rory thought, and cut his cable.

Katrina insisted his fall was her own doing, as did Ashley.

A double tap.

"When will the others arrive?" Katrina asked. She was on her feet, catlike, pacing surefooted on the flowing surface as if it were immobile.

"Others?" Rory asked.

"A-Z. Kelli and Calissa," Ashley answered. "They're coming by boat."

"Calissa!" Rory was on his feet now. He clenched a signal at her in code.

"Close by," she replied promptly, and Rory relaxed a bit.

"We gotta find that repeater," Alex groaned, climbing to his feet as well. "We gotta cut that signal." He pulled at his hair and growled in anguish. "I can't believe I missed it. I actually made it worse! Gawd! If this gets out global—I don't even want to think about it."

"How does it get *global*?" Rory asked him.

"No idea. This is new history," Alex answered with a shrug. "It's gotta be up there. Probably blasts to a satellite, then to all the airships."

"So maybe it's too late?" Katrina said, looking up at the spinning cloud cover.

"Rory," Ashley said, grasping his arm. "I need to see him."

"Your dad?" Rory fought back the thoughts of LF Winston being cut to ribbons. He refused to look at the blood spatter on his own clothes.

"No," Ashley choked it out. "Though we should take him with us."

That thought brought another wave of nausea.

"Then who?" Rory asked.

"Spexarth," she said gravely. She had an animal gleam in her eyes. "I want to make damn sure he's dead."

"And if he's not?" Rory asked.

"He will be," Katrina provided the inevitable answer.

64 New Arrival

The aether had dissipated, leaving the microphone room in a harmless white haze. It was hard to see, but it was no longer lethal. Spexarth's message, "Eat the Rich," echoed softly here. The broadcast was much louder in the larger outer chamber. Here, it seemed, Spexarth was among them, whispering his madcap message, even now.

They wandered around in the room of a thousand mics, sloshing in the water, tripping over cables and bodies. When discovered, each corpse was carried out to the larger room, arranged for removal when the ship would come. Rory and Alex moved through the task as if it were commonplace, but battlefield reconnaissance was still unsettling to her. Chavez and other men joined in, picking over corpses, rounding up weapons, patting them down for anything of use.

She thought it should be harder, since they knew most of these men. Rory had trained them all.

Soon she was led to the body she most dreaded seeing, that of her father. A makeshift shroud, now soaked in blood, wrapped around his body. She did not need to unwrap the swath around his face. She knew it was him by the frail body and the blood, so much blood, that pooled and moved all around him.

Ashley wept over him, undisturbed by the others. She knew they were giving her space. Anger welled in her and rumbled like the thunder. Spexarth's vile message continued to cycle her father's death sentence, a hundred, then a thousand times as she knelt there. They had not had a proper goodbye, yet again.

"Eat the Rich," the voice said again.

"Can't we shut that off?" she yelled.

"We'll find a way, Ash. First, I gotta find that mic," Alex called from the mist. "Maybe trace it, maybe change the message before it's too late."

She got to her feet, wiped her face, and composed herself. She did not want to be seen like this. They were all soldiers.

Rory was there, and he pulled her to him in a bear hug. He was her one solid thing in this sloshing ship, this hurricane of madness, this swirl of white foggy confusion.

"You should have Kat give you some rest or something," he offered. "When Zana gets here, we can get you something else."

"All I need is you," she said and nuzzled against him.

He clutched her more tightly, and they breathed together in a slow dance of ocean waves and the dying transpiration of the Undulatus. Ashley closed her eyes and wished it all away. She wished she could slow her pulse and count her breaths and just control herself like Rory was so good at. She wished she could Affect her own head or dismiss the pain in her ribs and collar and heart.

"How will you spot it?" Katrina was asking nearby.

"I will know it when I see it," Alex said, looking up as he came into their field of view.

"Eat the Rich," Spexarth continued. "Eat the Rich."

"You okay, Princess?" Alex asked, patting her shoulder awkwardly.

"Fine," she sniffed. "I'm fine."

"So many," Katrina said, nearly walking into them, as she spied the mics above, "hundreds, maybe."

They had been moving bodies and seeking the microphone for what seemed an eternity. They worked at it again, for what felt like another forever. In this place, where hurricane clouds and mystical waterfalls kept time, it was impossible to know for certain.

"Guys," Rory called to them. "I think I found it."

They had been seeking one in a thousand, their "eyes on the problem, not the prize," Rory said when they approached him. He was right. Spexarth's crumpled corpse was a signpost. Directly under it, he had found a few mics that resembled the one they sought.

Rory was more than a little surprised to find Spexarth's body, he told Ashley while they waited for the others to gather. He muttered that maybe Steve Spexarth was as invincible as Stan Combs, his nemesis who got away. Rory admitted he was worried that Spexarth, too, might never be discovered.

However, there he was, crumpled unnaturally from his fall, his face frozen in a horrible death mask of fear. Both she and Katrina had charged him with their full Affectations. He was most likely frightened to death, most likely his heart rendered in two. He died before he hit the ground, a bitter and terrible death.

It would never be enough.

Ashley spoke of a field autopsy, but even though she despised Spexarth, even at the sight of his dead body, she did not have the heart to do it. "How else will I ever understand? How was he able to trick me? Resist us?"

"I can tell you quite simply what was done to him," Katrina said. "He has been scraped."

"Scraped?" Ashley did not know what she was talking about. "Scraped?"

"Yes, scraped," Katrina said. "It is when one essentially has had a lobotomy."

"A back-alley lobotomy," Alex added.

"Like a Terminal?" Rory asked.

"Yes..." something registered with her, Ashley noticed, but Katrina continued. "It makes mud of the mind," Katrina said. "No one would do such a thing of their own choosing. He served another man who did this to him."

"Who?" Ashley asked, finding the prospect invigorating. She might yet have her true revenge. She fought the urge. Revenge went nowhere, but whoever was responsible for her father's death had to pay.

"I do not know who," Katrina said, "but I know that is very expensive and very, very painful."

"Getting scraped rewires the prefrontal cortex through manual means," Alex said. "It left him without a conscience."

"I know, I know," Ashley said. "I've studied it all, just never heard it put like that—scraped." She kicked his corpse again for good measure.

"Pitch this one in the ocean, then, Miss Winston?" Chavez asked.

"Yes, let's do it," Rory said, before she could deliberate more.

"Back at Corvo," Katrina added. "Let's find some sharks and watch."

They worked in twos, taking turns carrying Spexarth's body toward the shore. The others would be brought out in the same fashion. Alex said something more dignified would be arranged for LF Winston, though she could not imagine what.

Rory was in charge of shift changes, of course, for he had an unrivaled internal clock. She had challenged it in her head, with nothing else to do, by counting her steps on two shifts. They were within two paces from one another by her count. His accuracy, even in this strange setting, boggled her mind. It was something she liked about him, even in those gruesome circumstances: his quirkiness. It gave her something to think about on the long, wet walk back to Rory's boat.

She had come to ignore the storm, but as they walked toward the edge of the airship, it was more and more pronounced. Thunder and lightning, wind and the distant slap of waves all signaled they were making progress toward the *Obsidian*.

At least, Ashley thought, Spexarth's never-ending chant was fading into the background. On one of her shifts carrying, Ashley had the eerie feel that Spexarth was mouthing the words beneath the shirt they had pulled over his head to hide his horrible final expression. The jostling of the body and the ebb and flow of the airship skin beneath them was creating the effect, she told herself. Optical illusion. She had his feet, and she looked up the body to the covered head, then the arms, then studied Alex's back, as he was her carrying partner, just ahead. Only it wasn't Alex's back, was it? He was talking to Rory, to her left. It had to be Chavez. Hadn't he just had a shift, though, with Katrina?

Rory was at her side. He had noticed her curiosity, of course, as was his way. His whisper was a rumble lost in the thunder: "...each five shifts, different combinations... think through your partners... *think*." He did not take his eyes off the man ahead, even as he continued whispering to her. "Another chameleon, Katrina says."

"Family?" Ashley looked at Rory. Was he serious? She tried to keep her same pace and not let the shock register in her carrying manner. Hours now, this person had been among them, and she had not had the slightest indication! "*Dangerous*?"

Rory gave her a smile, saying, "*A danger foreseen is half avoided*." He knew it infuriated her when he would answer with one of his infernal quotations, but that also told her he was well aware and taking the intruder's presence in stride, watchfully aware.

Whenever she would change shifts, she would revisit the aches and pains of this adventure. Her ribs did not feel the weight of the carry as much as her collar, and that would flare only when she initially released the body's weight. At her every shift change, when she would first latch onto those boots and pant legs, Ashley was revolted. She had not spent so much time with a dead body, period, let alone one that had been her victim. She thought, maybe, it was the revulsion that had distracted her from the guest she had sometimes shared a carry shift with.

When they finally found the *Obsidian*, the corpse was strapped onto the back deck. They stood around on the ship awkwardly, exhausted, and without more to talk about, they settled to rest on deck cushions. Rory and Alex sought a change of clothes in the cabins. Katrina was more watchful than Ashley had ever seen her. She was sitting with Ashley and Chavez, but she was intently looking to the back of the boat, as if Spexarth would come clambering over the edge at any moment.

"What is it?" Ashley finally said in her ear.

"I have seen him," she said. "He is from the helicopter. And I have seen him before, on the airship where we first began."

"The *Arcus*?" Ashley was astounded. "He's been with us since the *Arcus*?"

Katrina shrugged. She looked at Ashley then, and a softness was in her eyes, almost a kinship. "We have been through a great deal together," she said.

It was just enough out of character that Ashley bristled. *Maybe this was the chameleon*? "If he's been around, hiding in plain sight, how do I know who to trust?"

"So, ask me anything," Katrina continued. "To be certain it *is* me."

Ashley thought a beat. So many things she wanted to know about her, so much mystery. "How do you do it? Get beat to hell then bounce back fighting. Have your head split open for brain surgery and just go with it?"

"I can tell myself, trick myself, to fight the pain," she shrugged. "This does not tell you that I am me, however. Try again."

Ashley sighed, relaxing a little, remembering her advice from what seemed weeks ago. She had a sure test to verify this was Katrina: some shared experience. "What did we eat that morning with Calissa?"

"Fruit," she smiled at the memory of the glorious fruit platter in Huacachina.

Ashley half-smiled with her. They savored the memory. It was another time, in a world of sunshine and warmth and flavor. Ashley felt something else in her memory, and she realized that in even sitting this close to Katrina—their thighs side by side and just touching—they were having a wash of the mind meld. And in that, she felt Katrina's flicker of belonging.

"What of him, then?" Ashley asked. "Is he one of us?"

"No." She was receding from Ashley's presence ever so slightly. Their connection was fading as Katrina hardened herself again for the situation at hand. "He is the one they called Mark Cox. He looks like a teenager, but he likes to fight. He finds things... amusing." Katrina was again fixed on the rear of the ship. "I don't know another thing about him."

"Skinny guy?" Ashley had a bolt of recognition. He had tended to her when she was locked in the *Arcus* storage room. He had been on the *Feldergarb*, too, the one who was poor at knots.

Katrina nodded, then raised an eyebrow.

Ashley followed her gaze.

"So, I'm found out," Cox acknowledged. He climbed the steps from below deck and approached them, a broad smile on his face.

"That's right, pal, so don't do anything stupid," Rory said, pointing a gun at him.

Cox put his hands in the air.

"Why the head games?" Rory asked.

"Yeah, and who the hell are you, anyway? You're not... historical... not familiar." Alex had emerged from the hull, too, and he was sporting a harpoon gun.

"Mark Cox," he said. "I've been around. I just blend in. I was even in the militia, Mr. Reed, clear back to Franklin."

"Why?" Rory rumbled. Ashley knew when his patience was getting taxed, and at that moment, he seemed to have none left.

"I've been dedicated to seeing that things work out well," he said.

"You suck at your job," Ashley said.

"Just wait," he said. "Can I put my hands down now?"

Rory looked at Katrina, then Ashley, then nodded. "I'm watching you, Cox."

"Oh, I know. You're so *observant*." He pointed over Rory's shoulder.

In a flash of lightning, Rory saw something approaching in the water. "Ship!"

"A-Z!" Ashley announced, feeling more relieved. The ship was more negative space and noise than truly visible. She could most easily see it by the plume of water in its wake. She glanced at Alex, adding, "And Kelli."

"And Calissa," Rory sighed, shouldering his rifle.

"And crew," Cox added, studying the approaching vessel. "Well, I guess I am sufficiently outnumbered then. Consider me harmless?"

"Never," Rory said, "but you can help tie them off."

65 Worse than Bad

Astar made introductions, proud of her nephew and his ship. Fazar's crew was introduced, too, and Rory took a liking to them. None of them were over thirty, but all four of them were very into sailing high speed yachts. Yannik gave them a tour of the engine room, showed them images in his HeadGear of the screws and the hull. Another talked of races they had recently won against highly overpowered competitors.

"It is all about the chemistry," Fazar said. "We work as one. It's our superpower!"

Rory mused over his own team, how well they had collaborated over the years. He would be sad to see this mission end—and he could feel, like he always could, the resolution was at hand.

He was going to miss them. He watched Zana and Alex swapping stories down on the rubbery surface of the *Undulatus*. He smiled at Astar coddling Fazar's crew on their yacht. He studied Kelli and Ashley, Calissa and Katrina—four powerful young women he would take as a team, had he not had such a personal investment in them. Best to have a team that could be changed out to suit the situation, he told himself, an expendable team. Interchangeable cogs.

They gathered around Astar, all fourteen of them, on the *Undulatus* surface. Together, they ate provisions she doled out. She polled them about their self-care. She cared for wounds Ashley and Katrina had inflicted upon one another, and she chastised them for being too harsh on each other. When Alex tried to get sympathy for an injury he revealed, Zana laughed it off as being the self-inflicted wound of a pity seeker. Rory wondered aloud if it was even a fresh wound.

Conversation turned more sober. Seven men had died here. Cox claimed another five or six had left with the chopper, posing an unknown threat. They discussed the best ways to get the deceased back to land, ultimately back to be buried in their own homelands.

Their talk did not get any lighter when Zana told them of Spexarth's broadcast and its effects already taking place. "The Interface is blowing up with stories," he said, "and now more and more CommCorp channels are carrying nothing but his vile message."

"Broadcasting 'eat the rich' just over and over?" Ashley asked.

"Yes, and it is like gasoline on a fire," Zana said. "When we came into the hurricane, we lost most of the channels, but I worry that it may be all that we hear when we return. Fazar says it is taking root."

"It is what LF was doing," Alex said, "or planning to, anyway. Expose us all to scopolamine and make a suggestion, globally."

"That is why he bought out CommCorp," Ashley offered. That was something Rory did not know, and yet it made sense: own the communications tool to broadcast the brainwashing.

"Yet he did not live even to regret it," Katrina said.

"And now Spexarth's message has been substituted," Zana said.

"Great. If we're to believe what LF said, the scopolamine is amplified many times more than its original potency," Alex stated. "A more powerful medium and message."

"So, we blow it all up," Kelli Chase suggested, looking toward the eye of the hurricane. "We sink this thing." She stomped on the rubberized *Undulatus*.

"That's what I said. I should have done it in the first place!" Alex agreed. "I can't believe I was so—"

A fireball erupted from the two ships, knocking everyone down. The blast was deafening. Rory's ears were ringing. He could scarcely hear the others yelling and crying out. Billowing black smoke was whipped around them, burning his eyes and throat. It smelled of burning plastic and fuel.

Rory crawled to his feet, scanning for Ashley. She was crumpled together with Yannik and Cox. He stumbled to them and lay on top of her as more explosions resounded from the ships. It was the fuel tanks now, and Rory felt pieces of the ships pelting his back. It fell all around them like debris from a tornado.

People were coughing. Cursing.

Acrid smoke was whirling in Rory's eyes. He fought it off and continued his watch.

Astar was crawling and calling out for Fazar and for Zana.

Rory made his way toward them.

Alex was there, too. "Calissa's with Kelli," he said. "They're fine."

"Astar!" Zana cried out, and they huddled together. "Fazar and his men—dead?"

"Yannik and the engineer are okay," Rory offered. "So's Ashley."

The fire cast an erratic orange glow over everything. It was whipped by the wind and reflected off the ocean.

"This is bad," Cox said, approaching with Katrina.

It was very bad. Their ships, their comms, their supplies—all gone. Rory doubted they had enough food and water to last any length of time.

"What weapons have we?" Zana asked.

A quick inventory revealed they had very few. Rory's pistols, assorted knives, and tools. Alex found the harpoon gun, but it was mangled and dysfunctional.

"Back there," Katrina remembered. "We have the weapons from Spexarth's men."

Rory's pulse quickened. There was an ample cache of arms near the corpses and the waterfall. They could get to them and at least feel that much safer.

"This was nothing random," one of Fazar's men said. "We have been blasted by something," he held out the object retrieved from their ship's remains, "some projectile."

"Where did it come from?" he asked.

"That direction," the engineer said. "I believe I heard it launch."

"So close," Rory assessed aloud. "Too close."

"Let me see that," Alex asked. He examined the fragment of the projectile for only a split second, then slid away from it as if it would explode again. "No!"

Astar glanced at him, then asked, "Who would do—"

Gunshots tore through them.

The rubbery surface of the Undulatus was hissing gas all around them.

Bullets were striking them too. Fazar cried out in agony. Cox was hit.

"Down," Rory roared, and everyone obeyed. He would not lose another man from gawking around like LF Winston had done.

After thirty rounds, the shooting stopped. That was just a warning volley, Rory knew.

Then all the HeadGear erupted with a high-pitched alert. The crewmen were raking theirs off their heads. Alex held his Stetson, or what was left of it after the explosion, at arm's length. Over all of the HeadGear, all at once came a loud pop, then a throat was cleared, and then: "WE'RE HERE FOR THE TIME TRAVELER. DELIVER HIM OR DIE."

Alex popped his head up, his torso, too, and he looked all around. He was a space-age prairie dog. Several more shots rang out, and he dropped back to the *Undulatus*. "Aw shit!" he cried out.

"Are you hit? Honey, did they get you?" Kelli was belly crawling to him.

"I'm fine, baby bunny," Alex said to Kelli, who was covering him with kisses. He kissed her once on the mouth then wriggled free. "I'm fine."

"Alex?" Rory rumbled. "Is it bad?"

"It's worse than bad," he replied. "It's the end."

66 So Much Worse

She could see it on his face. Whatever Alex had said had an effect on Rory like none she had seen before. He had switched in that moment. She could feel it from yards away. He was a solid mass of resolute power, but she ached to know exactly *what* he had resolved.

She was crawling toward him when Cox groaned her name. He was a gory mess, but his eyes were pleading. Urgent.

Ashley put her hand on his shoulder and tried to console him, tried to listen to whatever he was muttering.

"Don't do it," Cox said. "Don't waste the energy."

"I can make you feel better," she cried. "You'll be— "

"So much worse," Cox ground his teeth in pain. "It's going to get so much worse."

She looked beyond, trying to get a clear sighting of the men intent on taking Alex. "How? How could it get any worse?"

"I failed you." His eyes screwed shut tightly. He moaned. "*Everyone*."

Ashley Elizabeth Winston, heiress of the world's greatest economic empire, felt powerless. He did not want an Affectation. He was dying, and there was nothing she could do. She didn't even know him, but her heart was wrenching in two.

He clutched at her wrist, a spasm of an incredibly firm grip. "Spex... a puppet."

"Doesn't matter," she said. "We have bigger problems. Know anything about them?"

"No effect," he grunted. "We have no effect on them."

Katrina was with them then. She pried Ashley free. "I will tend him."

"Ashley!" Cox called as she was crawling away. He spat blood with the words: "Run... run out of time."

67 Unpredictable

Rory could not accept the assessment.

No matter how many times Alex explained, it did not align with his beliefs.

"It's over," Alex had said. "They have superior firepower. They have *prescience*, Rory. They know where this is going."

"I thought you said you didn't know this timeline? I thought you said—"

"Right. Right. *But they've been here before.* They wouldn't be so cocksure otherwise. There's at least a dozen of them out there, standing there in the open because they already know we're empty handed."

"We're not entirely—"

"No," Alex wasn't having it. He slapped away Rory's hand. "They don't care how many they lose, *or how many we lose*, so long as they get me!"

Zana dived into their huddle. "Two dead, two wounded, maybe more."

"Who?" Alex asked.

Rory knew the look on Zana's face. It wasn't SOP to ask. Neither was it standard operating procedure to frighten the others like Alex was doing with his ravings.

"Chavez and Boch," Zana said. "Both are dead. Boch was their helmsman."

"WE WILL PROVIDE NO COUNTDOWN," the voice droned over all the HeadGear. "PRODUCE THE TIME TRAVELER OR DIE."

Ashley had crawled toward them now. She was conferring with Kelli, also on the move. Consoling her. "No way, Kelli. We won't let anything happen to him."

"Course correction!" Kelli was screaming. "It's all we can do!"

Ashley turned to Rory then. "Rory? Rory!"

Rory looked away. His eyes stung from the black smoke. "*The only thing necessary for the triumph of evil is for good men to do nothing.*"

"It's not like that, man," Alex said. "Outmanned. Outgunned. Outsmarted."

The dozen men were standing in a half circle, not a hundred yards away. They stood between Rory and the weapons cache. He could just make out their silhouettes in the haze.

"I love you, brother, but I gotta go," Alex started to his feet.

In that instant, the *Feldergarb* screamed down, careening and smoldering. It skidded and bounced on the *Undulatus*, tipped on its side, sliding directly at the men Alex feared. They were firing on it with handheld cannons of green laser light.

Rory could hear men's voices crying out from the helicopter as the rotors snagged the rubbery surface of the ship and shattered. The broadcast on the HeadGear was now a garbled mess with sounds of the crash and gunfire. The voices emerging from the *Feldergarb* were not crying out in pain or surrender. They were shouting out the TurnCoat battle cries, all of them generously embellished with profanities.

It was the distraction Rory needed. He grabbed Calissa with one hand, Ashley with the other, and ran, dragging them to their feet. "Come on! Everyone. Come on!"

He was run-hopping on the trampoline-like surface, and this time he was getting it right. Calissa and Ashley got their footing gradually and ran along. Rory risked a glance behind and saw the rest of his party catching up. Farther back, the others were fighting hand to hand now with the men of the *Feldergarb*. Some of that crew was taking position to defend Rory's people as they fled.

"The portal," Rory snapped at Alex and the rest. "It's our best hope."

"Portal?" Ashley looked confused. "Which—"

"The nearest portal. Go!"

He threw her forward and unholstered his gun.

"Go. Go. Go!" he hollered at Fazar and Yannik. "Take the portal and get out of here!"

Rory ran toward the firefight, toward the flaming remains of the *Feldergarb*.

He was stopped by one of the men, one crouched in position. The man held a bazooka over his shoulder. "Reed!"

"Grimes!" Rory sloshed to a knee and greeted him. "So, you waited that out a hella long time!"

"You said *when it looked most grim*," Nick Grimes said, chewing on his cigar.

"It was pretty grim when Spexarth—"

"Bah. I had him figured out a long time ago," Grimes spat.

"It looked pretty bad with the Devil's Breath."

"We knew better," Grimes said smugly. "Thank Alex for the tip on the nose goo, though."

Rory grinned. "So, we don't need these bugs anymore, eh?" He removed his tiny HeadGear, fondly called the Lice by field men. Grimes pulled his off, too, and they tossed them aside.

"Your people safe?"

Rory looked over his shoulder. He counted seven figures at the portal. He trusted the others had already gone through. "Maybe. Probably. What do you got?" Rory nodded to the battle raging not far ahead.

"We got the element of surprise, Reed."

It was true. They were still outgunned. They were still likely to go down fighting, but Rory and the Turncoats had this one advantage: the unpredictable nature of man.

His clench was popping, and though he wanted nothing more than to join Grimes in the firefight, he stopped cold.

"What is it?"

"Clench," he said. "My daughter. Says they won't go without me."

"Then go," Grimes shrugged. "We got this."

"Fat and Happy," Rory said, offering his fist.

Grimes gave him a fist bump, and replied, "Fat and Happy."

Rory ran full tilt now, knowing time was not in their favor. He had to get them out and safe. If Alex was right, if the party pursuing him could regroup and retry indefinitely, they would figure out the ruse and outmaneuver the diving helicopter in the next pass. He still wasn't sure how that might work, but as he ran, splashing now in the stream heading into the portal, he did not care.

He didn't care how time travel worked.

He didn't care how portals worked.

He only cared about the safety of his girls, Calissa and Ashley.

When he reached them, only Alex and Kelli and Ashley remained. Everyone else had gone through, Alex told him.

"It's my turn to own up to this, Rory." Alex said. "If I go through with the rest of you, they'll keep hunting us down. They're—"

"I don't care," Rory said. He punched his friend square in the jaw, knocking him out cold, then forced him into Kelli's waiting arms. He shouted, "Take him before he gets away!"

Kelli smiled through her tears and shouted her thanks, then she dragged Alex into the portal, flashed in the surge of its light, and disappeared.

Rory turned to Ashley. Her silver white hair was whipping every way. Her smile was radiant. "Glad you could make it," she said over the sound of the rushing waters, the firefight, and the hurricane. Their relationship seemed always to take them to these extremes, and he thrived on it.

The remains of the helicopter exploded in the distance, casting a glow on her ScanTats. She was the most beautiful creature he had ever imagined. She crinkled her nose in a spritely smile and asked, "What?"

"If I haven't said it lately, I love you," he bellowed.

"You haven't said it at all, you oaf, but I get it. Big boys are—"

He reached out to pull her in for another hug, then shoved her with all his might, launching her through the portal and away to safety.

He cried out her name, then turned back toward the battle. He struggled to control his gasps and sobs. The green laser cannons were destroying everything. Everyone left was falling to them. The bazooka fire seemed inconsequential, as if they had predicted it, and they probably had.

They were advancing on the portals now, all twelve of the men.

They were not far away.

Rory scaled one of the black bubble hills, where he would make his last stand. "Hey! Up here!" he shouted. "Come get me!"

He was drawing their fire and attention. He jumped hard on the trampoline hill, bounding high in the air and laughing, then he slid down the other side. Again, the unpredictable. He pulled his back up revolver from his ankle holster and smiled at it.

He recalled a quote from Christopher Walken, then, something he'd filed away and never quite believed until now: "*At its best*," he shouted, "*life is completely unpredictable*."

They were closing in on him.

He had only seconds remaining.

He cocked both pistols, then whirled on the portal that glowed and gushed just fifty feet away. It harbored his friends, his family, and his love. Even as the green flare of laser was coursing his way, Rory let out a breath, counting it out patiently, and fired, emptying both guns.

His aim was true.

The tiny Tic-Tac that powered the Hot Wire shattered. The portal went black.

Rory Reed flopped down on his back against the hill, chuckling, knowing he had saved them all.

Epilogue

Winston Water Works had a working relationship with the law. Detectives retrieved all the remains of LF Winston's last Lost Journal within a week. Other resources were called upon to decipher his mad scratches, and still others were assembled to take action. Over the last six months, the "storm engine" as Winston had called it in his notes, that mighty coupling of airships, was brought down and dismantled. Remains of the *Undulatus* were scoured, sanitized of any evidence, and the ship was scuttled.

Not one body was found.

Once attention had been exhausted on that, the rest was more complicated. Most of the Winston fleet had been compromised. Millions who depended on the Water Works were enraged at the disruption. Winston Water Works had become an anathema. The airships were considered Earth's greatest source of water pollution, suspected of pouring down more trace of Devil's Breath. The people had spoken. The Weeklies, Ashley's legacy, was in ruin. The public had turned against her.

Their wrath, however, was nothing compared to that of the masses who had fallen to the never-ending broadcast message: *Eat the Rich*. Months had passed, and the movement was still going strong.

"We're still trying." Kyle closed his summation. "Every time we bring a signal down, another repeater takes up the lead. It's like taking a swing at Hydra. Cut off one, two more sprout up somewhere else."

"Ships still spreading the juice, Interface still spreading the word," Alex said, wrapping it up, "and we're all still on the run."

Alex flopped back down in his seat. He looked expectantly at Kelli.

She was in a posh leather office chair, a hot coffee in her hands. If this was life on the run, it was a pretty good life. The office was one of dark walnut and blood red carpet. Propaganda gyrated in vibrant HomeRoom feeds that covered a wall to her left. Across the room, a big TransCorp cabinet hummed and glowed.

Behind an antique desk so huge that would not fit in Kelli's bungalow, Ashley Elizabeth Winston sat cross-legged in a massive, high-backed chair. At least, she still looked vaguely like Ashley, though now a gaunt, hot mess. Her hair and nerves were frazzled. She was daydreaming, it seemed, absently toying with something on her desk.

She had the haggard look of a refugee.

The word made Kelli swallow hard. How ironic. They were refugees in a towering office complex far from the ravages of the civil war below. They were well-fed, clean and safe, yet they had to meet in sheltered spaces. As Alex had said, they would always be on the run. The *nouveau riche refugees*, Ashley and Kyle, were sharing this same space with her, a Turncoat, and with Alex, whatever he claimed he was.

Kelli was torn. The men and women scratching it out on the HomeRoom vids were her people, *good* people who had enough corporate control. The people of this office were scrappers, too, fighting for peace by regaining control.

By association, she was with them.

By her values, she was not.

It made her head swim.

"...don't you think so, possum?" Alex asked in her direction.

Kelli looked from face to face. They were looking for an answer.

"I think we already hashed this out," she said, standing. "What's really new?"

Ashley nodded her head once, more the bob of a sleep deprived soldier than the blessing of a Princess. "Nothing," Ashley said, clearing her throat.

"But..." Alex continued, "but don't you think the unrest is more civil? Don't you think there's been a change in the tide?"

She shook her head. Alex skirted past Kyle and maneuvered to the HomeRoom.

"Just look," he said, pointing at an image. "A month ago, this protest would have been a brawl. And this billboard would have been a bonfire."

No one spoke. He turned from the screen back to them and shrugged. "And CommCorps is resuming its sensational slop like old times. That's new, right?"

"Nothing from the islands?"

All eyes turned to Ashley. No one had anything to offer.

"Then nothing's new," she said. "Come back when you have news."

She flicked her hand toward the TransCorp device, dismissing them.

It had been a short meeting.

Ashley pivoted her chair around. She gazed out the floor-to-ceiling windows.

Kyle zipped his satchel and buttoned his suit. "Whenever you want to talk..." he offered the back of her chair, then slumped his shoulders. He busied himself with the portal controls.

Alex patted Ashley's desk as he passed. He extended a hand to Kelli, but she did not take it. He frowned at her but said nothing.

The blue white light pulsed as Kyle walked through the port and disappeared.

Alex tapped in their coordinates. "Let's go. Let her be."

"I'll be along," Kelli said. "Leave the numbers up."

Alex shrugged and, in a flash, was gone.

"Why are you still here?" Ashley asked of Kelli's reflection.

Kelli rounded the desk and wrenched Ashley's chair, bringing them face to face. "You think you're being—what—*noble* or something? A martyr?"

Ashley's eye roll infuriated her, and Kelli continued, "Listen. Reed was a good man. A great guy. I miss the shit out of him, but you—"

Ashley turned her chair to the desk, shearing Kelli's grip on it. She snatched up a glass disk and held it up. "See this?"

Kelli nodded.

"It's the last thing he gave me. It's a stupid antique telescope. It's all I have."

"It's not all you have. You have all of us." Kelli argued. "You've got the Family."

"I keep thinking, maybe it's a code. A clue," Ashley said, holding the disk between her thumb and forefinger. Her eyes were bloodshot and wild, and her breath was rancid. "I think he left me a clue."

"Ashley...I don't...a clue to *what*?"

"He had it delivered on my birthday," she chuckle-cried. "Somehow he knew all this was—" Ashley swung back to the desk and retrieved a little velvet bag. "See? Look what it says."

"Seymour?"

"*See. More... Get it*? He wants me to look for him." Ashley said.

"We're looking."

"No...he wants *me* to look for him. There's gotta be a reason." She blinked back tears and her mouth crumpled, fighting back a full-on cry, but she continued. "I think Alex is in on it. I think he did his time travel thing and showed Rory, and that's how Rory knew to leave me this."

Kelli tried not to show any emotion, but this was too much. Her girl had gone wild. She chortled and then winced instinctively, expecting the worst.

"What? *What did you think I was going to do*?"

"Hex me or whatever," Kelli said. "Screw me with your hoo-doo. I'm sorry, Ash, but I'm not—"

"Hex you? No way." Ashley stood and smiled a weird, wide smile. "I'm not going to hex you, Captain Chase. I'm going to recruit you."

"Recruit...me?"

"Yeah," she said. "We're going to find Rory Reed. Together."

Don't miss out!

Visit the website below and you can sign up to receive emails whenever Mark Landon Jarvis publishes a new book. There's no charge and no obligation.

https://books2read.com/r/B-A-QYDU-TYAGC

Also by Mark Landon Jarvis

Lightning's Hand
Bewildered

About the Author

Born when the world was black and white, when a phone was simply something one talked on, Mark Landon Jarvis appreciates modern technology and yet abhors its abuses. Most of his speculative work is from this vantage point of concerned enthusiasm.

Jarvis is from the rural Midwest. He lives on a hobby farm with his wife and four teens, along with seven goats, five dogs, four pigs, and a flock of chickens. He is a college professor and Spam connoisseur.

CPSIA information can be obtained
at www.ICGtesting.com
Printed in the USA
JSHW011101110623
42898JS00002B/3

9 798986 701219